BY NIGHT the STRANGERS

BY

HERBERT E. STOVER

CATAMOUNT
PRESS

an imprint of Sunbury Press, Inc.
Mechanicsburg, PA USA

CATAMOUNT
PRESS

an imprint of Sunbury Press, Inc.
Mechanicsburg, PA USA

For information about special discounts for bulk purchases, please contact Sunbury Press Orders Dept. at (855) 338-8359 or orders@sunburypress.com.

To request one of our authors for speaking engagements or book signings, please contact Sunbury Press Publicity Dept. at publicity@sunburypress.com.

FIRST CATAMOUNT PRESS EDITION: January 2023

Set in Adobe Garamond | Interior design by Crystal Devine | Cover by Lawrence Knorr | Edited by Sarah Peachey.

Publisher's Cataloging-in-Publication Data
Names: Stovert, Herbert E., author.
Title: By night the strangers / Herbert E. Stover.
Description: First trade paperback edition. | Mechanicsburg, PA : Catamount Press, 2023.
Summary: Prior to the Civil War, a young lumberman in western Pennsylvania becomes entangled in the Underground Railroad and the Abolition Movement, and finds himself defended by Thaddeus Stevens and sheltering the son of John Brown after Harper's Ferry.
Identifiers: ISBN : 979-8-88819-054-8 (softcover) | ISBN : 979-8-88819-055-5 (ePub).
Subjects: FICTION / Historical / Civil War Era | FICTION / Small Town & Rural.

Product of the United States of America
0 1 1 2 3 5 8 13 21 34 55

Continue the Enlightenment!

Front cover art: *The Underground Railroad* by Charles T. Webber, 1893.

To
KAY and BARBEE

Also by
HERBERT E. STOVER

Song of the Susquehanna

Men in Buckskin

Powder Mission

Copperhead Moon

THE AUTHOR of this story of the Pennsylvania hills in the stirring days immediately preceding the great Civil War gratefully and humbly acknowledges the help and direction furnished him by many persons conversant with local happenings during the time of the movement known as the Underground Railroad. They have shown him old maps, letters, diaries, old houses, and even caves, each having something to do in the days when lonely black people followed a star.

Specifically, he realizes his indebtedness to Colonel Henry Shoemaker of the Pennsylvania Folklore Society, the Library of Bucknell University, and the Extension Division of the Pennsylvania State Library.

With the exception of those of historic personages, all names used are fictitious.

CHAPTER ONE

FOR THE third night in succession, following the affair in Brown's General Store, Luke Hanley found it hard to sleep. In spite of the wide-open window in the room he occupied, the whole interior of the big stone mill was filled with a musty heat gathered during the day. He sat on the edge of his cot and mopped perspiration from his head and chest with a corner of the cotton blanket, using his left hand to do so and holding his aching right one across his bony knees.

Wide awake now, he knew he could not sleep because of the trouble in the store. Fred Horton had been a stranger to him, but there was nothing strange about the foul remark or the girl's name. They had been uttered loudly enough for any customer to hear if there had been one in the store. Luckily no one had been present outside of Luke, the drummer to whom the words were said, and Brown, who had been somewhere behind the place. Horton went down at the first blow and remained on the floor, rubbing his chin and mouthing curses while his assailant walked out. It was that same night, too, that Luke had noticed the other sound, and he found himself listening for it again.

Minutes dragged by. He was about to swing his feet from the rough floor back onto the cot when he heard it, and there was a light pricking of the hairs along the back of his neck. The rapid, walking steps of a spirited horse were approaching down the creek road from town. The bridge planks rumbled, then the animal's pace quickened until the drumming of a gallop came back from the ridge road, growing fainter and fainter, being lost finally in the distance. Luke rose and walked slowly to the window.

Tiny creakings from inside the building sounded as though the timbers talked to each other. Outside were the common night noises: the chirping of crickets, the light stirring of breezes in the dejected leaves of the trees, all against the steady background of falling water, where the millrace flow had been diverted from the big wheel and fell with soft splashing on the rocks below before hurrying on to the creek. There was no moon, and the dim starlight above the trees made the shadows about the stone mill heavier.

Luke was there a long while, his lean body shivering a little under the touch of the quickening breeze. This was the third time he had heard the sound of a horse at night, at first furtive, then hurrying on its way, and it had brought back vividly the twelve-year-old memory of a hurried horseman carrying the news of the death of Luke's father at the hands of an anti-Abolitionist mob. Standing here in this old mill, he could still feel the frantic clutch of his mother's fingers on his shoulder and hear the broken, choking sound of her voice as she questioned the impatient messenger.

Few people here in quiet Crossville rode horses and even fewer by night. Doctor Forney always used a buggy. There was something sinister in the night riding of this unseen horseman, something that did not fit into the character of this neighborhood where people slept soundly at night and traveled leisurely by day. It was a long time until sleep finally came to Luke.

A high sun streaming in his window roused him just as a hard rapping came to the outside door. Half-dressed and still sleepy, he opened the mill door and faced the one man of Crossville whom he most cordially disliked, John Caines, carefully groomed even at this early hour. Among many interests of this man was the local hotel where he lived with his daughter, Linda. There was none of the girl's soft full features in her father's too-regular face, but the color of their hair was the same—a deep lustrous black. Luke's high-boned, expressive face was hard. His rumpled red-brown hair stood in a shock above his forehead, and his gray eyes frowned. There was no friendliness between the two men.

"Yes," Luke said shortly, "what do you want?"

"Come with me," Caines said grimly.

Luke followed his visitor outside and along the path that circled the mill to the triangle made by the race and breast of the dam. There, a bit to the side of the well-traveled walk, crushing down ferns and low bushes, was the body of a man Luke identified at once as Fred Horton, whom he had knocked down in Brown's store. For a moment, he and Caines stared at the inert body and the bullet wound above the right ear.

"Shot himself," Caines grunted, "and good riddance. Go down and get Squire Jacoby. I'll stay with the body."

Returning to his room, Luke dressed slowly so he'd have more time to think. Then he went up the road to the village of Crossville. Squire Ernest Jacoby was already in his tiny office, so cluttered it looked like the birthplace of confusion.

"Squire, Fred Horton's shot!"

Jacoby was a huge, heavy man with a broad, noncommittal face under a thatch of white hair. He looked keenly at his early visitor and spoke mildly. "You shoot him, son?"

"No, Squire, he shot himself. Come along."

Jacoby took time enough to put on his seersucker coat and a broad-brimmed, much-soiled straw hat which he removed, scratching his head in thought.

"There's no county coroner. That means a Justice of the Peace must serve. Run along, son, and get Ben Thatch, Ezra Corman, and John Caines—"

"He's at the body," Luke interrupted bluntly. "He found it."

Jacoby shifted his thick fingers from his hair to his chin and looked more thoughtful as Luke continued.

"Caines routed me out of bed to tell me. I slept late."

"Then pick up John Roudabush and Bob Hendricks. That'll make four. Don't talk—just tell them I want them in a hurry."

It took most of an hour to find and dispatch the men to the scene of the suicide. Four wives heard Jacoby's summons to their husbands, and by the time Luke and the last man, Bob Hendricks, arrived at the dam, a small crowd of the curious had collected. Luke heard Jacoby's final question put to Caines. "Why were you out so early, John?"

"Cornmeal," the hotel man replied. "The cook told me last night we were out, and I thought there might be some at the mill, even if it wasn't running."

Jacoby swung his heavy face toward his recently arrived messenger. "Any cornmeal there, Luke?"

"Yes," the young caretaker replied with some reluctance. "There's a little in the number four bin. I've been selling some, now and then."

Jacoby looked down at the dead man a moment, then spoke to the bystanders. "Folks, Doc Forney's coming, and he'll want to be private-like. I'm sending over to the county seat for Nedrow, the county attorney, and most likely, he'll have some questions. There'll be a meeting in the schoolhouse right after dinner tomorrow. We'll have a verdict then."

Luke returned to his room in the mill, thinking hard. He had seen a few dead people but never one who had been shot. Like most of the folks in the village of Crossville and the little valley which lay south a score of miles from the great lumbering region of central Pennsylvania, he had heard a lot about the reputation of Fred Horton. The man had broken several homes, and he was reputed to have more than his share of enemies who hated him with good cause. Ten years past, he had left town, returning only recently, unsummoned and unwelcome. There were some who would have willingly killed him. It was odd that he should have put an end to himself. Even stranger to Luke was the fact that he had not heard this shot fired so close to the mill, especially since he had slept so fitfully.

It was nice to have things to do about the mill so he was busy. John Caines' peremptory manner irritated him, and the violent death so near shocked him. So, he welcomed cleaning some bins and conveyors. When his work was finished, he climbed into the little cupola on the roof from which there was a good view of the town. The main street was L-shaped, with the schoolhouse, where the meeting would be, on the corner. Caines Hotel was at the upper end of town, with scattered houses between it and the school building. Half a mile to the north were roughly broken mountains. Luke's attention was focused on the hotel. When a small figure appeared on its porch, he wondered if it could be Linda Caines. This morning was the first time he had encountered the girl's father since Caines had directed him to keep away from both his daughter and the hotel.

Anyway, Luke thought grimly, there were always young men hanging about Linda Caines, and she wouldn't miss him much. He hadn't the money to show a girl a good time with buggy rides, dances, and things. Girls like Linda demanded entertainment. John Caines did not want his daughter to waste her time on a combination watchman and student.

That evening, Luke tried first working on surveying problems assigned to him by Professor Blake, who was teaching him. Later, he tried a map with no better success. His hand was still sore from the blow he had struck Fred Horton, making it hard to handle either a pencil or a mapping pen.

At about nine-thirty, he walked over to town and passed the Caines Hotel. Through the big parlor window, he saw some young people gathered about Linda, who occupied the organ stool. One of the men bent solicitously over her, ready to turn the music for her. A grim mood seized Luke as he realized how poorly he would fit into such a scene. He was just a gangling man from the lumber country who had come up with the fool idea of bettering himself by becoming a surveyor while he earned his keep watching the old Potter mill.

* * *

There was no horseman that night, and in the morning, the Breitman boy appeared with a message from Squire Jacoby. "He wants you should come up right away."

Luke tried to think of something he might give the freckle-faced youngster for his trouble, and the lad saw his dilemma. "The squire gave me a nickel. You better hurry."

Jacoby was alone in his office and curtly directed his visitor to close the door. Luke took the indicated chair and waited.

"Where were you the night Horton was killed?"

Luke frowned, then his hand came up in his habitual gesture of running his fingers through his hair when puzzled. "I'm not rightly sure, Squire. Tried to think this morning. Professor Blake gave me a map to make, but my hand was sore, so I went uptown and bought some tobacco. Likely I read a while before I went to bed. That's my habit."

Jacoby smiled, and there was an expression of relief on his face. "Guilty men usually have good alibis. Honest folks just find it hard to check back over what they did. Now listen carefully, son. The day you hit Horton, you told me that you'd never seen the man before."

Luke nodded promptly. "That's right, sir, but he wasn't over ten feet from me when he shot off his mouth and—"

Jacoby's hand lifted, interrupting. "Keep remembering that. Don't mention the name of the woman Horton was maligning. Clean forget that much." He pulled open his desk drawer, fumbled in the papers, and tossed a short-barreled, walnut-stocked pistol on the desk pad while Luke stared in surprise.

"That's mine. Squire, where—"

Jacoby turned the weapon about with his forefinger. "Yes, I knew it was yours. It's the one your father took on trips, but he left it at home when he went to Exeter where he was killed. John Caines says he found it in the weeds close to Horton's body and that it had been fired lately. How did it get there?"

Luke picked up the pistol and stared at it as if looking for some record of its activities. Then he spoke emphatically. "That gun was on a shelf in my room. I put it there close to ten days ago when I had killed a rat with it. And, sir, I haven't touched it since." His eyes widened. Putting the weapon back on the desk, he leaned forward. "Squire, look. If Horton killed himself with that pistol, part of the exploded percussion cap would be on the nipple. There's no sign of a cap. Did Caines handle that gun?"

"No, son. He saw it in the weeds and didn't pick it up. He showed it to Bob Hendricks, who gave it to me."

Jacoby seemed to understand the confusion in his visitor's mind and tossed the weapon back into the drawer, pushing papers over it. A moment later, when he had found his keys, he locked the drawer. "Son," he said softly, "I called you in to put you on your guard for the afternoon when Nedrow comes. I knew your father and have known you for years. Nedrow'll not understand as I would. He'll want to know why you didn't hear that shot, and he'll find out you knocked Horton down. Doctor Forney will tell there were a lot of bruises on the body. Horton took a beating before he died. But unless John Caines mentions it, Nedrow isn't likely to learn about your pistol."

"But Caines will tell."

The squire smiled and shook his head. "No, it could be he knew whose name Horton was peddling." The old man rose, and Luke followed suit. "Luke, the jury will find a verdict of suicide. Only Hendricks, Caines, and I know about your pistol. There are young married men in Crossville who'd have killed Horton if their wives had talked. Maybe one of them was suspicious. All the dead man was fit for was to die. Now, remember, hold in that hair-trigger temper when Nedrow asks his questions. You didn't know Horton. You didn't hear a shot. Keep your fingers out of your hair or he'll think you're nervous. Tell him you're a lumberman here in town to study surveying. Say you are the caretaker of the mill, that your parents are dead. Now I have a report to make out."

Luke was worried about the pistol because he realized how it could have been taken from the mill. There had been just one visitor, not counting John Caines' morning call, in the past ten days, and that had been Linda Caines, who had accompanied him to his place on a dare. That was exactly four days ago.

She had come in with her usual gay manner and laughingly inspected his room, criticizing his housekeeping. She didn't think he had made his bed well, and his few dishes, although clean enough, were not properly arranged on the shelves. He remembered that she had taken the pistol down with the remark that guns did not belong among housekeeping things. Then he thought she had replaced it, but she could have slipped it into her dress pocket. He had been too excited by her visit to observe closely or to remember much. But even if she had taken it, that did not explain how it came to be beside the dead body of the libertine now decently prepared for burial in the local undertaking parlor.

In his room once more, Luke checked and found the space between the tea canister and a jar of cherries empty. That was where he kept the pistol. It was hard to think of Linda Caines with a gun in her soft white hand. Squire Jacoby was hinting at murder—at least he had mentioned that there were those who might have wished Horton dead.

* * *

County Attorney George Nedrow drove a team of buckskin ponies hitched to a buckboard that sagged badly under the weight of the corpulent young lawyer. Close to ten o'clock, he clattered into Crossville and thereafter busied himself asking questions and soaking up gossip. At twelve, he repaired to the Caines Hotel and ate hugely of a complimentary dinner specially prepared for him.

The single-roomed schoolhouse had filled quickly with the gossip-hungry and excited adults of the town. Sunbonneted women occupied one side, shirt-sleeved men the other. Luke was a little late and had to take a seat up front on the right side of the room. Squire Jacoby was behind a table facing the audience, and Nedrow, already perspiring through the armpits of his seersucker coat, had ensconced himself behind the teacher's desk, his bulk neatly filling the chair. He was questioning John Caines, who sat partly facing the audience and partly the attorney.

Luke could look across the front of the room and out the window at the dusty schoolyard, where a single dejected white hen scratched languidly in the dust of her own making. Nedrow's team was tied to a hitching rail directly across the street. Luke kept his attention in that direction because Linda Caines, the only woman in the room with an uncovered head, occupied a front seat. Her heavy black hair was drawn back severely from her almond-shaped face and fastened in heavy coils at the nape of her small neck. A tantalizing, half-promising ghost of a smile played about the girl's full lips. It seemed as though she had felt it her duty to be there but was really not interested in her surroundings. Luke did not permit himself to look her way after his first glance. There was a sick feeling in his stomach as he realized she could have taken the pistol from his shelf, but why?

John Caines was his deliberate, careful, unemotional self and told his complete story without interruption. He spoke of his early visit to the mill and how he had been shocked at what he found. He was dismissed without questioning and with thanks. After all, the county attorney could have no wish to antagonize a man reputed to be influential in the county. Eben Brown, the storekeeper, came next and explained, on being questioned, that he had been too far back in the room to hear what had been said by the drummer to cause Luke Hanley's resentment.

"The young man you mention is in the room?" Nedrow asked, and Brown pointed to Luke, whose neck reddened as the glances of the men and women in the room rested on him. Brown was then excused.

Doctor Forney explained the nature of the gunshot wound which had killed Horton and stated that the body had been bruised. Following him, Luke was called to the stand, which was a kitchen chair.

Luke disentangled his long legs from their cramped position under the desk and walked forward to take his seat with the apologetic stoop to his shoulders so common to tall men. He knew from Squire Jacoby's warning that he was probably in for a bad time and that the audience sensed excitement. His main perplexity was what to say if asked about the pistol, and his quick side glance showed him Linda was now looking out the window. Nedrow ran several routine questions together.

"You are Luke Hanley, caretaker of the Potter mill, twenty-three years of age, born and reared fifteen miles east of Crossville?"

Luke nodded. Nedrow frowned and questioned further. "Roused by Mr. Caines, you went to Squire Jacoby, telling of the discovery of the body of Fred Horton?"

"Yes."

"Since the deceased was found close to the mill, you must have heard the shot. Did you?"

"No."

Nedrow's tone with his next question was loaded with sarcasm. "Isn't it strange that a young man with presumably sound hearing heard no shot, Mr. Hanley?"

Luke felt a stiffness in the muscles of his face. Nedrow was playing with him, leading him to make a spectacle of himself. But he answered evenly. "I heard no shot."

"You knew the deceased, Fred Horton?"

"No."

The attorney looked delighted and leaned forward as if to intimidate the witness with his very weight. "Yet you have heard Mr. Brown's testimony—"

Jacoby suddenly slapped the top of the table. The attorney looked surprised and stopped.

"Nedrow, these men have not testified. Don't you know the law? None of them were under oath."

The county attorney gulped. His face reddened, then, ignoring the interruption, he faced Luke again. "Mr. Brown stated that you viciously attacked this same Horton whom you say you did not know. Is it your custom to go about beating strangers?"

Luke shook his head and then explained. "I had never seen him before. It's true I had heard about him and realized who he must be. Then he made a dirty remark about a woman, and I knocked him down. I—"

Nedrow jerked forward, interrupting. "What woman? Who was she?"

Luke's eyes went cold as he stared back. Squire Jacoby had warned him not to mention the name, but he would not have done so anyway. He had no intention of curbing the anger that now seethed within him, and his answer was slow and insolent. "None of your damned business."

A gasp of astonishment swept through the women's section, and the men shifted about in their places. Nedrow was a lawyer and a county official accustomed to being treated respectfully, but he recovered and shot his comment at the grim-faced young man staring at him.

"Horton was bruised from a beating. Probably you made a second attack. This time you shot him to protect the woman you are guarding, to still his tongue."

Nedrow's pudgy hands were waving to emphasize his accusation, and Luke was fascinated by his vehement gestures.

"Hanley, tell us where you were the night Horton was shot!"

Nedrow shouted his question, and the audience sat open-mouthed. Luke managed to keep his face expressionless. His mind was confused to the point where he was not sure he could tell the exact day on which they had found the body, much less the details of what he had been doing at the time.

The attorney was waiting with triumph on his heavy face when a calm but clear woman's voice cut into the tension. "Mr. Nedrow."

He swung his head in surprise. Linda Caines was standing beside her seat. The light wool shawl she wore was pushed back from her slim neck, and sunlight touched the smoothness of her hair. She was half smiling.

"Yes, Miss Caines," the attorney managed to say, "what is it?"

"Just this; Mr. Hanley was with me, sir."

A quick stir passed through the audience, and the lawyer, plainly confused, stared at the poised young woman facing him. It was then that he made his blunder. "How long?"

Linda Caines hesitated for only an instant. Squire Jacoby, scowling, half rose. Then the girl pitched her reputation into the balance and smiled as she did so. "Why, nearly all night, sir."

After those words, she sat down.

The room was deathly still. John Caines sat immobile, with strained features. Nedrow mopped his perspiring face with a huge handkerchief, realizing what he had done to his own ambitions by stripping away the good name of the daughter of the man reputed to own the county offices. Jacoby broke the tense silence with a thump on his table. He ignored the flustered lawyer.

"Ladies and gentlemen, the jury finds that Fred Horton committed suicide. This meeting is adjourned."

John Caines rose and offered his arm to his daughter. She placed the tips of her fingers upon it, and together they walked from the room before the confusion of talk broke out. Luke remained where he was, too upset to know what to do. Linda Caines had saved him from a critical situation, but he was appalled at the price she had paid, and she had dared to lie for him.

Jacoby picked up his papers and stepped over to the County Attorney. "Now, you damned fool, get back to the county seat. You've made enough mess for one day, and I hope John Caines nails your stupid hide to the courthouse door."

Luke stumbled through the empty aisles on feet that usually carried him surely among brush and rocks. Instead of the road, he went through the alleys and used the path back to the mill. Everyone in town would be talking, tearing Linda to pieces. Nearly everybody knew John Caines had warned Luke away from his daughter. Linda had told her preposterous story, and there would be talk of clandestine trysts and all the foul ideas gossips can assemble.

Less than an hour later, John Caines arrived and entered the mill without knocking. All his control was gone. His face was distorted with rage, and his voice trembled as it threatened. "Get out of town!" he yelled. "If you're here in the morning, I'll shoot you like a damned mangy pup."

Luke stood, surprised at his own restraint as he faced the irate, bitter man who, of course, had right on his side if his daughter's story was to be believed.

"John," he said calmly, "you know damn well Linda lied to shut up Nedrow. I'm getting out of town, but it's for her sake, not on account of your threats."

Caines stepped forward with one arm upraised as if to slap the younger man's face, and Luke's self-control snapped. He grabbed the arm, twisting it.

"Caines, you've made your jumps. You ordered me out of your hotel and gossiped about me like an old woman, so I hear. You've talked about my dead father. Now get the hell out of this mill and my life. Something rotten's happened here in Crossville, and I think you're at the bottom of it."

The hotel man was not lightly built and was supposed to have been a real rough-and-tumble fighter when younger, but Luke's savage thrust sent him reeling through the open door and down the short flight of steps.

Luke had little appetite for his scanty supper. When it was finished, he made bundles of his few belongings. One held books and instruments loaned to him by Professor Blake. Both Blake and Squire Jacoby, who had found the job as caretaker for his friend's son, would be disappointed, but there could be no staying in Crossville with its embattled gossips. Luke had finished packing when a light step sounded on the gravel outside. A moment later, he flung open the door, and Linda Caines entered. Exhausted from hurry, she dropped into a chair.

"Luke," she said breathlessly, "I had to see you and ran most of the way."

He bent over her. "Linda," he demanded, "why did you do it? Why?"

She stood up and placed both hands on his shoulders. "You helped me first shut Horton's mouth. I can't help what people say or my father's raging. And I can't explain things or what I'm afraid of, but I want you to go away, quick." Her fingers tugged nervously at his shirt sleeves. For the first time since he had known this girl, he read real alarm in her eyes.

"I'm going." He gestured at the bundles. She was so close he slipped his arms about her shoulders. "Linda, you're crying. What's wrong?"

She shook her head vigorously and wiped her eyes. "I said I couldn't tell you because I know only half the facts. But get away. Father and Nedrow have been together. They'll do anything now, Luke."

He shook her lightly. "I'm leaving for your sake, Linda, so folks won't be watching to crucify you. Never mind about your father and that fat lawyer."

Her bare arm slipped about his neck. He found the full richness of her lips, and for a long moment, they clung to each other.

"Someday, Luke, maybe someday."

He kissed her again. She slipped from his arms, pulled the shawl closer about her slim shoulders, and left as she had come.

* * *

Jacoby was again in his office early when Luke called on him. The squire promised to deliver Professor Blake's things and to contact another man to take care of the mill, after which he indicated a chair.

"I took for granted you'd leave when you came in with those bundles, son. It's a pity. I knew and loved your father, and when you came here, I felt there was a real future for you. Surveying is a shade better than swinging an axe." He waited a moment, then continued. "I hate to see a boy cut loose from things. You lost your home when your mother died. Now you have no ties, no anchor, and that's bad for a young man. Your father had two anchors—his home and the Abolition cause. I wish you had something like that. The cause needs men, Luke."

He waved a ruler at his visitor's frown. "Naturally, you are bitter about it. He was away from his home a lot and left you and your mother pretty poor when he died. Yet a man is neither as great nor as important as the cause to which he gives himself."

The squire saw that he had lost his visitor's interest and changed his tactics, speaking in a lighter vein. "Your troubles began when a young woman wrapped you around her finger. Maybe if I was twenty-three, tall and lanky, with a shock of hair that wouldn't stay combed, and a girl wanted to wrap me, well, I'd just let her wrap."

He opened the desk drawer, took out the pistol, and tossed it to Luke. "That gun didn't kill Horton, but so long as it's here, it's evidence. You take it. John Caines was asking to have it yesterday evening."

After Luke had thrust the weapon into his pocket, Jacoby took three crumpled dollar bills from a vest pocket and passed them over. "That much is coming to you from Potter, son. I'll get it back from him."

Both stood and looked into each other's eyes as they shook hands.

"I'm obliged," Luke mumbled. "There have been so many things."

Jacoby started to reply but instead nodded his head and sat down as Luke walked out, carrying his meager bundle.

CHAPTER TWO

FORTY MILES east and north of Crossville, after five days of leisurely travel, Luke still retained his own small store of silver and the crumpled bills Squire Jacoby had given him. Each day, he stopped and worked for bed and board. He enjoyed splitting wood, milking cows, and working about the farm stables. Best of all, he liked the haymows, where he usually slept, with their smell of cured forage. At night, the barns were filled with the stirring of animals, and the creaking of beams reminded him strongly of the old Potter mill. His plans were still sketchy and consisted merely of keeping busy at odd jobs until winter work in the pine woods upriver opened.

Now, in the early afternoon, he sat on an old pine stump where the road forked, mildly disturbed by the realization that it did not matter in the least which way he chose. The branch to the left climbed boldly along the side of the ridge and turned about a sharp boulder a few hundred yards from where he sat. It was the better of the two roads. The right-hand way crossed a narrow pole bridge and wound up among hemlocks. Its travel marks were light, and the road itself was not much wider than the spread of the wagon tracks printed on it.

Luke wasn't particularly tired, but he was hungry, even though he carried in his bundle a store of cold food given to him by an earnest housewife at the last farm where he had stopped. What he wanted was to sit down, stretch his legs under a table, and talk with folks while they ate. There should be a checkered cloth on the table and a castor set in the middle, proudly bearing cruets of vinegar, homemade ketchup, and thin wine, as there used to be on his mother's table. He shrugged his shoulders, knowing that what bothered him was just plain homesickness.

There was no sense in sitting there mooning. He would think of Linda Caines, and that way lay misery. Squire Jacoby had talked about an anchor, but so far, Luke had encountered nothing heavier than his old knapsack. He had learned that hard work and walking kept him from thinking too much. The right-hand road was good enough. There would be farms up on the high flats. The bridge poles rattled under his feet as he crossed.

* * *

Luke was right. There was flat land at the top of the grade, and the going was good if a bit sandy. Here were plenty of deer tracks and, once in the gutter, the sharp, clear print of a turkey's foot.

In another half hour, after cutting through a grove of small pines, the road turned toward the right and passed a farm, where fields of late-summer green stretched away to bounding timber. Beyond that lay pine-covered hills broken by deep gaps. Substantial farm buildings stood close to the center of the cleared land, and a good lane through a cornfield led to them.

Luke was halfway to the barn, from which came the sound of pounding, when a huge black dog stepped out of the corn and barred the way.

Luke looked at him and grinned. "All right, watchman, take me to the barn."

The animal fell in and walked beside him until they passed the picket fence about the house yard and approached the barn. This was a solid-looking structure of logs and sawn boards. Close to it lay a pile of white pine billets and the tools for making split shingles, complete with a shaving horse.

On impulse, he stripped off his knapsack and jacket and hung both on the fence. Then he picked up a mallet and froe and set to work. In minutes, he had split out a dozen clapboards, after which, using the sharp drawknife, he set to finishing the shingles from the clear pine.

It was interesting labor. The clean shavings fell away, and the pile of shingles grew higher. He did not notice anyone approach and was startled when a cheerful voice greeted him. He looked up into the face of a tall, thin man dressed in worn clothing. Luke liked the friendliness of the man's eyes.

"Thanks for the shingles," the man said, extending his hand. "I'm Jim Haliday. Can I do something for you?"

"No," Luke said, rising and shaking the proffered hand. "I was just passing through. When I saw the shingle-making tools, I just had to turn out a few. My father and I used to make and sell them; the name's Luke Hanley."

Haliday picked up one of the finished pieces of wood and examined it critically, after which he checked a second and a third, tossing each back on the pile. "They're good, butts even, no feathered ends. You ought to see the ones my boy Hugh turns out. No two of them's alike. He's only a mite worse than his dad at it. Both of us get in a hurry, and that don't turn out good shingles."

He mopped his forehead on his sleeve and continued. "I put off this roofing job till the summer crops was in. Now the corn's pressing us, and the way I'm going, this roof'll take me the living month. Come on up to the house, Hanley. I got me an idea."

A pleasant brown-haired woman met them at the picket fence gate, and Haliday spoke to her a trifle apologetically.

"Emma, this is Luke Hanley. He says as how he's just passing through, and he makes good shingles. I was figgering on asking him could he help with the barn roof."

Emma Haliday, obviously his wife, gave Luke a warm hand after she had wiped it on her apron. "Glad you came along," she said with welcome in her tone. "Jim, you better ask him if he'll stay. Likely you forgot that part."

The two men grinned at each other, and Emma smoothed her hair with her fingers. "Bring your things in, Luke. I see by your face Jim has a new man, and he'll be glad to be rid of them shingles. There's ham and beans for supper."

Haliday made one comment as they returned to the bark. "Emma's a manager, she sure is."

For what remained of the afternoon, Luke reveled in his job after he touched up the edged tools with a whetstone. Occasionally, he stopped long enough to carry a bundle of his finished shingles up the ladder to Haliday, who was nailing them in place. At such times the farmer would talk for a minute.

"We got two children, Hugh and Hester. You'll see them at supper. Hugh went to town. Hester is out riding somewheres."

Within the hour, a light team drawing a spring wagon trotted up the lane and stopped close to the shingle-making operation. A rangy, black-haired boy alighted, and Jim Haliday introduced the young people. Hugh, for it was the son, unhooked the team aided by Luke, then he watered them at the big trough.

"Nice horses," Luke commented, and the boy smiled.

"We like to keep them nice. I'll finish unhitching; it's close to supper time."

Luke returned to his bench, feeling he would like these Halidays. Even Corbet, the black dog, approached in a friendly way to watch the shingle-making for a while before curling up in a pile of shavings.

Luke was getting hungrier. He was splitting out clapboards, his mallet blows smothering other sounds. When he looked up, a horse had stopped close to him. The rider, sitting astride, was a girl who made a generous showing of bare rounded knees and small feet shod with coarse shoes. She dismounted with an easy grace amid a flutter of petticoats, then looked at Luke.

"Who are you?" she asked bluntly.

The girl's face and hands were deeply tanned. Shoulder-length yellow hair hung loosely about her small face, and deep blue eyes looked frankly into Luke's gray ones.

"I'm Hanley, Luke Hanley," he answered, grinning. "I'm the new shingle machine. I suppose you'll be Hester."

She shook her head and showed white teeth in a smile.

"No, I won't be. I *am* Hester."

Mrs. Haliday had come to the fence and was now shaking a finger at her daughter, having heard the interchange. "Hester keeps forgetting she's past sixteen and almost a lady. Daughter, Luke's come to help your father with the barn roof."

Hugh came up and took charge of his sister's horse while the girl, going toward the house, tweaked her mother's hair as she passed.

Haliday, approaching, said to Luke, "It's queer about children. Hugh is quiet, all but shy. Hester tears round on a horse. She can beat Hugh shooting, and she's the best fisherman in these hills. Supper's about ready. You call me Jim."

The family and the new man sat down to a meal that was not only plentiful but superbly cooked. The tablecloth was red-checked, and in the center was a polished pewter castor. Oddly, it was Hester who said grace. It was not a prayer; instead, she repeated the soldiers' psalm, and there was a vibrant, moving quality to her voice. Halfway through the meal, Luke suddenly stopped eating, and Mrs. Haliday noticed.

"Anything wrong?"

He shook his head and explained that this was the way his mother always set the table and that he had thought of it when on a mountain farm. "She ought to be where there's people, lots of them."

That ended the talking. Afterward, they worked busily until they had sawed enough straight-grained pine blocks for their shingle-making.

* * *

The next morning, Luke was busy in his regular place beside the pasture fence, splitting clapboards and shaping them into shingles.

Tom was a little, evil-minded black bull. Haliday had repeatedly warned the family about the animal's disposition, and Hugh, for one, treated the bull with respect. Hester, however, delighted in entering the stables and whistling, a sound that infuriated the beast until he'd bellow and paw the floor with his forefeet. This morning, he had been turned into the pasture for some exercise.

It was very peaceful and quiet. Haliday and his wife had driven over to see a neighbor. Hugh was behind the barn from Luke and the pasture field, mending harnesses. Busy with his tools, Luke heard nothing amiss until the high screeching bellow of the bull brought him to his feet. Hester, in a bright dress, was in the middle of the pasture. Vaulting the low fence, Luke started toward the girl. Tom, from the side of the pasture, had started his charge, probably excited by the bright shade of Hester's dress. Man and bull were running toward the now-frightened girl from different angles. She started to run and, tripping over a rock, went sprawling. The drumming of the bull's hoofs was loud in Luke's ears, but he did not waste time looking round until he reached the scrambling girl. Snatching her up, they gained the partial safety of a stump while the charging animal rushed by.

Hugh had heard. With the black dog Corbet, he entered the field, carrying a pitchfork he had snatched up. The dog distracted Tom's attention, and Hugh finished the rout with the tines of his fork, herding the now subdued animal back to the bars and then to his pen.

Luke walked with the silent, disheveled girl to the fence near the house. His face was grim, and so were his words. "Never again, young lady. You know better than to cross a field where a bull is loose. Stay out hereafter."

She looked at him, pushed the hair back from her face, and brushed some dirt from her skirt. He wondered if she was about to cry or whether she would thank him. For the moment, he felt mildly heroic, and either gesture on her part would seem suitable. When she remained silent, he lifted her over the fence. She took a dozen short steps toward the house, her trim back held straight. Then she turned swiftly, put out her red tongue at him, wheeled, and darted inside the house.

"She'll come to real trouble someday," Hugh commented. "Let's not say anything to the folks about it. Mother worries a lot. Mebbe you should have used an axe on that bull critter."

Before supper, when Luke was washing his face in a basin kept on the back porch, he saw Hester feed Corbet. Pieces of chicken, cake, and beef went into the black dog's little trough. George, the small farm shepherd, had to content himself with plain beef. Luke continued his splashing lest the girl noticed that he had watched.

Harvesting the corn was the next big farm job, and there was a lot of it. Luke fashioned several of the bucks used by the cutters to support the stalks of corn they cut until there was enough for a sheaf which would be tied with long straw. He was finishing one of these bucks, Haliday was out in the field with a load of manure. Corbet lay near Luke on a pile of shavings. The big dog got up and growled as an open buggy drawn by a black horse came up the lane and stopped by the yard fence to allow a heavily built man, who wore a wide-brimmed hat, to alight. He tied his horse and approached Luke.

"Is this the Haliday place?"

Instinctively, Luke did not like the man. His red face was hard. There was arrogance in the way he spoke and a hint of swagger as he walked up. A heavy gold watch chain was draped loosely across an ample paunch; he looked like an older, harder Nedrow.

"Yes," Luke told him curtly. Corbet stood, and when the visitor started toward the barn, the dog stepped in front of him, a deep growl rumbling in its throat.

"Get out!" the man snapped. Corbet stepped aside but walked beside the visitor as he took more steps toward the barn.

"You, call back this damned dog."

Luke shook his head. "He wouldn't listen, but watch him. He's hell on strangers. Haliday's coming. Better stand still."

Jim's team clattered into the barnyard. He leaped down from the wagon and came forward to stand before the visitor. The usual welcome was entirely absent from the farmer's face and Luke, watching, was surprised to see it hard and cold.

"Bay's the name," the big man explained. "You have a nice farm here. Mind if I look around?"

Haliday shook his head. "Help yourself. Corbet'll go with you. Don't make quick motions, Mister Bay. The dog's nervous."

Not five minutes passed before Bay, followed closely by Corbet, returned from the barn. The dog's tongue lolled out, but he carried his tail upright and stiff as a ramrod.

"Your damn dog's nasty," Bay snarled at Haliday, who had remained close to Luke. "Why don't you keep him tied?"

Jim stepped a little closer to the angry man and leaned on the handle of his manure fork. "Corbet lives here; you don't. Mebbe they tie you up when your home down at the county seat."

His big soiled hand shot out and grasped the lapel of Bay's coat. "You ain't fooled me a bit, Mister Deputy Marshal. You was sent up here about strangers that come by night, and I hate a snooper. Get the hell off my property, and don't come back 'less you have a warrant. It's no matter what John Caines and his new lap dog, Nedrow, say."

Corbet, hearing the anger in his master's voice, would have attacked the man, but Jim caught his collar. Bay hurried to his horse, untied him, then scrambled into the buggy and was off, fast. Jim released the dog, and Corbet looked up at his master as if he shared a joke with him.

Unnoticed, Emma Haliday had appeared. Her face was white. Jim went to her and patted her shoulder. "Mother, hunt me a bone for Corbet. That feller as just left stirred up his appetite."

Luke thought a lot that night. The mention of Caines brought up Linda, the warmth and softness of her lips, and the kindness of her voice. Evidently, Nedrow had promptly made his peace with the hotel man. At first, he had thought the deputy marshal's visit had to do with him, but he dismissed that thought. This was the first time he had seen anyone made unwelcome here at the Haliday farm, even if it was just a peddler or a tramp.

"Strangers that come by night" was an odd phrase. Haliday had literally hurled the words at the big marshal. Luke remembered that the officer had seemed to want to look about the place rather than talk to the farm people.

* * *

Later, Luke was roused from a light sleep by the sound of low voices coming through his open window. Slipping from his bed, he walked quietly to where he could listen better. Once before, he had heard night voices here, but he had attributed them to late visitors just leaving and had paid no attention.

Shadows were so deep under the trees that he could see nothing, but the trample of hoofs told him there was a horse down there. Haliday had just finished speaking, and the voice of a stranger cut in.

"Well, Jim, he was just suspicious. Mebbe he wanted to put the fear of the law in you. Bay's new on the job."

"No," Haliday argued, "he figgered he'd find something on the place."

"It could be your new hired man," the voice commented. "Does he know about—"

Part of the words were spoken too low to be heard, but the final one was "stranger."

Haliday appeared to consider quite a while, and Luke strained to catch what the farmer would say.

"No, Bay didn't have Luke in mind. I never told the boy about things up here. He's had enough troubles of his own."

The men were walking away from the house, and nothing more could be heard. Downstairs, a moment later, an outer door closed softly. Luke returned to his bed, puzzled that there should be a mystery here on this peaceful farm. Later, he slept so soundly that Mrs. Haliday had to call him twice to come to breakfast.

CHAPTER THREE

BAY'S VISIT was not mentioned in the Haliday home, though Luke fancied he noticed a tension not apparent before. Nothing was said of the other visitor who had come by night. All the men were now busy in the cornfield. Luke liked striding along, swinging a sharp cutter against the heavy stalks. Then he racked handfuls of heavy stems, laden with corn ears, against the bucks for tying later, a job done by either Jim or Hugh since Luke could not seem to master knotting the straw binder used.

Haliday was a forehanded man. When all the corn was cut, he immediately prepared for the husking. Now even the women helped during parts of the days. A dozen sheaves of corn would be pulled together and set in a small circle where the huskers worked. Hugh elected to go along the edges of the fields in the hope of seeing wild turkeys. Jim hauled in the husked ears, and usually Luke and Hester operated together.

At first, the girl could beat Luke, but he learned rapidly how to overtake her efforts, and his strong wrists gave him a real advantage. This day, they had built a high breastwork of sheaves to keep off the wind and kneeled side by side, tearing off the husks with steel hooks and tossing the yellow ears into a pile. Luke found a red ear and glanced at his companion, who appeared not to notice though a slow flush crept along her neck. Half an hour later, he found a second red ear. Holding it aloft triumphantly, he caught Hester about the waist, expecting to hear her laugh at the old custom. But her eyes widened slowly, and her lips were just parted.

Luke was bending for his kiss when she shook her head vigorously. "No, Luke, don't. Let's not spoil—"

He released her before she finished, scarcely catching the last low words, and went doggedly back to work. He had begun the incident in fun, but the girl's attitude had changed things. He was afraid that his clumsiness had destroyed the fine sense of comradeship that meant so much to him. They worked together another hour when Hester rose and stretched her supple young body.

"Got to go in now and help Mother, Luke."

He scrambled up from his cramped position, and she suddenly thrust out her small, firm hand. "We'll just forget," she promised, "clean forget."

He took her fingers, and they closed tightly about his. Then she left. Halfway on her trip to the house, she started to whistle, but Luke did not recognize the tune. He continued to work but was exasperated. Hester had made a great deal out of what he had meant to be a gesture of fun, and it irritated him.

Anyway, he was glad that he worked alone during the afternoon, for it gave him a chance to take stock of himself. Luke felt that perhaps here on this farm he could find the anchor that Squire Jacoby had spoken of. He liked these people and their complete acceptance of him. But he knew how often his mind strayed back to Linda Caines, her soft lips, and the unarticulated promise in her eyes. He also realized that any of the Halidays could break this thinking: Jim with his deliberate speech; Emma with her motherliness; Hugh with his friendliness; and especially Hester. She was so alive, so vibrant, giving companionship rather than allure. He had seen her with her yellow hair tossed back from her face, the wind molding her dress against her strong rounded body, and he had felt her beauty deeply. The thing to do was to count her as a sister; that relationship was safe, even if a bit empty.

Evenings in the Haliday home were the best part of the day. Neighbors often dropped in for an hour's visit with good talk about crops, livestock, game, or cooking. But the five of them were sufficient. Luke would help Hugh with his arithmetic. Occasionally, Emma would play the organ and insist that the young people sing to her accompaniment while Jim sat in a corner, smoking and grinning with pleasure. Dominoes was their only game, but Hester was so good at it that the young men hesitated to play with her. The girl was also the family barber, cutting the men folks' hair. Luke liked to sit in a kitchen chair, a towel about his neck, while she snipped away with scissors sharpened by Jim for the job. Hugh was indulging in long sideburns, and Hester threatened these each time she wielded the scissors on him.

Luke was busy with the last of the corn fodder, helping to haul it into the barn, when a visitor came and talked a long time with Jim down by the watering trough. Luke heard the man's voice just once, but he recognized it as that of the midnight visitor to whom he had listened, talking under his window.

That evening, Haliday fell from the haymow to the barn floor, badly wrenching his back. The family made him comfortable on the couch behind the stove. Sometime after supper, when Luke was fashioning a tiny basket from a peach stone, the injured man stirred and spoke almost sharply.

"Luke, are you the Right Sort of People as your father was?" The other members of the family stopped what they were doing.

Luke tested the edge of his clasp knife with his thumb. The question puzzled him. "Why, Jim, guess I don't know just what you mean."

Mrs. Haliday's brown head bent lower over her knitting while her husband explained.

"My friend, this is a station on what folks call the Underground Railroad. Most escaping slaves go up New York way through Williamsport, and some travel up the Loyalsock Creek east of the city on the old Indian path. But, Luke, the slave catchers have been so busy those ways, ain't too safe anymore. We're trying to work out a safer road to New York State. I'm a conductor. Runaway slaves come here at night. We keep them one day, then hustle them down to Mr. Brookland at Spring Haven. He's our big man and sends the black folks on in any way he holds is safe. That's why Bay was snooping round here; he's suspicious."

Luke put away his knife and nodded. Of course, he had heard stories about the Underground but had thought little about it. Now he understood the expression "strangers by night."

Haliday was continuing. "Three or four of these people will come here tomorrow night, and I'm laid up. They'll have to be moved in twenty-four hours, and it takes two men. I don't want Hugh tackling such a run alone. Would you be willing to take my place?" Hugh's eyes were bright in the lamplight. He was watching closely, eagerly, and Luke grinned at him.

"Sure, Jim," he promised. "I'll go if Hugh'll show me the ropes."

Haliday's voice was graver, and he kept glancing at his wife. "I got to tell you, it's all against the law. If they catch you with runaways, it could mean six months and up in jail, plus a thousand dollars fine for each runaway. Any officer from a constable up can make the arrest, and I've got some enemies that try to watch. It's kind of a dangerous job."

Emma laid down her knitting and lifted a face drawn with concern. "I'm so afraid, Jim. Someday they'll take you. If you go to jail, what's to become of us and the farm? There'd be heavy fines."

The injured man on the couch was silent a few minutes before he put a question. "Emma, these poor folks follow a star. That's all they know, and they're strangers in a pretty dark night. They got to trust folks along the way. Let one station fail them, and they're lost; it's back to slavery for them. I've seen you feed, nurse, and clothe them. Do you want me to fail them at this late date?"

Without answering her husband, Emma picked up her knitting with trembling fingers. Half an hour later, Luke noticed that she had unraveled what she had finished in the interim and was doing it over. She was disturbed, and there were sharp lines on Jim's face that had not shown before.

"Hugh," he directed, "use the light wagon. Put in some oats and a couple bundles of Luke's shingles. There's but three runaways likely to come. The load will help you cover if you're stopped."

The boy rose to go upstairs. In a corner by the stairway stood a double-barreled shotgun, always kept loaded for hawks. As Hugh passed, he touched the weapon and glanced at his father. Jim nodded grimly, but the mother had not seen the byplay.

After the chores were finished in the morning, Hugh and Luke went over every item they would need. The spring wagon was greased and checked carefully down to the curtain snaps. Next was the team harness, examined as to each strap and buckle. There was a small feed bag for each bridle, and Luke was curious about them.

"So's we can slip one over a horse's nose and keep him from whinnying," Hugh explained. "There's times when we have to lay mighty low. Tonight we use the Pine Station road. It's rough and steep in spots, but we can walk the passengers up hills. The only thing is that it's narrow, and we can't let ourselves be trapped where we can't turn out. I'll handle the team, you handle the shotgun, and we'll take George."

Luke grinned, and Hugh shrugged his shoulders. "That George dog can smell a constable five miles. The gun's just for bluff. Most folks around here carry a gun at night; there's bears and lots of snakes."

Luke thought of his pistol but promptly determined not to take it. There had been trouble enough about the little handgun. Anyway, he was doubly glad that Caines did not get it.

Supper was a quiet meal, but it was easy to see a large quantity of food had been cooked, enough for several families. The runaways were expected by midnight, and the young folks played dominoes to pass the time. It wasn't much after ten o'clock, however, when there was the sound of a rig outside, followed by a rap at the door. Mrs. Haliday raised her hand to her throat.

The rap sounded again, and a rough voice called, "It's the right kind of people."

Hugh admitted a short, stocky man who wore an overcoat as much too long as his cap was too small for his bald head.

"Hello, Abel. You're early," Jim greeted. "You know the family. The other is Luke Hanley, who'll ride with Hugh now that I'm laid up with this back. Luke, this is Abel Thorn from down Yankee Run way."

The newcomer finally got his cap off, then scratched his head. He was plainly troubled. "Jim, these folks outside have to move on tonight. This new man Bay's snoopin' about, and we'd better git 'em on to Brookland. He kin handle the marshal."

"You ready, boys?"

Both young men nodded at Jim's question, and Emma rose.

"Bring them in, Abel," she directed. "They must be fed, and you look hungry, too."

In spite of himself, Luke could not help staring at the frightened faces of the three black passengers who entered and lined up awkwardly along the wall with their hands tucked behind them. Two were women, one much older than the other. The man looked as though he could be the older woman's son. It was evident that the young woman was the driving spirit of the trio. She had an attractive face and alert eyes. Now she smiled and introduced her companions and herself.

"Folks, this is Mother Amy. Jerry here is my man, and I'm Claudy. We don' aim to make too much trouble, jes wants to git on. It's still a fer piece till we kin figger we be safe."

Hester led the three visitors and Thorn to the table. Then she and her mother served the food. "Coffee will come in a few minutes," she promised. "I know you like it, Abel."

There seemed no end to the hunger of these hunted people, and they ate with the concentration of those who find meals few and far between. At his end of the table, Abel Thorn was matching them, having disposed of three cups of coffee together with two huge bowls of soup made thick with meat. Jim Haliday said nothing, merely watching his guests. When his wife and daughter were busy serving, he motioned to Luke and Hugh.

"Luke, handle the gun. I see it's been slipped outside. Be sure to take George. He'll give warning. Keep his collar on. If they stop the wagon, he'll pitch at them and you got to grab him. Make the folks walk through the gap where it's narrow."

They were moving away when he motioned Luke back and Hugh to go on. He spoke in a very low tone. "Better watch that Claudy. She's got a kinda roving eye. Women like that make trouble sometimes."

Luke didn't know exactly what he meant but went out to the waiting wagon. George, the small shepherd, was already in his place on the front seat where he would sit between Hugh and Luke. The shotgun was on the floor where it could be reached in a hurry. Abel Thorn helped his charges into the back of the wagon, fastened the snaps of the cover, and came up to speak to Hugh.

"Good luck, son. You've made the run before and know how to save your horses iffen you got to make a run fer it." The stout man was serious and nervous.

After they had pulled away from the buildings, Hugh poked his friend in the ribs. "They all try to scare us. I think it's fun, slipping along in the night, dodging the constables and their friends. You'll like it by and by."

The steady tramp of the horses and the roll of the wheels made little dull sounds in the sandy road except when a tire or a horseshoe struck a stone. There was no sound from the passengers. Luke had been over part of the road they were following with Hester and knew it to be monotonous, a slow winding way through woodland where the timber was thin and stunted. By and by, he gave himself up to drowsiness and did not wake until Hugh nudged him. The moon had come up, dimly lighting the scene. A break showed in the mountain range ahead.

"Hold the team," Hugh directed, passing over the lines. "George and I'll do some scouting. The gap's just ahead."

He returned a quarter of an hour later so stealthily that Luke did not guess his return until George leaped up to his place on the seat.

"People have been through here tonight," he said. "There's dust smell in the air, and George winded something. I'll walk ahead; you follow with the team. Let the horses have their heads—there's a bad drop to your right. Count to two hundred, then start."

Hugh's dim shape vanished in the shadows as Luke started his count. At a hundred and fifty, he paused momentarily, thinking he heard a sound on the road over which they had just come. After listening a moment, he recognized nothing distinct, so he resumed the count. What he thought he heard was probably breeze puffs in the leaves.

Hugh was waiting at the foot of the grade. "Didn't find a thing, but George is still uneasy—"

He broke off suddenly. His voice was sharp now though still pitched in little more than a whisper.

"Something is coming. There's an old lumber road just ahead. I'll lead the team. Let the lines loose."

Hugh was little more than a boy, but he certainly knew this territory like the back of his hand. In minutes, he had the horses and the rig off the road in a thick grove of pines. Both now heard distinctly the occasional clink of horseshoes coming down through the gap. Hugh slipped the feed bags in place on the horses' noses.

The approaching animal moved slowly as if it had been given free rein. There was no stir in the wagon while the two young men waited, holding the heads of the horses close to their jackets. Then the stillness was broken by the chirp of a little bird disturbed on its perch.

"Hester," Luke whispered. "She's out there; followed us."

He left their animals and ran back to the road where the indistinct shapes of horse and rider loomed against the sky.

"It's Luke," he said in a low tone, walking close, and the girl's voice answered.

"Help me down."

He reached up and, for a moment or two, held her warm body close in his arms. Her breath was against his face, and her lips brushed his cheek as he set her down.

"They're ahead of you, Luke. Four of them."

Hugh approached in time to hear the remainder of the warning.

"Ed Cathcart came to the house a little after you boys left and said that Bay and three others went down this way early in the evening, right after dark. Ed didn't think there'd be passengers tonight, so he took his time telling father. Well, you'd gone, and I was afraid you'd run into a trap."

Hugh swore softly as he listened. "You shouldn't have risked coming, Sis. The road's bad even in daylight."

Hester laughed. "Star's sure-footed," she assured him. "What'll you do with your passengers?"

For a few minutes, the three young people discussed the situation, and Hugh made the decision.

"If they're down below us, they've heard the wagon. Sound carries far at night. I'll lead the passengers through the woods, and Luke will take the rig on. If he's stopped, he has shingles and oats for Mr. Brookland. I'll have my people close to the big dead chestnut on the main road just west from where you come out on it. Wave your handkerchief if things are all right."

Both men wanted Hester to wait until daylight for her return, but she merely laughed at them. Hugh returned to the wagon to explain to the runaways. When they had gone off into the woods, Luke lifted Hester back into the saddle, holding her tightly as he did so. For the second time, her lips brushed his cheek, then he found them and bruised them with his own while they clung together. Finally, she drew away, and her voice was unsteady as she warned, "Watch where this road comes into the pike."

Then horse and rider moved up the gap into the darkness. Luke's mind was in a whirl. Tonight, here on this wild road, he had ended the happy comradeship about which this girl had warned him a month past in the cornfield. He had felt much this same hunger for Linda Caines, but there was a difference. Linda knew men and their impulses; Hester was so much younger and unused to men. He thought of her gaiety and her bird songs.

"You damned fool," he muttered to himself. "You double-damned fool." Jim Haliday had told him how well he had gotten on with Hugh and Hester.

Luke stumbled and plodded down to where the team was tied. George growled when he climbed into the seat, then pushed his shaggy body close as Luke slipped an arm about the animal's neck.

"Hell, George," he whispered. "You got no problems. All you have to do is be a good dog."

He had driven what he supposed was a full hour, and there were signs of morning in the eastern sky as he reached a road running east and west and turned to his left. Five minutes later, they were all about him, mounted men who had come out of the brush. One caught hold of a bridle, stopping the team.

George growled, and holding the reins fast, Luke leaned down to pull out the shotgun. His right hand went round the throat of the stock, and his thumb was ready to cock the hammers when a dark lantern opened, and the yellow light searched the front seat.

An authoritative voice snapped, "Put that gun down. We're officers of the law."

Luke's answer was the double snick of the hammers as he cocked both. That voice belonged to the swaggering visitor to the farm, Bay.

He remembered vividly the day Corbet and Jim Haliday had practically chased the man off the premises.

George was becoming a problem, growling savagely. Luke's hands were full of reins, the dog's collar, and the gun. He was ordered again to put down his gun. They were using the lantern to look into the back of the wagon, and the spirited team was getting restless.

"Get away from my team!" Luke yelled. "I can't hold this dog forever."

To his surprise, the man holding the bridle released it, and as the horses surged forward, he heard a voice mumble snatches of sentences. "Haliday's team all right . . . shingles and grain . . . no evidence. Guess he's slipped . . .

The dead chestnut was only a mile along the road, and it was light enough for Luke to show his handkerchief. Hugh and his charges emerged from the brush, and the drive was resumed.

Hugh chuckled at his companion's story. "So it was Bay again. I wish I knew who was with him. We have folks up in the hills that'd sell their grandmothers if they could get a price."

For a while, he drove fast and whistled through his teeth. Then he slowed and began talking. "You know, Luke, there's thousands of dollars reward offered for men in this Underground, people like John Brown and this man, Remington. But the highest price is for Harriet Tubman, a black woman."

Luke snorted derisively, still feeling irritated at having been stopped so summarily. "Well, sheriffs and law officers ought to be able to pick them up pretty easy."

Hugh's reply was a short laugh. Then he explained. "No, men like Brown and Remington will shoot. When they run batches of runaways, they pass out corn knives and pistols to the men, black pepper to the women. When you figure Brown lately ran a string of twenty-eight all the way from the deep south to Canada, you got to reason that the ordinary sheriff just isn't willing to take on a force like that. Harriet Tubman, she's different."

Luke was becoming interested in spite of himself and turned to face his companion across the back of the shaggy dog. "How is she different?"

Hugh nodded. "You ought to be interested. My father says yours died for the Abolition cause."

"Listen, Hugh, that was my father, not me. Tell me about Harriet Tubman."

"Well, my father and I went down country where she was supposed to come. There was a lot of folks in a big house, mostly white people. She wasn't there at first, and the folks just sat around visiting. Then she come in, and I'll never forget her. She was a big, rawboned woman dressed in a shabby outfit. When she had taken a chair and pulled off her sunbonnet, she talked. I can't remember the words she said. You just kinda felt her spirit and that no danger could stop you whilst you were helping runaways. My father says she goes right down south like Remington does. Only, she's a woman alone. She gets a party of runaways together and leads them north. Father says the reason she gets away is because she's never afraid. She thinks God guides her. The southern anti-Abolition societies will pay ten thousand dollars for that woman, dead or alive."

Hugh put on the wagon brake as they descended a long hill with a deep, tree-filled hollow to the left. George sat up and looked from one to the other as if expecting something.

Luke put his arm across the dog and asked a question. "Folks like them back in the wagon—don't they ever fuss around or ask questions?"

"No," came the answer after a moment. "No, not much or often. Sometimes a woman like that Claudy will open up. Luke, these folks are scared clear through. They've been on the road for close to a month, in danger all the time. By and by, they get numb to it and act like hunted animals. They just huddle together and try to keep out of the way and out of sight. All they've got is the little hope that they can follow the North Star to Canada. It's like religion to them."

Hugh flung out his arms. "Luke, I wish I could be like Remington and go down south, be a sort of raider. I'd want to bring a dozen at a time all the way. Once Remington stopped at our house. He's a small, ordinary-looking fellow. He let me shoot his revolver a little, then Hester beat me, using the same gun."

CHAPTER FOUR

THE DESCENDING road made a final sharp turn about a ridge point, and before them, was a large farm stretching east and west of the public road that divided the fields. Here was the vivid green of wheat waiting for the snows and neatly cleaned, lush cornfields and pastures where cattle grazed.

"That's Spring Haven, where Brookland lives," Hugh announced, pointing with his whip.

A huge stone barn was directly before them, but Luke's eyes were on the house. Dwarfed by the vase-shaped elms and the pyramids of pines and hemlocks that made the lawn like a park, the building was made of stone with wide chimneys lifting at both ends of the rambling structure. It fitted into the landscape as if it had always been there, like the rising hills across the creek to its rear. A graveled driveway that left the road between two stone posts wound in through the trees to the front porch of the house.

Hugh swung his team off the road toward the barn. The horses had just stopped when two men, both approximately Jim Haliday's age, appeared. They were smiling and looked oddly alike with the same small stature, sandy hair, and weathered faces.

"Climb down, boys. We'll take over," one of them called.

"Al and Ad, this is Luke Hanley with me," Hugh introduced. "Luke, meet the Jenkins cousins."

No sooner were the two young men off the seat and given a short handshake when one of the cousins climbed up and took the reins. With his free hand, he patted George, who wagged his tail vigorously. The other Jenkins opened the big barn doors, and the wagon with its team and passengers disappeared when the heavy wooden leaves swung quietly shut. Luke and Hugh walked toward the house.

"Funny, George didn't make a fuss. He's touchy with people," Luke commented to Hugh, who grinned.

"They raised him and gave him to us. But they get along with any animals from dogs to nasty bulls."

The wide stone-flagged porch was before them, and Hugh was about to sound the brass knocker on the polished walnut door when it swung open and a tall, lean man stood in the doorway.

"Mr. Brookland," Hugh said, "this is Luke Hanley. We brought down some people."

Brookland was taller than Luke. In spite of the gray at his temples, his face looked young. He probably was not ten years older than Luke. He was dressed in soft, worn corduroy, and his smile deepened the wrinkles at the corners of his eyes. He offered to each man a big, well-kept hand.

"Glad you came, Hugh. Hanley, your name's familiar, and I'm glad you're with us. Come in, men. The air is a bit sharp." He held the door open while they entered a wide hall where heavy walnut furnishings were ranked along the walls. Hugh, from former visits, seemed to feel at home, but Luke felt awkward as he followed their host into a huge living room where a roaring birchwood fire burned in a fieldstone fireplace that looked like the entrance to a cavern beneath the dark oak mantel. Paintings hung on the walls, and bundles of Indian arrows and bows stood together with fine-looking rifles and fowling pieces in the corners. To Luke, the room was a showplace where he could have spent hours just looking.

Brookland indicated chairs and put cigars on the table. He seemed very pleased to see his guests. "How are the folks, Hugh? I'm glad your father seems to have picked up a recruit in Hanley, here. The Right Sort of People surely need recruits now with a new deputy marshal loose. Did you have any trouble coming down?"

Hugh did most of the talking, telling about Bay's visit to the farm earlier and explaining why they had come through a day earlier with the runaways. He left out nothing, including Hester's warning.

Brookland frowned at this. "Don't frighten your mother, Hugh, but don't let that girl ride the hills too much alone. Some of these slave hunters are hard citizens."

It was plain that the boy enjoyed the confidence and responsibility this tall, urbane man put in him. Brookland was talking. "You're not a bit too early. Maisie has a young wild turkey we'll have for supper. The Jenkins boys have a good store of victuals in their kitchen behind the barn. I'm sorry we can't have our visitors here in the house, but there might be callers who would not understand and might carry news."

Hugh and Luke slept most of the afternoon and were glad for the chance since they had been awake all the preceding night. When they woke, their host showed them about. Luke was interested in the small grist mill a short distance down the creek.

"Only one thing wrong about here. The copperheads come off the ridges in dry weather. Then we have to watch where we walk," Brookland commented.

The dinner was an excellent meal, with the tender young turkey as the main dish. A tall, light-haired woman did the serving and evidently was the cook, from the pleasure she showed at the comments made about the dishes served. Brookland was a perfect host, talking of many things, but he never mentioned the people in his barn. He said that his father had owned this place, and it had run down. Brookland had loved it as a boy and had remodeled both the house and barn and developed the fields.

"The Jenkins boys worked for my father, and I don't know what I'd do without them. They can farm well, carpenter, break stock, swing axes, and shoot rifles." He waved his hand in a gesture toward the big farm. "When you boys are older, you'll realize that land gives a man an anchor. I used to travel a lot, but now I'm content here on the place."

Luke remembered Squire Jacoby's statement made months before that a young man should have some kind of anchor. The Haliday farm had offered peace, good work, and fine companionship, and he would have been glad to go on living there. But now he thought of Hester last night, the warmth of her body, the sweetness of her lips, and the storm she roused in him. Hugh broke into his thoughts with a question about the runaway slaves they had brought and their chances of going north.

"They'll be all right," Brookland answered. "I'll take them myself. But things are getting tighter with a deputy marshal named for this section. Pennsylvania has kept too much to the letter of that infernal Fugitive Slave Law of 1850. New York doesn't pay much attention to it. Up there, a black man can often testify for himself before a magistrate. He can't here. That's why these kidnappers of our black friends get away with the deviltry so easily."

Holding his cigar in the long powerful fingers of his right hand, he leaned forward over the table. "Both of you know the main Underground route comes up the Susquehanna through Williamsport, then north along the railroad to New York State. There's another a few miles east up Loyalsock Creek, following the Indian path and the old Gennessee road to the same state. Law officers and professional slave catchers hang around down that way like buzzards. So I want to develop a new route. We're close to the town of King's Shore, ten miles west of Williamsport. Runaways come to us over the mountains west of the Susquehanna. I could slip these people up to my lumber jobs on the West Branch of the Susquehanna close to Hyner Run. But above me are the John Caines operations, and I don't trust him or his men. Now, across the Tiadaghton from King's Shore is the Coudersport Pike running northwest. It's a lonely sixty miles with no houses and plenty of room to dodge officers. I want to establish two stations along this route so we can feed and lodge the runaways. My camps at Hyner Run could keep these places supplied. There's a logging road from there to the Pike."

He pushed back his chair, reached into a desk, and found a piece of paper on which he sketched rapidly with a pencil. "Here is Spring Haven. From here we go north through Antes Gap. King's Shore is directly ahead, four miles from here. We turn left, dodge the town, follow the river a mile, and reach where the Tiadaghton comes in. Just over the river from there is the Sanson farm, where I keep wagons and horses. Three miles north of the farm is the Pike. We'll make one station in the woods twelve miles up the road. The other will be at the Dyer farm, fifteen miles farther on. I need two men; when I find them, I'll be set."

Hugh, who had listened politely, excused himself as Maisie cleared the table. Luke and his host smoked quietly for a time. When Brookland spoke again, he completely changed the subject.

"Luke, you're not a complete stranger. Squire Jacoby, your friend and your father's, gave me your complete story, and I know from Jim how welcome you made yourself on his farm. It looks to me as though you're trapped by circumstances, if not worse."

Luke frowned at the turn in the conversation, but he read genuine concern in the fine eyes of the man talking to him. "Not trapped," he mumbled, "I just blundered."

Brookland shook his head in sharp negation. "We all make blunders. Linda Caines saved you from something we do not understand, and she paid a stiff price. Her father wanted you out of Crossville. He could have threatened the girl. Certainly she thought it tremendously important to break up that interrogation. Lord knows what she knows or suspects."

Luke, startled, stared at his host.

Brookland dusted the ashes from his cigar and found it had gone out. "Someday, friend, I'll find out about things, and there are ways open to me that may be closed to you. Remember, you just stepped into a situation in Crossville that none of us understands. Meanwhile, there is work to do—work your father would have approved. I want you to take one of those stations on the Pike."

The proffer was just what Luke needed at the moment. It would give him a chance to think things through, and it would save him the embarrassment of facing Hester until he was sure of his feelings for the girl. He had no great conviction about runaway slaves, but as with Hugh, some of its excitement had taken hold.

"Sure, Mr. Brookland. The farm work's finished for the season."

Later they went to the barn and found the runaways comfortable. Claudy was quite gay. Brookland talked with them for a while, giving the assurance that their troubles were nearly over.

Jerry suddenly became eager. "I jes can't be took, Mister. You see, I tried to git off right after me and Claudy was married."

"Show your back," his wife directed. The man pulled up his cotton shirt and showed a network of badly healed scars from the lash.

While he was pulling down the garment, Claudy talked. "After they ketched him, he was tied up in the town square so lots of folks could watch while the town constable lashed him with a blacksnake whip. So we traveled hard this time. Like to hev played Mother Amy out, but they'd hev hanged Jerry did they ketch him."

Brookland's steady eyes met Luke's for a moment, and the Jenkins men stood near the door.

"Don't worry, folks. So far, the Jenkins boys and I haven't lost a passenger," Brookland said. "When we get you to Lymansville, you're safe. It's close to New York State."

Since the runaways were a day ahead of schedule, it was necessary to wait at Spring Haven until the following night. Meanwhile, the refugees were fitted with warmer clothing.

Brookland had an errand in the town of King's Shore. He directed Luke to make himself at home on the place. Hugh was returning home, but he talked to Luke a bit before leaving.

"Mr. Brookland wants me for that first station. I got to see if I can talk the folks round. Mother worries, but Hester might talk her over."

With time on his hands, Luke wandered about the big place, spending much of his time in the mill. The dusty smell of its interior brought back memories of Crossville: Linda Caines in his arms while she begged him to go away, the dead body by the mill race, the inquisition in the schoolhouse, and what Jacoby had said about the pistol. He could no longer believe Linda took the weapon nor that she would have killed a man, but he understood part of John Caines' murderous attitude toward him when he came to the mill. The hurt to Caines' pride must have been terrible. Luke could remember the faint scent of Linda's hair and the soft willingness of her lips. He shook his head sharply. In spite of everything that had gone before, he had held Hester close, had crushed her lips with his own, and felt the girl's eager response.

"Damned fool," he groaned aloud.

Brookland and Luke had dinner together that evening. When they finished, Luke was ready with a question.

"What interest does John Caines have in this runaway slave business?"

Minor Brookland's face hardened at once, and he spoke speculatively. "I can't be sure. The man's in everything: lumbering, hotels, politics. He buys votes like cigars. But I can't see how he has made so much money so fast in legitimate business. The men around him are tough, some of them should be in the penitentiary. That blacksmith, Axelroth, looks like a murderer to me, and he's Caines' right-hand man. His master is hard, cruel, and dangerous."

Brookland rose abruptly, stepped to a window, and watched while a top buggy passed. Then he returned to his chair. "There are men making money catching runaway slaves, and they pick up free blacks and sell them back down south. A good black man could be worth a thousand dollars. The law won't permit a black man to testify on his own behalf. My friends tell me these freedmen are being picked up from Philadelphia to the Mississippi, most of them in Pennsylvania. We hear dark stories of Caines in the hills. Luke, your guess is as good as mine. If he's in this devilish man-snatching business, the sooner he's dead, the better for freedom."

He nervously lighted his cigar at the fireplace. "John Remington, whom you'll meet someday, told me personally that he'd shoot Caines sometime. Remington's pretty close-mouthed, so he must have had a reason for his threat." Moving to a more comfortable chair, Brookland relaxed and smiled at his visitor. "I talk too much, Luke, but this cause means a lot to me. We ride tonight. Let's get some rest. After Maisie's dinner, I can sleep."

Starting at eleven o'clock, Brookland, the Jenkins cousins, and Luke led their passengers past the gap on foot and on through sparse timber to where a boat was hidden in the water birches. It took two trips, but eventually, all of them and the baggage they carried were safely over the broad river.

"Just a mile now to horses and wagon," Ad Jenkins told Luke.

The Sanson farm Brookland had mentioned was a small place where two young people appeared, carrying a lantern to welcome them. Luke thought Brookland must have been here during the afternoon, from what they said.

"All's set. Horses fed and watered. Three days' grub is stored under the hay in the wagon, Mr. Brookland," the young farmer announced. "I'll drive the Jenkins men back to the boat."

"Thanks," Brookland told the efficient young farmer. "If you pick up a warning or something, you can overtake us on that mare of yours."

The former slaves sat in the wagon box on straw. Luke rode beside Brookland on the wagon seat. Under the driver's legs was a shotgun, pushed back against the base of the seat. In addition, the lantern back at the farm had shown a suspicious bulge beneath Brookland's corduroy coat just under the left armpit.

The sandy road followed the big creek, almost a river at that point. At a bend of the stream, the road turned westward, passing a white church and a cluster of houses. Beyond the village, they entered the timber. After a mile or so, Brookland pulled in his team and stopped.

"Take the gun, Luke. There's somebody ahead. We'll get out."

It wasn't a dark night, and since they had been away from lights for hours, they could see pretty well. In a minute, Luke heard the sound which had alarmed his companion—the shuffling of feet in the sand and an occasional hiccup. Not far from them, a figure was approaching, weaving from one side of the road to the other.

"Drunk," Brookland grunted and stepped in front of the fellow so suddenly that he all but fell forward.

"Brother," he mumbled, clutching Brookland's coat to keep from falling, "you damn near scairt me to death. I'm lost, travelin' round and round. Show me where that church is and I'll get home."

"You need another drink," his accoster suggested. "Maybe a little more liquor'd clear your head."

The man staggered back a step and then grabbed for his former hold. "Where'd I git it? Where—"

A small bottle was thrust into his hand. "Take a shot of this, brother, then I'll lead you down the road a piece."

The already drunken man drank freely from the bottle, then he docilely allowed himself to be led past the wagon and into a lane at the end of which a light showed. Back in his seat, Brookland chuckled. "If he empties that bottle, he'll think he's struck by lightning. That was brandy."

The road was climbing now, and the moon was out, lighting the timberland through which they passed. Luke carried the gun across his knees and noticed that his companion had become silent. The genial host was gone. This man holding the leather lines was alert and watchful of even slight sounds. He bent forward a little as he drove. Just after they had topped a grade, he pulled in the horses and placed a hand on Luke's knee.

"It don't fit, friend. That man back there wasn't drunk in spite of his breath. He was coming out of the woods. Listen, there's a logging road ahead. Take the rig in there. I believe the drunk was a spy and remember he walked past our wagon. They may be after us."

Luke slid over as Brookland dropped off the wagon. This was the same maneuver Hugh had used a few nights past. The moon helped, and inside a quarter of an hour, the team and wagon were off the road in dense timber shadows. When Luke got down, he reassured his passengers.

"No danger, folks. We're just trying to be real careful."

"We's used to that," Claudy answered. "We kin wait."

After he had tied the horses, Luke took the shotgun and went back to the road, where he hid himself behind a big rock. Time dragged as it usually does when one waits and listens. The horsemen, though, were closer than expected. One moment the road was empty, the next, three bulky, mounted figures were silhouetted against the skyline as they passed. Luke made his position more comfortable and waited. The riders were scarcely out of earshot when they returned and pulled up not twenty feet from where Luke crouched with his gun.

A heavy voice demanded: "You're sure it was Brookland, Ben."

The answering voice was unmistakably that of the drunken man of several hours back. "Sure, I know the stuck-up cuss too well. Besides, who in these hills would carry brandy but him? The young fellow with him carried a gun, don't be forgettin' thet."

After the men were silent a few moments and the horses had milled around a little, a third voice spoke. "There's a woods road takes off here somewheres. Mebbe the wagon's down there."

Luke eased back one hammer of the gun with the vague idea of firing into the air to create a diversion, but the authoritative tones of the first speaker cut in emphatically. "Listen to me, men. We don't foller Minor Brookland down any side road for a ten-dollar fine or so. That man'll shoot. He was in the army once. Might as well say as how we've had our ride for nothing and collect our expense money tomorrow. Thet'll be one dollar apiece. Besides that, Ben got him some high-toned drinking licker. Let's get home. There'll be other times."

Brookland appeared in easy spirits a few minutes after the horsemen had gone. "That was Wash Turner from the village through which we passed, he and his posse. No trouble anymore from them this trip. The only problem is, how did they know we'd be coming tonight so they could put out a spy and be all set to take us?"

At daylight, they stopped by a chattering stream, and Claudy prepared an excellent breakfast from the stores they carried. Brookland, using bits of meat as bait, supplemented the meal with a catch of small trout that the girl fried nicely in bacon fat.

"Claudy," Brookland told her, "guess I'll have to take you home with me. My Maisie's leaving, and I need a good cook."

The girl rolled her eyes and giggled. Later, she looked at her husband thoughtfully.

They remained in this camp until after lunch. The afternoon trip took them through the great pines. From the hills, they crossed the land spread away in all directions, a great sea of trees that softened the outlines and seemed limitless. The road wound through a colonnade of brown trunks. A glance at the sky gave one the impression that he was traveling at the base of a deep trench. The farther they drove into this timber, the quieter all became as if some brooding presence lurked under the tall trees.

"This is the Black Forest," Brookland commented to Luke. "It's timber that will never be cut, too far from market and no stream to float out the logs."

The timber finally thinned to hardwoods and pitch pine. They turned into a narrow road to the left. "This will be the Dyer farm, Luke. We'll spend the night under a roof."

Two empty log buildings stood close to a big spring at the edge of a farm overgrown now with weeds and brush. As soon as a fire was going in the stone chimney, the cabin became more cheerful. Once again, Claudy showed her skill as a cook.

"I work't in the big house," she explained. "They was mighty pertickler."

The evening was pleasant for the runaways relaxed, feeling they must be coming close to the end of their long journey. Even Mother Amy joined the general talk before the fire.

"This'll be your station, Luke. Will you be lonely here?" Brookland asked, and the younger man shook his head.

"No, sir. I'd like it here."

Much of their baggage had been brought into the cabin. On the top of some blankets lay a small, cheap harmonica at the sight of which Jerry's dull eyes brightened. He looked at the instrument until Brookland noticed and nodded his head affirmatively. Sheer joy showed in the man's eyes as he placed the instrument to his lips and started playing softly. He was really good at it and gave forth tune after tune, old hymns, plantation melodies, and plaintive bits he probably composed himself.

Close to noon of the next day, Brookland and Luke delivered their charges to Mr. Erritt at his place, which he called Hillside. The runaways were exuberant when told they would be in New York State in another day. Mother Amy muttered a prayer. Jerry fondled the harmonica Brookland had given to him. It was Claudy who let herself go. She took several steps into the room, began a tuneless chant, and started dancing. Wilder and wilder she became, her dress whirling about her bare legs and her eyes rolling. Abruptly she caught hold of herself, stopped dancing, and dutifully seated herself beside her husband.

Before leaving, Brookland drove into the village of Lymansville, where he purchased several bales of wool. It took him and Luke only two days to return, including time spent selling the wool in King's Shore. The Jenkins cousins were delighted when the wagon rolled in on the driveway, but they asked no questions.

CHAPTER FIVE

SEVERAL DAYS after the return to Spring Haven, the weather turned sharply cold, but there was still little snow. Since nothing more was said about the station on the Pike, Luke grew more and more restless. He did not want to go back to the Haliday home just yet, for there would be little work there for an extra man. He could go up the river, but woodsmen would not be in demand. Finally, he mustered the courage to approach his host.

"Mr. Brookland, I'll have to find work somewhere. Since I drifted into this country, I've been sponging on the Halidays and you."

The big man laughed. "I apologize. But I was watching you, Luke. You kept a grip on yourself and you were good to our passengers. I'm about ready to go up the Pike so we can get things in shape before heavy snows fall. Your job will be at the Dyer farm, where you'll take care of what we send you. The teams will shuttle back and forth when we're fully organized. It'll be something like stage runs."

The statement partially satisfied Luke, but his other bother was his lack of money. Brookland seemed to read his mind.

"Another thing, friend. Money isn't scarce with us who work the Underground, for the city Abolition societies keep us pretty well supplied. You'll get wages—mind you, not for running slaves, but for being caretaker, driver, and hostler. We can't pay a man for lawbreaking."

He took two five-dollar gold pieces from his pocket. "The rate's forty dollars a month and found. Here's your first week's pay. Now I want you to run up to the Halidays' and pay Jim for horse feed and other expenses he's had."

That excuse was all Luke needed to make up his mind. He found the Haliday family glad to see him when he arrived, and he felt his coming broke a tension in the home. Emma was more silent than before, however. Hester was preoccupied and gave Luke no chance to see her alone. There was no hint from her about what happened that night below the gap. At supper, Luke explained Brookland's plan concerning stations, and Hugh kept his eyes on his plate.

Finally, Emma laid down her fork and spoke in a strained voice. "I don't like it. There will be trouble, arrests, fines, months, maybe years, in jail. They'd take the farm and the men folks away. Now, Luke, you're pulled into it." She ignored Jim's all but imperceptible gesture to stop and continued. "Things are different with a man like Minor Brookland. He has money and big friends who'd get him out of trouble. They never jail folks like him. It's just working folks like us that get hurt."

Jim pushed back his plate, and his face was solemn. "They come knocking, Mother. The star they follow leads to our place. All they got in the world is trust in folks like us." He stood up abruptly. Luke had never seen this quiet, self-contained man like this, striding up and down, talking. "I hate slavery. Mebbe you folks didn't see Jerry's back. Years past, I was down south and got a belly full of slavery. If we was black folks in the South, Emma, they could sell you, use you like a cow to breed more slaves. Damn it, don't squirm. I've seen worse. Hugh'd make a good fieldhand. Hester would be some ornery young devil's plaything like that girl we took through last spring. The whole thing's hellish. I'm just a mountain farmer, but here's something the Lord has put in my hand—"

"Jim!"

Emma Haliday's cry stopped her husband. "There's no use," she said and dropped her head on her arms, shaking with sobs.

Luke helped Hugh with the barn chores in the morning and made him take one of the gold pieces he had received from Brookland. After protesting, the boy pocketed it, then jabbed his fork hard in a pile of hay.

"I can't tell Mother. She's too worried and worked up. But I feel like Pop, and I'm going to man a station if Brookland wants me. Only I'd like better to go down south like Remington and fetch up a dozen at a time. That way, a man could fight his way through."

He tossed the hay into a manger and faced Luke abruptly. "It's this Bay that spoiled things. And somebody's paying folks up around here to carry news to the law. Likely we're being watched. Someday I'm gonna unload a shotgun into that Bay's backside. That'll keep him from riding for a spell."

The remark worried Luke. He knew the excitement of night driving and the appeal of possible danger. This would be stronger in Hugh, who was younger. The boy was entirely capable of carrying out his threat. Now Hugh added some peculiar reasoning.

"He wouldn't shoot back. You see, them lawmen know they can't fine a dead man."

They finished their work with no further talk, seeing to it that all racks were crammed with hay and each feed box got its proper amount of corn or ground grain. The whole barn was filled with the cheerful sound of animals eating amid the fresh, clean odors brought in from harvest fields.

Minor Brookland made a surprise visit that evening and was his charming, cheerful self. His assured manner did much to lessen the tension. He was certain there was little danger on the Pike because it was not heavily traveled and officers would not lurk on it.

When he drove away later in the night, both young men went with him. Hester had not given Luke a minute alone with her, but she had been most gracious to Brookland during his visit.

The departure from the Sanson farm for the Pike took on the character of a real expedition. Sanson stored materials for the Brookland camps upriver, so there was plenty of food and equipment to load a big wagon. Over the food, blankets, and extra clothing, a canvas cover was pulled tightly, then on this, hay was piled until there was a good three feet of it. Ad Jenkins, Luke, Hugh, and Brookland made up the party. The day was cold, and they drove openly since there was nothing illegal in their load.

* * *

The first station was farther out the Pike than Luke had expected, and it was to be a camp in a narrow ravine. The canvas spread over the food and equipment was to serve as a tent. The screening pines and hemlocks hid the spot from the road. Hugh and Jenkins remained to set the place up comfortably.

Luke and Brookland did not reach the Dyer farm until nearly dark, but it was simple to make it habitable since there was a good roof. Brookland spent the night with him, and they talked a long time before retiring.

With long legs stretched out toward the blaze and his body completely relaxed, Luke's employer explained the plan he expected to follow.

"We'll arrange to run our passengers, when we get them, out of Spring Haven on Mondays and Tuesdays for two weeks. That'll mean that you receive them Wednesdays and Thursdays. At the end of two weeks, we'll reverse the times so curious folks won't know just when to watch. We'll use two good teams and shuttle them back and forth. Feed and supplies would make it hard to use too many horses. Likely Erritt will help later and come down to you for people. Wagonloads back would be wool, which is profitable and an excellent way to account for Brookland wagons on the Pike."

He lit a fresh cigar and looked sharply at his companion. "You'll find Erritt a reliable man. It's the Halidays that worry me. I'm willing to take chances like you young fellows do. But Emma Haliday is frightened, and that makes Hugh edgy. If he used fine shot on a constable, it would be bad, and if an officer was killed, it would just about close up the Underground. That's one reason I want Hugh out here in the woods. He's less likely to run into trouble. Abel Thorn'll help Jim Haliday while the boy's gone."

Changing the subject completely, he surprised Luke. "Tell me more about this business with Linda Caines and Horton. I want to fill in the blanks."

It seemed entirely natural to sit here by the fire and talk with a man who really invited confidences. Luke supplied a lot of details, after which his listener drew a long breath.

"It beats me why a fine girl should take the step she did unless you, my fine-fisted friend, were in more danger than we know. Linda Caines must be a wonderful person and an equally wonderful friend."

Luke studied the play of the flames about sticks of wood a while before he commented. "It all bothers me, Mr. Brookland. When I was with the Halidays, I could forget Crossville and be happy. But when I was alone, I couldn't keep from figuring that Linda possibly thought I was jealous and had really shot Horton. When I dropped that thought, I figured she took my pistol. That she should use it was preposterous. Now I feel John Caines got it some way and was going to plant it so I would be blamed for murder. But why would he do that before the meeting in the schoolhouse when Linda talked?"

Brookland tossed his cigar into the coals.

"Luke, John Caines must have had a reason to run you out of Crossville. True, his daughter's confession hurt his pride, but he was plotting before that happened. Also, he and Nedrow are now supposed to be hand-in-glove when they should be enemies. Just take this for granted: you're a young man in your twenties, and you have a bitter enemy in John Caines who has a lot of influence behind him."

"Hell," Luke snapped angrily. "All you people warn me about the man. He doesn't look dangerous to me. I threw him out the door and the mill didn't fall down. If it hadn't been for Linda, I'd have stayed in Crossville."

Brookland grinned into the angry face of his companion and got up. "I'm not too old yet, friend, to know how you feel. Let's let it ride and get to bed. I have a long drive in the morning. Only one last thing; if you ever threaten John Caines, don't leave him alive. I believe that this county, this state, and maybe this nation could well spare the man anytime."

With this surprisingly vicious comment, Brookland took his blanket and rolled up on his straw pallet, leaving Luke with the feeling that this ordinarily quiet, poised gentleman would be more dangerous to his enemies than John Caines could ever be.

* * *

The horses were hitched, and Brookland sat in the driver's seat. He had been sleepy at breakfast, but now he grinned. Reaching behind him into the wagon, he handed Luke three books.

"They'll help pass the time. Remember, it will be Brookland to Hugh to you to Lymansville and Erritt's place. Let's keep things ready."

After the last sound of the wagon had died away in the hills, Luke examined his books. The first was a surveyor's manual. Now he could continue the studies that had been interrupted at Crossville. The second was a copy of Walter Scott's *Rob Roy*, and the third was a worn Bible with the name Minor Brookland on the flyleaf.

There wasn't a great deal of work to be done about the place other than to gather great heaps of boughs for beds and pile the shed high with firewood. After a few days, Luke fashioned a crude calendar so he could keep track of the days passengers might arrive. Late one forenoon, he saw the first snowflakes. By mid-afternoon, the ground was well covered, and the smother of flakes was so dense he could see only a few yards across the clearing. Darkness came early, and Luke read a long time by firelight, hoarding the small stock of candles brought here.

He slept fitfully, and each time he roused, he went to the door and looked out. The snowfall had thinned enough, so he saw a dim, white world with all the rough places neatly rounded. It was so quiet that he caught himself straining to listen for sounds hidden behind the soft whisper of the flakes against the house boards.

The storm continued the next day, and with nightfall, the wind lifted, drifting loose snow against the windows and walls with the sound of light surf. In occasional lulls, Luke caught himself listening again and he knew that was a bad thing. A man alone must not do it. Yet once, when he looked out the door, he thought he saw a figure moving in the white smother. His uneasiness increased, but now he was thinking of Hugh with his meager shelter of tent cloth. The cold was mounting. Minor Brookland probably knew what he was about, but certainly no one would move on the Pike in such weather. Luke had his doubts about the efficiency of such a business as it was planned.

Following his breakfast, he decided to go back and see how the boy in his camp was making out. After all the Halidays' friendliness, he owed at least that much to them where their son was concerned. Luke felt partially responsible for the fact that Hugh had become a station keeper in that lonely place. In preparation, he took a full box of sulfur matches and a small bundle of mixed birch bark and pine shavings so an emergency fire could be started in a hurry. A paper parcel of bread and meat went into his pocket, and a belt axe completed his equipment. After a glance outside, he closed the door while he pulled on an extra coat. He was now wearing all the clothing he had.

The savage wind had practically cleared the lane out to the Pike, but it was different on the road. Drifts had piled so high that he had to detour through the timber, and walking became steadily harder. The cold was so great the snow creaked under his feet.

Luke had covered close to five miles before he fully realized how dangerous his venture was. After circumventing a particularly long drift, he had difficulty finding the road again. He was getting tired and knew that if a man got lost out here in such weather, he would most likely freeze to death.

When his mind was about settled to turn back, he came upon a straight stretch of the highway marked by low trees on either side. Here the snow drifted to a deceptive level, and he found himself floundering in it up to his waist. An attempt to detour led him too far back into the timber. Then, as he bent his head, concentrating on pushing against the wind with his shoulders, he stopped abruptly. Over the sound of the storm, he heard a high-pitched, eerie wail. Through the thickening snow, a dark figure was approaching, one that fell forward, rose, and came on, taking more and more time for each movement.

Luke's first thought was of a bear, but he realized that any respectable member of that animal family would have been sound asleep for months. Then he figured it must be Hugh, as the object made a final desperate wallowing effort, then dropped and was still.

He hesitated only a moment, then floundered forward through the drift. Kneeling beside the quiet figure, he found a still, partially-conscious black man struggling to regain his breath.

"Outa, outa—"

The panting words came stiffly as the man twisted and gained a sitting position. One reason for his exhaustion showed then. He carried a child, heavily swaddled in blankets.

"Mealie and I's jest played out," he panted, trying to shape a smile on his cold-stiffened face.

Luke's first gesture was to strip off his own outer coat and pull it across the thinly clad shoulders of the man.

"Hold tight," he directed. "Get your breath. I'll have a fire in a jiffy."

The only available shelter from the piercing wind was the lee of a big rock, and here Luke built his fire, thankful for the dry kindling he had carried. When the first blaze had been made strong with piled-on broken branches, he helped the stricken man and his burden to the reviving circle of heat. The stranger sat, spreading huge hands toward the blaze, still holding the closely wrapped child on his lap. Once, he pulled away the blanket cover and revealed the patient but almost wizened face of a little girl.

"Mealie ain't but three," he explained. "I'm Fred. We been travelin' too far fer her."

Fred ravenously devoured the lunch Luke gave him, sharing with the child what parts of it she could choke down, and Luke ate a piece of bread to gain the strength he knew he would need getting back to the farm.

"I'm one of the Right Sort of People," Luke assured the man. "Now let's get back to the house if you're strong enough."

The answering smile was doubtful. "Mebbe I kin, sir, was you to help me a little. Mealie ain't real heavy, but—"

Luke took the blanketed bundle from the arms of the weakened man and plowed forward, breaking track. He was careful to keep the flap of the blanket over the child's face to cut the force of the stinging, wind-driven snow.

The trip back over the miles to the lane was a cold and breathless nightmare, with the snow a savage antagonist that fought to pull down a man's strength. In moments of regained energy, Fred would break the way a few yards, then Luke would take over. Their eyes ached from the wind and snow, and they wasted no time talking. Breath was too precious, and they tried to make no unnecessary moves.

Luke, still carrying the child, had just enough strength left to push open the cabin door. Then he fell forward on the floor. Fred must have made a quicker recovery, for when his rescuer opened his eyes, there was a blazing fire going. Little Mealie, still wrapped in the blanket but with her head uncovered, lay before the fireplace, and Fred was grinning.

"Jes made it, Mister. Only jes."

Heat, rest, and food did wonders for the men. They dragged one of the bough pallets close to the fireplace so the heat would reach it, and the child lay there, her tired eyes on the leaping blaze. Unbelievably tiny, she seemed to have an adult's understanding of their desire to help her and would try to smile each time they did something for her comfort. When she attempted to speak, a spasm of coughing followed.

"She's hed her a cold most a week and was always puny-like. Mealie ain't but a bit more'n three, and she's walked a lot lately."

Clumsily, the men prepared some gruel using water and bread. The child tried to drink the concoction, holding the cup with hands like those of an old and fragile woman. She could not get it down and laid back on the pallet.

"Was we to hev warm milk now," Fred mumbled desperately, and Luke, dismayed, stared at him. Milk, which would be life to the child, was forty drifted snow miles away.

Both men sat up during the night to watch and help. During the long hours, Fred told his story. He was from a plantation in the Deep South and had been the plantation blacksmith. His pretty wife was younger and loved a good time far too much. Their only child was frail Mealie, whose mother had resented her because, in so many ways, she hampered her pleasure. The master was a hard, cynical man. One day, Fred left his forge to get a file he had left in his cabin. Standing outside, he had heard voices he recognized as those of his wife and the master. He heard enough to realize the woman was asking the man to sell the child, Mealie, because she would never amount to anything.

"Then, I jes walked in. They was on the bed with Mealie shet in a closet out of the way. Mister Bright hed him a pistol and come at me. I paid him no attention but slapped her oncet. Next, I hit him hard. Pretty soon I seen he'd never git up, fer his neck was twisted. I tied her up, took Mealie, and come off. We bin travelin' ever since."

Luke listened to the incredible story. The child, unloved by her mother, lay between them, and Fred went on. "They turned loose the dogs, and I shot one of 'em with his pistol."

After some fumbling in his clothes, he took out a double-barreled derringer and handed it to his host. "Never kilt nobody before. I jes hit him hard. They kept atter us fer days and days. Mealie wuz hungry, but she didn't whimper none. Mister Brookland sent us along fast because they wuz offerin' money fer me. The boy at the camp sed as how I mus' stay two or three days. When he went out to git wood, me and Mealie come away."

Sometime near morning, the little girl who had come so far on this desperate journey opened her eyes. She moved her frail body a little and seemed to be trying to talk.

Then, she died.

His own face wet with tears, Luke took her tiny hand from her father's huge one and tucked it under the covers. Fred broke, his big body retching with sobs. His thick lips were mumbling, "Jes too little . . . jes too little. She tried so mighty hard."

Watching him, for the first time Luke now understood the hatred for the institution of slavery held by his own father and Jim Haliday. They knew its terrible abuses. Here was a father and a tiny child hunted like beasts because the man had struck down an unnatural mother and killed her paramour. Here was the cause that sent black people north by thousands on the desperate journey toward freedom. Here was the cause that was moving thousands of men in the North to try to wipe out this curse upon the nation.

The blizzard had spent itself during the night. Luke chose a place on the south side of a great pine where the sun would rest kindly, even on a cold day. There they buried the child after Luke read from Brookland's worn Bible. The ground had been hard, but the grave only needed to be small. When all was finished, a puff of wind sifted snow across the tiny mound.

CHAPTER SIX

FRED'S DEMEANOR puzzled Luke. He had run away from Hugh's camp in his eagerness to get to freedom. He had carried his feeble daughter over the terrible miles. Now, after several days of natural brooding over the child's death, he did not mention going on, even though the storm had blown itself out and the weather had moderated considerably.

"Fred, one of these days, we'll have to move along through the woods to the next station. That's Lymansville. After that, New York State, where you'll be safe."

The big man shook his heavy head and spoke dubiously. "I 'spect so, Mister."

Other things bothered Luke, especially Hugh. A team must have brought Fred and Mealie to the camp in the ravine. It should have been Hugh's business to bring the horses on up if the road was passable, but no team came. Brookland must have been particularly concerned about this fugitive to have sent him along in the bad weather.

The third day after the storm Luke went out to the Pike and was just in time to hide when what looked like a logging outfit came in sight and passed by. Four heavy horses were hitched to a sled piled high with a burden of feed and gear. There was a third team of big horses fastened to the tailgate with leading straps, and five men rode the load. Luke was tempted to show himself and ask passage for Fred since he knew most lumbermen were friendly to runaways. He thought better of it in a moment, remembering that Fred was a hunted man, wanted for murder. At any rate, the passage of the outfit showed the road was open.

Trouble struck without warning. Luke had chopped wood most of the morning and, after lunch, had flung himself down on a pallet to take a nap. Fred had cooked the meal and washed the dishes. He was fairly cheerful now and seldom made references to the dead child. However, Luke had occasionally caught the man looking at the derringer pistol, testing the lock, and examining the single brass percussion cap still in place on the unfired barrel. Luke had offered ammunition and had shown the man just how to load the weapon, but he had not done so.

Luke overslept and was roused by heavy pounding. He remembered Fred's custom of putting the heavy bar across the door when they were both inside the building. This was probably Hugh, for there was the sound of horses tramping outside. A glance at Fred told him something else. The man was gray with fright. He held his pistol but did not seem to know how to handle it, and he was mumbling.

"Open the door," Luke commanded. "Likely it's Hugh from the other camp."

Fred stepped closer, held his finger across his lips, and whispered, "It's the patrollers, Mister Luke. They's come fer me."

The rapping was now accompanied by vigorous kicks against the panels, and a voice bellowed, "Open in the name of the law! There's a murderer in there!"

Fully awake now to the danger, Luke took a hasty glance through a crack and saw three horsemen, two of them dismounted. All were armed. Luke's axe stood outside the door, and one of the men snatched it up, ready to break their way in. Fred was gibbering when his companion leaped to the corner where the loaded shotgun stood.

"Get away from that door!" he shouted. The answer was a shot. A bullet ripped through the panels high up, struck the stone fireplace, and dropped to the floor.

As he lifted the gun, Luke remembered that it was loaded with a light charge, not nearly strong enough to drive shot through the door. His mind was searching desperately for something to gain time while Fred escaped. Then he heard a triumphant yell.

"There he goes!"

When Luke darted to the now-open rear door, he saw what had happened. Fred had leaped out and was running across the open field for the timber. He had gone a hundred yards when the man who had remained mounted spurred his horse. As it leaped forward, the rider lifted a pistol and fired. Fred made two more frantic leaps and pitched forward, face down in the snow.

Luke was overwhelmed with a rage that did not count consequences. He had just seen a man shot down like an escaping beast without being given a chance. He crossed the room in two bounds and jerked the bar away from the front door. The other two men had mounted and now were fifty to seventy-five yards from the cabin when the shotgun came up and roared.

The man who had shot Fred yelled, and his horse nearly unseated him. All three men swung their mounts toward the lane, and Luke fired the second barrel. Still not satisfied at the rout he had caused, Luke reloaded the gun and dashed after the posse. The tracks in the snow on the Pike told him the men had gone down it at a furious pace.

To his amazement, when he returned to the cabin, Fred was sitting up on the snow with bewilderment on his features.

"Fred," Luke called, "aren't you hit?"

The man got to his knees and then stood up shakily. "Dunno jist yet. I tripped, but I'm bloody."

Luke helped the man into the cabin. When Fred pulled off his shirt, there was a bullet cut through the skin just under one arm that bled freely but was extremely shallow. He yelled when it was doused with the woodman's specialty—turpentine. He also had the start of a good lump on the forehead where he had struck something hard in falling.

He grinned at Luke as he wriggled back into his clothing. "Sure was lucky, Mister Luke. Thet patroller wanted his bullet through my back."

Fred had lost the pistol in his dash, but he found it and reloaded it as soon as the weapon was dried off. "Didn't remember I hed it," the big fellow remarked ruefully. "Now let's git us away from here, far, before they come back."

"No, Fred, there's no hurry. I put a load of shot in one, and they won't be anxious to try it again. Anyway, we'd have to wait till we won't make tracks or they'd follow. We could fight them off if we stayed in the house."

Fred did not comment on whether that was a wise decision or not, but he borrowed his companion's jackknife to whittle out a ramrod for loading the derringer.

Just at evening, he made a surprising announcement. "Mister Luke, them men figgered to shoot me like a sheep-killin' dog. Next time, I shoots back. I don't want to go up north, and I got nobody but me now. You folks is helping other folks thet follers the star. I'm gonna stay and help."

Luke looked at the man in astonishment. He was powerfully built, his chin was strong, and there was a different look in his eyes.

"Yessir, I aims to help."

Luke grinned at his determination. There was no use in telling him this shooting today might throw all of Brookland's system out of gear for months, even years. Those discomfited horsemen would not take defeat lightly. The pursuit of Fred had been all the more determined because he had left a dead man behind. It was possible that Brookland, the Halidays, and most likely Hugh might be under arrest.

Abruptly his rage returned, and he shook Fred's shoulders.

"Sure!" he shouted. "You'll help and we'll shoot hell out of the next bunch that comes riding in here with pistols in their hands. If only to God I'd have had a rifle today."

Fred released himself and raised a heavy warning hand. "Mister Luke, don't. Ef a man gits him too mad, he's kind of blind like. So it wuz when I came off with Mealie, and now she's dead. We gotta git us cooled down some."

The sunny days passed until there was a threat of more storm, yet there was no snow, while one gloomy day followed another. Luke explained that there was a settlement of black people up the West Branch of the Susquehanna and that the little creek which rose here on the farm emptied into that river. As soon as there was snow to cover their tracks, they would go that way. The distance wasn't more than a long day's march for a good man.

* * *

One bleak night, both men were sound asleep, neither having thought of keeping watch, when a rapping at the door brought them both to their feet. There was light enough in the room from the fireplace for Luke to find his shotgun and for Fred to locate his pistol. Luke walked to the door and stood beside it.

A voice called, "Open, friend. I'm from the Right Sort of People."

That was the password all right, but anyone could have given it. At Luke's gesture, Fred, with pistol ready, stood on the other side of the door as the bar was lifted. In the poor light, they could see that the man who stepped between them was a bit over middle height, rawboned and roughly dressed. Fred shoved the muzzle of his pistol into the visitor's ribs, but he spoke quietly.

"Put it down, son. I'm a friend."

There was enough reassurance in the man's voice to make Luke put aside his gun and light a candle from the coals in the fireplace. Their visitor bore the marks of hard travel, and he was not heavily dressed. Frost showed on his mustache, and his face was reddened and chapped by the weather.

"It's cold riding your hills tonight, friends. Maybe you'd put up my horse and me for the rest of it," he said as he spread big red hands to the fire.

Fred tossed more wood on the coals, and when the flames licked up, the horseman turned himself slowly about so the welcome heat would touch every part of him.

"Well, boys, you haven't run me out, so I figure I stay. How about the horse?"

Fred lit the lantern, and all three went out where a big bay, reins dragging in western fashion, stood close to the door. The stock of a short rifle protruded from a saddle boot, and there was a big blanket roll tied behind the saddle. In the shed, the newcomer rid the horse of its gear and fastened a blanket on his mount while corn was put into the feed box and hay stuffed in the manger.

"Tobe don't often get it so good," the rider said as they walked back to the cabin, where he dumped the saddle and the gear he carried on the floor near the door. Inside, he turned to Luke.

"I know who you must be, young man, and I have a message for you. It's important. You can call me Owen Smith, though that's not my name nor can I tell you my business. That way, if you're ever asked questions, you won't have a thing to hide."

There was power and calmness in the man's voice. He looked young, but there was already some gray at his temples. His cheekbones were high as an Indian's, but his eyes were the prominent features of his countenance. Set deeply, they were gray and as steady as a rock. Looking into them, one felt they would always remain unmoved no matter what they saw.

"Some southern folks and a court officer came up this way after a black man who killed his master. One of these men got shot. When they got him back down country, they used the telegraph to set the sheriff in this county on the man that did the shooting. They thought the black man was dead, shot when escaping. Some of the right sort of people heard the news and told me to warn you away. The sheriff's not too anxious to do his job, but murder's murder. It could be he'd get here before another night passes."

He turned to Fred. "You ought to get yourself up Keating way. Some of your people are there. Don't move farther on till this thing quiets down."

"They shot Fred, you know, Mr. Smith," Luke said quietly, and the visitor bowed in understanding.

"So I would suppose. There was one professional slave catcher in the trio, but the man hit was a deputy sheriff."

He was rubbing his big hands at the fire again and accidentally brushed back his coat enough so that the light picked out a glimpse of the cylindrical nipples of two walnut-stocked revolvers thrust through his belt.

"You hungry?" Luke asked, and Smith's smile was wide with friendliness.

"Now that's a good word. I ate at early noon, but I'm always hungry. My father says that thin people, like gaunt horses, are heavy feeders."

He ate hungrily, without selection, seeming to relish all Fred set before him. When he had finished, the three drew up before the fire, and Smith took out a huge tobacco pouch and shared its contents with his hosts.

"Fred ought to know where that tobacco comes from. It's south Virginia leaf."

Smith talked about the Underground Railroad. He praised Harriet Tubman for going south and bringing people north with her, and he spoke of New York State as being almost as safe for a runaway as Canada. Abruptly, his brows drew down, and he pointed a finger at Luke. "You ever hear of the Knights of the Golden Circle?"

Luke shook his head, and Smith spoke carefully.

"It's an organization for the extension of slave territory. Now there seems to be organization behind these slave catchers. There are times when I wonder if this outfit might have a man somewhere in central Pennsylvania. Too many runaways are caught."

In a moment, he changed the subject. "Boys, I routed you out of bed, and I've a long ride tomorrow. Let's sleep."

He laid both revolvers and his rifle on the table. Minutes later, both Smith and Fred were snoring, but Luke lay thinking. Shooting an officer was serious business. He was really in trouble this time.

* * *

The first thing the next morning, Smith went to the barn to feed and rub down his horse. There was a light snow falling, and when he came in, he offered advice. "Good day to travel, boys. That snow'll cover tracks."

When the three sat at the rickety table for breakfast, Smith bowed his head and said a short grace in his deep calm voice, after which he ate heartily. Before he put on his coat, he took out two gold coins and gave them to Fred.

"Take these to the Keating folks. They're mighty poor. Anyway, it'll make your welcome surer."

Much as small boys will do, Luke and Fred trooped after Smith when he went out and mounted. He picked up his reins, held them at chest height, and touched Tobe with his heel.

"Goodbye, boys. The Lord be with you, and don't forget—He made the North Star."

The big horse trotted up the road and was lost to sight in the softly falling snow. Luke had the feeling that Smith was one of the most remarkable men he had ever known. He had come in the night, made himself a friend in a few hours, and gave both a warning and confidence, to Luke, at least.

Fred spoke first. "Wonders me who thet man is. He ain't Smith, so he said."

They wasted no time hiding some of the materials about the place and getting together food and blankets for their trip. Luke divided the one box of matches, and each took a short length of candle to help start fires. There was one hand axe Luke wanted Fred to take, but Fred preferred a big, wicked-looking butcher knife. Luke carried the shotgun while Fred took his pistol and a small supply of ammunition for it.

It was a simple trip down to the river through wooded hollows along the little creek. They parted early in the morning after a night spent in the brush; Fred to go westward to the Keating country, Luke downriver for a talk with Minor Brookland.

"Be careful," Luke admonished Fred at parting, but he grinned, showing his white teeth.

"Come a right smart piece by myself already, Mister Luke. You look out fer yourself. I's worried about that shooting." There wasn't a great deal of snow along the river, and Luke traveled fast, carefully detouring the few houses. At a place where the river showed ice and boulders, he crossed to the south side where there would be no people.

Here he followed what was probably an old Indian path. Often when he went over outthrusts of the mountains, he stopped and looked across the river at the bold hills, the dark green of pine timber, and the occasional coves pushing back into the mountains.

The rough going and the long detour to get past the county-seat town of Point Haven made it necessary to spend another night in the woods. He was growing more and more uneasy about the situation. It seemed to Luke he was always getting involved and never in his own interest. In Crossville, Horton's death and Linda Caines' statement had ended his plans for becoming a surveyor. This Underground had broken the peace he was beginning to find with the Halidays and now had probably made him a man sought for the serious crime of shooting an officer. Furthermore, the encounter at the Dyer farm could well have wrecked Brookland's plans.

Discouraged and tired, he arrived at Spring Haven late in the day and was welcomed by the Jenkins cousins with what seemed like subdued enthusiasm. They volunteered no information except about the weather and some fine Jersey heifers born on the place. Leaving them, Luke walked slowly along the drive to the house where homelike spirals of smoke lifted from both tall chimneys.

Brookland's handshake and cry of welcome sounded sincere and warmed Luke a little. "You're just in time, friend. We've been expecting you, and there is a visitor. But come in here a moment."

They went into a room usually used as an office, and there, the first question put to Luke was about Fred and what had become of him.

"On his way to Keating. They shot him down, but he wasn't hit hard. Smith thought, too, that was the place for the man to go."

"Smith," Brookland said, leaning forward. "So he came down from Lymansville with a warning, did he?"

"Yes," Luke rejoined. "He was a quiet man with a deep voice and steady eyes who prayed at the table."

"Don't describe him further. I hoped he would be up in that country. Never mind his name. He's wanted in the South, and they tell me there's a big reward for him. Let's have the rest of your story, just what happened."

Luke rapidly detailed the happenings at the Dyer farm; the storm, his attempt to reach Hugh, and finding Fred and his child in the drift. He detailed little Mealie's death and the attack on the father that followed.

Brookland's hands jerked in a quick gesture. "We tried to keep the child here, but the father would not give her up. There's a reward of two thousand dollars out for him, dead or alive, and they're still hot on his trail. The officers bullied the Halidays and badgered us until we ran them off. Hugh landed in jail for two nights until I could bail him out. Of course, Fred knew that if they picked up the child, they would use her to get hands on him. She was sick, and he was afraid about that, too."

Luke, remembering the scene in the cabin, rose and paced back and forth for a moment. "It looks as though I made a mess of your plans, sir, with the shooting. But I'd seen the child die, then saw Fred shot down when that horseman could have caught him in a minute. They came to kill, not capture."

"No," Brookland interrupted emphatically. "Those slave catchers have learned some caution. Don't blame yourself. Remember, a shotgun rides in every wagon when there are runaways in it. We'll go through peacefully if we can, but we won't give up our charges." He patted Luke's arm. "Come, we have a visitor—or rather, you have."

They crossed the dark hall and entered the living room, where a woman dressed for riding stood at a window, looking out at the stream. She wore breeches and a crimson shirt. A leather jacket, gloves, and a cap lay on a chair near her. Luke's breath caught in his throat. There seemed to be a drumming in his ears as he realized who the visitor was.

"Linda!" he cried, "Linda!"

She turned slowly. Her heavy hair was drawn back as usual, but the great coils at her slender neck were looser. The bright shirt was open at the throat, and there a miniature on a slender gold chain rested.

Oblivious to Brookland's presence, he crossed the room and took her hands. In a moment, she released them and put them on his shoulders while she smiled into his eyes. "Luke, you look better. Even that stoop to your shoulders is gone."

With her so near to him, all his old hunger for her surged through him. His doubts and speculations about her went out the window. He lifted his big hands and, in the next moment, would have crushed her slim body close had it not been for the forbidding signal in her eyes.

"I've been trying everywhere to find you, Luke. I came here from Point Haven, hoping you just might be here. They are after you. Mr. Brookland agrees with me—you must leave the country."

Here it was again, a warning. He was suddenly angry and snapped part of a question. "Your father—"

Linda stopped him by taking his shoulders and shaking him lightly. "Never mind him, and wake up! You shot a deputy sheriff. There's one warrant out for that and another for aiding a criminal to escape."

Brookland broke in. "She's right, Luke. Miss Caines has ridden hard to warn you. You owe her so much you must listen."

Luke's mind was in confusion. There were the scenes in Crossville dominated by the fact that this lovely girl before him had paid a bitter price to get him out of what she realized better than he did was a dangerous situation. Now she was helping once more.

"Where do you want me to go?" he asked of both of them, and Linda answered.

"I don't know, Luke Hanley, and as long as I don't, I won't need to lie. But make it far, out of the state at least."

She picked up her jacket, and Luke had the grace to hold it for her and to see that she had her gloves and the little cap that matched the jacket.

Brookland spoke again. "Miss Caines must get back to Point Haven, Luke. See her out to the barn. The boys will have her horse ready."

His friend had graciously given him an opportunity to be with Linda alone, and he was grateful. Hidden by the bole of a great elm, his strong arms swept her close. For a moment, she strained against him, then for fleeting seconds, gave him the warmth of her body and the richness of her lips.

"Be careful," she whispered. "Things are . . . Be careful."

The sound of a horse tramping broke them apart. Linda gathered her reins in a gloved hand. Ad Jenkins gave her a hand, and she went into the saddle with a supple swing of her body. The horse shot down the driveway, scattering gravel, then turned into the dusky road, and she was gone. Luke realized that he had not even thanked her and swore at himself under his breath while Jenkins looked at him, smiling.

The other cousin, Al, driving a fast horse hitched to a light buggy, set Luke down at the Haliday home a little before nine o'clock in the evening. Hugh was in Williamsport, and Jim went out with Luke to speak with Jenkins, who had just turned his rig around. When the driver was gone, Haliday cautioned Luke.

"Don't say much about runaways, son. Emma's all worked up."

Even during the short time they spent together, Luke caught the strain in this home that once had been so carefree. Jim talked about crops, the barn, and the livestock, while his wife and Hester knitted industriously with their heads lowered, saying nothing.

When Jim finally rose, his wife spoke sharply. "That marshal was here today."

Jim offered an answer that sounded feeble and evasive, and Luke replied without explanation on his part. "I suppose he was, but I'm leaving in the morning. I just wanted my things."

"Mebbe that would be safest, son," Jim commented. "They're hot after you since you shot Brost. Now I'm going to bed, but wait a minute."

He walked over to a cupboard and took out a cigar box Luke recognized as the family's money container. "Here's some money, Luke. It's your wages. I put it in this envelope a couple of weeks past."

The women had left the room without even a "goodnight." Jim waited a moment, then left while Luke stood by the table, holding the envelope in his fingers. Finally, he stepped outside to freshen his thoughts in the crisp night air.

The moon swung high above the frosty fields, and he strode along swiftly. Corbet emerged from his small house, touched his hand with his nose, and walked beside him. When Luke returned to the house, he saw Hester standing on the porch in the dim light with a soft shawl across her shoulders.

"The marshal wasn't the only one," she said without preamble.

Luke looked at her but did not speak. He had caught the malice in her tone.

"Your Linda came looking for you. She's a—"

Hester did not finish, and presently he was alone.

He ate an early, quiet breakfast with Jim and Emma in the kitchen. The food stuck in his throat, and before the pair finished, he was up and had slipped into his jacket.

"I helped bury Mealie," he told them bitterly and, with no other word, walked out. His shotgun blast had brought down a cloud of trouble and had finally destroyed what was left of the shreds of welcome left for him here on this farm. On the porch, his fingers touched the envelope of money Jim had given him in the evening. He thought a moment, then opened the door he had closed, stepped inside, and laid the envelope on the table.

Corbet accompanied him to the turn of the road, where he sat down upon being ordered to return home. From the next bend, Luke could see him sitting there, a dark shape against the early brightness of the morning.

CHAPTER SEVEN

LUKE ENTERED the office of the commandant of the little navy yard so quietly that the naval officer, bent low over his writing, apparently did not hear him. Captain George Caris continued to scratch away with his pen, holding his head so close to the paper that his neatly trimmed beard nearly touched it. Luke, in spite of his obviously new civilian clothing, stood rigidly at attention until the captain looked up and faced his visitor. Then, he saluted formally.

"The captain sent for me, sir?"

Caris leaned back in his chair and grinned. "Very nice, very nice." His grin widened. "But civilians do not salute; you are no longer in the navy with that discharge paper in your pocket."

His voice gibed a little.

"Our carpenter's mate, first class, had politician friends and so gets a full year clipped from his enlistment."

Luke's face reddened, and he tried to remonstrate. "Mr. Brookland—"

He was interrupted with a waved hand and a different tone of voice. "It's all right, Luke. Brookland and I have been friends since you were a bit of a boy. You and I have been shipmates for a good stretch at that. Let's see, a year before the mast at sea; now two more years and one month in this navy yard. Sit down. I want to talk."

The officer filled and lit an evil-smelling pipe while his visitor cleared a chair of a litter of papers and seated himself.

"Minor Brookland is a big man and will grow bigger. He understands people and has told me all the troubles that have come your way. It's nice that you are going back to him, for I believe he needs you pretty badly. He's a real lumberman, and there may be a chance for you to better yourself financially. War's in the air, son, and all the spars and ship timber we can get out of your Pennsylvania hills won't be nearly enough. It's not commonly known, Luke, but we need your hard pitch pine for gunboats."

He blew smoke at the ceiling and, for a moment, gave his attention to the mingled noises coming from the nearby yard; the screech of saws, the pounding of hammers, and the slam of boards and timbers.

"In eight months, I retire from the navy. Then I expect to start a small shipyard with some friends. I've a hunch that, in a year or so, anything with a bottom that'll carry something a little bigger than a musket will be worth its weight in silver. Furnish me pitch pine planking of random widths, twelve to twenty feet in length, and I'll guarantee you twenty dollars a thousand feet for it laid down at your Pennsylvania river market at Marietta."

Luke, knowing lumber, looked doubtful. "Mr. Brookland might be interested. If I had the time and money, I'd give that a whirl. Pitch pine is a weed on some of those upriver hills. But, all I have is three hundred dollars, not enough for mill, wages, and equipment until I sold lumber."

Caris changed the subject. "You have been a good man. Three years have squared the shoulders you brought us. There's a different look in your eyes, and you've handled men well here in the yard. Only your deviltry has kept you from a commission."

"Yes," he said shortly when the younger man raised his eyebrows. "I recommended you, but you had been in three or four of those slave scraps. They accused you of starting around a dozen runaways north. Some men feel pretty sure you started that riot at the slave sale in Turnersville. Son, slaves are property, and southern slave owners wag the tail if they're not the dog in national affairs. You and your redheaded pal, Darnly, cost the folks close to twelve thousand dollars when those runaways got off. So there was that, and when I recommended you, they dug up the fact that your father had been an Abolitionist. Go home, son, and get your mind on lumber rather than the Underground Railroad."

The captain rose and shook hands with his visitor. Then he made a startling statement. "Goodbye and good luck. By the way, your man, Fred, has the new route working fine."

Greatly puzzled, Luke walked out into the sunshine. Captain Caris was a hard, efficient officer who drove men in the yard as he did at sea. After his warning about the Underground, his statement indicating his knowledge of affairs up the Susquehanna came as a surprise, and there could have been a hint in it of something that a commissioned officer would not have offered openly.

For a moment, Luke closed his eyes to the bright Virginia sunlight. Up there on the river were the pine-covered hills, the blue flash of clear waters, and the smells of farmland mingled with those that drifted in from the woods. In the night, there could be the soft roll of wheels on sandy roads, the driver busy with his team, and the man beside him alert for ambushes.

* * *

A week later, a train deposited Luke in King's Shore, and he walked leisurely up through Antes Gap. When he sighted the roofs of Spring Haven, he stopped to admire the big trees, the loom of the stone buildings, and the spring-fed stream behind them.

Minor Brookland met his guest before he was halfway from the road to the house. There was little change in the man after three years. Dressed in worn corduroys, his hair had touches of gray at the temples, but there was youth on his deeply tanned face. The two men gripped hands. They were equally tall, but Luke was the heavier of the two. His shoulders were carried back squarely, reflecting his naval training, and the lines on his face had stiffened.

Brookland's voice was warm, and there was real feeling in his words. "I'm so glad you've come. I've been looking forward to seeing you."

"Not more than I have looked forward to coming, sir. Thanks for getting me out," Luke replied.

His host turned toward the house. "After all, I really got you into the mess," he said. Then he turned toward the barn and called. Both the Jenkins cousins appeared, and this time they were friendly, with a welcome even more effusive than their employer.

"Boys," Brookland promised, "whet your appetites and eat with us tonight. We want to welcome our prodigal, only it'll be roast beef, not veal."

When they entered the house, cigars were set out, but the host excused himself because he had to run into town on business. "We'll talk after supper when we have time. There're three full years to cover."

Left to his own devices, Luke moved restlessly about the lower floor of the big house. He remembered vividly the living room where Linda Caines had waited. Now it looked empty without her vivid presence. He moved to the entrance hall. There he stopped before a great walnut coat rack. Light from a transom was reflected in its mirror. Looking at the array of hats, coats, and walking sticks, his quick eye picked out something he recognized instantly. On one of the brass hooks hung a light, vividly colored shawl. He looked at it for some time, then took it down and passed it through his fingers. The shawl belonged to Hester Haliday.

Often through the long years, he had thought of the girl as she had been that night on the road and how she had avoided him later. Hester was a strange combination; her friendship was a wonderful thing. It was odd that it could change so quickly to a coldness that hurt. He was just replacing the shawl when the door opened to admit the owner of the house. He looked from Luke to the scarf, then spoke softly as if answering an unasked question.

"Yes, it belongs to Hester. Someday I hope she will return and claim it."

A black man named Morris had replaced Maisie as cook, and the meal was excellent. Its main feature was a huge beef roast surrounded by baked apples and potatoes. There were peas cooked to a mush and heavily seasoned with pepper. Big silver pitchers held tangy cider. The four men ate heartily with little talk until the dessert of apple pie served with cheese was brought on. After that, there were cigars. Then the host leaned back.

"Now talk, Luke. The boys and I want to know what happened after you left."

It wasn't hard to talk to these men. They listened closely and sympathetically as he began.

"After I left the Haliday farm, I cut across the hills and then followed the river. Close to Sunbury, I got on a late raft and went down to Marietta. Some navy men were there buying spar sticks, and I went with them to Baltimore, enlisted, and had the luck to land with Captain Caris, who you know, Mr. Brookland. We were at sea for a year—the Mediterranean coasts, west Africa for months. There I saw the slave ships, and we went ashore, checking the registration of vessels anchored and waiting for their cargo. All of them were under foreign flags."

He shook his head vigorously. His sun-bleached hair and cold eyes gave him a sinister look under the candles, and his hands tightened into fists. "God won't need to damn a slave trader. He's damned already while he's alive. The taint is on him like the odor that clings to the ships they sail. It's foul, reeking, sickening."

Morris had entered the room to remove the dishes from the table and had heard the last remarks. He said nothing, just went about his work calmly. Luke changed his story to a lighter vein.

"We came back to the Chesapeake and the shipyard until the arrangement was made for my discharge. That was straight carpentry. I handled gangs under Captain Caris's orders. The captain claims there is going to be war. Pitch pine planks for gunboats will bring twenty dollars a thousand feet at Marietta."

Brookland asked a question about which sizes of timber were best for spars, and Luke illustrated, holding a wax candle.

"To be a standard, the spar has to be ninety feet in length and twelve to eighteen inches in diameter at the thin end. The stick has to be evenly tapered. Usually, the butt fifteen feet has to be shaped with axes. Longer spars are only bought on special order."

Another hour of lumber talk passed pleasantly with these men who all had experience in the woods. Then the Jenkins cousins declared they must get to their quarters. Luke and his host repaired to the living room. On the way, Brookland picked up Hester's shawl, looked at it a moment, and returned it to the hook.

"Luke, our experience with Fred just about wrecked our plans. They watched us all like hawks. Then, near that spring, three runaways showed up at Haliday's. I had warned Jim to be careful, but Bay surprised them. There was an arrest and a prompt trial that showed the hand of Nedrow. Jim's fine of three thousand dollars wiped out his life's savings. He wouldn't take any money from me and he was short two hundred eighty dollars.

They levied on his place and it's to be sold at sheriff's sale soon. I managed to get Hugh out of jail, and he joined the regular army. The only break was that neighbors carried off Jim's stock and implements—'borrowed' them. Jim hates me now but only a little less than Emma does."

"In heaven's name, why?" Luke questioned in surprise, and Brookland cleared his throat, speaking almost harshly.

"Hester. She left home two months after you went away. Her mother had ideas—you might as well face it—about the girl and you."

Anger tightened Luke's throat, but he was so anxious to hear the story this keen-eyed, kindly-faced man would tell that he kept silent.

"This is confidential, Luke. Jim doesn't know it, but before Emma married him, she came close to making what would have been to her a tragic mistake with a man. It has never left the background of her thinking and has made her suspicious of the motives of men. She started doubting her daughter after she carried that warning to you. Hester stood her mother's accusations for a time and then left home."

The smoke from Brookland's cigar lifted in a lazy spiral toward the paneled ceiling, and he watched it for a moment.

"The girl came to me. There was no other place to go, and I helped her to get upcountry to some people in Lymansville named Prentis. They were old folks who ran a small hotel. First, Hester worked in their kitchen and dining room. Later she became an entertainer with that remarkable gift she has for mimicry. Her singing voice is excellent, fit for the stage. Later, the Prentis folks treated her like a daughter. I think when Prentis died, the girl inherited the hotel. At any rate, she's comfortable financially. But what the girl did seems worse to the mother than what she suspected before Hester left home."

Luke got up and paced the room excitedly. "There was nothing between Hester and me. I kept myself in hand—"

"I know," the older man interrupted," and so does Jim, who leads a dog's life now. They live close to Point Haven, and he works when he can find something to do. In ten days or so, that farm will go for two hundred eighty dollars. Likely John Caines'll gobble it up. Folks are afraid to bid against him, and the sheriff is his tool. The Halidays wouldn't use the farm if I bought it."

Luke sat down and faced his friend. "Mr. Brookland, I came back home with one thing in mind. I felt my hasty shot at the Dyer farm had broken up your plans. Likely lots of runaways have been recaptured because of me and that shotgun. I came back to help runaways, sir. On the African coast, I saw the slave trade like I told about tonight. Down there at the navy yard, I saw a lot of slavery. I thought when I came back, you'd set me to work. I'm older, harder. Guess I see things the way my father did, and he died for what he believed. Now there's this Haliday mess. Shouldn't I straighten it out before—"

Minor Brookland stared at the young man and spoke softly. "Thank God, Luke. What you've said is so much more than I had hoped. And I need a man, someone who has the courage and the wit to handle things." Suddenly he checked himself and then shot a question. "What do you know of the Knights of the Golden Circle?"

Luke's eyes widened. "Sir, that's the question Smith asked in the Dyer cabin. It's a secret order to extend slave territory. Its members are sworn to secrecy to do what is ordered. There was some talk about it around the navy yard."

Brookland was nodding. "Luke, there's an organization behind this slave catching, this kidnapping of freedmen. My friends in Washington tell me more recaptured slaves and freedmen are reaching the slave auctions than we can move to safety. This is my suspicion, and it's between us. I think John Caines is behind most of this deviltry, and I have the feeling he is the agent, at least in these parts, of the Knights who want to break up the Underground. Luke, if we can beat that man, the road to freedom opens for every runaway that reaches us. I believe Remington had his suspicions years back when he spoke of shooting Caines."

"But the Halidays. What about them?"

"We'll begin there, Luke. We must block every move of the slavers. If the Halidays lose their place for good, other farmers will be afraid to shelter runaways. Your first job is to block that sale somehow. Then I'm going to send you upriver. You'll be a lumberman like the other folks up there. Caines' operations will be close to you, and you'll be in position to act when necessary." Calmer now, they talked for an hour longer, mostly about the Haliday situation.

"It's late now, Luke. Ad Jenkins will drive you up to the farm in the morning."

Luke did not sleep for hours. He was thinking of John Caines. What Brookland said fit into what Luke knew of the man. Caines had become wealthy and powerful in a very short time. Something must have been behind him. Luke tried to fit the Horton death into the picture but could not.

* * *

The next day, Ad Jenkins drove fast, using a little gray mare, but Luke made him stop a half mile from the farm.

"I'll walk in," he told his companion, and Jenkins nodded. "You'll find it a sorry place to what you knowed. Lots can happen to a farm in a year or so."

Luke walked slowly up the lane where Corbet had met him so long ago. Neither all he had been told nor his imagination prepared him for the ruin he faced. What had been well-tended fields were high with weeds. Doors on the outbuildings sagged on their hinges. Window panes in the house were broken, and apple trees in the new orchard were uprooted. Under a maple tree, Luke stumbled over a board crudely lettered with a "C" and saw that it had been the headboard of a small mound.

Pushing his way through a heavy growth of ragweed and thistle, he entered the big barn door and stood a full minute looking about before he realized that he was not alone. In a far corner, seated on an upturned half-bushel measure, was a man whom he recognized in spite of the changes in his appearance.

"Jim!" Luke cried out, crossing to the farmer and dropping his hands on the bowed shoulders.

Haliday rose as if very weary and shook hands listlessly. "Been quite a time, Luke. Quite a time."

Together, with neither man knowing just what to say, they walked to the doorway and surveyed the desolation of the fields and the wreckage of the once neat buildings.

"Tell me about it, Jim."

Haliday motioned to some shingle billets, and they sat down facing each other. The farmer began talking with desperate eagerness to get his story out. "Spring after you left, Bay caught us with three passengers in the house. I don't know if somebody told on us or what. Hugh went to jail for a couple of days after he knocked one of the raiders flat. The United States Commissioner fined me twenty-nine hundred dollars and said he wouldn't throw me in jail. Brookland got Hugh out, and he went off."

He drew a long breath. "Me and Emma had a little over twenty-five hundred dollars. She had a hundred dollars more of egg money. John Caines was in town and paid the rest so I'd keep out of jail. I had no money to pay him, so he levied on the farm. The sale's soon. I can't say just when. Dates mix me up some."

The muscles on the kindly farmer's face were twitching. "Neighbors borrowed the stock, and I gave them bills of sale. It was a little crooked, but I couldn't stand to see the horses sold away. Nedrow down at the county seat complained, but I got mad and told him where he could go. Selling them horses would be like . . . like selling a member of the family."

He wiped his eyes unashamedly on his sleeve.

"Me and Emma live up the river now. I'd ask you up there, but Emma's kinda set against you, Luke. She's powerful unhappy about this Underground stuff. We're all alone now that Hugh's away."

"Thank the Lord, Jim. We can get the farm back. Here's three hundred dollars. The judgment is only two hundred eighty dollars. The neighbors will bring back the stock."

Haliday's thin features hardened, and there was wild light in his eyes as he stared at the yellow banknotes.

"No, Emma and me won't be beholden to you. The same goes for Minor Brookland. Both of you brought sorrow on our house." His grimness broke as quickly as it had appeared. "We still got that money you didn't take when you went. There was times when we came close to spending it, but it's still at the house."

"Corbet, Jim. Where's he?"

"One of Bay's men shot him. I buried him under the maple. He was a good dog, but he pure hated Bay."

Luke suddenly swore viciously. Bitterness and futility all but choked him. He wanted to take Haliday by the shoulders and shake sense into him. He wanted to go down to Williamsport and find Marshal Bay or anyone on whom he could vent his anger. When he quieted down, Jim rose stiffly, looked about the barn, and then walked down what had been a lane across the fields.

* * *

Three days later, driven by another idea, and without having returned to Spring Haven, Luke got out of the stage at Lymansville after a long slow ride up the Pike and walked slowly up the steps of The Stagecoach Hotel.

The long ride had given him time to think, for most of the way he had been the sole passenger. His mind was on Hester. Whatever her trouble with her mother had been, that was the heart of the matter. She was the thinker of the Haliday family, the strong one. It was up to her to suggest some procedure that would save the farm.

The hotel clerk was a big man with a protuberant stomach and a watch chain reminiscent of Marshal Bay. "Yes, sir, we have a room. Number four. It's the only one left. Tomorrow is the big time in town."

CHAPTER EIGHT

LUKE AVOIDED his fellow guests in the crowded little hotel as much as possible and asked no questions about the girl he had come to see. But in the morning, he had another errand: visit Hillside and talk with Erritt. With Brookland, Luke had visited the place after dark, and now he wanted to know more about it.

The farm was off the highway some little distance at the end of a long lane. Luke had followed this only a hundred yards or so when a big, bearded man stepped from behind a red oak.

"You got a match, stranger?" his big voice boomed. "Been hunting and am fresh out of a way to light my pipe."

Without speaking, Luke passed over a box of sulfur matches and noted that the man stood squarely in line, blocking the way. Now he spoke, grinning. "Friend, I know what you're hunting, but I've been here before. I'm the Right Sort of People."

The sentry shot out a big hand which Luke accepted. "I'm Ben Wattles, and I told Sam this sentry stuff didn't amount to much. This is the first I've had a chance to ask for a match in a month. The slave catchers just don't like coming down this lane. Let's go to the house."

It was an interesting place. Between the buildings and the highway was a wide field where brush and weeds were allowed to grow and flourish until they formed a screen. The rambling house was set on a sharp hillside. It had probably begun as one log cabin, but now there were four sections joined to each other by a long, narrow porch that ran the length of the log and plank structures.

Samuel Erritt was a short man who greatly resembled the Jenkins cousins in features but who was much more stockily built. He came across the wide living room with a deceptively light step that belied his weight. A stocking cap was pushed well back on a head of closely cropped hair, and his eyes were as sharp as a hawk's. He wore a flannel shirt open at the throat, and his trousers were lined inside the thighs with leather.

"Hanley, I'm glad to see you. I hope you've come to help." His grip was hard, given by hands that were large for a man of his height. There was warm friendliness in his voice as he went on. "Over three years it's been since I asked Smith to warn you. Let's sit down and talk. Again, I hope you've come to help."

Luke took the proffered chair. "Yes, I came back from the navy to help. Just now, though, I've got a side job that has to be managed. At the moment, I'd like to know what's happened on the Underground and whether you think the law will make something of that shooting years back."

Erritt smiled and crossed his short legs. "I think you're pretty safe now, my friend. It isn't likely the folks at the courthouse will bring any action against a known friend of Brookland, especially when that deputy wasn't hurt much. But times are bad. They capture as many of the poor souls as we get through. Farmers along the routes are getting afraid to harbor runaways."

"That's it," Luke interrupted. "Brookland and I want to straighten out that Haliday business. John Caines—"

It was Erritt's turn to interrupt. His face hardened, and he swore savagely. "That man. I believe he has something to do with our troubles. He could be behind whatever organization is kidnapping free men and capturing runaway slaves. He owns the sheriff, everything but the judge in your county. Next time John Remington comes this way, I won't stop him."

Luke remembered Brookland's remark about Remington's threat.

Erritt had not finished. "Maybe someday a tree will fall on the man. He's a lumberman, you know." He grinned suddenly, but there was no mirth in his expression. "You've studied surveying and know your algebra. Remember: some problems are solved by addition, some by subtraction, some by elimination. I feel ours would be worked out nicely by elimination."

"No," he said a little later on, "we don't have much, if any, trouble from here to the New York State line. Folks about Lymansville are not friendly to slave catchers. Over at Wellsboro, they took runaways from a sheriff's posse and sent them north. No, the trouble is down your way, Hanley."

Luke changed the subject and asked directly about Hester Haliday. "She's quite a girl, inherited the Prentis place when the old man died. The old lady Prentis lived there with her. The girl's popular, does a lot of singing."

He waved a thick hand deprecatingly. "Guess I don't know too much about young women. Yes, I know the trouble her father had with the law. Lots of the boys hang around this Hester. One of them is Rush Geen, who owns a livery stable. He generally sees to it that the girl isn't bothered with rough stuff. Old George Brendy, who travels with him, was supposed to be a lawyer once."

"Runs a livery," Luke remarked, and his host laughed.

"He does have a place. Lots of New York horses come down through here, and Pennsylvania horses go north. Geen is in that business and makes money at it. He's always ready to let me have horses when I'm pressed. Rush could be a real help if Hester wants him to do something."

He changed the subject abruptly. "There is a big affair in town tonight, a sort of party for men going into the woods for the season. The lumber bosses have bought out the bars, and there will be free liquor. But before they open up, there'll be a supper in the town hall. You'll see your Hester Haliday then. She will sing."

Luke left Erritt's place late in the afternoon, having received a last bit of advice.

"If I was you, I wouldn't waste too much time on the Haliday affair. It's all very logical to say you and Brookland'll get on the runaway job after you've boosted the morale of people who might use their houses as stations. But, after could be a little late for folks that follow a star. I knew your father, Luke. You can be a power to us."

Luke took a nap at the hotel before supper time. Then he found the town hall and dutifully paid his fifty cents for a blue pasteboard ticket.

"That'll give you supper and let you dance," the rather grim-looking woman who took his money advised him.

The meal was served at long tables, with most of the food in great dishes that were passed up and down. Men ate in typical lumber camp fashion, doing no talking and giving their entire attention to the excellent food. Dessert was a huge dish of vanilla ice cream, a rarity in the lumber country.

The meal finished, men and women stood about while the tables were dismantled and the floor was cleared for dancing.

At eight o'clock, the musicians appeared: two violinists and a third with a bass viol. After they had tuned up, some of the older folks took to the floor and danced gravely through the first number. Later, as the music quickened, there were more young people out until the floor was well filled with couples. Still unwilling to ask questions, Luke was about to leave when an intermission was announced.

"After that," the spokesman said, "Miss Hester, our mountain nightingale, will sing for us."

Applause lasting minutes ran round the room. Then a door to one side of the little stage opened, and Hester Haliday entered the room, stepping immediately to the platform.

Luke found himself staring at the girl desperately. He had not seen her for more than three years, and he remembered her sweetness as well as the scorn with which she had sent him away. She had been so much the dominant one in the Haliday family. He had thought of her so often during lonely watches at sea and later when he was in the South.

She had matured and seemed taller, carrying her slim form more easily and with new poise. The yellow hair she used to wear loose to the wind was now piled high on her small head. Her brown dress had short puffed sleeves exposing her arms, and it was cut low enough to show her white throat, where hung a small locket supported by a narrow black ribbon. Involuntarily, Luke moved forward until the press of the crowd blocked his way. The girl on the platform was smiling, entirely at ease.

"Friends," she said, "you look too solemn. Sing with me, and you'll feel better."

The small orchestra noted her signal, and she began singing "Pop Goes the Weasel," with her audience helping enthusiastically at the accented parts. The next song was "Wait for the Wagon." When that was finished, she came forward a little, and there was a soberness on her face as she sang alone.

The song was "Home, Sweet Home." Luke stood, gripped by the beauty of her voice as it soared and fell through the movement of the music. Before the last verse died away, women were sobbing. Near Luke, a man brushed his sleeve across his eyes. The audience gave her the perfect approval of complete silence when she finished.

Luke took a long breath, and then, from far across the fields, a whippoor-will called, followed a moment later by the "Bob White" whistle of a quail. The audience was loosening up at the familiar sounds. Now an angry cat squalled on a back fence, and a small dog promptly barked in reply. The girl continued to imitate the creatures of the out-of-doors until she interrupted her program with the aroused chatter of a red squirrel. When the applause stopped, Hester concluded her program by singing through the first verse of "From Greenland's Icy Mountains," after which she led the audience through the remainder of the old hymn.

This time, there was little stir in the audience though the girl had departed. When the violins began a dance tune, Luke went out.

It was dark after the light in the rooms, and he walked slowly toward the Prentis Hotel. The gleam from a wall lamp showed a wide porch, and he was just in time to see a girl's figure mounting the steps. Luke started forward to overtake her and had not noticed anyone else until three men blocked his way.

One of them demanded curtly, "You following that girl?"

Luke did not hesitate. He plunged ahead but was held fast by strong grasps on his arms and shoulders.

"Nobody bothers Hester," the voice declared, and Luke twisted about.

"Let me go, you damned fools. Mind your own—"

The hotel door opened, and Hester stood framed against the light. In another moment, she ran down the stairs and approached the group.

"Luke!" she cried, "Luke Hanley, is it you?"

"Yes," he snapped, "now wait till I get rid of your guard."

She was in the midst of the group, evidently recognizing the men in spite of the dim light. Her voice was sharp. "Let him go. I'm tired of being shepherded, Rush. This man's an old friend, Luke Hanley, from back home."

The hands released Luke, and the man who had done the talking spoke apologetically. "The town's full of strangers, Hester. Things are getting a bit rough, so we watched."

"All right," Hester said more kindly. "Now go on back downtown. Luke and I must have a talk."

She led her guest back to the hotel and into a pleasantly furnished living room. Through a side door, the end of a bedstead showed.

"I'm sorry about the boys, Luke. That was Rush Geen and his friends. Things do get rough about here sometimes, and Rush has been very kind and thoughtful. Now, it's been three years. Tell me everything—all the news."

"There's not much," Luke replied, taking the chair she indicated. "I went downriver and right into the United States Navy. After sea duty for a year, I went into a navy yard and have been there since. Minor Brookland got my discharge to supervise some lumbering. I didn't come about myself, Hester. It's about your folks and the farm."

The girl frowned and shifted her position so her face was no longer in the bright light. Luke told her bluntly what he had found and the hopelessness of the situation so long as her parents would not accept help.

"It's less than three hundred dollars, and I've offered the money. John Caines will get the place if your father won't listen to common sense."

An odd look, almost like a shadow, passed over the girl's face. After some minutes, she began to talk. "It began with mother. Perhaps all the trouble rests with her. She was desperately afraid of the runaway slave thing. Father wouldn't give it up. Then, you came."

She paused again, and the line of her lips had narrowed. "She thought things had happened between us. She knew your character, Luke Hanley, and your playing fast and loose with women. So I left home. Twice I sent money; they returned it."

Luke looked at her, remembering with a sinking heart what Brookland had told him of Emma Haliday. He understood only partly what this girl's mother had done to her with her accusations. He wanted to say something to break through the barrier between them but could not shape the words. So he frowned and tried to ignore what she had said.

"It's the sale, Hester. I have three hundred dollars, but the farm'll bring a lot more. John Caines—"

"Yes," she interrupted. "You talk of John Caines. Perhaps you've forgotten what you did to him through his daughter." Hester saw that she had hurt her visitor badly. She leaned forward. Now her tone was placating. "One of Rush Geen's men was a lawyer. He's George Brendy. Liquor ruined him, but if there's a way, he'll know it. I'll have him come in when it's morning."

Luke rose and moved toward the door. Hester had greeted him friendly enough. Now he realized that was to put him at his ease so he would not suspect that she was about to hurt him. She had walked with him to the door. Suddenly he gripped her slim shoulders, and her body stiffened.

"Let me go," she hissed. "I've lost a lot through you and won't have you mauling me. Save that for your Linda, who probably likes to have men do that."

Luke was thoroughly angry and released her before the temptation to shake her became too much for him. "Hester, I'm the one who lost. Three years of my life went through the business I got mixed up with right there in your mother's home. I can't help her or your ideas. All I want is to clear up the farm mess. And I don't want your friend John Caines to get one damn rod of the place."

He slammed the door and walked back to his hotel, tempted to return to Spring Haven. When he undertook coming up here to Lymansville, he had felt sure Hester might have some plan. She had always been the brains of the family. Now he saw she had become an imbittered young woman. If she had ever had any affection for him, that was surely dead.

In the morning, he felt better, and breakfast was waited on by a tall, strongly built man whose voice he remembered from the night before.

"I'm Rush Geen," he introduced himself, and Luke looked coldly into the friendly face of the dark-haired, brown-eyed man.

"Well," he replied, "keep on being that, only don't lay your hands on me again."

There was a touch of anger, quickly mastered, on the visitor's face, and he spoke quietly, ignoring the gibe thrown at him.

"Mister, I didn't come to quarrel. Hester wants us. George Brendy has gone to her place and she's asked for us. That's my business here, and it's all that counts."

The two young men walked to the Prentis House in silence and were admitted by Hester. A third man, well up in years, sat in the room's most comfortable chair. When introduced as George Brendy, he partially rose from his seat and proffered a limp hand to Luke. The lawyer's clothing was badly worn. His string tie was pulled to one side and partly covered by a straggly beard. But, when Luke and Geen were seated, he came directly to the point.

"Mister, if you've got close to three hundred dollars, hand it over. We'll see that Jim Haliday gets back his farm at the sale. You get back down country and leave it up to Rush and me. If we can't, you'll get your money back."

Still angry at Hester now that he saw her again, Luke counted three hundred dollars from his wallet into the dirty hands of George Brendy and walked out with no word of farewell. Two hours later, he was on the stage bound for King's Shore. Brookland was at home when he finally reached Spring Haven, and to him, Luke detailed his experience with Jim Haliday and what had happened at Lymansville.

Brookland nodded when Luke finished. "Once I knew George Brendy. He has been a lawyer, drunkard, horse thief, and camp cook, but he has brains. If he's on the job, he just might manage it. Nevertheless—"

He stopped, crossed to a desk and took out some money he gave to Luke. "There's a thousand dollars. I got it out of the bank yesterday. You take this to the sale. Bid up to that much. We can't let John Caines have the place. If Jim Haliday chooses to be stubborn, we'll set up a real Underground station there. It's a key point."

When Luke made no comment, Brookland frowned. "I know what hurts you, my friend, for the same thing hurts me. You've carried a picture of Hester in your mind for years. Now you find her so sadly changed, how much perhaps neither of us really knows. Let's you and I hope she changes back. Her mother hurt her terribly. A girl has the right to expect her mother to hold faith in her to the last. Anyway, you found a real artist if you heard her sing."

Luke's answer was a nod, and Brookland changed the subject.

"The Jenkins boys will want us for supper this evening. They have some venison steaks and have been asking when you will return."

* * *

The morning of the sale was sharp, almost frosty, and a good-sized crowd had assembled by the time Brookland, the two Jenkins boys, and Luke got there. Soon, Sheriff Clayton Webster and some other officials arrived and took their positions importantly on the back porch of the house. The farmstead was pretty well filled with buggies and spring wagons belonging to the hill people, many of them Haliday neighbors. The odd thing was a string of good-looking saddled horses tethered close to where Corbet was buried. A casual but alert-looking young man stood close to the horses. Luke counted eight of them. Jim Haliday was there and stood to one side in the background. After a few minutes, Luke recognized Rush Geen and George Brendy, who stood close to the porch with companions.

The sheriff made his announcements pompously. The purpose today was to sell the Haliday farm, terms cash, to the highest bidder in order to settle a judgment against the place in the amount of two hundred eighty dollars. He already had a certified bid for that amount from John Caines in the amount stated.

Geen and Brendy had moved closer. The one-time lawyer looked shabby in a short overcoat and a battered hat pulled low over his forehead. Sheriff Webster, looking dapper among these plainly dressed people, lifted a stick in place of the customary auctioneer's gavel and frowned when Geen asked him a question. The official had a little difficulty hearing, for he asked the horseman to repeat and it was done in a loud voice.

"I asked, is the sale to be made to the highest bidder?"

"That's the law," the official snapped, "and I already said so."

Geen smiled and held up his hand. "So, Mister Sheriff, if nobody tops the claim of John Caines, he takes this place for two hundred eighty dollars?"

A murmur passed through the crowd. Sheriff Webster forced a smile and gave a bluff answer. "That's the law, brother. But it ain't likely this really fine piece of property will go for chicken feed like that."

Geen dropped back a little, and Ad Jenkins caught Luke's arm excitedly. "Look, there's a bunch of men with Geen. You can pick them out."

He pointed and it was easy to note that four hard-faced, determined-looking men stood close to Geen and Brendy. Each carried a heavy riding crop.

"Ladies and gentlemen," the sheriff intoned, "it is now eleven o'clock, the time set for this sale. Make your bids promptly. Be ready to settle for cash. We have one bid for two hundred eighty dollars."

Luke pushed forward in the crowd, ready to begin his own bidding backed by Brookland's money. Ad Jenkins stuck beside him.

"Two hundred eighty-five," Geen's voice cut in.

Near Luke, a man raised an arm excitedly as if to bid, but the nearest of Geen's company stepped close and laid a mittened hand on his shoulder. The would-be bidder wheeled angrily, saw the accoster's face, and subsided.

"Two hundred eighty-five," Webster shouted. "Come on, folks, give us some common-sense bids."

In five minutes of shouting and calling for bids, the official became thoroughly angry as he received no response. "Listen, you folks. I came here to sell, you to buy. I didn't come here to—"

This time George Brendy interrupted. "Mister Sheriff, is this claim for two hundred eighty dollars the only one against this property?"

Webster mumbled something, consulted one of his aides, and then answered, "Yes, I guess so. Why?"

Brendy was stroking his wispy beard. "You shouldn't guess, Sheriff. You ought to know. Maybe these folks are uneasy about other judgments and afraid to buy. I understand that Mr. Haliday has paid all claims against him except the sum you mention. He was fined for helping runaway folks escape north to freedom. Now another question. If somebody pays more than John Caines' bid, who gets the money? The county or Haliday?"

The crowd was instantly noisy and restless. One man near the porch spat tobacco juice just below the sheriff's stand.

"Something's going on here!" Webster cried. "Somebody's trying to put something over."

Brendy was now out front, and his voice was caustic. "Tell them, Sheriff. The money'll go to John Caines. You're selling his place, not Haliday's."

"Who the hell are you?" demanded the court officer, and Brendy grinned.

"I'm the attorney for the man who just offered two hundred eighty-five dollars. Sheriff, you have a bid. Sell the farm."

Webster's voice was lost in the murmuring confusion before him. He started shouting, "Two hundred eighty-five dollars, two hundred eighty-five dollars."

In the subtle way common to crowds, an unspoken warning had passed through this one. Brendy's questions were probably not fully understood, but no one present seemed to want to risk a bid. Geen and his men formed a short arc directly in front of the porch. One of Geen's thumbs was hooked in his belt; he stood with his coat brushed back a little.

"That's the bid, Sheriff. Two hundred eighty-five dollars." Brendy, at Geen's side, waved a handful of banknotes. "That's your bid, Webster. Sell the property."

The badgered official looked into the faces before him, noted the little phalanx about the bidder, and the now uneasy crowd behind them. He had not anticipated any trouble and here he was beyond any help or advice from those who controlled him.

"Two hundred eighty-five dollars, second and last call. Two hundred eighty-five dollars; are you all done? Sold to, sold to—"

Brendy stepped forward with his money. "Mr. James Haliday. Now here's your money. Let's make out the papers."

A roar of approbation lifted from the crowd. Jim Haliday was half carried, half pushed to the porch where Sheriff Webster's aides were filling out the deed. Jim was too stunned with surprise to say anything until he moved away, clutching the deed in his gnarled fingers. Luke, standing well back, felt his elbow jostled, and Brendy was there, proffering money.

"Mister, you gave us three hundred dollars. Rush and I had some expenses, but here's your change."

Luke stared down at the wrinkled currency in his hand. When he looked up, Brendy had gone. Brookland approached, smiling.

"Come, Luke, let's get away. We don't want Jim to guess we had anything in this. Rush Geen turned the trick using Brendy's brains."

They were almost to Spring Haven when he made another comment. "Brendy knew his crowd. Let's not forget how it reacted when he mentioned the reason for Haliday's trouble."

He smiled and slapped Luke's knee. "Today may have been worth more than helping a dozen unfortunates to New York State. We'll count the day to profit."

CHAPTER NINE

WHATEVER EFFECT the events of the Haliday sale might later have on the efficiency of the Underground Railroad, it almost immediately improved conditions for the Halidays. Ad Jenkins was a curious man. The sale had been held on a Tuesday. On Thursday, as he said, he was "scouting" up in the hills and saw that the neighbors were bringing back their "borrowings"—the horses, cattle, and implements belonging to the farm. Emma and Jim had returned to their home and were being welcomed.

Brookland commented on hearing Ad's story. "They'll be all right now. Jim's a good farmer. Of course, it will be lonesome for them, but I'm glad Hugh's in the army. He's hot-headed, and I was afraid he might do something drastic to Marshal Bay. Hester, of course, is making a career for herself."

Luke made no comment, but he felt a deep relief. He knew the shot he had fired in defense of Fred had hurt these friends. Now, he had done what he could to put them on their feet again. Perhaps the Hester of the mountain farm who had ridden fast horses and whistled to the quail in the grain fields was gone forever. That night so long ago in the dark gap of the hills, she had been warm and sweet in his arms, stirring him tremendously. Now she had become a poised, cold, young woman with a bitter tongue that could and did hurt.

* * *

Two days later, after dinner, impatient at inaction, Luke spoke to his friend. "Mr. Brookland, I know you got me out of the navy for a real purpose, and I've just been marking time. Now the Haliday thing is settled, perhaps I could go to work."

Brookland smiled and drew strongly on his cigar. "You're always eager. But I've been hesitating. The last time I sent you out, it took three years to get you back."

Luke leaned forward. "Sir, I'm older now and know what I want. What you said about Caines being head of whatever organization there may be among the slave catchers strikes me as true. I want to go after him, hard."

Abruptly, the older man's eyes met those of his eager companion, and he spoke almost cryptically. "Not in the way you may be thinking. We'll let that to John Remington or Brown. Remember, Caines is inside the law, and he all but owns the officers in this and nearby counties. You have heard, of course, that he has moved from Crossville and lives now between the county seat and his lumber camps up the river. You'll have to be careful."

For a moment, the two men stared at each other sharply. In spite of age and coloring, there was a strong likeness between them. Both were spare of flesh; Brookland the taller, Luke the heavier. Both had level mouths with a little more kindness about Brookland's lips. Both carried the promise of action in their eyes, but the older man had better control.

Luke blurted his answer. "No, between us, I don't want to shoot John Caines—yet. I want to break up his organization, whatever it is. I want to block him and make it risky to snatch runaways. I want to put the risks on the other side of the fence.

Grimness stiffened his face as he continued. "At first, the excitement of helping the runaways appealed to me as it did to Hugh. Then I saw little Mealie die and her father shot down like a mad dog. I wasn't an Abolitionist as my father was and didn't consider the sacrifices he felt he must give until he finally died. But, as I told you, I saw the Gold Coast and the Portuguese ships standing out to sea with their loads of human misery. You tell me that, here in Pennsylvania, one out of two runaways is caught and that hundreds of freed slaves are kidnapped. Sir, that damned law of 1850 denies a black man everything in the line of freedom except what we men, outside the law, can grab for him."

A little embarrassed by his long monologue, Luke stopped. Brookland had been studying his face.

"It could be you can match John Caines. That's the principal reason I worked to get you back here. Now my main camp, as you know, is on Hyner Run. That's the beginning of the high pine country. Pine Bend, Weston, and other lumber towns are above. Go up there and report to Ben Royal, my camp boss, who'll help you. Get into the towns, meet people, take your time. You'll be on the Brookland payroll. Outwardly, you're a wood hick, kind of an understudy to Ben Royal. That's about all. Of course, the men in my camp will help. It's not too far from my place to the Pike and then to the Dyer farm. There's one freeman on my payroll up there."

Without seeing Brookland in the morning, because he was still asleep, Luke walked to King's Shore and took a train from there to the county seat town of Point Haven. From there, his pockets crammed with cold food from a restaurant, he took the woodsman's path west and north, walking easily, enjoying the sense of freedom. He spent the first night in the brush.

Looking up at the stars high and bright above the mountains, he heard about him the tiny whisperings of the forest, and Luke felt more contented than he had been for a long time. The course ahead of him was no longer confused. With Brookland, he knew the job was to stop John Caines. Actually, he had really little acquaintance with the man, but in spite of the smoothness and poise usually shown by Caines, Luke knew how the man's veneer could crack under strain. He had seen him that morning in the old Potter mill when his face was a mask of murderous fury.

Still wondering about Caines, Luke fell asleep. Toward morning, he dreamed. Once again, a horseman was running his mount along the hill road, and its drumming hoofbeats finally woke him to a bright, unbelievably fresh morning.

Luke was getting up into the great white pine country, which each spring sent down the broad reaches of the West Branch of the Susquehanna its fleet of rafts to the lumber market of Marietta. He had made good time. It was only a few miles to Hyner Run on which he would find the Brookland logging camp.

Even though he walked leisurely now, he reached Hyner Run about noon and crossed the stream on a footlog close to where the teams and wagons forded the stream in low water. From the Jenkins cousins' accounts, Pine Bend was about ten miles farther upriver. Determined to have a look at it, he went on and finally saw the village ahead of him beyond a bridge over what must be Young Woman's Creek. A short distance across the stream and still well removed from the town was a huge structure Luke took to be a hotel. Most of the houses stood along one street, but well behind them toward the mountains, a wagon road all but detoured the place. Luke took this road, remembering that the Caines operations were farther upriver.

Around a turn a half-mile from Pine Bend, he came upon a small field where there sat a mixed log-and-lumber blacksmith shop, judging by the dark smoke lifting from its chimney. He had turned toward it and was almost to the wide doors when a man carrying a riding whip in a gloved hand came around the building. He led a saddled horse and stopped when he saw Luke. It was John Caines. Both men looked at each other. Both were surprised, but Caines recovered himself immediately.

"Ah," he said smoothly. "You are back."

Luke nodded and spoke civilly. "Yes, having a look around before I go into the woods."

The blacksmith, an incredibly dirty man whose breadth of shoulders made him look short, came out and stood listening. When he pulled off his cap and mopped his face with it, he showed a head almost devoid of hair. Caines did not look his way.

"Likely you want the Brookland camp. It's east of here. One of my own operations is farther upriver. We're proud of our new spool road. We don't cut spars—just saw timber."

For a few minutes, the two men talked of lumbering and the weather. Then Caines mounted and rode away toward town. Luke stood, deciphering the sign over the shop. "Axelroth," he read, then looked sharply at the dirty man and asked a question in one word. "Axelroth?"

"Yes," the smith grunted, "what's it to you?"

Luke, satisfied that his interview with Caines had passed off well enough, grinned at the stranger. "Not a damned thing, brother. Not a thing. Maybe someday I'll want you to sharpen my pocket knife. When it gets dull, then I'll hunt you up."

Axelroth's scowl came quickly. He knew he was being baited, and the hammer held in his right hand lifted slowly.

Luke warned the man, "Keep your shirt on, Axel. It's pretty dirty at that."

This encounter pleased him even more than his interview with Caines. Feeling pretty cocky, he turned back toward Pine Bend. A look at the Caines operation could come later. Just now, it would be worthwhile to inspect the town. He did not see the smith staring after him nor hear him say as he spat into the dust, "So that damned fresh pup's the Hanley man."

* * *

Pine Bend's one street was all but deserted as Luke walked past general stores, barbershops, and two frame hotels. In spite of its beautiful location along the river, the place was drab and seemed trapped between timbered mountains and the broad sweep of the river.

A scant half-mile east of the town was the building that had first attracted Luke's attention but which he had missed on the back road. Now he saw that it was set a half-dozen rods from the narrow road. It was a big two-story building. In front of it was a long hitching rack, and the rear of the structure looked as though it was fitted out to take the place of the usual summer kitchen, woodshed, and spring house. Behind it was a barn. Just under the eaves of the long front porch was a wide, crudely lettered sign: Tammie's Place.

Luke walked up slowly, mounted three wide steps, crossed the veranda, and entered a wide door that stood ajar. He came upon a huge room littered with small tables and heavy chairs. At its back was a bar made of dark wood. In the mirror behind this were reflected the neatly racked bottles and glasses. His first impression was that the room was empty until a woman's voice hailed him.

"All right, brother. Now close the door. I can't warm the whole county with one stove."

Startled, Luke turned toward the west window, where a woman was just getting out of a deep wing chair. A broad plait of yellow hair almost as wide as one of Linda Caines' was wound about her head. Her eyes were a deep blue, and she was smiling at her visitor's discomfiture, showing small white teeth. She was stout but not clumsy, and her loose sleeves fell back from fully rounded arms when she raised her hands to rearrange her hair.

Luke stammered, "I'm sorry, I didn't mean to—"

She had crossed to the bar and turned toward him. "Well, if you're that mixed up already, it ain't whiskey you need."

The woman stepped through the bar gate and worked busily for a moment, then set a filled glass before her visitor. "Here. It's ginger beer mixed with wine we make ourselves." Luke lifted the glass, noting how clean it was, and sipped the drink slowly. Half finished, he shoved a coin across the dark wood.

"Name's Tammie," she offered, "and don't say 'Tammie what?'"

He started his reply, but she stopped him.

"Let me do a bit of guessing. You've been in the army or navy from the way you walk, been drilled a lot." She took another good look from his head to his shoes. "Navy," she concluded triumphantly. "You looked to see if the glass was clean before you drank. Army don't give a damn."

Luke laughed. "You're right on both counts. Captain Caris drilled us a lot, and it was the navy. I'm Luke Hanley on my way to the Brookland camps."

Some of the friendliness left her face. "Luke Hanley," she said softly. "Luke Hanley."

He set down his glass and looked at her, puzzled. "You know something about me, Tammie?"

Her plump palm smacked the bar smartly for emphasis. "Not a thing, brother. To me, you're just another lantern-jawed hick, bound into the timber to bump knots with a dull axe and eat salt pork for breakfast. Saturday nights, you'll step out a little, drink whiskey, and get the hell knocked out of you in a rumpus. That's a hick for you, just hired from the neck down."

She was polishing the bar vigorously as she delivered her tirade. "You got seventy-five cents, it'd buy you supper, bed, and breakfast. I put up hicks going into the woods but not out. Most of them is lousy then."

Luke had intended on going on to camp, but the woman amused him so he took out the money and gave it to her. "You're hard on hicks," he told her, and she smiled.

"It's a hard country, brother. I was just trying you for size."

Supper was an excellent meal. The food was well-cooked, and the waitress was clean and neat. She wore her skirt short without embarrassment. Luke ate with real appetite, for this was his first square meal since leaving Point Haven two days before. After supper, he stood on the veranda and looked about. There were still some leaves clinging to oaks and chestnuts, making a bright contrast to the deep green of the pines. Restless, he walked over to Pine Bend, loafed about a while, and returned to Tammie's Place to find it booming. The big room was crowded with lumbermen and local farmers. This noisy, boisterous crew did not appeal to Luke, so he went to his room, got out his surveyor's manual, and gave himself over to study.

It must have been close to ten o'clock when hurried steps in the hallway were followed by a nervous rapping at his door. He opened it to admit the girl with the short dress who had waited on tables at supper time. "There's bad trouble downstairs," she stammered. "Mister Hanley, mebbe if you was to go down—"

Luke looked into the loose, frightened face. There was something wrong—she would not meet his eyes. "All right, sister," he agreed finally. "But, I'll bet Tammie didn't send you."

The neat barroom was a scene of confusion, but the barkeeper, a big vacant-faced man, showed little sign of being disturbed. Nearly a score of roughly dressed men sat at the tables or lolled against the bar. There seemed to be only six who were causing trouble, and they were grouped about one table. Luke's first glance told him they had a bearded man flat on his back on the table. He was yelling, partly in fright, more in sheer rage.

"Buck," one of the men holding the victim called, "better gag the damned noisy fool. He's likely to upset somebody. Somebody hold this candle."

The big man who answered to the name of Buck fished out a dirty handkerchief, tossed it on the victim's face, and then brandished the candle given to him.

"Men!" he yelled. "This here's a singeing party. It's good fer hair, chapped hands, and dirty feet. We figger this buzzard's jest a roosting place fer graybacks. Gather round, folks, while we burn the biting devils out of house and home."

Luke suddenly looked at the man stretched on the table and saw it was George Brendy, Rush Geen's friend who had saved the Haliday farm. His clothing was torn from the struggle he had put up, and his shirt was ripped badly, showing his bony torso. Luke realized many of the men in the room regarded what was going on as just rough horseplay, but there was a viciousness about the way Buck was proceeding. As Luke stepped forward, he heard his own name pronounced but did not see who had spoken.

One of Buck's companions whirled halfway about at the sound, and Luke realized there had been a reason for his being called downstairs. He suspected a trap, and the only escape from it would be quick action. Buck's huge hand with its blackened nails lifted, and he threw the lighted candle at Luke, who dodged it by diving low. When he came up, his blow starting from the floor landed flush on the side of his assailant's jaw. Buck's legs buckled, and he fell on hands and knees. As he lifted his head, a second blow caught him directly on the Adam's apple.

"Run for it, Brendy," Luke snapped to the man on the table, who promptly rolled off and disappeared through the legs of Buck's companions, now rushing in for the kill. Luke had seen many roughhouses among sailors and knew it was a disaster to go down where his attackers could use their heavy shoes on his face and ribs.

Buck, still gasping, had regained his feet. "Get back," he mouthed. "I'll kill the bastard. Hanley, git ready to pick yer teeth off the floor and an eye with it."

Luke's fingers snatched an axe handle one of the men had dropped. He had time to make one slashing blow that probably broke Buck's right hand, for he howled with pain. Next instant, Luke's weapon was snatched from him and slammed home on his head. In the momentary blackness, he remembered the counsel of an old sergeant at arms.

"Keep in close when they're too much for you."

He brought his boot heel down on the instep of one man, pulled his head low, and jerked up against the chin of the staggering man with such force he heard teeth click. He at least had the advantage that each of his blows struck an enemy while his adversaries had to look out for each other in the melee. But he was taking a lot of punishment. He saw the axe handle, bent to get it, and an upswung chair crashed down on his head and shoulders. As he dropped, his last thought was that he was going down under those heavy, flailing boots.

He did not see the outer door open, and it seemed a long time until the crash of a pistol shot cleared his head. Onlookers and participants alike were stunned with surprise. One of the men who had entered was Rush Geen. He was accompanied by a man who held a pistol waist high, its muzzle flicking from side to side like a snake's tongue. George Brendy entered, and Geen spoke to the crowd.

"My friend came in for a drink, and you damned stinking woods lice stood by while John Caines' ape, Buck Fletch here, mauled him. It took Hanley to save him."

Buck stood close to the bar, holding his injured hand. One of his men close to Geen made a threatening gesture, and the horseman promptly knocked him senseless with a revolver barrel.

"Bob," Geen directed, "here's my gun. If any of these cattle move, shoot." Rubbing the knuckles of his right hand, Geen stepped toward the now frightened Buck. "I've heard about you, Buck. Tonight, you've hit your last man. You bullied my friend to bait Hanley. Caines wanted you and your gang to handle him."

Fletch did the only thing open to him. He rushed Geen, who side-stepped and dropped the charging bully with two blows to the back of the ear. Geen dragged Fetch to his feet by his hair and, this time, cut the man's face again and again with slashing blows until it was a gory mess and he dropped to the floor, groveling.

"Get him out of here," Geen directed Fletch's friends. "Tell him he has till tomorrow morning to get out of the country or I'll cut his heart out."

* * *

The young horseman insisted that Luke go out with him and his friends. At the hitching rack, he explained. "Hanley, George went in there for a drink. They weren't after him. Fletch is Caines' woods boss. I figure he started a rumpus to pull you into it. Carry a pistol after this and use it. A fellow like Fletch would put your eyes out. Next time you see Buck, use an axe on him, not a handle. Brendy and I are much obliged."

The three men shook hands warmly before they mounted. Brendy touched Luke's shoulder. "Someday, I hope to help you, Hanley."

Luke stood a while in the darkness. He was awed by the efficiency and ruthlessness of this man, Geen, who had been Hester Haliday's self-appointed bodyguard in Lymansville. The man's hands had moved with the skill of a professional prizefighter.

The soft fall of horses' hoofs died away to the westward. Luke's steps made little shuffling noises as he returned to the hotel, where he climbed the stairs to his room.

Most of an hour passed as he lay on the bed, smoking and thinking about what had happened. Geen had been sure the attack lay at the door of John Caines. Had it succeeded, he would now be a bruised, battered, and even crippled man, perhaps a blinded one. It was pretty certain the whole affair had been a trap. Brendy was the bait; likely, the girl who had come with the message was part of the plan. The door opened, interrupting his thinking. Tammie, clad in a voluminous wrapper, came in and looked at the man on the bed. He returned her stare soberly but said nothing.

"You all right?" she queried, and he touched the lump on his head gingerly with his fingertips.

"Sure," he answered mockingly. "Sure, I'm fine, Tammie. Why did you send the girl? You should have come."

She did not answer but stepped out of the door and returned with a basin and cloths. She skillfully applied a hot compress to his bruises. "I didn't," she said. "But I knowed she was sent. Mebbe I thought a grown man could smell a rat dead that long. Likely you're just dumber than I figured."

She shrugged her shoulders as Luke swung his legs from the bed and spoke irritably. "Mebbe, mebbe, mebbe. I don't care for the mebbe's. Rush Geen said John Caines was behind the rough stuff tonight, that he likely wanted the hell knocked out of me." He grabbed her shoulders and looked into her face. "Where do you stand in this business, Tammie?"

Her smile, as she released herself, showed her teeth. "Me, Buster, I'm the Good Man, kind to all devils because I don't know who's coming for supper."

Some of Luke's bad temper evaporated. "Tammie, one of these days, I'll lay you over my knee and give you a back-handed blessing."

She was serious now and came closer. "Friend, how well do you know this Geen man?"

After Luke explained that he had met the man in Lymansville, she lifted her plump hands and examined them carefully before dropping them to her sides. "If I was Buck Fletch, I wouldn't stop short of Canada. He bullied an old man, and that man was George Brendy. Geen would kill for that old lush any time."

"Well, Tammie, who is Rush Geen?"

"Buster," she rejoined, "don't ask fool questions. We know a lot about you up here; how you was run out of Grossville, how you left the county two jumps ahead of the law. We don't think for a holy minute you're up here to bump knots. You straddle a railroad that sometimes runs up the Pike and sometimes goes through here to Keating. Now, on top of this, you ask who is Rush Geen."

Perhaps some of Luke's surprise was mirrored on his face as she lifted her plump arms to fix her hair. "Rush Geen is a liveryman from Lymansville. He buys and sells horses up and down the country. And, Luke Hanley, my suspicious friend, he's the coolest, hardest man in these mountains. At that, I'm kinda glad he owes you something. There's too many people that don't."

Luke followed her to the door, where she stopped, set down her basin, and took him by the shoulders. "Listen, Luke Hanley. Stick to cutting timber. Never mind these strangers that come by night and just get you into more and more trouble."

Suddenly she rose on tiptoes and kissed him. Then she went out, forgetting her basin and the cloths piled in it.

CHAPTER TEN

LUKE FELT stiff and sore in the morning after his encounter with the Caines' woods boss and his henchmen. Brookland had emphasized that he should take time to learn the situation. So, instead of going to the camp, he walked into Pine Bend again. Remembering his encounter with Caines and Axelroth, he continued his walk but found the blacksmith shop closed.

Above the smithy, the curve of the mountains was beginning to crowd the road toward the river. Close to ten miles above the village, he came to the beginning of a huge lumbering operation that must belong to John Caines. Along the riverbank was a stretch of landings on which logs were already piled high to wait through the cold months for spring and flood water. There was no one about. Luke was free to inspect more carefully.

Soft spots in the roads had been carefully corduroyed with small logs, adzed flat for a smoother surface. The feature of the place was the spool railroad. The rails were straight logs carefully spliced together at the ends and reaching back toward the mountains. The sleepers were great bolts of chestnut logs, impervious to rot. One of the trucks had been lifted from the rails. It was nothing more than two heavy bolsters connected with a white oak coupling pole, adjustable for length. The four wheels resembled huge thread spools, which were set loose on the axles to accommodate the varying tread of the rails. John Caines had solved the problem of the long haul from the hills, which took men, horses, and time. As Luke stood inspecting, he heard a rumbling noise back at the mountain and identified it as a log slide. Caines did not need to wait for winter and iced roads; his operation was in full swing, capable of gaining months on other lumbermen.

There was nothing to be learned by looking longer. Luke turned and walked slowly over the way he had come. In Pine Bend, he visited both general stores, buying some tobacco and a woolen shirt. At Tammie's, he turned in and found her cleaning up bottles behind the bar.

"I've seventy-five cents more," he told her with a laugh. "I want another of those suppers."

She took his money, picked up a glass, and polished it before putting it on the rack. "You'll have company for supper, Luke. He was asking about you."

When he walked into the dining room, a man sat at a table in a corner. He turned, and Luke recognized George Brendy, Rush Geen's friend. The one-time lawyer was surprisingly genial, insisting that Luke share his table, and the two men ate with excellent appetites.

"Tammie's cooking," Brendy commented. "I'd ride miles out of my way to get a bite of it most anytime."

The lawyer carried the weight of the conversation. He was an enthusiastic fisherman and interested in ships when Luke said that he had worked in a navy yard. The meeting had been a friendly and enjoyable one in the beginning. But finally, the few other diners had left, and they were alone.

Brendy crumpled some bread, then, looking down at the cloth, changed the subject sharply. "Hanley, don't be offended when I tell you it's pretty well known why you're up here. A man like you doesn't need to work by the day in the woods. Brookland's smart—he sent you into Caines country because he thought you had some chance to knock out the man who dominates this upriver region. Hell, he owns it like he does the county officers."

Brendy stopped, probably to see how his companion was taking it. "Could be you'll win. But it's also mighty probable that he may. There are some things about Caines we could use—if we had evidence. Lacking that, he is inside the law and riding high. His weak spot is the love of his daughter, and I'm told relations between them are pretty strained."

Luke could not entirely conceal a start at the mention of Linda, but Brendy continued, drawing down his heavy brows. "Now, that's about enough talk of speculations. Let me be specific. You'll find everything you do blocked, interfered with. Somebody'll be watching what you do, what you say. Sometimes I'm not sure why John Caines is so set against you, but I'm sure it isn't all because of a few black folks in the brush. When something happens, hit back hard. Don't get mixed up in brawls; they'll try to cripple you."

Brendy suddenly rose and stood beside the table with a crooked smile on his bearded lips. "Hanley, you can use what I've told you or just say to hell with it. What I said is partly for you, partly for me, because something about you makes me feel you might stop Caines. God, how I'd like to see that man broken and whining like some others I know."

He walked out of the room without another word, and Luke sat at the table, his mind in turmoil at what he had heard. Linda had been mentioned, and he had tried to put her out of his mind. There were too many other men of position and wealth in her life for him to hope, yet she had done so much for him. Between them, too, was this enmity between her father and himself.

It was surprising how much Brendy knew and how he summed up things. There was something in Caines' life, the ex-lawyer hinted. Luke shrugged his shoulders. Brookland had told him to go slow, but he could do one thing Brendy had suggested—strike back hard.

In the morning, he started his interrupted trip to the Hyner camp. Where the road climbed over the ridge point, he stopped again to study the terrain.

The river dominated the scene, but the mountains set their feet directly against the stream, crowding the water into deep, swift stretches then, stepping back, opened to broad coves of flat country running back to higher land. The blue-black of hemlocks screened the rough places on the hill except where occasional gray rocks showed through like old bones half hidden in shadows.

Ben Royal welcomed him on Hyner Run before the log and slab buildings that made up the Brookland camp. He was a widely built man whose beard and hair were streaked with gray. His face carried a worried look, but his eyes were friendly and a little relieved. "You're just in time to meet the men, Hanley. They're in the dining room, and there's a visitor to see you."

However, the men had finished the meal and had trooped into the lobby, a huge room with straw- and blanket-filled bunks on three sides and a huge pot-bellied stove exactly in its center. From wires stretched just under the ceiling, socks and underwear hung, drying.

"Men," Royal introduced. "This is Luke Hanley, a friend of Mr. Brookland's. He's to be a kind of assistant to me. Luke, you'll get to know the names of these briar pullers soon enough. Now, I'll get you some supper."

* * *

"That's a good crew. They keep their mouths shut. Dave, the black man, is treated just like the rest. There's only two rum hounds," Royal commented as they entered the dining room.

There were long tables and doors that opened to the kitchen, the lobby, and a small room that would be the office. To Luke's surprise, at the end of one table were three black men eating busily. He had just started toward them when one jumped up with a cry of eagerness.

"Luke, Mister Luke! Am I glad to see you!"

It was Fred, neatly dressed, eager, and eyes shining as he and Luke gripped hands and pounded each other on the back.

"We has been waiting. Heard you was coming." Gesturing to the other black men, he introduced them.

"Ned and Charley, this here is Mister Luke. He got me away from the patrollers years back. Now you is safe."

The men looked up, grinned, and began eating again. Then Luke, Royal, and Fred sat down while the cook served them. As they ate, Fred explained the situation.

"I helps run things down Keating way. These boys came over the old Karthaus road. Their master has offered five hundred dollars fer each of 'em. Charley's a smith. So the boys kept off reg'lar routes, and they just ought to git on to Lymansville kinda fast like."

He smiled, showing his white teeth. "I'm talkin' free like, but Mr. Brookland said you was comin'. God knows how we needs the like of you along this here river. I can't be from home too much."

Royal interrupted when he had his pipe filled and going. "Fred's not told you all of it. When he was away last week, three slave catchers slipped into the village behind Keating. They took a man and likely he's across the Pennsylvania line into slave country now. When Fred's home, he can stand off such men. He's routed a couple of gangs like that. So he ought to get back there."

"All right," Luke promised. "I'll take them up to Erritt if they'll keep their mouths shut and do just what they're told." Both black men looked up and nodded their closely cropped heads while Fred smiled.

"They's good boys. Yes, I was off when they ketched Tom Barney. He hed him a wife and two little folks. The day they got him he was huntin' butternuts on Piney Island. We followed, but they put him on a train at Point Haven."

Royal broke in again. "They took Tom before a Justice of the Peace. Under the law, he couldn't testify. They said he was a runaway though we all know Tom had lived up this way all his life."

Both Luke and Fred looked at each other grimly while Royal finished. "We used to hire some of the Keating boys, and they worked first-rate in the woods. Now I'm kinda afraid to hire them for fear of these damned kidnappers. Dave is the only one we have now; can't spare him, he's too good with a peeling axe. But I can't watch all the time."

The three talked on for a time while Fred told of his work. Since his own escape, he proudly said he had helped thirty-two runaways to safety. "I better go now, Mister Ben and Luke. I jest can't rest easy away from home." He shook hands all around, picked up a light double-bitted axe from a corner and went out.

Later, in the office, the two white men talked. The fugitives were curled up on the dining room floor, well-wrapped in blankets.

"Luke, I don't think even Minor Brookland knows how bad things are. Them kidnappers hang around Keating and other places like wolves do when the deer are yarded. No able-bodied black man or good-looking black girl's safe. Between us, the folks in Keating have shotguns now, only they're afraid to cut loose unless Fred's there."

* * *

In the morning, Royal, using the camp's spring wagon, took Luke and his charges by lumbering roads to the Pike and then on to the Dyer farm. Since the runaways were both strong young men, they agreed it would be safer to make the remainder of the trip to Lymansville on foot. Royal left them to return to his work.

After Luke's charges were slumbering peacefully on brush pallets, he stepped out into the moonlight. It was easy to find the little mound beneath the big pine. Fred had come a long way to place the last of the season's flowers on the resting place of the child who had been too tired and frail to go farther. Luke lifted and replaced the cluster of yellow witch hazel.

He lay sleepless a long time on his pallet. Tomorrow he would be in Lymansville where he might see Hester. He thought of her that day in the cornfield when she had asked him not to mar their friendship. Her back had been carried so straight when she went toward the house. But when he did sleep, he dreamed of Linda Caines and the cryptic smile that so often rested on her full lips.

Charley roused him in the morning with a shake followed by a wide grin as Luke opened his eyes.

"Mister, was I to sleep that sound like, the patrollers'd have me half-way to Virginny 'fore I woke up right."

Charley had prepared a good breakfast of bacon, coffee, and toasted bread, so all three started the long walk to Lymansville well-fed, rested, and hopeful. There was little likelihood of meeting any of the danger men on foot could not avoid, but Luke carried his father's old pistol loaded with a single buckshot. Through the years, since it figured somehow in the death of Fred Horton, Luke had practiced with the weapon until he had become an excellent shot.

They were careless and so walked into a surprise that might have proved disastrous. They had come down a steep hill with a turn in it. At its foot was a narrow bridge and a small clearing beyond. Charley saw them first, gave his warning, and dived into the brush. There were two mounted men down there and three led horses. They carried guns across their saddlebows and rode easily, eyes searching the road ahead. One was a slim, Indian-looking youth; the other was George Brendy. Luke did not reveal his presence, and none of them came out of the brush until the small cavalcade had climbed the hill and disappeared southward.

"Sure looked like patrollers," Charley declared after Luke explained who the one man was. Yet, somehow, he was uneasy about the incident and was glad when he turned over his charges to Erritt, who gave them a cordial welcome at Hillside.

"You're all right now," he assured the runaways. "The fact is, you were when you landed in Luke Hanley's hands."

Later, when the two friends were smoking cigars by the fireplace in the evening, Luke was surprised at the station master's knowledge of his coming and going.

Erritt explained. "News always did travel fast in these hills. There's always more grapevine than telegraph, and we've got both. Word flashed upriver that somebody was coming who'd break up this kidnap stuff. You know, I think Brookland started that to take the boldness out of the man snatchers. You showed up in Pine Bend and spoiled Buck Fletch, which makes you a marked man."

Luke felt irritated at being advertised so thoroughly.

Erritt continued. "Brookland could have picked a man who looked and acted like a woods hick, but he sent you. I figure it is warning, like I just said. You've got a certain set to your shoulders and a cold eye. The thing I'm afraid of for you is a bullet from the brush or a ganging up of these toughs like there was down at Tammie's Place that night."

Luke laughed at Erritt's tone, but the man was in earnest.

"Don't laugh. If a man threatens to do people out of a business that brings in thousands of dollars a year, he just can't reasonably expect to stay safe."

The way this experienced station master talked, the Underground had changed much in the past few years while Luke had been away. It had been rather casual, its danger nominal. Now there were times when it was a desperate undertaking. Runaways and their helpers had died in the brush from shots fired by officers.

* * *

Luke stayed at Hillside overnight. In the morning, after saying good-bye to his host, he went into town. Seeing the livery stable, he turned in and found Geen, who was most cordial. "I wish George was here. He'd want to talk with you."

He waited a moment then spoke again. "It's all right to tell you. George has the notion that somebody's watching the Pike. It could be for runaways or something else, but he had the fool idea he might smoke them out, so he's riding for a couple of days."

Luke waved a hand deprecatingly. "I'd like to see him, but just now, I'm interested in seeing horses."

Geen's face brightened, and he took his visitor through the well-equipped barns. There were six horses in good box stalls. These made up two light teams and one heavy one that would have delighted any lumberman. Neatly washed buggies stood side by side with their shafts lifted high and all harnesses oiled and polished. Luke complimented Geen on his place.

"Glad you like it," the liveryman said. "Any time you need anything, George and I will be glad to help."

"You have already, Geen. That gang had me pretty foul till you stepped in. Yes, I might need you badly."

"We figured you might," the horseman said shortly.

Luke was outside when Geen called him back with an unexpected statement. "Hester Haliday is at home today. It's none of my business, but did she pay back your money used for the farm?"

Luke's surprised look probably answered the question, and Geen nodded. "I'll have to speak to her about that. She always has money. Times are hard, and a man can always use cash, especially if he can't work regular."

Luke did not linger. Geen's assurance grated on him a little, even though he realized the man meant well. He went up to the little hotel where he rapped on Hester's door.

In the few minutes he waited, Luke thought of what had happened here the last time he had called. There was no sound reason for his coming today. Certainly he was no longer the impressionable boy she had kissed and confused. A light step sounded, and the door opened.

"Why, Luke," said the girl in a neat print dress, greeting him with a smile. "This is nice. Come in."

He entered the now-familiar room and, passing a table, caught the scent of sweet fern. There was a spray of it in a vase, and the nostalgic perfume carried him back to the farm and this girl standing on a hill, letting the wind have its way with her hair. She politely indicated a chair.

"I'm glad to have a chance to thank you, Luke, for helping the folks. Rush tells me they are back home again, thanks to you."

As abruptly as the perfume had stirred him, Luke knew another thing. There was no real feeling behind this poised young woman's words. She was saying conventional phrases, and he had strong doubts as to how much she might care for her parents and the old home in the mountains.

"I'm so grateful," she continued, "I suppose you're up here on business, or—"

His frown checked her, but he spoke smoothly, almost confidently. "No, not business. You see, I haven't any. I'm just sort of shiftless like I was when I came to your home. Sometimes I make trouble for people, get sorry, and am on my way again."

The girl's temper was rising, as shown by the tightness at the corners of her mouth, but she held the fixed wooden smile. Luke knew his performance was silly and that Hester Haliday wanted him to go. But he could not understand why this slim girl could rouse his exasperation so quickly.

He rose. "I'll be going now. It would be wrong to stir up more trouble like you said a while back."

Her eyes were snapping. There was a hint of high color in her cheeks, but she maintained polite control. "You must come again, Luke. In the spring, I'll be singing in Reverend Hartzell's revival. Come up. It might do you good."

His fingers were on the doorknob when Hester exploded. Her lips drew back from her teeth, her eyes blazed, and her voice rasped. "Get out, you shiftless bully. Get out!"

Her fingers snatched the nearest thing to her, the metal vase that held the sweet fern, and hurled it at his head. Luke dodged, then caught her slim wrist. She struggled, but he wrapped long arms about her and kissed her lips again and again until she relaxed. One of her arms lifted as if to entwine about his neck. He saw tears in the corners of her eyes, and her head, with its soft, fragrant hair, rested against his shoulder. Releasing her abruptly, he went out.

Luke was a good half-mile out of town before he cooled down enough to realize what he was doing. He was thoroughly exasperated at himself because of the way Hester could move him. Since he was now close to Hillside, he went there again, making a thin excuse for his return which Erritt apparently accepted at face value.

"Your boys go out tonight. Geen wants you to stop at his place. He wants to give you a lift as far as the Dyer farm, from which you'll cut across country to the Brookland camp."

Luke walked down to the livery, and Geen seemed pleased. "Give me five minutes, Hanley, and the boys will have the team hooked up. I'm going to King's Shore, so I can set you partway to the camp."

The turnout was a fine buckboard and a pair of bays unmatched in anything but gait. The two horses trotted together like a machine.

"I can't sell these horses," Geen commented. "Folks want matched colors. But I like to drive them. They work together." They were probably five miles out of Lymansville, where farms were giving way to brush and timberland. The horses moved easily, and both men leaned back in their seat, relaxed. The crash of a shot came from the brush. Luke felt the seat jerk at the bullet's impact, and the frightened horses bolted.

The sudden plunge forward almost unseated the surprised men. Geen sawed his lines and brought the team under control promptly. Then he handed the reins to his companion.

"Hold them," he directed, leaping to the ground and pulling a revolver from under his coat. When he reached the spot from which the shot appeared to have come, he searched the brushland with shot after shot until his weapon was emptied. His face was grim when he returned to the rig and busied himself reloading his revolver, fitting the tiny brass caps in place with care.

"Spoiled your buckboard seat," Luke commented. "Which one of us did the fellow want?"

The horseman returned the revolver to its holster. "I don't know. Could be this is the ambusher George was talking about. Yes, I have enemies—" He stopped and frowned, seeming uneasy. "From what's happened lately, Hanley, it was likely you he was after. Somebody don't want you round, damned bad at that."

Luke nodded. He had been under fire before, in landing parties and riots. This time, he felt an unreasonable exhilaration. Surely he was getting somewhere if it was so vital to have him removed.

The team trotted on, and the two young men talked of fishing, gravely discussing the merits of braided horsehair lines over linen ones. Geen took him into the lane to the Dyer farm, and Luke got out. From there, it wasn't a hard tramp to the Brookland camp. Before Geen started off, he leaned from his buckboard.

"Hanley, you locate one of those kidnapping gangs, and I'll bring the boys. After today, I'd like to hand those fellows a little red-hot hell. They're getting too free with their shooting."

CHAPTER ELEVEN

THE DAY Luke returned to camp, the weather set in cold, and the overcast sky promised snow. Ben Royal was a weatherwise man.

"We'll have to hit it," he said to the men. "This is timber weather."

Before the week was out, there was from a foot to eighteen inches of loose snow in the woods. Water from a small stream was diverted to flow over the roads, icing them for the heavy loads of logs being taken down to the landings where they would be kept until spring when the rafts were made up. Brookland's timber was excellent, and now the snow cushioned the fall of the great pines that would be shaped into spars. Tom Short and Ed Coser did the final shaping of these valuable timbers. They were the best axe men in camp and proud of their skill.

A week after the first snowfall, Ben Royal's cousin, Dan Pritchett, arrived. A small, active man about Luke's age, he was an expert black-smith and soon became well-liked by all the men in the camp. To Luke, he became a companion almost at once, and often the two read late at night in the office. Dan liked the only novel in camp, the copy of *Rob Roy* Brookland had given Luke.

"Friend," he said one evening, "I'll make you one of them big Scotch claymores. Then you'll challenge Caines to a duel and split the old cuss."

Luke looked at the young smith sharply, then filled and lit his pipe before he spoke. "Mr. Brookland talked to you?"

Pritchett nodded. "Sure. He sent me to be a sort of papa's little helper."

"Thanks," Luke said dryly. "Anyway, I don't seem to need any help; all I do is work in the woods. Maybe papa's little helper can tell me what I should be doing."

Pritchett pointed with his pipe. "Just keep your eyes peeled. No run-aways'll be traveling in such weather, but they can hit at you. Maybe they'd mess up this camp, keep you too busy to hit at them. All you can do now is sit tight. Of course, if you want to run up and burn Caines' camps, I'll go along. But he owns Pine Bend, and they've got lots of coal oil. Likely they could set a pretty big fire themselves."

Generally, Luke worked with the cutting crews, but his main concern was locating spar trees and marking them for the cutters. Brookland wanted a hundred of these sticks. The work was hard but exhilarating. There was always the song of the saws, the measured axe strokes, and the smell of pine in the frosty air. The food served was good, if a trifle monotonous. Brookland's men, contrary to most lumbermen, quit each day a half-hour before sunset. At that time, axes were ground and saws filed.

"Grind on your own time" was the motto on most lumber jobs, but Brookland's men boasted about this consideration of their boss in their interest. Evenings were a little dull but short because the men retired early. The huge lobby stove was always fired hard, and the room would often be full of steam from drying clothing hung close to the ceiling.

Ben Royal wasn't feeling well and he was worried. "Things are moving good, but look out. Something is bound to happen, and it's whiskey I'm afraid of. Lots of the men drink hard. Now, there's Tom Short and Ed Coser. You won't find better men, but Tom's helpless after his first drink and Ed will back him up. Christmas is coming, and every damned hotel in these parts will set up the first drink to any man who wanders in."

A week before the holiday, Brookland arrived with a sled-load of extra food, candy, and a present of two pairs of socks with a silver dollar tucked into the toe of the fourth sock for each man. He also brought a demijohn of excellent whiskey.

"Ben," he advised Royal, "watch that stuff. See that each man gets a little. I'm afraid it may set some of them off."

"Tom Short, for one," Royal commented.

On the promise of a big dinner, the men worked in the morning on the log rollways close to camp. The principal reason for keeping them busy was to get them out of the cook's way.

The meal was excellent; roasted chicken and pork, pickled eggs, sweet potatoes, boiled beans, and corn. Each man got a quarter of an apple pie for dessert, and beside each plate was a small bag of striped stick candy. When the heavy meal was finished, Luke and Dan distributed the gifts to the delight of the men.

Afterward, Ben Royal served the whiskey. "This is Brookland's treat; tomorrow, we'll chop pine."

Most of the men dozed in their bunks through the afternoon while the more ambitious walked about the camp. It was close to four o'clock when Luke missed Tom Short and his crony, Ed Coser. He reported to Royal at once.

The boss lay on his cot and looked sick. "Tom and Ed are gone."

Ben rubbed his eyes and groaned. "Sneaked off to town," he said savagely. "There goes a week's work on the spars. They'll be stiff drunk."

He stood, tried to walk, and sat down again.

"Luke, I'm too damned shaky. You and Pritchett go down to the German Arms in town. I warned that barkeeper never to give either of those men whiskey. You brace him. Take the sleigh and the horse, Tobe, to freight the two damned fools back here. I promised Tom's wife to keep him sober this winter. You boys bring him back if you have to knock him down and drag him."

Luke and the young smith left camp right after supper, but it was already dark, and they had a slow horse.

"The German Arms," Luke said after a long silence between them. "Don't Caines own that place?"

"I guess so," Pritchett replied, "but Ben said we had to brace the barkeeper. That could be real interesting."

Luke snorted, remembering the fight in Tammie's Place. He was also pretty sure that if Tom Short had been drinking during the afternoon, he would likely be involved in trouble before they got there.

The horse was extremely slow, and the night was bitterly cold. At hills, both men got out and ran alongside the rig to keep warm. It was past eight-thirty, closer to nine o'clock, when they reached Pine Bend and tied up their horse.

This saloon was a big one, boasting the longest bar on the river. Luke had heard the men talk about it, though he had never been inside. Now the two men reconnoitered the place carefully. A party seemed in full swing inside, for there was the sound of violins and the stamping of a dance. Every window of the structure was alight. Dan Pritchett almost fell over a man slumped down in the shadow. To their great satisfaction, it proved to be Ed Coser, a maudlin drunk.

Luke dragged him to his feet by his collar. "Come on, Ed. I've got a sleigh here for you."

The drunken man lolled against him. "Can't. The man said he'd bring another bottle. Gotta wait fer Tom."

Luke shook him hard. "Another bottle?" he demanded. "Who gave you a bottle?"

Coser simpered like a silly girl and held on to Luke's lapels. "The nicest man, friends. He give me a bottle, he give Tom a bottle. Tom's got damn near all mine."

"Who was he?" Luke demanded, giving the drunken man a harder shake.

Coser's head wagged back and forth, and his mouth hung open. Finally, he managed another statement. "Nice man, store clothes. Said he had jobs fer me'n Tom."

There was nothing to be gained by further questioning, so they dumped the man into the sleigh box, covered him with blankets, and then went back into the hotel. With Pritchett close on his heels, Luke pushed through the dancing, howling throng to the bar, where he signaled to a man who was racking glasses. Just then, Pritchett caught his elbow and pointed. Tom Short sat at a table, holding onto a girl's arm as she stood close to him. With the other hand, he tried to pull a bottle from his coat pocket.

The barkeeper was bending forward, and Luke pointed to the woodsman. "Ben Royal told you not to sell that man liquor."

The man looked in the direction indicated and shook his head. "Tell Ben I didn't. He came in here with a bottle. He's been raising hell all evening. I'd be obliged if you got him out of the place."

The girl had freed herself even as Luke and Dan moved toward Short's table. The big man gained his feet and started to follow her, waving a quart bottle in one hand. Luke blocked his way.

"Out of the road," Tom yelled, "gotta find my girl. She's slipped me."

Pritchett caught his arm. "Come on, Tom. We'll help you."

Short's reply was to send the smaller, slighter man sprawling against the wall, and Luke's gorge rose. He drove a straight right against the woodman's jaw, dropping him to his knees.

There were stories up and down the river about Tom Short and his abilities as a barroom fighter, but he was drunk tonight. He waved his bottle, a dangerous weapon, as he came up and charged. Luke stood his ground, rocking the big man back and forth with punishing blows. His own anger was bitter now. This drunken fool had involved him in another barroom fight. Paying no attention to Short's windmill swings, he went in close and sent a hard left to the Adam's apple. When his victim was gagging for breath, he jerked his knee into the man's groin, then knocked him senseless with a savage right under the ear. With the help of several men who had seen the fight, they dragged Short out and dumped him into the sleigh.

Luke thanked the men. "I sure wish I knew who gave him that bottle."

No one answered. They were driving out of the yard when a man stepped from the shadow.

"Mister," he said in a low tone, "I heard you back there. Carl Williams gave your man the bottle. He's one of the bookkeepers up at Caines' Number Three."

As furtively as he had appeared, the informer slipped away in the darkness, and Luke swore savagely. This was it; wherever he, Luke Hanley, was, there would be trouble. For a moment, he had a mind to yank Tom Short out of the sleigh and beat him some more.

Pritchett seemed to understand his mood. "You can't blame Short too much. He's just a damned fool that was never weaned from a bottle."

Both Short and Coser worked the next day and had a big spar tree down when Luke approached them about three o'clock. Short's face showed bruises, and when he saw the man who had beaten him, he stopped working and stood, tightly gripping the handle of his newly ground double-bitted axe. Short could swing that tool accurately enough to split a match stem. Still, Luke walked up to within three feet of him.

"Tom," he announced calmly, "you came at me with a bottle. You ever raise one of your damn filthy hands against me again, and I'll cut your face off with my fists. I'll do the same thing if I ever see you sucking at another one of John Caines' bottles. Now get back to work. We don't pay men to nurse an axe handle. Use it."

Short took a long look at the bony features held so close to his own, then he glanced at the axe as though he did not realize he held it. In another moment, he returned to work. But it was plain the big axe man harbored a savage grudge that his smaller partner in work and play probably encouraged.

The camp crisis came late in January. Ben Royal had been more or less ill all winter and was finally compelled to give up. He had to go downriver to his home for regular treatment by a physician, and he was so weak, he was compelled to be taken down in a sleigh.

"Luke," he said on leaving, "you'll have to take complete charge. Look out for whiskey. We're a little behind in the logging and can't afford to lose a man or a day. Better start Fred Orvis and Ben Charles on the big sticks. Short and Coser are up to trouble."

* * *

Brookland came up after a few days, and he and Luke had a long talk. "Anyway, Luke, there won't be any runaways until the weather opens. Do the best you can with Short. Get him straightened out and he'll be your best man. He wasn't playing with Caines. To him, a bottle is a bottle."

He leaned back in his chair and blew a smoke ring. Then he smiled. "Caines hit at us, Luke. You got any plans?"

It was Luke's turn to grin. Before he spoke, he got up and assured himself none of the men were near. "Dan Pritchett and I have been doing a little work in the shop. I wouldn't want to worry you about our using some of that big iron pipe and a little blasting powder."

"No," Brookland said hurriedly. "No, I wouldn't want to worry about anything but men that get a bit too reckless."

The next night, Luke and Pritchett lost about all their sleep. It was a long tramp, especially since they carried a homemade bomb made of iron pipe. Three days later, Pine Bend was still talking about a mysterious explosion that had wrecked a big tool house up on Caines' Number 3 and destroyed a couple hundred dollars worth of rope and tools.

Pritchett was thoughtful the day after their night foray. "Let's not waste any of that pipe on what it was bought for. I got a competitor up here, a fellow called Axelroth. Somehow, I don't like the man. Three feet of that pipe properly stuffed would raise his whole damn shop without raising his feelings."

Luke grinned. "It's an idea, Dan. It's a good idea."

In mid-February, Luke had to drive upriver to Weston for some hardware and was gone the greater part of the day, all night, and well into the next morning. He returned to a dead camp. Short and Coser were drunk in their bunks, and all the others, except Pritchett and the cook, had been drinking hard. The two men had seen to it that the horses had been fed and watered.

Luke was furious. Entering the lobby, he pushed through the loafing men and yanked Short from his bunk to the floor. Then he pitched a bucket of cold water over the man, but he was too far gone to do more than gasp. Hen Bettelyen was watching, fascinated, and Luke turned on him.

"Well, Hen, where did the stuff come from?"

Bettelyen weaved back and forth on unsteady legs. "Chipped in a dollar," he mumbled, but there was no sense in the man.

Three valuable days were lost by the escapade, but with his first anger spent, Luke realized there was no sense in riding the men, though he did keep a close watch on Short and Coser. The work of getting out saw timber for the rafts was going "suspiciously well," as Ben Royal phrased it.

The brief month of February had ended, and the homestretch of the winter's work was before them. The day had been an unsettled one, with occasional flurries of snow. That night, Luke was restless and sleeping in the men's lobby because it was warmer there. He got out of his bunk quietly so he would not disturb anyone and pulled on his heavy socks. The log sleds had been hauled up to the landings the night before, but he could not remember if they had been unloaded, and he wanted to know.

He moved quietly across the lobby, through the dining room, and raised his hand to the latch of the office door. His rubber shoes were in there, and he wanted them. Last evening, he had pulled them off while he worked on the payroll. The office held a small safe that contained whatever funds were necessary for the operation. The main sum in it was made up of the men's wages, held there for safekeeping. Each man owned a big envelope into which he would put his monthly pay. They often made a ceremony of asking for their "poke," then carefully counting the accumulation.

As Luke touched the latch with fumbling fingers, there was a sudden stirring inside the office, a slight metallic grating that stopped him momentarily before wrenching open the door.

For an instant, there was silence. Then, against the dim light from the window, Luke saw a dark figure and leaped forward. Powerful arms met his rush and hurled him back. He lost his balance, stumbling over a chair. He was coming up when the blow of a club dropped him to his knees. The outer door was jerked open as he fought his way to his feet. He could see the figure outside, running for the brush. Luke fumbled in the desk and found his little pistol. Propped against the doorjamb, he fired at the vanishing shape. Then, a swimming nausea caught him, and he fell, not hearing the camp come to life.

He was sick when he became conscious. The intruder had used a pick handle on his head. The men found that the safe door was about wrenched off. The robber would have succeeded if Luke had not surprised him.

He was better by noon and surprised that the men, on going to work, had left Tom Short to care for him. The big fellow was seated by the stove, chewing tobacco and spitting into the open firebox door.

Luke beckoned him over. "Tom, you and the cook lug that safe over under your bunk. It'll have to be in a more protected place."

When the job was done and the cook had returned to his kitchen, Short stood beside Luke's bunk, a stubborn, surprised look on his broad face.

"Hanley, you didn't figger I was at that money box?"

Luke swung his legs over the side of the bunk, sat up unsteadily, and faced the woodsman.

"Tom, you're a damned fool for whiskey. If we could wean you off a bottle, you'd be a number-one man. Hell, you're no thief. Now get back to the woods and quit nursing me. We're way behind in the work. You and Ed help them boys I put to working on spars. Watch so they don't ruin the sticks."

He sat on the edge of the bunk, laboriously pulling on his pants while Short walked to the stove and stood a moment with half a grin on his face. He spat copiously and accurately into the fire, then stalked out.

On the following Saturday, Tom came to Luke, acting mysteriously and insisting that Luke bring along his pistol. A few minutes later, they were hidden in the brush near one of the landings. The wait was short before Hen Bettelyen approached furtively, casting many glances back at the camp to assure himself that no one was watching. When he was certain, he walked to a pile of brush, plunged in his arm, and pulled it out, lugging a jug stoppered with a piece of corn cob.

"The pistol," Tom hissed. "Shoot the jug when he lifts it." Luke nodded and cocked the weapon under his coat to hide the slight sound. The distance was not much more than twenty yards. Bettelyen removed the cob stopper and swung the jug up to drink from it. The little pistol cracked, and the woodsman fell backward, deluged with whiskey and pieces of crockery. He was on his feet in a moment.

"My God, I'm shot!" he yelled and started to run madly up the drag road while Tom Short hugged himself in silent laughter.

"Hanley," he said a moment later, "I wanted you to see I didn't bring in the likker last week."

The two tall men looked into each other's eyes before clasping hands. "Give us time, Tom, and we'll really get to know each other," Luke promised.

The terrified and subdued Bettelyen sneaked back into camp that evening, and Luke ordered him to go to the office at once. During the interim, he had talked to two of the other men.

"Hen," he said to the man, "your wife's related to Axelroth, the blacksmith."

Bettelyen nodded, and his prominent Adam's apple went up and down as he swallowed nervously.

"What did they pay you to bring in that whiskey?"

The man began stammering his innocence, denying that he had any part in what happened until Luke stopped him.

"Hen, we lost the work of eighteen men through you. I'm afraid we can't afford to have a man on the job who gets paid by both Mr. Brookland and John Caines. Here's your time." He handed Bettelyen his poke taken from the safe, then leaned forward. "Now get the hell off this job. I hate a sneak."

Three days after the occurrence, Luke called in Pritchett and Tom Short. "Boys, I'm going down to Pine Bend tonight. I'll stop at Tammie's Place. Maybe she knows how Bettelyen got started. Now, if you went along, have you any ideas?"

Short rubbed his big hands together and glanced at Pritchett. "Dan, here, has an idea. He'd like to see what Axelroth's place looks like after dark. Anyway, I could use a couple of good horseshoe nails. The boys like to make good luck rings with 'em."

Luke stopped at Tammie's Place, and the others went on. He was delighted to find the change in Short. Brookland had been right in his estimate of the man.

The three men had left the camp pretty late, and Tammie's Place showed only a few lights. Luke went up the steps and entered an apparently deserted room. Then a voice startled him, and he wheeled.

"Don't be nervous, friend. Too bad the boys ain't here. They'd be glad to see you."

It was Tammie seated in her wide chair by the window. Luke crossed the room, pulled up a chair, and sat down facing her.

"My, my," she chuckled, "he's so friendly and sociable. Could be he's had whiskey trouble, like I heard. News just gets round. Now me, all I sell goes over the bar. More profit that way."

"Tammie," he said, "you're trying to tell me something. Thanks."

She rose, and Luke followed her to the bar, where she set out a glass of wine for him and took one for herself. They sipped thoughtfully for a moment before she spoke. "Luke Hanley, I own this place. My business comes from the camps and, once in a while, from the railroad men that work downriver from here." She twirled her wine glass and did not look at him. "There's trouble on the river, black folks in the brush, men hunting them for rewards. On top of that, these damned lumbermen are at each other's—"

She clutched his sleeve and spoke heatedly. "If you, John Caines, and that filthy Axelroth would just take hands and walk over the ice into the river where it's good and deep, we honest folks could make a decent and peaceful living."

He patted her arm. "I can swim, Tammie."

"Figgered you could." She nodded and looked straight into his eyes. "Likely John Caines can, too."

Luke pulled out some silver to pay for the drink, but she declined abruptly and walked with him to the door. When he opened it, she shivered in the cold rush of air, and her voice was bitter.

"Wasn't going to tell you. Figgered you was too damn independent. Somebody came to town and asked about you. Stop at the second house from here, and don't say Tammie sent you."

Outside, Luke pulled his coat closer to him and hesitated. He was not sure he could trust Tammie. It was plain she knew everything that was going on in this locality. Tonight, she had practically told him she had no part in the camp troubles.

Frozen snow creaked under his shoe soles as he walked. By Tammie's directions, he found a double house where a light showed on one side through drawn blinds. He stepped up and rapped.

There was hurried movement inside. A lamp was turned higher, then a throaty, familiar voice that thrilled him down to his cold feet, called, "Who's there?"

At his answer, the door opened to a lit interior, and framed against the light was the slim figure of a woman in a dressing gown, with long braids hanging in front of her shoulders. It was Linda Caines—the first time he had seen her in years. He gathered her close in his arms and hugged her. After a moment, she disengaged herself and closed the door.

"Luke," she chided. "I knew you were back, but you have not come round to see me."

She found a chair and, taking his hands, pushed him into it. He reveled at the smooth touch of her fingers against his own weather-roughened ones.

"You're cold, Luke. There's coffee on the back of the stove. We'll have some together."

Over the cups, they talked, and she was so full of questions that he had little chance to ask her any.

"You know, Luke, it's been good for you. No more stooped shoulders. You've grown up."

There was an infectious quality about this girl and her voice. She was genuinely glad to see him. Where Hester Haliday had held him off, Linda was all friendliness. They spent an hour together. Linda explained that she had come up to see her father and that this house belonged to him. Ordinarily, she lived in Point Haven. "I keep moving. There are always good horses, friends, excitement."

"And men," he said jealously.

She lifted her face with eyes shining, and her lips parted a little. He thought she was about to say something and, reaching out, caught her hands. Minutes passed before she withdrew her fingers.

"Luke, Father will be here soon. Maybe you'd better go."

He rose. "I'm always dodging him. Why should I keep on running? I'm a man now, not a boy to be chased about."

"Do it for me," she said simply. "A good friend won't make trouble for a girl."

They walked to the door arm in arm, then she put her hands on his shoulders in a remembered gesture. "Luke, there are so many stories. Please, for my sake, stick to lumbering. I'm afraid for you, and a time may come when I can't help—"

He did not let her finish but put his arms around her shoulders and thought of the things this slender, dark-haired girl had done for him. Linda Caines, the beauty with so many admirers, had everything. Yet she had risked her reputation for him. He freed one hand and patted her hair.

"Spring's coming, Linda. I always feel taller when I have been with you."

Their lips met softly. There was not much light at the doorway, but Luke thought he detected tears in the girl's eyes.

Short and Pritchett met him a short distance down the road, and they were exuberant.

"Luke," Pritchett exclaimed, "smell the liquor on our shoepacs. Tom and I liberated close to thirty gallons of the stuff tonight."

"Stumbled over it in the dark," Short cut in. "It's going to be damned dry about that blacksmith shop for a spell." He struck his palms together. "And you know, we didn't find a damned horseshoe nail."

Luke felt, as they walked on, that they were paying debts right along in this "eye for an eye" business.

CHAPTER TWELVE

WORK ON the Brookland lumbering operation kept Luke too busy to worry about the warnings given to him by both Tammie and Linda. Both women seemed to know his major interest on the river was not straight lumbering. Now, however, with Ben Royal still quite ill, the task of getting out the timber rafts had dropped entirely into his lap, leaving no time to bother about runaways, and, fortunately, none appeared. Nor did any of the annoyances which had occurred earlier happen now. Caines' men were probably busy, too.

There had been a marked change among the men since the attempt at the safe. If the money had actually been taken, it would in all likelihood have broken up the working force at the Brookland camp. Now the men laid the attempt at the door of the men farther upriver, especially since it was rumored that the blacksmith, Axelroth, had suffered some time from a sore shoulder. Luke's bullet may have hit the man if he had been the robber.

Another factor worried Luke. Times were hard, and he did not think Brookland could afford to miss the early lumber market on the river, especially since he had a shipment of spars. With the labor needed to shape them, these sticks were an expensive proposition. Even Caines had abandoned cutting them.

Spring promised to come early. Bare spaces showed at the southern bases of the big pines. Snow became mushy overnight, and there were bald spots on the iced roadway. Red maples flaunted scarlet buds against the white of paper birches. Each morning, when the men came out of the dining room, they would stand for a few minutes looking out at the river. Excitement was high when they saw water over the ice.

"She's about to pull," Ed Coser said with conviction one muggy morning, and his companions nodded a grave assent.

Ed was right. That night, the ice went out. Close to twelve o'clock, reports like cannon fire routed half-dressed men from their straw-filled bunks to run out barefooted for a look at the river. Tom Short led them in a howling cheer. Luke broke out the small supply of whiskey, and all hands drank in celebration.

A week before, all cutting crews, with the exception of the spar men, had been taken from the woods to broach the log landings. Now inside Brookland's boom at the mouth of the creek, a carpet of brown white pine logs rose and fell in the backwash of the great river.

The men had donned the spiked shoes and stagged pants of the riverman. Each wore a wide studded belt, heavy suspenders, extra woolen shirts, and high-crowned hats with matches stuck into the bands. The working costume of these men was dictated by the exigencies of their labor. Cant hooks and pike poles had become the tools instead of saws and axes.

Each raft was to be four sections in length, making the finished floater a full hundred feet long, with the whole bound together by limber oak lash poles held fast by wooden pins driven into auger holes in the logs. Sections were fastened to each other with heavy grab chains. When the rafts of saw timber were complete, fifty spars were rolled in place on top of each of them, and the rivermen grumbled.

"Them damned long sticks make the rafts stiff," Tom Short remarked, but Luke realized that these spars, at twenty dollars a thousand feet, meant the winter's profit. Saw timber usually brought twelve dollars for the same amount, that and less. It was true that the sheer weight of these ninety-foot timbers brought the rafts all but awash. There would be a danger of tearing apart or hanging up on mid-current rocks.

The river had become a tremendous brown flood, stretching from mountain to mountain, inundating low brushland along its course. Whole uprooted trees drifted past in great patches of white foam.

The Brookland rafts were finally ready. Everything was loaded in the small shelter cabins on each floater. This meant food, tools, and extra clothing. Snubbing ropes were neatly coiled on deck, and the great guiding sweeps were greased well with tallow at the pins on which they turned. Cooking would be done with fires built on sand boxes. There was a small supply of whiskey on each raft to be used when men were drenched. Oddly, Luke knew that the only men in the crews who could swim were Pritchett and himself. But in that icy torrent fresh from snowfields, no strength could keep a man alive long.

The last supper in camp was a special occasion, with tables groaning with food the men liked, and the dessert was huge sections of mince pie plentifully laced with cooking whiskey.

"Me," Lias Bredney declared when he had waded through his piece, "all I'd ask is a whole pie, then I'd be damned good and drunk."

Luke's treat for the men was a box of cigars obtained in Pine Bend.

"Tom's river boss," he told them unnecessarily. "We shove off at daylight."

After supper, there was considerable daylight, and Luke went to the office, where he had some paperwork to finish. He heard horses moving but paid no attention until a man stood at the outer door, blocking out his light.

"Get out of the light," he said without looking up. "I can't see."

"You're Luke Hanley?"

Luke looked up at the unfamiliar voice. The man in the doorway was a stranger. Dressed in corduroys, his open coat revealed a revolver tucked into his trouser band. A wide hat shadowed his face, and a drooping mustache hid his mouth.

"Yes," Luke answered shortly, "what do you want?"

The visitor jerked a paper from his pocket and slapped it against his free palm. "Deputy Sheriff Moore. This is a warrant for the arrest of Luke Hanley. The charge is assault on an officer with deadly weapons with the intent to kill."

Outside behind the deputy were two other men seated in a spring wagon, with a third man holding the lines over a team of bays. Luke's mind flashed to the Dyer cabin and a fugitive man running for his life. He felt something of the wild rage that had made him shoot that day, but more, he now felt an empty sensation in his stomach. He had ceased to worry about the occurrence; this was the hard blow—Caines' trump card. Sudden panic was upon him, and he bent forward over the desk to conceal his feelings from the officer whose hand went to the revolver butt. The threat helped Luke master his momentary weakness.

"Pull that gun, Moore, and I'll stick it down your damned throat."

Rising, he jerked open the dining room door and bellowed for Tom Short, who came so quickly he could have been eavesdropping.

"Tom, they're taking me to the county seat."

The big woodsman stared at him in horrified surprise. "But the rafts start in the morning?"

Luke nodded and crossed to the open safe that had been returned to the office for security during the drive. "You're river boss, Tom. Take that money with you as expenses on the trip. Take good care of the men. You are short-handed anyway. Make your tie-ups early, and look out for those spars. They make a raft unwieldy like you said."

The two big men looked into each other's eyes for a moment. There was a wild temper in Tom's expression, but Luke shook his head almost imperceptibly. There had been no time to think, and even if he escaped this posse, he could be picked up with the rafts anywhere on the way downriver. He was sure Caines was behind this arrest, and the man had timed things beautifully. Luke picked up his battered hat and his worn jacket and stepped through the door with the deputy following.

By now, the crew had boiled out of the camp and surrounded the wagon and Moore as he appeared behind Luke. One of the men in the rig got uneasy and pulled his revolver. Short was close to him and, snatching the weapon, held back the hammer while he thumbed off the caps and then tossed it back. "No guns, sonny, or we'll sure beat the hell out of you."

"Good luck, men," Luke said to the crew. Then he went to the wagon and climbed up beside the driver. As soon as Moore was aboard, the team started downriver at a smart pace while the lumbermen watched until it disappeared in the timber along the river.

The posse had fed and watered their horses shortly before the arrest, for they made the long drive back to Point Haven with no long stops despite the atrocious condition of the road, which occasionally forced all hands to walk short distances. Even the driver then led his horses. The men were surly but shared their lunches with the prisoner. A little after one o'clock in the morning, a sleepy, mud-spattered cavalcade clattered into Point Haven and on to the courthouse that also contained the county jail.

The timing of the arrest seemed to have been made to coincide with the session of the Grand Jury the following day.

That body's procedure with Luke was short and severe. First, he was interrogated briefly as to his name, age, and service in the navy. Then he was bound over for court, which would convene in ten days. Bail was fixed at three thousand dollars, and since Luke had neither money nor a bondsman, he was committed to the county jail. The prisoner said little during the proceedings, bottling up his wrath. He did hear one of the older jurors whisper to a neighbor, "Yes, it's Hanley's boy, all right. Looks like him, too."

The first days of imprisonment were hard for a man who had never been confined to close quarters. On a ship and in the navy yard, he had been quartered with others with whom he had shared room. Here in his cell, there was room only for his cot, a bucket, and a straight chair. The cramped quarters got on his nerves. At night, he would wake with sweat pouring off him and his hands pushing against the wall nearest his cot. It took three days for him to get control of himself. The trick was to sleep a great deal and keep from thinking too much. He was worried about the raft, but Tom Short was a good riverman, and it wasn't likely there would be any further interference. All the deviltry had been aimed at him, Luke Hanley. He felt a little bitter about Brookland, who had not appeared, and his future looked grimmer the more he thought about it. Someone, and that would be Caines, was determined to get rid of him. He had been forced out of Crossville, he had lost the pleasant associations of the Haliday farm, and he had been driven into the navy. A bullet near Lymansville had been meant for him, and Caines' bullies had planned to maim him in the fight in Tammie's Place.

The jail was well kept, and the food plain but wholesome. The two attendants were fair enough, although they showed little interest in the prisoner. At his request, one of them brought him a book, a dog-eared copy of *Ivanhoe*. He tried to interest himself in it, but his mind would swing away to Tom Short out there on the river and to the two pilots, Norman Henry and Fred Harry, swinging their weight on the sweeps as the rafts swept down the flooded river.

On the morning of the fourth day, the attendant took the prisoner to a bare reception room. To Luke's surprise, there sat George Brendy, who had so strongly advised him to be careful. With him was the cold-eyed Rush Geen. They shook hands cordially.

Geen did the talking. "Just got the word on Wednesday, day after they took you," he explained almost apologetically. "We got to your camp on the evening of the next day and have been busy since."

Luke fought back his impulse to ask questions, for he did not want to interrupt Geen, who stepped to the door where the attendant stood. He looked at the man a moment, then calmly closed the door in his face and returned.

"Hanley, they sure messed things up for you and Brookland. A gang of toughs hit your camp the night you left. Tom Short was hurt pretty bad. Pritchett has a game arm. Both your pilots was manhandled, rough."

Luke jumped up at the news and strode up and down, swearing savagely. "So they hit the men. They hadn't any stake in it. Where in the hell's Brookland? He's got to know."

"He knows," Geen said dryly. "They fixed the first raft, cut the lash axles, and the timber's all over the West Branch Valley. Them timber thieves will have good picking. We got there in time to help fix up the second raft. It's on the way to Marietta with both crews aboard. Brookland left for Lancaster the minute he heard you was arrested."

It was stunning news. Half a year's work was lost, all due to Luke's presence. He had brought Brookland only bad luck, exactly as Hester claimed he had done to her. Deep down in his mind, however, was the feeling that Caines must have more against him than this slave-running business to take such savage measures. Luke looked into Geen's stern face, then over to Brendy, who was fishing a wad of greenbacks from his pocket.

"Here's the money you put up for the Halidays, Hanley. You'll need it for a lawyer."

Luke took the money, then passed it back. "Men, I can't take your money. You've done enough."

"It's not ours," Geen explained. "Hester sent it."

The sudden warmth that started in Luke died as the horseman finished his statement.

"Brendy and I advised her it was a good time to pay you back. She was a little put out but sent it along just the same."

Luke balanced the wad in his hand, half in mind to ask them to return it to the cold girl up in Lymansville. But these men had ridden hard and done all they could to help. Geen was speaking almost casually.

"Someday, I'll have to do something to John Caines."

"Shut up, Rush," Brendy snapped. "This is no place to discuss plans. They can hear through them thin doors. Likely Brookland went to get a real lawyer. He has connections and could get a change of venue when this case comes up."

Geen was suddenly impatient and got up. "Anything outside you want, Hanley? Mebbe you can think of something."

Luke struck his hands together as an idea hit him. Caines had struck hard—perhaps he was up to something else. "Listen, friends. In my own troubles, I clean forgot something. Maybe they arrested me so they could hit and wreck the camp. Do you suppose they might have raided the Keating country and carried off some of them folks?"

Geen smiled. "That was the first thing Brendy, Erritt, and I figured. No, they didn't. Erritt and I have men up there now, watching. They're pretty rough customers and will shoot. You don't need to worry about that end or other runaways. We'll take over for a while."

It was time for the visitors to leave. As they shook hands, Luke said, "I don't know how to make things right with you men."

"Mebbe we have a stake in this, too," Geen offered soberly.

Things were about as bad as they could be; the men beaten, the raft lost. So far, it had been a long, bitter road from the old Potter mill in Crossville. Luke took out and counted the money, wondering about the relation between Rush Geen and Hester.

Ivanhoe paled again as entertainment, but Luke had learned that the older of his attendants tied trout flies and liked to teach others. He was about to propose the matter of learning. Then, in the evening, when he expected the guard, Brookland turned up with a man a little older than Luke, who was introduced as Jonathan Shaw.

Luke's boss had no reproaches. "No, I don't blame you. After all, I got you into most of these messes. We'll worry about the logs when you're out of this current trouble. That's why I brought Jonathan and was slow coming to see you."

Brookland's tanned face was earnest. Luke had the feeling that this calm owner of Spring Haven was a bigger man than any of them dreamed. He sat close and put his fingers on the younger man's knee.

"This trial is a bigger thing than either of us. It will be watched nation-wide, North and South. There's war in the air, and it's time a Northern court shows our Southern friends it will not convict a man for helping runaway slaves."

He paused and glanced at Shaw before proceeding. "Jonathan here is a member of Peters, Shaw, and Stevens of Lancaster. They are lawyers. His stamping ground is Lancaster. Don't worry about expenses. The Philadelphia Society for Total Abolition, for which your father worked and died, is paying all costs."

He smiled and waved his hand. "Not because Luke Hanley or Minor Brookland matter too much. The principle does. People in the North must not be left afraid to help runaways. You must be cleared."

The jail attendant appeared. Brookland remained in the waiting room while Shaw accompanied Luke to his cell, where they sat down, Shaw on the chair, his client on the cot.

"Now," the lawyer said, "Let's talk."

Luke warmed to the man at once. Like all good lawyers, he was an excellent listener, asking questions only when necessary to get clearer information from his client. Brookland must have supplied Luke's background pretty thoroughly, even to a full account of the happenings in Crossville and Linda Caines' confession.

After an hour, Luke grinned ruefully. "Well, sir. I've talked about myself until I'm black in the face. Let's talk about you, Mr. Shaw."

The lawyer waved the pencil he used to make notes. "I'm not on trial, my friend. You've helped me a lot with information. Now, I'd like to discuss the important matter of trout fishing. How is it on your Hyner Run?"

They talked for another half-hour entirely about trout and tackle. Shaw had a new line from England. "It's made of silk, and it's braided. Also, I have a new rod of Greenhart. It won't set as Lancewood will."

He rose to leave. "I'm going now. Remember, we'll handle everything. Your part is to sit tight. Answer questions truthfully, but don't volunteer anything, no matter how important it seems, and don't be surprised at anything. We'd arrange bail, but it will look better at the trial if we can show you languished in jail because the bail was set so high."

He shook hands, fished a small book from his pocket, and tossed it on the bed by Luke. When he was gone and the attendant had relocked the door, Luke found the book to be Walton's *The Compleat Angler*.

The visit left the prisoner excited, a little relieved, and restless. The matter of bail didn't look too logical to him, but he was satisfied that his friends were doing all they could. From this day on, there were plenty of visitors. One was a reporter from the local paper who wanted details about Luke's troubles, but the prisoner explained that his lawyer had forbidden him to talk much. The Methodist minister was another caller who guardedly talked for some time about slavery and the Underground Railroad.

Saturday morning, to his surprise and consternation, four ladies dressed in black silk and wearing intricate bonnets were in the waiting room, representing some church society, when he was taken there.

"We've brought you a pie," the chairperson said, presenting a huge napkin-covered plate of pastry. "After all, we feel there is some relationship between the church and these poor black people in the southland. Don't you think so, Mr. Hanley?"

He was embarrassed. His clothing was worn and shabby, and his hair, as usual, needed a barber. "Yes, ma'am," he agreed. "Thank you for the pie."

They all shook hands with him on leaving, and he agreed to leave the pie plate and napkin with the jailer. He noticed that they had observed his clothing critically.

Gifts came in until it was evident Point Haven was interested in the man now in the local jail and did not consider him a dangerous criminal.

He shared the provisions with the attendants. One of them said to him, "You're getting popular. There was a box of cigars, a shirt, a necktie, and a lot of fruit. All you need is a key and you can walk out of here."

On Sunday morning, a visitor was brought directly to his cell, and Luke was delighted to see that it was Squire Jacoby from Crossville. Luke pumped the old man's arm vigorously, then pushed him to a seat on the chair, demanding that he talk about Crossville.

"Things don't change much over there," the white-haired man said. "You know Caines moved out and has a man running the hotel. Our man lives all over: in Weston, Pine Bend, and Point Haven."

After a pause, he asked a pointed question. "Did you hear a horse late at night when you were at the mill?"

Luke was surprised but told of the two times he had heard the nocturnal rider and how it had brought up memories of the time his father was killed.

"That was hard, son, hard on you and your mother. Your father left in a hurry for that meeting, and the bullet that hit him was fired through a window. The man who fired was probably a professional killer. But, Luke, who tipped off such a man or society that your father was coming? Somebody from home sent that word. Also, remember how Fred Horton was killed? He did not commit suicide."

Luke's thin, weathered face was intent as he leaned forward, but the squire anticipated his question. "That's all I'm going to say except this: neither your father nor you deserved a murderous enemy, but you both have them. When you get out, will you go on with the Underground work?"

The younger man frowned. He had not thought much about such things lately. Personal troubles had been too close. Jacoby was probably going to warn him. He had stood up, waiting for a reply. When it did not come in a moment, he spoke.

"Well, son, I wanted you to know your friends haven't forgotten you. I'm glad for the way you have developed. It looks to me as though you had found an anchor like I mentioned years past. There's a proverb you ought to think about; 'Yesterday and tomorrow are just as important as today.'"

Alone again, Luke thought of the squire's last statement, which he did not fully understand. The attendant appeared shortly afterward, and the two worked on a Black Gnat fly until noon.

CHAPTER THIRTEEN

COURT WEEK in Point Haven had all the allure of a county fair to the upriver people, with the added attraction that the entertainment was free. People from all the nearby sections would come in for a day or more to spend part of their holiday walking about the streets and the rest of it in court, allotting their time in accordance with the interest of the cases being tried. On the bright May day, when Luke's trial came up, the spectators anticipated a spectacular performance, judging by the charges against this desperate man who had shot an officer. Town rumor had it that there would be surprising developments and a famous state lawyer would be there.

County Attorney Nedrow went bustling about, weighted down by his poundage and present importance. There was a knowing look on his face when he declared to newspapermen that he could answer no questions and could only say that the case of the Commonwealth versus Luke Hanley was first on the docket.

Hitching racks for blocks around the brick courthouse were solid with tied horses that Monday morning, and the stone steps of the building were crowded with people waiting for the courthouse doors to open. No one seemed to appreciate the excellent view of the tree-clad hills across the great river and the mountains beyond them. The throng was about equally divided between men and women, and there was a small sprinkling of children. Town folks wore their conventional garb, and those from the hills were usually dressed in rough work clothing, sometimes colorful and picturesque.

Since his first visit, Attorney Shaw had been with Luke only three times. In each instance, he had checked some part of the shooting story up there on that lonely snow-swept farm. He was interested in the fact that the shotgun had been lightly loaded, so not a weapon one would choose to shoot a man with the intent to kill him.

"Did they mention a warrant when they roused you?"

"No, they just demanded that the murderer come out."

"They mentioned no names?"

"No."

"The fact is that you, Luke Hanley, did not know these men. They were strangers outside your house, threatening you in the night."

"Oh, Fred and I knew who they were, all right."

The lawyer ignored Luke's remark, made a tent of his fingers, and resumed. "Two men in a lonely mountain retreat are roused from slumber by men breathing threats, and a shot is fired through the door. The—"

"It wasn't night, Mr. Shaw."

The lawyer continued to pay no attention to interruptions but went on, building up his story. "The frightened black man runs out and is shot down. Believing you would be the next victim of this murderous crew, you, Luke Hanley, with the fear of death in your heart, discharged a weapon at your attackers."

Shaw grinned widely at his perplexed listener. "My friend, I could get your famed desperado, Lewis, off on a self-defense plea like that. But, my impetuous friend, I am not primarily interested in clearing you. Our country is drifting toward civil war. This trial will test the mettle of Northern folks. Fred means little more than you, but the principle of citizens in the North aiding frightened runaways to reach freedom, even in violation of the infamous law of 1850, means everything."

In charge of Deputy Sheriff Moore, who had arrested him, Luke entered the courtroom through a small door to the left of the judge's bench. To pass that, he had to face the audience momentarily and was embarrassed by the stares turned on him, especially since he was still dressed in the rough working clothes of the camps. True, he wore a borrowed coat over his check shirt. His face was neatly shaved, but his hair still needed a barber's attention. Brookland had suggested a new suit, but Shaw vetoed that promptly. So Luke looked the part of a tall, spare, powerful young man, just in from the woods.

Judge Adam Faris leaned back in his armchair behind the dark wood of the courtroom bench. He was a frail-looking man with the drawn features of a semi-invalid. The heavy hair combed back from an austere forehead was almost entirely gray. The jurist resided in a northern county of this judicial district and enjoyed the reputation of a fair but cold man. Certainly he was in the pay of no one nor under anyone's influence.

Luke slumped in his chair, still painfully conscious of the eyes turned upon him. The scene reminded him of the Crossville schoolhouse, where Nedrow had conducted his abortive investigation, only there were twenty times as many people, and now he was really under arrest, charged with a serious crime. His brief glance told him Squire Jacoby was seated well up front. In the back of the room, near a window, a girl was seated beside a young man. Luke recognized Hester Haliday and Rush Geen.

After the court clerk had finished reading the charges against the prisoner of assault on one Henry Borst, a deputy sheriff, with intent to cause great bodily injury or death, both Nedrow for the county and Shaw for the defense declared themselves ready to proceed.

Preliminary business dragged along until it came time for jury selection. Nedrow was pompously businesslike, exuding the impression that this was an open and shut case that would take little time. Shaw, on the other hand, acted the very pattern of a clever irritant, taking his time when Nedrow hurried, then being far too apologetically polite when the county attorney showed signs of impatience.

"Your Honor," Nedrow addressed the court, "I am anxious to get this case moving. It is so evident that this trial is merely a matter of form since the law in the matter is so explicit. Almost any group of these talesmen would suit me."

Shaw was on his feet so quickly the judge had no chance to reply to Nedrow before he was addressed again.

"Your Honor, if the court pleases, a man's liberty is at stake and his good repute as a citizen. Further, a great principle is to be considered by this jury; whether or not a free citizen of our Republic may defend a poor stranger who, following a star toward freedom, knocks at his door at night. Too much care cannot be taken when such great issues are at stake."

Nedrow squirmed with chagrin at the opening he had given his opponent, and Judge Faris's lips twisted as though he was about to smile when Shaw took his seat.

The full panel was complete by noon, and during the hour's intermission, both Shaw and Brookland talked to Luke. The lawyer was emphatic.

"Don't get impatient. I'm dragging the trial deliberately, tearing away at Nedrow's patience. He's probably a good lawyer, but he's pompous. He may lose his temper. I'm sure there are no strings on that judge, or he'd have shut me up this morning."

Brookland, continuing to look out the window, commented, "Nedrow won't bring up the Crossville matter when he tries to take Luke apart. His engagement to Linda Caines was announced two nights past at a dinner in the Union Hotel."

Luke sank back in his chair as if he had been struck. Linda, who had been in his arms only a few weeks past; Linda, who had warned and saved him time and again though she faced shame doing it. It was unbelievable that she should marry this political "fetch" dog of her father's. Shaw stared at the stricken man a moment. When Luke looked down at the pattern of the floor carpet, the lawyer shook his head at Brookland.

The last of the qualified jurors took his seat in the box close to three o'clock, and Nedrow finished his opening speech in exactly thirty minutes by the courthouse clock. After that, the judge adjourned court for the day, and the disappointed audience trailed out the courthouse doors to the street.

Luke had no wish for company but paced his narrow cell, trying to compose himself and adjust his thinking to the blow he had been dealt. Shaw's delaying tactics had made the trial doubly irritable, but he did not care now. Linda Caines had been a popular girl with plenty of admirers who were more handsome and better off financially. Perhaps Luke had never really aspired to marry her because he knew he did not fit into her circle. But from the very beginning, when he had gone to Crossville to study, she had been kind. He had tasted the sweetness of her and had held her close in his arms. Yet, he had never dared to speak of love to her, even during those embraces. Now she was out of his reach.

For the first time during his confinement, he tested the rusty bars of his cell window. They were so flimsy that a strong man might bend them. There was nothing the matter with his strength. Tonight, when everything was still, he could escape. Captain Caris would see that he was reenlisted and assigned to sea duty. Once he was out of the country, his enemies would be satisfied.

The attendant coming in with the evening tray was voluble, even though he noticed what Luke was doing. "I wouldn't if I was you." He sat in the doorway while Luke fumbled with the bars.

"They say in the sheriff's office that the jury likes you men, and that makes things better for you." He grinned, showing the loss of back teeth. "Mister Hanley, we got a bet running. It's even Stephen now between guilty or not guilty. It irked me a bit."

Luke looked at the man without the will to ask which way he had wagered. At that moment, he didn't care greatly how the game went, but it was exasperating to know that the fate of a man could be a sporting proposition. The attendant got up and took the tray closer.

"Kind of a thing you can't bet. I seen that Brendy give you a wad of bills. Likely it went to the lawyer. If it didn't, you could get yourself a bet."

Luke studied the attendant a minute. People in such positions were always more observant than was suspected. For himself, he had almost forgotten the money. Now he took it out and counted off two worn dollar bills.

"Here, Purvis. Cover your bet. Say, leave my door unlocked so I can stretch my legs. You can lock the corridor."

He stepped out with the man who had not finished his comments.

"About that Geen. Every damn officer in this county is scared of him. I'll bet two dollars he could take a string of a dozen horses right through Point Haven in broad daylight, and the sheriff and his boys would be out feshin'. He was in court today with a mighty pretty girl. Wonder if she's his wife?"

Luke tramped the corridor for hours that evening. Later, he slept but did not rise refreshed, nor was he ready when the deputy came for him.

Court opened promptly at nine o'clock. Nedrow, immaculately dressed, began solemnly and ponderously. "If the court pleases, I shall present the Commonwealth's witnesses in rapid order so we may finish by noon or early in the afternoon. It is my desire to save time and costs to the county."

Judge Faris inclined his head, and Nedrow glanced at Luke. Shaw was reading some papers and did not look up. The names of the witnesses meant nothing to Luke, but he recognized the faces of one or two who had been in Tammie's Place the night of the fight over George Brendy, when Fletch had come to grief. They testified to seeing the prisoner as a participant in a barroom brawl. A third man corroborated their testimony.

The fourth witness was a stranger who gave his name and then his residence in a small town in Maryland. Under Nedrow's questioning, he said he recognized Hanley as one of a group of sailors from a shipyard who had disturbed the peace and resisted the local authorities. Captain Caris had paid the fines and promised to discipline the men. The prisoner had seemed to be a leader in the trouble.

Nedrow looked triumphantly toward the crowded room. Shaw had declined to cross-examine the first three witnesses, but now he rose, bowed to the judge, then faced the witness. "Will you state the nature of this disturbance?"

"The sailors tried to break up a public sale."

Shaw smiled. "Thank you. Now, one more question. What was being sold that stimulated these sailors to violence?"

The witness hesitated, looked toward Nedrow, and glanced at the expectant crowd. He gulped several times.

Shaw moved closer and spoke quietly. "It was a sale of slaves, of human beings, was it not?"

The witness inclined his head, and his mumbled "yes" was all but inaudible.

In a murmur that ran through the room, Nedrow called another witness, Deputy Marshal David Bay, who testified that he had seen the prisoner on various occasions and that he appeared to engage in questionable activities. At this point, Shaw interrupted apologetically with a word to the judge spoken in such a low tone as to be inaudible to the audience. The judge frowned and tapped the desk with his gavel.

"The attorney for the defense requests that I make clear that, as a United States Marshall, his duties are to carry out federal law."

Shaw added, "In this case, the provision of the Fugitive Slave Law of 1850 was initiated and ordered—"

"Mr. Shaw, confine your remarks to the defense. The court's capable of making what it considers a sufficient explanation."

Shaw sat down, looking humble, and Nedrow directed the witness to continue.

Bay told the story bluntly. He, Henry Borst, and another man had followed into the hills a desperate black fugitive who had killed his master and for whom a reward was offered. The posse had approached the Dyer farm cabin and demanded that the murderer come forth. The fugitive had been struck down when attempting to escape, after which the prisoner had assaulted the posse with a gun, wounding Henry Borst.

Shaw did not cross-examine, and Nedrow called Henry Borst. This time, there was a commotion in the crowd as the once-deputy sheriff took the stand and was duly sworn in.

Yes, he recognized the prisoner. Yes, Marshal Bay's story covered the occasion. He further testified that, of the three, he had remained mounted and that the third man, Marcus Guston, had rapped on the door, demanding that the murderer appear. When the fugitive attempted to escape, he, Henry Borst, attempted to fire over the running black man's head. It was then that Luke Hanley appeared and discharged a shotgun at him, causing a severe and painful wound. Further, this same Hanley had pursued them to the Pike, firing his gun and yelling.

Nedrow waved a pudgy, challenging hand toward Shaw and asked a question. "Will you cross-examine?"

Shaw rose slowly, moved toward the witness chair, and stood quietly for what seemed like a long minute. He carried a sheet of paper and spoke to the man pleasantly. "There were three of you in the party?"

The witness nodded, appearing to enjoy the publicity he was receiving.

"Marshal Bay is present, you are present. Where is the third man, Marcus Guston?"

Borst stared at Shaw, then at Nedrow, who got up and spluttered something about an objection.

Judge Faris shook his head. "The witness will answer the question."

"He's in jail down in Carlisle."

It was necessary to quiet the audience with the gavel. Luke, sitting quietly during the testimony and interchange, had noticed that Hester Haliday was again present, but he did not see Geen.

Shaw was looking with mock sympathy at the witness. "You were a deputy sheriff?"

"Yes."

"Your posse at the time of the encounter was off the public road on privately owned land?"

"Yes, I guess so."

"You then had, no doubt, a properly executed warrant?"

"No, but the fugitive was a murderer. There was a reward! He—"

"Exactly," Shaw countered. "You stated that you fired over the fugitive's head. Where did you suppose he carried it?"

Borst's face reddened with rising anger, and Shaw smiled.

"Don't tell this intelligent jury, Mr. Borst, that he carried it under his arm like a bird does when he sleeps. Your shot hit the fugitive in the side. You are probably a poor shot.

"The hell you say?"

Nedrow's violently raised hand checked Borst from going further in his outburst, and Shaw proceeded calmly.

"Mr. Borst, I am trying to bring out the facts. After you fired your pistol over the fugitive's head, presumably under his arm, you were yourself attacked and shot?"

"Yes, he fired three times."

Shaw clicked his tongue sympathetically. "Dear me, you must have been injured terribly." The witness tried to speak, but the lawyer went on. "Is it not true, and remember that you are under oath, that two evenings after you sustained these terrible wounds, you went coon hunting with one Calvin Keve and that your party killed three coons and consumed two quarts of whiskey during the hunt?"

Nedrow roared an objection which the judge sustained, but the deputy's red face and surprised confusion had answered Shaw's question so far as the audience was concerned. Even two of the jurors were smiling.

The big clock indicated eleven, and Nedrow rose.

"Your Honor, copies of the deposition made by Marshal Bay and the members of his posse at the time of the crime have been made available to this court and may be had by the jury. I have shown the defendant as a disturber of the peace and one who uses deadly weapons when thwarted. It is common knowledge that the defendant fled the county after his crime, thereby confessing it. It was committed against sworn officers of the law. The hint made by Attorney Shaw that these officers carried no warrant may be ignored. They pursued a desperate man who had killed once and would do so again. Further, they acted under a federal law that permits and directs citizens to apprehend fugitive slaves. They sought, as I said, a murderer—"

Shaw leaped to his feet, holding up a hand in interruption. The judge frowned, and Nedrow looked astonished, for he knew the defense lawyer was clearly out of order.

"My apologies, Mr. County Attorney. You state there was a reward offered for the apprehension of this fugitive?"

"A witness has so stated. Is that all you wish to know?"

Shaw ignored the sarcasm. "Has this reward been withdrawn during the four years which have passed?"

"Yes."

Judge Faris pounded with his gavel. "Attorney Shaw, you have been out of order several times. We have been tolerant because you are new to this court. No further outbreaks will be tolerated. Mr. Nedrow will proceed."

"Therefore," the district attorney intoned, "gentlemen of the jury, your course is quite clear. The defendant attacked officers of the law with a deadly weapon, as has been proved by testimony. I demand, in the name of the Commonwealth and under the federal statute of 1850, the full fine and imprisonment specified for those who aid runaway persons. Your Honor, the Commonwealth rests."

He sat down heavily and mopped his face, a gesture which brought back to Luke the scene in the schoolhouse at Crossville. Now this stout, perspiring pomposity was to marry Linda Caines.

When Shaw and Brookland visited with Luke during the noon hour, the lawyer spoke bluntly. "Luke, this afternoon is the critical time. Keep your shirt on no matter what happens. If you don't, I'll put you on the witness stand and let Nedrow get you so damned mad you'll throw something. Or do you want to take the stand?"

"No," Luke said bluntly. "I've been enough of a show as it is."

* * *

Court convened early. Several jurors looked as if they had hurried their lunches, for they held toothpicks in their mouths. Every seat in the room was taken. Squire Jacoby sat just across the railing from Luke. Now there was another lawyer seated with Shaw. He was an old man with strong, thin features and a wide mouth that looked like a bar across his face. Heavy gray hair was flung back from his forehead.

Judge Faris had an announcement. "The attorneys for the Commonwealth and the defense have agreed to forego the usual summations following the presentations of the defense. The district attorney is now permitted to sum up his case, briefly." The judge consulted a note on his desk and read without looking up. "This afternoon, the defense will be aided by the senior member of Attorney Shaw's firm, Mr. Stevens."

Abruptly, Judge Faris stopped and stared at the old man who sat with Shaw. There was surprise and incredulity on the judge's face. He glanced at his paper again, then looked out over the audience. "The Honorable Thaddeus Stevens, member of the Lancaster County bar and senior senator from Pennsylvania."

Not too many in the audience understood, and the man with Shaw did not look up as the judge finished. "Mr. Nedrow, you may proceed."

In spite of his surprise at the judge's announcement and the impressive opposition he now faced, Nedrow made a good job of summing up for the state and asking the jury for a guilty verdict.

When he rested, Shaw thanked him for taking so little time, then he addressed the court and the jury.

"Your Honor and gentlemen of the jury, cross-examination has shown many things about the credibility of the Commonwealth's witnesses and the character of their depositions. The defense has but one witness, a man who has come here in grave danger to his life and liberty. He has risked all this to repay the man who did so much for him. Fred Brooks!"

Luke came half out of his chair. Squire Jacoby's long arm reached across the railing and yanked him down. The big man entered the room by the door through which Luke had been led. He was decently dressed, and his big face was sober. This time, it took a full minute to quiet the crowded room. Fred was led to the witness chair and raised a big hand to take the oath when Nedrow jumped to his feet, protesting violently. "This man is a fugitive slave—he cannot testify."

Shaw's colleague rose and bowed. "Your Honor, the distinguished county attorney is only partially right. The man cannot testify for himself, but he may do so for another when his own status is not being considered."

"There is such a precedent," Judge Faris agreed. "Mr. Nedrow, I shall give you the reference later."

The county attorney would not be mollified. "Your Honor, the man is a fugitive from justice."

"Is there now a warrant out for him, Mr. Nedrow?"

"No."

"You stated this forenoon, before I warned Mr. Shaw, that the reward for the capture of this man had been withdrawn. There exists now no warrant for his arrest. The witness may be sworn in. Proceed."

Shaw walked close to the chair and faced his witness. "You are the man, Fred, who was on his way north with your child, Mealie?"

"Yes, sir."

"Tell the court, Fred, how you met this man, Hanley, who sits over there."

Fred looked across the little space, caught the shocked expression on his friend's face, and smiled. "Yes, sir. Me and my little girl, Mealie, was in the snow on thet lonesome road. She was feeble like, and we hed come a fer piece. Guess I hurried too much lest the patrollers might ketch us. I give out, jest fell down in the snow. Mister Luke, over there, found us, built us a fire, and mighty near lured us to his house."

He continued his story, telling about the death and burial of his little girl. "She was jest too little and tired to keep on," he said solemnly, and Luke remembered the sprig of witch hazel on the tiny mound. Fred continued with the account of the appearance of the officers and the shot through the door.

"I jes' pitched out and run. The man was comin' on a big horse and shot me. I fell down 'cause I figgered I was dead. Twas then Mister Luke chased the patrollers off. Mister, they hed a mind to kill me."

The big room had been eerily quiet except for the sound of labored breathing. The juror in the front row, who had munched away at his tobacco through the trial so far, had stopped, his mouth open. When the big man finished, Shaw asked a last question.

"You followed a star, Fred, like the Wise Men of old."

"Yessir, the North Star. But, if it hadn't been fer Mister Luke, it'd hev gone clean out fer me."

Nedrow had the grace, or perhaps the wisdom, not to cross-examine, and the witness was escorted from the room. Before the door closed behind the man, Luke glimpsed Rush Geen in the hallway. Shaw bowed to the court and jury. "Your Honor and gentlemen of the jury, this case is so important that I have asked the senior member of our firm to present the remainder of the case for the defendant before this bar. There is more than just a man being tried in this courtroom today. We are defending the principle of the free man's right to aid the stranger at his door without regard for race, color, or condition of life. I present, gentlemen, the senior senator from Pennsylvania, the Honorable Thaddeus Stevens."

The older man rose stiffly to his feet, and his step dragged slightly as he approached the bench and bowed to Judge Faris. Then he faced the jury.

"Your Honor and gentlemen, my associate has handled this case to your satisfaction, I am quite sure. But it is so important that I have come up here to add my feeble words to those said by Mr. Shaw. The defendant, Luke Hanley, has suffered much. His father was shot down years ago, defending the cause of our enslaved brothers. You have seen this young man brought into court for saving from death a man who followed a star. Luke Hanley has good cause to hate African slavery. As a sailor, he had seen the black ships leave Africa with their cargoes of human misery.

"Gentlemen, Fred sought only liberty. He carried his little girl in his arms over the frozen hills until his strength failed him and his child died from the effect of exposure. He was succored by Luke Hanley, who risked his own liberty to perform an act of mercy."

Stevens leaned forward and flung the hair back from his forehead. "A score of years ago, I said in our state legislature that we must stand on higher ground in our thinking. Today, I say to free men all over this broad land that there is a higher ground and a higher law than that cited by our distinguished Mr. Nedrow. It is the law of humanity."

He turned slowly from the jury, to the judge, to the audience, and finally back to the waiting twelve men listening intently. "You read your Bibles, I know. Centuries ago, Wise Men followed a star and found the full freedom which only the Lord Christ can give. This humble black man who today risked his liberty to save a friend, followed a star in the direction of the freedom he sought for himself and his child.

"Gentlemen of the jury, what a calamity it would have been if anyone had stopped the Biblical Wise Men in their quest. What a calamity it would be if Luke Hanley or any other man was punished for helping a brother follow his star. The defense rests."

Judge Faris crumpled a sheet of paper in his hand and had to clear his throat before speaking. "The jury will retire and consider a verdict."

The twelve men rose stiffly and filed out behind a bailiff. It seemed the door had scarcely closed when they filed back, and Judge Faris turned to the foreman.

"How say you, gentlemen of the jury, in your judgment of this case?"

"Not guilty of the crime as charged!"

CHAPTER FOURTEEN

THE FORMALITY of Luke's discharge from custody by Judge Faris was lost in the roar and confusion of an approving crowd, many of whom pushed forward trying to congratulate him. The tipstaves and clerks had a hard time clearing the big room. Shaw and Luke thanked the jury, and then the lawyer led his half-dazed client through side doors into a small office where Brookland stood at a window. On opposite sides of a small table were Squire Jacoby and Senator Stevens.

Luke came forward and faced the Great Commoner. "Sir, I am very grateful—"

Brookland swung from the window, his face twisted in anger, interrupting the young man with a pointed finger.

"That's a damned polite lie, Luke, and you know it. You're not grateful. You might feel a little better when I tell you Rush Geen had Fred out of town fifteen minutes after his testimony was finished. A lot of people have done things for you, and the big worry to all of us was how soon you'd lose your temper and blow up. Through the whole trial, you sat trying your damndest to look guilty."

Luke turned on his friend, the pent-up emotions of the past few weeks contorting his lean features. "Listen to me, Minor Brookland. Just now, I don't give a damn whether I'm free or not. Yes, I owe you a lot. Through me, your lumber job was wrecked, the men manhandled. But like you and Shaw said, I wasn't on trial; nobody really gave a hoot about me and the jail I faced. The senator didn't come up from Washington on account of Luke Hanley. You figure they were after the Underground when they struck at me, but I know that was only part of it. This is a fight between John Caines and me. Just now, the bone he and I are picking happens to be runaway slaves. One of these days, I'll come downriver floating on my back. They hitched me to murder before I'd ever seen a runaway and chased me out of my home country."

He choked momentarily from rage. "They sicked their bullies on me in barrooms, shot at me from the brush, and started me toward the penitentiary when I struck back. Minor, they're after me personally, and that makes it bad luck for anybody who hires me and for every place I stop. I sat here in a courtroom while every stinking, curious loafer stared at me. Hell, I was a horserace with people betting which way I'd go, upriver or down to the penitentiary."

Luke was nearly exhausted by his harangue, but he wanted to continue when the deep voice of Senator Stevens interrupted him.

"Son, you are both right and wrong, but remember, no man is bigger than or as important as a cause. Yes, it's true; Luke Hanley didn't predominate today. The effort was made to show Northern people that aiding runaway slaves is both safe and a duty in spite of vicious laws. Through what you may have suffered, people know that mercy still pays and meets the approval of most. You are too young and hotheaded to realize that whatever you have done, whatever you have endured, has helped a national cause. Today, you have opened many doors along Mason and Dixon's line to strangers who come by night."

He smiled, his deep-set eyes holding Luke's attention. Then he gestured toward Squire Jacoby. "The Squire and I are old friends. We were in the State Legislature together. He's told me all about you, my young friend. I met your father twice. He was a man of great soul and sympathy. Now here, you damned fire-eater, is the job to which you should be dedicated. Make this country along the West Branch so hot for slave catchers that they'll run howling to their Southern leaders with their tails between their legs. If John Caines is their top man, knock him out of the game. You are big enough and strong enough and have friends enough. Make sure every starved, scared runaway that hits our West Branch of the Susquehanna feels he's reached the Promised Land."

Stevens rose and, dragging a foot a little, walked to Luke, his hand extended. "Son, as a lover of liberty, I'm grateful to you."

They clasped hands, one white and fragile, the other brown and strong. The senator shook his leonine head. "If I were younger, I would give a lot to 'ride the river' with you. When you've laid John Caines on his back, send me word. I'll furnish the lilies."

With his crippled foot thumping on the bare floor. Senator Thaddeus Stevens walked from the room while the others rose and watched him go. Jonathan Shaw gathered his papers into a big envelope, and Jacoby motioned Brookland and Luke to sit with him at the table.

"Both of you shot off a good bit, and we'll lay that to the tension under which you have been. Both of you have been right. If your collars have cooled down, listen to an old man."

The two friends, lately so angry, now grinned at each other, then sat facing the squire who spoke cautiously. "It's probably true they, and that really means John Caines, are after Luke for more than the Underground work and want him out of the way, probably dead or in the penitentiary. The county authorities made no attempt to bring him back when he went to the navy, and they had three years to do it. But as soon as he returns, things happen. The thing that bothers me is that somebody had it in for Luke's father. Ostensibly, he was shot down as an Abolitionist leader. I think, personally, though I have no real evidence, that the murder was done by a hired thug, paid and advised by someone in Crossville. Abolitionism wasn't such a hot thing in those days that a man would be shot for making a speech."

Jacoby got up and paced the room a moment before he confronted his friends. "It could be I'm just old and suspicious, but I want Luke to be careful, mighty careful. Some say the story will continue until we have evidence. You can't keep a little deviltry secret forever."

Attorney Shaw had clapped on his hat and picked up his envelope when Luke stopped him and took out his money. "Mr. Shaw, I'd like to do something about your bill."

The lawyer grinned, and his face was all friendliness. "Like you said a while ago when you were ranting, this wasn't your trial. The Abolition Society of Philadelphia will pay for it. They are never short of money, but reckless young devils like you are scarce. Now the fearful will take heart, and people will help runaways."

He shook hands vigorously with all of them. "Remember, gentlemen, Luke owes me a week's fishing at his Hyner Run. To this, you are witnesses. Luke, next time you're in jail, call me any time. With that temper of yours, I wouldn't be surprised."

Jacoby left them on the way to the hotel. Luke told Brookland he was going upriver to salvage some of the things from the wrecked raft, and the lumberman agreed.

"The water's still high enough for a float. The other raft sold well now that logs have hit almost spar prices. Don't worry—I broke even on the winter's work."

Luke wanted to leave at once, but his friend demurred. "Hester Haliday sings tonight in Fellows' Hall. It's her first time in Point Haven. Let's go. I doubt that Jim and Emma will come."

* * *

The hall proved to be large, but it was already nearly filled when the men entered and took seats pretty well forward. The program was for the benefit of the town hospital. The chairman of the board spoke for a few moments and announced that refreshments would be sold on the first floor following the entertainment. After a short pause, he stepped forward a little on the platform.

"Now, ladies and gentlemen, I have the unusual pleasure of presenting to you our Pine Woods Nightingale. The northern part of our state has been ringing with praises of her artistry, but this is her first appearance here in the county seat. Ladies and gentlemen, Hester Haliday, who will sing her way into your hearts."

A small orchestra was seated on the platform, and Hester entered from the wings, bowing to the patter of applause. Tonight, she was dressed in a dark gown that accentuated the whiteness of her throat and bared arms. Again, her hair was piled high on her small head, and she had the poise of the professional entertainer.

The girl held her audience from her first bars of music, and her lovely voice was in complete control. Luke felt a lump rise in his throat as she sang familiar melodies, and Brookland's face was set. He did not realize time was passing until he was standing while Hester led the audience in singing "Auld Lang Syne." Then he followed his friend's long strides into the aisle to go out.

At the foot of the stairway, a rough hand caught Luke's shoulder. It was Rush Geen, who nodded curtly to Brookland but spoke to Luke.

"Hester wants you backstage. It's important."

She was waiting, seeming nervous when the three men joined her. She smiled, however, when they congratulated her and then plunged immediately into her reason for summoning them. "Mr. Brookland, Luke, a man came in from Lymansville just before I sang, and I saw you both in the audience. He said slave catchers raided homes in the Keating section and carried away three persons."

Her eyes were wide, and Luke was reminded of the night she brought the warning to him and Hugh in the mountain gap. Her smooth arm lifted as she fussed with an ornament in her hair. "Two of them are girls. That's why I'm so scared. They are said to be half-white. The boy is in his late teens."

Geen frowned and rubbed his chin. "The kidnappers have all of two- or three-days' start. That means they could be downriver and have bypassed this town. My horses are with Brendy and two men four miles west of here at Quinn's Run."

"Let's start," Luke said to Rush. "You'll know where to go."

Hester's evident anxiety swept away all his resolution to move cautiously and his hesitation at ever again having anything to do with runaways. The lamplight glinted on her hair, and her lips were slightly parted. Brookland stood beside her, looking down. As Luke followed Geen from the room, he saw Hester glance up into the lumberman's face, and he had the feeling that Brookland had said something she challenged.

The young men set a fast pace to the hollow above the town where George Brendy sat alone before a tiny fire. He rapidly explained what had happened, and the one-time lawyer, poking the flames with a stick, commented cynically. "If it's that Pine Valley crowd and they have girls, don't look for them to travel fast."

He got up and stuffed articles into saddlebags with the ease of long practice. One of Geen's men had gone into town. The other came up now, and Geen directed him. "You boys stay with the horses. Luke here hasn't a gun; give him yours. We'll take the three best horses."

Luke tucked the long barrel of the revolver into his trouser band with some misgivings. In five minutes more, they rode east at a fast clip to Point Haven and then detoured the town.

"I'm chasing a hunch, Hanley," Geen remarked. "Those kidnappers likely came downriver on horses, but somewhere in the next valley or the one beyond, they'll have a wagon waiting. I know all the back roads. My figuring is that by tomorrow night, they'll be camped in the Long Narrows, likely close to Crabapple Mountain."

About noon, the three horsemen rode into a farmyard where a house and barn stood backed up against the woods to one side of the narrow road beyond which lay the fields. The layout was such that a man could sit on his front porch and see his whole farm at a glance. A stout man with a face well-weathered by wind and sun, who reminded Luke a little of Erritt, approached, and Geen greeted him as he swung from the saddle.

"Hello, Tate."

They shook hands, and Geen introduced Luke, finishing with the statement, "Tate Gannon here raises the best oats in the county."

Luke's hand was taken in a powerful grip, and he noted that the farmer moved with surprising lightness. He whistled, and a boy who, in a wild way, resembled Hugh Haliday, appeared and took the horses to the barn.

"I've got extra ham fried," Tate announced hospitably. "Come in and help eat it."

The big kitchen was neat and clean, but no woman appeared, and Tate served the meal. The boy returned to the house, ate rapidly, and went out again. Then Geen asked his question.

"Four white men and three black folks crossed the valley. Is that right, Tate?"

"To most anybody else, I'd say I ain't seen nobody," Tate said. "To you, I seen the Baumheits. They had six horses. Two were in the wagon, two rode, and the others led."

Geen thought hard. He looked sharply at his host. "They'll cross to the Long Narrows and camp a day or so at the old Midway dam."

Tate nodded. "Yes, there was two girls. You know what that means. Recall that story about the wench last fall?"

Geen pointed out the window toward the mountains to the south and explained. "The Baumheits are from up Pine Valley, and they follow a regular run. They go through that gap you can see, then over and through the ridges and camp somewhere. That's the time they put the fear of God into whatever black folks they have picked up. After that, they take their catch to Midburg where there's a United States Commissioner. One of the gang swears the black folks are slaves that escaped from him down Maryland way. The official gets his fee, and the black folks are on the way to the block, even if they were born in the North."

He half rose from the table but sat down again. "Tate, I guess this time we'll make it the last run for the Baumheits. I keep remembering how Clate Baumheit, when he was drunk, bragged about what they did to that woman they kidnapped. This time they have two girls."

Their host looked at the three men a moment, then took a deep draught from his coffee cup. "All right, Rush. Bring the folks here. I'll see that they get back upriver."

Luke asked no questions, being content to follow the leadership of this man who seemed to know exactly what he wanted and how to accomplish it. But he wondered at Tate Gannon and whether this was an Underground route about which he had never heard.

* * *

They crossed the valley and followed twisting woods roads through the hills. About dusk, they emerged on a high summit and looked down toward a pine-bordered sheet of water beside which the flicker of a campfire glowed. After a minute, they saw there was a second fire and figures moving among the trees.

"That's their camp," Brendy said. "Let's work our way down."

Geen pushed back his hat, swung a leg across his saddle, and spoke to Luke, assuming Brendy knew how to go about such things.

"We'll approach through a gap just above here. Then we'll blacken our faces. I don't want anybody to recognize you, Luke. Those folks will watch the road where it comes off this hill and the Narrows road. We'll come in on their blind side."

They angled along the ridge eastward until they entered a gap where a big sand spring bubbled up. Men and horses drank, then the riders used the ashes of an old fire to blacken their faces. Close to an estimated half-mile from the old dam and the camp, they tied up the horses.

"Be careful talking," Brendy warned. "Voices carry far in the nighttime."

Ten minutes of walking brought them to the edge of the Ham, where they could see the camp well-illuminated by the two high fires. Back in the timber loomed the dim mass of a covered wagon, and near it were the moving shapes of horses. Close to one fire was a black boy, his feet hobbled with light rope. Between them and the blaze of the other fire, a man who looked older than Brendy, squatted on his heels and poked sticks into the blaze. A hulking young man emerged from the shadows and approached the older one.

"You," the squatting man snarled scornfully, "you in the brush and Hen in the wagon. You'll sure raise hell with us yet."

He rose and spoke almost kindly in the direction of the shadow. "Come on out."

A girl, probably in her late teens, hanging her head and fussing with her disordered dress, appeared and slid herself onto a seat beside the boy on a log. In the firelight, she looked almost white. Not more than a minute passed when a second young man, almost a duplicate of the other, sauntered into the light.

The older man snapped at him. "Where's the girl?"

"The spitfire's in the wagon, tied up."

Evidently, the old man was the leader. He spat into the fire to show his disgust. "This is the last time for this kind of stuff. There was that wench last fall, now—"

He did not finish, for Geen and Brendy stepped into the firelight, covering the three men with double-barreled shotguns.

"You're right, Pop," Geen snarled. "This is the last time and the last raid."

He jerked his head toward Luke. "Get the girl in the wagon."

Enough firelight shone into the end of the wagon cover for him to see a girl lying on some blankets. She was almost naked and tied hand and foot. When Luke crawled in beside her, she cringed away from him.

"It's all right," he said. "Here, I'll cut those ropes."

She was free in a moment and sitting up.

"Put on your dress and come on," he directed, and she joined him outside the wagon in a minute.

"Go to the fire."

Watching the girl stumble forward nearly proved disastrous. To Luke's left, the fourth member of the gang stepped into the half-light behind Geen and Brendy. He held an axe swung high, ready to throw it at Geen. Luke yelled a warning and leaped toward the fellow, but the axe had been thrown. Missing Geen, who had jumped to one side, it struck the fire and sent sparks flying. Luke brought his man down, gasping, then hammered two blows home under his ear. Geen did not hesitate but swung up his gun barrels and felled the man before him like a pole-axed beef.

For the second time, Luke saw the ferocity and skill of the horseman's fighting. Geen kicked Pop into the fire and used his gun barrels to stagger the third young man. He recovered, however, and rushed his antagonist. Geen dropped his gun and methodically pummeled the man's face into a gory mess, then dropped him with a slam to the throat.

Minutes later, they had the quartet tied up. Then they pulled the wagon across one of the fires, and the blaze caught quickly on the straw in the box until the whole was a huge torch in the darkness. Brendy gathered up the team harness and tossed it into the fire.

"Now," Geen addressed his prisoners, "get up and strip."

Pop obeyed with no question. One of the others hesitated. Geen snatched up a horsewhip that had dropped from the wagon and sent the lash hissing against the man. He howled and stripped off his clothes. In minutes, the four were naked, and Brendy pitched all their clothing into the furious fire.

"Start walking, you Baumheits," Geen snarled, raising his whip toward the naked, shivering men. "Remember, there's a little matter of rape in this. By God, I'll lash the meat off your filthy backs if you don't move fast."

Brendy herded the captives into the road, where he turned them west toward Pine Valley. When they were dim, trotting shapes, he fired his shotgun after them and was answered by a yelp of pain followed by silence.

Close to noon again, the cavalcade moved into Tate Grannon's yard. Geen had brought away the Baumheit horses. The farmer fed the animals, then cooked a big meal for all hands.

"Looks like them kids had a hard time, Rush. I'll hide them a couple of days, then get them home."

When Luke and his friends rode on, they were mounted on horses captured at the Baumheit camp. Geen commented, "Horses are my business. I don't think that outfit will try to get them back. They handled those girls pretty bad, and they're smart enough to tell."

"Just who were those fellows?" Luke asked, and Brendy replied.

"The two big young ones are Baumheit brothers. Pop's their uncle, and they all live together on a fine farm in Pine Valley. The man who used the axe is a stranger. Most of the folks in that valley are tarred with the same stick. A black person don't count with them for as much as a cow."

"Do you think they'll go to the authorities?"

Brendy rode for a while in silence before committing himself. "I doubt it. There was a lot of talk last fall about that black woman they mishandled. Now this rape of two girls on top of that would be bad, even for them. Also, I don't think they'd risk losing another wagon and horses. I figure they're about done with such business."

Luke rode thoughtfully along for a time. This was the way to handle kidnappers. Serve out quick hard punishment. News of what happened back there at the dam would get out some way. People would talk. He rode close to Geen and voiced his thoughts.

"They knew just when to strike. Fred was away, and most everybody was down at the courthouse."

"Including my watchers," Geen said angrily. "There's no doubt about it, Hanley. There's a big organization behind slave hunting. Those Baumheits figured on getting four thousand, maybe more, for those three young folks. And they'd have split some of that money with the organization that tipped them off on the right time to kidnap. Things won't settle till the kingpin gets the fear of God throwed into him. By this time, I'd know where to hit if I was you."

CHAPTER FIFTEEN

LUKE AND his companions separated on the outskirts of Point Haven, but before they parted, he and Rush Geen talked for a few minutes.

"I'm still in your debt, Hanley. That fellow with the Baumheits would have finished me with that axe. I forgot there were four men." He grinned, and they shook hands.

For the first time, Luke realized he really liked this coldly efficient young horseman. Perhaps it was the man's recklessness that appealed to him.

"Too bad you must walk, Hanley, but I can't risk running this string of horses through town. Some folks might think I didn't get them honestly."

Brendy's broad wink was the best comment on the situation, and Luke was tempted to tell how the jail attendant had said Geen could ride through Point Haven with stolen horses and the officers would go fishing to avoid doing anything about it.

Once in town, he went over to the Carman House, where he wrote a short letter to Brookland, advising him that he was going upriver to attempt to salvage some of the logs lost at the time of his arrest. As Brookland had said, the river was still high enough to float a raft. When his letter was finished, he leaned back in his chair. There was no question that the raid on the Baumheits had been a success. Thinking of his own troubles resulting from using a shotgun on Borst, however, he was worried about what effect Brendy's shot in the darkness might have, and he was not too easy in his mind about that string of horses. Geen had rendered excellent service to the cause of freedom, but he had been well paid for it.

Luke was about to get up and mail his letter when a young man entered the lobby and headed straight across to him, smiling as he came.

"I'm from the Clarion," he announced. "My name is French, and I'd like an interview with you, Mr. Hanley."

Luke looked at him in surprise and laid his letter back on the desk. "With me," he said. "Why?"

The reporter fished out a pad of paper. "You're a pretty well-known person now with state senators coming up to defend you. The story of that has reached the national papers. We gave that good coverage, for it isn't often that a man like Thaddeus Stevens comes up here. People are talking about you."

Luke had to smile at the eagerness of his inquisitor, but he did not want to be interviewed or questioned. "I suppose they are talking, Mr. French. I'm sorry, but I didn't read the papers. You see, I was busy being tried."

French laughed and asked a string of questions about Luke's background and his plans, all of which he avoided as much as possible. He explained that he was simply an employee of Minor Brookland and planned to salvage logs. Then the reporter shot a surprising question.

"Know anything about this raid on the black folks at Keating, Mr. Hanley?"

Startled, Luke picked up his letter, glad for a chance to move and so cover his momentary confusion. This man was going to entangle him in the slave question if he could. "What raid?"

French looked at him a long moment, then appeared to have made up his mind.

"On the second day of your trial, three teenage black people were kidnapped from their home near Keating. There is a rumor that a party of professional slave catchers from Pine Valley brought these young people downriver. Another rumor has it that the victims have been released. People are calling at our office, asking for news. John Caines was one of these when he went through town this morning."

Luke's face hardened. That was sheer gall on Caines' part, and it angered him into speaking recklessly. "Better ask John for news. He does get around, you know."

French realized that he had offended and tried to cover up. "I mentioned it because he is a big man and likely to become a bigger one. It seemed nice that he was interested in these obscure young people. Two of them were girls, by the way. Don't you like John Caines, Mr. Hanley?"

"On the contrary, Mr. French. You may quote me as saying I love the man. Evenings up in the woods, I sit around thinking wonderful thoughts about him." He rose to his full height, patted the puzzled reporter on the shoulder, and stalked out of the hotel.

In the morning, he rode west on a three-car construction train, and the conductor was voluble about the railroad's progress up the river. "Give us a year or so and we'll be connected with Erie and the lakes. Western grain will come down through these hills."

"How about lumber?" Luke queried. "Will it haul logs?"

"No, not likely. The river's still the cheaper way for them. But the road will handle sawed stuff. The fact is, we're carrying some of it now from close to where we are building. Good dry stuff at the end of construction would pay its shipment very well." He spat over the side of the car. "This war talk is sending up the price of lumber. We're paying close to double the old price for ties."

Luke left the train at the end of the steel track and walked on, thinking about the railroad. Its construction would be costly because the mountain spurs left little flat land along the river. There were big creeks to bridge, great gullies to cross. If lumber could be shipped by railroad, it would mean a steady year-round market rather than a glutted two-month one each spring when rafts went down.

He made good time and walked into camp shortly after dark. Ben Royal, a bit thin but otherwise well again, was delighted at his coming, and the men, hearing his voice, crowded into the office to greet him. Those who had been hurt when the camp was raided were pretty well recovered. The men, with Royal, agreed that some of the lost logs could be salvaged.

"Luke," Royal suggested, "take the batteau. Use Tom, Pritchett, and the two pilots. That's five men. Pick up all the logs marked with our three-star brand, no matter who claims them. Work the river as far down as Scootac Creek."

After the bountiful supper the cook set out for him, Luke and Royal talked.

"Ben, I've been wondering about these timber thieves we call Algerines and the way they pick up logs. They must sell to somebody. I'm going up and have a talk with Tammie. She might drop a hint."

Royal refilled his pipe and commented, "Somebody buys them, but it ain't Tammie. Use one of the horses; you've had a long walk."

An hour later, Luke tied his horse to the hitching rail at Tammie's Place. There were no other animals tethered there and, when he entered the big room, no customers. But Tammie came from the back and welcomed him effusively.

"Lordy, but I'm glad to see you, Luke. Especially since you ain't carrying a shotgun. This is Wednesday, the day we keep closed."

He caught her by the shoulders, whirled her about several times, then kissed her, surprised at the warmth of her response.

"Tammie, I want some of that blackberry wine of yours and a session of talk. Get it quick before I get mad and kiss you again."

She got the wine, and the two sat down facing each other.

"Luke, I never heard anything like that Stevens man. It was so crowded I couldn't get into the room. Heard him from the hall. When he talked, I felt like getting me a gun and going down South to shoot me a slave owner."

Luke fidgeted. He did not want to talk about the trial. "Maybe you wouldn't need to go so far, Tammie. Anyway, Stevens didn't come up here just for me."

Tammie eased herself back into her chair and sipped the wine in her glass. When she spoke, she ignored the first part of his statement. "No, mebbe he didn't come just for you, but now you've got a name on this river. Folks talk about you—some good, some bad. A while back, you was just a wood hick with a dirty face and stagged pants. Now you're the man with the shotgun that makes his own laws."

He frowned. All the foolishness and fun had gone out of him. "Listen, Tammie. I came to talk business. Tomorrow morning I start to find the logs we lost when I was arrested. I figured you might tell me something because I've had a rough time. I lost Brookland's raft. That might wash me up from getting to be a boss. Who buys the timber these Algerines pick up?"

The woman took a deeper draught from her glass, emptying it of all but the dregs she swirled about a while. "Well, I shouldn't be talking, but they say there is a big drift of fourteen-foot logs in the eddy at Baker's Bend. Most of your logs was likely sixteens. These logs ain't marked yet, and old Mose High's said to have a pretty big woodpile."

She got up, and Luke followed her to the bar, where she rinsed the wine glasses.

"I'm no fortuneteller. Could be the answers you want will come when you don't want 'em. Don't try to rush things or me." Her smile showed nearly perfect white teeth. She changed the subject. "The railroad is buying a lot of land for right of way along the river. Better get some to sell."

It was plain she wasn't going to tell him anything important. Anybody could know about the logs down at Baker's Bend. She went to the door with him, where he kissed her lightly.

"Wish I could figure women, Tammie. Maybe you told me something tonight, maybe you didn't. I'd like to know about women, I surely would."

She patted his shoulder with a plump hand and drawled, "You seem to be trying, friend. Trying hard."

On the way to camp, listening to the steady clop of the horse's hoofs, Luke thought through his visit. This big blonde woman stimulated him, and somehow, she loosened the tensions in him so that he felt freer, happier after a visit with her. She had been frank about the logs at Baker's Bend but had not even hinted that she knew how the river thieves disposed of their timber. The talk about the railroad did not seem to fit in, and he wondered why she had brought up the subject.

By the time he stabled his horse and rolled himself into the blankets on his bunk, his good humor was gone, and he was thoroughly angry at himself for being simple enough to think Tammie would tell him one thing she did not wish to reveal or even hint at anything which might indicate she was taking sides in a controversy.

He swore under his breath, pulled the blankets higher, and finally slept.

* * *

The double-ended batteau looked overloaded with grab chains, coiled rope, boat hooks, peavies, and the food and gear of five men, besides the crew itself. The river had fallen about three feet from flood height, and so, in the first mile, they found logs stranded on the banks. These were rolled into the water, fastened with grabs, and towed behind the batteau. They tied up the first night six miles downriver, where a little stream entered from the north.

"Tomorrow could be hot," German, one of the pilots, said. His partner, Harry, nodded, and Luke knew they were not referring entirely to the weather.

"Yep," Norm agreed, "we'll be at the bend where old Mose High hangs out. He'll be waiting with a cap on his gun."

Again, Luke realized the pilots were talking for his benefit. He had heard some of the stories about the old riverman and his half-wild boys who lived by salvaging logs from broken rafts and then selling them back to the owners or, what was of greater interest to Luke, to others.

It was a bright morning when they rounded the first bend, slowly picking up logs until they were towing a full section of a raft. Then came the second and wider turn of the river above the mouth of Baker's Run. On the south side of the big stream, low in the break of the hills, stood a cabin and outbuildings. In the stream itself, piles had been driven, and these were joined by chains, so there was a tight, strong boom now completely filled with white pine logs.

Luke spoke to the batteau rowers. "Pull in to the shore, boys, and tie up."

Norm German handled the tie-up of the boat and their little raft. When Luke went ashore, Tom Short followed, but Luke spoke sharply to the big man. "No, Tom. I'll handle this myself. He'd bluster if there were two men."

Short pushed his hat well back on his head and deluged a laurel bush with tobacco juice. "Well, Mister, it's your funeral. Old Mose likes to chew 'em up fine." He pulled his hat into position and issued a flat statement. "Anyway, if we hear a noise, we'll be down."

Luke grinned and waved a hand airily as he walked along the narrow path. At the boom, he stepped out on the logs. All were prime sticks, and he found one shaped with axes to a uniform taper. It had been cut from the butt of a spar. Counting rapidly, he computed the volume of the impounded logs. The lower end of the boom was flimsy, made merely of ropes and poles. Satisfied, he strode toward the landing where a man sat in an old armchair, holding a rifle across bony knees.

Luke did not pause until he was off the logs within a dozen feet of the armed sentinel. The man had once been tall and powerful, but now his shoulders were bent. The hat pulled low over a small-featured face hid all but a few wisps of gray hair, and the leathery cheek of the old man bulged with a huge cud of tobacco. "Stop right there, stranger, or I'll shoot."

Luke came closer and saw that the hammer of the gun was being pulled back slowly by a dirty thumb.

"The hell you will," he answered the warning.

"This is my property," the old man spluttered, and Luke jerked a thumb toward the boom.

"And my logs. You can have your land, but what's left of that pine belongs to me." His quick glance searched the premises and took in a woodshed piled high with blocks. Walking slowly and completely ignoring the man with the gun, he passed the house and approached the site. He felt a cold touch in the middle of his back when his quick side glance showed him the brass cap on the gun nipple and the hammer fully back like a vicious snake's head.

He turned and met the advancing owner of the place. "Well, Mister, you either got in your winter's wood early, or you're fixing to make shake shingles."

High swung the gun in a short arc. "Don't touch my firewood, or I'll bore you."

"Put that damned gun down, High. You old horse thief, you've got fifty thousand feet of Brookland's logs out front. You sawed off two feet from each to hide the three-star brand. If you hadn't been so damned lazy, you'd have split that wood to kill the brands; you might have got away with it. Now, I'll send you straight to jail."

To Luke's surprise, the tips of High's soiled mustache twitched. When he sat down on a chopping block, there was a glint in his faded eyes. "Well, me and the boys was pretty busy. Hed to go to court to see them try a feller as looked like you a lot. Could be some of them logs was yours, but we fished them out of the river and finders keepers. What you going to do about it?"

Luke looked sharply at the old riverman and grinned. "High, I figure you sold them logs and don't care too much about them. Else you might have used that gun. You sold them to—"

"Stop right there. We ain't namin' no names. Yep, I got the money in my pocket and thet timber kinda spoils my view. It's in my road. Besides, I likes to spit in the water, and I can't till them logs is clear gone."

Suddenly, he thrust the gun into Luke's hands, and two young men came round the woodshed from the rear. One carried a crippled arm at an unnatural angle.

"Boys," High quavered, "I been overpowered. This long-legged splinter hound tuk my gun off me, and he's about to clear every log out of our pond."

Neither youth appeared impressed with their father's statement, though both carefully spat tobacco juice on the ground. High spoke sharply to them. "Stir yourselves. Help them fellers upriver raft the stuff. There mightened be any time to waste."

In less than twenty minutes, Luke's crew with the batteau and the collected logs came down. The impounded logs were pushed out with pike poles while Luke and High watched from the bank. When the boom was empty, High boarded the forming raft and directed the placing of lash poles and a set of sweeps that materialized from behind the woodshed. When everything was finished, High led Luke back to the house.

"Now, Mister, don't git funny idees. Not many folks run Mose High. I knowed you in court, and I knowed you here. You put a load of shot into that Deputy Borst. Mister, it was him that hit my Eddie with a club and gave him thet crooked arm when they hed an argument about a deer."

He waved a dirty hand toward the raft. "We got five dollars a thousand for them logs. It's paid. Now I don't care a good wind-blowed damn whut happens to the stuff. When the man shows up, I'll say you stole the whole damned business, even tuk my gun off me. He jest ain't fixed to call me a liar."

Luke looked around. "Maybe there's something we could do for you. Ask me, anyway."

The riverman gestured toward the batteau, now unnecessary since the raft was all the transportation Luke's crew would need.

"Ours is stoved up bad. You won't be needin' it. And we could use a hundred feet of that three-quarter-inch rope you got piled in her."

The boat was pushed over at Luke's prompt order. "She's yours, so's the rope, High. Now, could I hire your Eddie to make the run downriver? We're short-handed. It's a dollar a day and found."

No answer was necessary. The crippled boy dashed into the house. Emerging in five minutes with a blanket roll, he leaped from the shore to the raft. Luke sent Pritchett back to the camp; Royal would need him, and High's other son set him across the river with the batteau.

Despite his crooked arm, Eddie High proved a real find. He had a quick sense about tricky currents and a keen eye for anything that even resembled a shoal. By the time they passed Point Haven, both pilots, Harry and German, stood back and gave the boy a chance to steer. Tom Short, who had a weakness for young people, fashioned a laurel wood pipe for Eddie, and now he smoked instead of chewing.

Eight days after leaving Baker's Bend, Luke, bound north from Marietta where they had sold the logs, got off the train at King's Shore while his crew continued on to Point Haven. He wanted to see Brookland as soon as possible. For once, he had good news. The lumberman greeted him warmly and led him into the office room, where Luke took out a sheaf of bills and slapped them on the desk.

"There she is—eleven hundred dollars. Those salvaged logs brought close to spar prices."

Brookland gave a low whistle of astonishment. He picked up the money, then laid it down while he took a paper from a pigeonhole in the big roll-top desk. "More good luck right here. This and what you brought puts me in good shape again."

Luke glanced at the paper and saw it was a check for four thousand dollars. His friend explained. "That's for the railroad right of way over my river lands. The company now owns a strip all the way up and a little past Pine Bend, where the Caines lands begin. He owns ten thousand acres in a strip right along the river, and the road has to cross all of it."

Luke shook his head ruefully. "He'll be hard to deal with."

"So is the railroad," Brookland rejoined. "Attorney Shaw is handling the land procurement for the company. Of course, they could use eminent domain, but that means delay while viewers fix damages, and Caines could control any set of local men the county would put on such a job."

Luke finished his cigar with real appetite. It made him feel good to know that Jonathan Shaw would come to grips with John Caines. He would be betting on the young lawyer.

Brookland picked up a letter. "War's not far off, I'm afraid. This slavery squabble cannot go on much longer. There is open fighting on the Kansas prairies. Southern leaders talk secession and ride roughshod over Congress and the president. This letter is from Captain Caris, and he wants to remind you about the yellow pine; pitch, we call it. He says he is out of the navy and can market all the dry yellow pine planks we can get him at twenty-eight dollars a thousand board feet."

It was Luke's turn to whistle his surprise. "That means there is a young fortune just east of your white pine cutting." Then his face fell. "I see the joker. Pitch won't run. It's so heavy, it'll sink. Besides, we have no sawmill."

Brookland pulled some paper toward him. He held a pencil in his hand. "I'm not bothering with the pitch pine business, but let's figure a bit." He worked for a few minutes and then looked up with a question. "You have still got three hundred dollars?"

Luke nodded, and his host continued.

"There's about a hundred more coming to you as wages. I'll sell you the stumpage on a hundred acres at a dollar and a half per acre, only the pitch, you realize. Old Man Ely, who stole all that wild cherry above Driftwood, had a pretty good up-and-down mill he offers for a hundred twenty-five dollars. He was so sure I'd buy it that he moved the whole business just north of the Dyer farm. You could put that mill on Rattlesnake, just a short distance below Hyner."

Luke's eyes were shining. Here was the thing he really wanted opening before his eyes.

Brookland had not finished. "I'll go in on the venture and pay two men for a year. One should be our man, Clyde Brown. He's a good worker, but I'm always worried about kidnappers. With you, he'd be safe. Every other month, you boys will work for me, which will pay your living. I'll take double the wages paid you when the lumber's sold. Also, I'll furnish teams to haul your planks to the end of the railroad."

Luke was on his feet, almost shouting with pleasure. "I'm in business, Minor." He caught himself at the familiarity and colored. This was the first time he had addressed his friend by his given name, but Brookland was smiling.

"Good, Luke. I wondered if you'd ever break down and remember I'm only ten years older than you. I was getting a little tired of the 'Mister' role with you."

Luke was so elated that he refused to stay the night. He wanted to get upriver fast and then to Lymansville to buy the mill. While he waited for a train at King's Shore, he remembered this was one of the few times he had talked with Minor Brookland that the matter of runaway slaves had not been discussed. He frowned. After all, he would be upriver at a place where he might help. He would also be situated where he could strike back at Caines. But even these issues seemed tame alongside this chance to get somewhere.

"I'm in business," he whispered under his breath as the train rolled into the station.

CHAPTER SIXTEEN

LUKE WENT upriver in a mood that surprised him, for it was so new in his experience during the last ten years or so. He had a sense of real freedom. True, he had not felt exactly tied in the navy as there he had only to obey orders. There was little emotion in those years except when he had seen the slave ships and again when he had witnessed the sale of the unfortunates in the towns near the navy yard. Before his flight and again since his return, he had been caught in a tangle of woods work together with whatever his conscience dictated he should do about the runaway slaves. Even his relations with Hester and Linda merely confused him. Now, he had a clear-cut chance to do something to further himself in the world, and the prospect was intoxicating.

Early summer was delightful, with the leafy deciduous trees wearing fresh, almost yellow, green against the background of the pines. The river had been dropping steadily but still showed occasional whitecaps where rocks thrust up in the channel. When he was directly across Baker's Bend, he saw a small figure on the wharf and signaled. A boat pushed off at once. The oarsman was Eddie High, who said his father would be glad to see Luke and had been talking about him only that morning at breakfast.

The old riverman seemed pleased with his visitor and roughly expressed his approval at the treatment his son had received on the raft. He would not be put off, insisting that Luke stay the night.

Supper was a bounteous meal, though Luke was sure the meat was out-of-season venison. There were dandelion greens, prepared as Luke's mother used to do, and there were baked potatoes and green apple pie.

High's wife was a tall, silent woman who beamed at her visitor's compliments on her cooking. The sons ate rapidly, saying almost nothing. The father did the talking for the family. When the meal was finished and the two men sat on the porch smoking, they discussed Luke's pitch pine venture.

"Hanley," High said after some deliberation, "fetch your mill to this side. With me and the boys helping, we could make a pretty thing."

"You have no timber," Luke countered, and the old man chuckled.

"There's any God's amount of it back in the hills. We could steal enough to make us rich. None of these lumber folks pay any attention to pitch."

He changed the subject abruptly with a shocking surprise for the younger man. "John Caines is after Dan Parvin's senate place."

Luke merely stared. State Senator Parvin was almost a tradition in this senatorial district. By virtue of his office, he was one of the most influential men in this great lumbering country and had held the position so long that he seldom had an opponent in an election.

"Parvin, Honest Dan Parvin," he said. "Mose, Caines can't beat him."

"No, he won't need to. Dan's been sick a lot, and he's old. Talk is that he'll resign soon and that the governor'll appoint Caines. The big shot's from the next county. Him and Caines has been friends, and our lumberman would be God Almighty. Has a pretty big chunk of votes he can swing."

High let his news sink in and then continued. "Caines is eatin' high on the hog these days. Came here the other day and wanted to know about that timber. I told him these damn woodpeckers cut my boom, and all his logs went to hell downriver."

"Won't he sue you, Mose?"

The question was answered by a derisive snort. "Him? D'ye spose that man'd risk goin' to law about fourteen-foot logs? He jest looked at that empty boom, mindin' me of a cat switchin' her tail, madlike."

Luke smoked steadily, looking out over the river and thinking about John Caines. Probably the appointment to the state senate was in the man's grasp if he wanted the position. It would give him tremendous power and prestige in a country where every second woodsman worked on a

Caines job and where the county officials were his henchmen. Luke was concerned about the effect it would have on the Underground. If Caines was really head of the organization of slave catchers and kidnappers, additional political power would end the chances of ever helping runaways to escape upriver. Now Linda was to marry Nedrow. Surely her new fiancé had paid a price to be so thoroughly acceptable to this cold, ambitious man who coveted Parvin's senatorship. High interrupted his thinking.

"Let's go to bed. Every time that man's named, you cloud up. Most of us up here know he's been ridin' you. If I was in your shoes, I'd stop him from doin' it even if I hed to use a gun."

Luke turned to his companion and studied the wrinkled face in the light from the doorway. "Why has Caines got it in for me? Tell me that."

The riverman knocked the dottle from his pipe and replied at once. "I ain't sayin' I know, and I ain't sayin' I don't. I lived on this here river long enough to keep my mouth shut till the right time comes along, and it gin'rally does. Somehow you got in his way—thet's the only thing as counts with that bird. Git in his way and he's out fer blood, and it ain't healthy. Thet's all I'm gonna say right now."

In the morning, still cheerful about his future prospects and with High's promise to help set up the mill, Luke was ferried to the north shore of the river. In the Brookland camp, which he reached in a couple of hours, Tom Short and Pritchett were enthusiastic about the pitch pine operation.

"There's acres and acres of the stuff," Ben Royal declared. "There's places where it stands thicker than white pine. You can get it off the mountain by a slide. The logs won't be so big that you can't hand log a lot of it, saving team work. Come spring, the railroad end will be within five miles. Out will go your planks for that twenty-eight-dollar price."

Royal had a last word with Luke before they went to bed. "You want to go to Lymansville. Take a horse and the buckboard. I hate to bother you, but one of our night strangers is up the hollow. He wants to get up to Lymansville. Looks a bit like they chased him out of Keating."

Luke made no comment though he did not welcome the job. Every time he turned, this Underground lifted its head, and just now, he wanted only to get started on his lumbering operation.

The black man was waiting up the road a mile from camp in a tiny bark shelter originally placed there by lumbermen in case of rain. He was a wizened, tough-looking, middle-aged fellow, reticent at first and evidently suspicious of Luke. Patient questioning as they drove along over the rough road brought out much of his story. Fred had run him out of the settlement. Now he was bound north, partly to escape, partly to see a woman.

"Name of Claudy," he confided a little later, to Luke's surprise. "She's up here somewheres, and I'll find her. Fred run her off, too."

Luke listened but made no comment. Claudy was the name of the young woman with the party on that first trip he made for the Underground, and he vividly recalled her dance of joy when they had finally reached Hillside and Erritt. She had been the spokesman for both her husband and her mother, and there had been an attractive quality about her face with its searching bright eyes. Luke's companion had not finished.

"She and me was fixin' to live together, and I wasn't married to thet Lottie woman. Fred jest didn't like Claudy and said as how we both hed to git out. Claudy lost her first man. He was tuk, and she got away in the bresh."

Luke drove along, listening to the steady trotting of the horse and wondering a little at what might have happened up there in Fred's bailiwick. Certainly the big man would have had a good reason for his action, and Luke was not at all sure he liked this cringing man by his side.

Sam Erritt was glad to see Luke but looked askance at the passenger he had brought, studying him a while before putting him in one of the smaller cabins.

"Something shady in that business," he declared when Luke had given the story told him by the fugitive. "I hear this Claudy woman's been seen in lumber camps as far south as Weston. Likely she went to Keating from there. But why? We sent her out of here with her husband, and they tell us he was recaptured somehow. She did come back to Lymansville and worked in the Prentis House a while till she got nice clothes. It could be she's tolling men along and turning them in to the slave catchers."

Luke was sure his friend had not finished all he could say about this matter, but Erritt changed the subject. "I promised to take in the protracted meeting this evening. You go along over. Hester Haliday will sing, and there are two or three good preachers."

Luke repressed a smile as he remembered Hester's invitation to come up for these meetings on the score that they might do him good. He surely had not planned on going, but he went along with Erritt.

This was like the other occasions when he had heard the girl sing. She knew how to handle an audience. Tonight, she was dressed demurely, and the spell of her voice was as strong on Luke as it had been the first time he heard her. Like Brookland said, she could have a real career on the stage.

When the meeting was over, Luke and Erritt were making a slow way through the crowd in the aisle when Luke felt his sleeve plucked. Turning, he found it was Hester.

"I saw you from the platform, and I'm glad you did come. Run in tomorrow so we can talk."

She turned to Erritt with a smile and talked with animation. Luke continued to be puzzled by this slip of a girl who could ride a wild horse or sing a song equally well. One month, she could be coldly savage in her attitude; the next, she could be concerned about the kidnapping of black girls and youths.

"Luke was a member of our family," she was saying to Erritt. "I'll look for him in the morning. Good night, gentlemen."

An amused smile showed on Erritt's broad face. Later, at Hillside, they talked a long time about the pitch pine enterprise. Finally, the station keeper changed the subject cautiously. "You know Hester Haliday well?"

Luke shrugged his heavy shoulders. "Who does? She was a sweet, fine girl back on her father's farm when I worked there, but now—"

Erritt tapped out his pipe. "She owns the Prentis Hotel now. As you know, Mr. Prentis and his wife treated her as a daughter. Prentis died and Hester bought out the widow before her death."

He raised his eyebrows at Luke's sharp glance. "Oh, everything was on the up and up, my friend. She is one of those people who can make money. Every time she opens that lovely mouth of hers to sing, she's paid. She got ten dollars for this evening. A moneymaker she is and as cold as a

Potter County trout stream in April. Geen made money for her in horses. Likely she staked him. Now she owns a little sawmill out of town a ways. Also, she makes that hotel pay."

Luke did not comment. He was thinking of the poverty of Hester's parents on his return. True, they were home once more, but the mother had aged ten years in three, and Jim was an old man now, his spirit quenched.

Erritt realized he was taking a chance with his next statement. "Maybe you're in love with her, and I'm hurting you. Rush Geen was, and she damned near wrecked him, cold and hard as he is. Even now, he'll still go through fire and water for her. Watches over her like a big brother."

Luke did not answer. His long, hard features hid what he was thinking, and Erritt got up to pace the floor, talking as he did so.

"In my young days, women were women. Now this lumber country has two of them, both beautiful, both able to turn any man's head and both better managers than any man I know. They are Linda Caines and this Hester I'm talking about."

He pointed a finger at Luke and stood with his short legs astraddle. "Linda Caines' father is a crawling snake, but his girl's just opposite. I know she keeps a string of men buzzing about her and that she's engaged to Nedrow. Maybe Linda Caines is wild; if I was a girl with her looks, I'd see what the world had to offer, too. But, brother. I'd rather take my chances with Linda Caines or Tammie down at Pine Bend than with our psalm-singing little Hester."

With no further comment or even a good night, Luke's host stalked out. Nor did Luke see him when he ate breakfast or fed and harnessed his horse. The woman who served breakfast said she did not know where her employer was.

The horse plodded up the street of the town at a slow walk, passing the tabernacle where the services had been held the night before. There, an old man was listlessly picking up litter among the seats. Two blocks farther, Luke turned in to the Prentis House hitching rail and tied his horse.

All the buildings on the place were substantially built and in excellent repair. The yard was neatly raked. Luke walked slowly back toward the barn, admiring things. Directly behind the one-story kitchen was an outside pump and a small watering trough. As Luke stopped to study the layout of the barn, he heard a door open. Turning, he saw a girl come out, go to the little trough, and begin splashing water over her face and shoulders. She seemed to be wearing a single scanty garment, and when she straightened up, with a shock, he recognized Claudy. She saw him in the same instant, turned, and entered the kitchen like a scuttling rabbit.

Minutes passed before he went back, walked up the steps, and rapped at Hester's door. It opened immediately, and she was there, smiling.

"You're early, Luke, and I'm glad," she said animatedly. "I saw your rig, and since I wanted to run over to my mill, I thought you'd take me."

He assured her he would be most willing but apologized for his slow horse and buggy.

She laughed. "Remember the old spring wagon down home? Don't apologize." She had caught up a shawl and then touched his sleeve lightly. "Come on, Luke. I'm anxious to be outside. A ride will do me good."

From the time she stepped into the buggy, she monopolized the conversation and was once again the good companion. She seemed to have forgotten the warning given him and Geen that night in Point Haven. When a woodchuck sat up near a stone wall, she whistled at him until he was confused and puzzled, turning his head slowly as if wondering why he, a watchman, should be warned by another chuck. Hester laughed aloud at his discomfiture.

Eventually, she looked toward Luke directly and asked a question. "But, Luke, I know you didn't come to town just to see me or—"

Her eyes partly closed before she finished.

"Or, did you?"

His face colored, and he moved in the seat. "No," he said at last. "I came up to buy a mill."

She ignored his confusion in a quick interest, asking a host of questions such as a lumberman might have done. In half an hour, she had all the information he had about pitch pine prices, with the name of the man from whom he expected to buy the mill together with what he expected to pay.

"Pitch is interesting," she said. "There's lots of it up here. Planks could be hauled out over the Pike by wagon."

Hester's lumbering operation was located behind a small farm, which certainly wasn't as neat or well-managed as the Prentis House. None of the men they saw were friendly, and the foreman, a dour man, looked as slovenly as the operation he managed. After an hour, they turned back, and when they had gone about a mile, she touched the lines.

"Stop a minute. Let's talk. What do you think of my setup?"

"Not good, Hester. You can't make money with men like that. Our Ben Royal would fire every man I saw. Get Rush Geen to send you a foreman."

Her small mouth was set grimly. "You're right. Hugh will be out of the army in a few months. He's coming up here to help me run things. I can't bother Rush too much. He hauls my logs to a mill west of here. Our lumber is sold locally for houses and barns."

They drove on for a while. Luke wondered how she had made money if her other ventures were as poor as this lumbering one appeared. On top of a hill in sight of Lymansville, he pulled the horse under a great spreading chestnut. This slim girl beside him had changed sharply since they had started out.

"Hester, this morning you were the girl back home, the one who came over the mountain in the dark. Now you've changed again—"

Her look stopped him, and her voice was low, as though she found it an effort to control it. Even her eyes looked different, darker. "That's the second time you've told me I've changed. You are right. I was a child on that lonesome farm. You were something new, that was all."

Her lips curled, and there was no mirth in her light trill of laughter. "Perhaps for a while I did think you were sort of wonderful. Then that Caines girl appeared, the one you laid around with at night, and she boasted about it in public."

"Stop it," he demanded. "Stop it!"

She paid no attention. "You were such bad luck to all of us. The family ruined, Hugh leaving home, then I, when Mother thought I'd stooped to something with you. You were a big shot, running the Underground for Minor Brookland. I went to your trial, hoping—" She was all but hysterical with fury. "Those filthy runaways beggared my father. I pitied the women, but I hated the men."

His powerful hand clamped down on the girl's slim wrist. He was beginning to understand Erritt's hints of the night before. Claudy was in her house, even now. In a few hours, this blazing little beauty would be singing hymns in a revival service.

"Hester, God help you. I think I know what you've been up to, how you made your money. That Claudy is with you. You've been playing with John Caines, helping the slave catchers. Only one thing keeps me from believing all of what I've said."

Her face looked hard.

Luke was so disturbed that he breathed as though he had been running. "It's the fact that you warned us about those girls the Baumheits kidnapped."

Her small face twisted, and her words came in jerks. "The women . . . the men, filthy, hulking, pawing . . . breeding. When I was fourteen . . . he . . . I got away."

She grabbed his arm with both hands, her nails digging through his sleeve. "I'll send every black man that comes my way back where he belongs, to work and rot and die."

She twisted, snatched the whip from its socket, and leaped from the buggy. Luke followed her.

"Don't touch me," she warned, "or I'll cut your eyes out with this. Someday I'll settle you, Luke Hanley, with your mind only on chasing women."

Suddenly she flung down her weapon and ran, her skirts held high and her slim legs flying. Unreasonably, through his anger and sick surprise, he saw another picture: this same girl in the pasture field, running from the enraged bull. This time there was no saving her.

Luke was stabling his horse at Hillside when Erritt appeared. The station master watched him for a little while before he spoke.

"I see you found out, my friend. It shows on your face."

Luke nodded miserably, and Erritt continued thoughtfully but not unkindly.

"The man you brought up slipped away, but he stole three dollars from my cash box before he went. I'll bet he and Claudy are on their way south somewhere. Maybe over toward Driftwood. John Caines' runners will have him in a day or so and add another thousand dollars to their organization's cash box. John'll get his forty percent. Claudy will get a new dress and a new man."

They went into the house. In spite of his hurt, Luke wanted to know more, and Erritt was full of information, answering at length and explaining.

"Yes, there's really an organization. It's not like it was before you left for the navy. Then, Brookland and us could plan and run a regular route. Now, we just have to grab a runaway and do our best. Of course, we're fairly safe in Lymansville, but they catch them in this country, too. They take these black boys out over the old Karthaus road, right behind Keating, not more than twelve miles. Luke, I firmly believe John Caines is the Pennsylvania head of those Knights of the Golden Circle. He's politically ambitious, and his work has won him the support of some Southern senators. He expects to get Parvin's seat."

Luke frowned, recalling what Mose High had said about the senatorship. In Erritt's words, he was beginning to see the shape of Caines' ambitions, and it brought him little comfort. The station master's lips made a grim straight line.

"There's only two things; war's just around the corner. If it comes, John Caines is done. He'd have the wrong friends politically. Besides, there won't be an Underground. Runaways will just need to cross the border and be safe. The other is, and I don't care a damn if it shocks you, to put a bullet through the man. And, Luke, there are men who'd be glad to do it. Up in this country, we play rough."

In spite of himself, Luke's mind flashed to Rush Geen and the occasional savagery he showed.

Erritt's hand dropped on his friend's shoulder. "Don't worry too much about Hester Haliday. She can't do much. I keep thinking about what her family went through. It soured the girl on the whole Underground business. Maybe she had other reasons."

He mused a moment, and Luke thought of her remark about black men who probably had come to the farm.

"Minor Brookland's just like you and Rush, Luke. He's loved that girl for years, and he's a wonderful man. If she married him, it would save her."

* * *

Later, Luke went uptown to get information about the owner of the mill he had come to buy. His name was Ely. While Luke waited in a saloon for a word with the busy bartender, a sudden fight broke out that developed into a free-for-all. Luke tried to edge out of it and had nearly reached the door when someone threw a heavy chair. It caught his head, and he went down, knowing nothing until he woke in a bed at Hillside. Erritt explained to the groggy patient that Rush Geen had pulled him out of the melee that had all but wrecked the place.

"Doc Hentz says there's no concussion, but he has your stomach plastered where somebody kicked you. You don't know it, but you been out close to two days now. You're a hellion to get into trouble. Rush Geen wants to see you in the morning."

Geen turned up close to nine o'clock, and Luke was so much better, he had shaved and dressed. The horseman produced a paper. "There's your bill of sale from Ely for the mill and the old man's receipt. You owe me a hundred dollars. I beat him down twenty-five."

He stopped Luke's thanks. "I was looking out for myself. You pay me a hundred twenty-five, and I'll set that mill down at your job. I'll go down the old road from the Dyer farm with it. My teams need work. Is it agreeable?"

Delighted, Luke counted out his money, which Geen thrust carelessly into his pants pocket.

He grinned. "I was pretty sure of things. Two teams went up to the Dyer place this morning." He sobered, came over to the bed on which Luke sat, and leaned against the wall. "You might as well know this. I knew somebody had to move fast and so I did it while you were out. After Ely had his money and I had his receipt, he got a second offer of a hundred fifty dollars for his machinery, and he was wild; tore into me like all get out. So I told him off. The sooner that mill's down the Pike, the better."

Luke nodded in approval. His head still ached, but getting the mill made him feel better. He asked idly, "Wonder who wanted that mill?"

The horseman's voice was cold with his answer. "Hester Haliday!"

Neither man commented, but when Geen was about to leave, Luke stood and looked at him. "Rush, I'm beginning to wonder what the hell I'd do without you."

His friend chuckled deep in his throat. "Don't know how you get along downriver, Hanley, but here in Potter County, you sure need helping."

CHAPTER SEVENTEEN

LUKE WAS still sore and stiff when, after three days, he got down to the Brookland camp. Then, in company with Tom Short, Pritchett, and Clyde Brown, he went down on Rattlesnake Run, where Rush Geen's teams had placed the mill machinery. In three days of commuting from the Brookland camp to the new site, the four men had thrown up a small cabin and cleared the spot where the mill would stand. Pritchett checked everything and came up with a statement.

"That's a pretty tricky outfit to set up. Tom and I talked a lot while you were gone, and we just don't have a damn bit of know-how for such a job. Let's go down and get that old devil of an Algerine, Mose High. He knows how such mills tick."

Pritchett, with Luke's approval, undertook the errand and returned with High's promise to report the following morning.

"He was just doing some serious drinking when I got there, and he was out on his chair, sitting on the landing. He'd take a big drink, then a shot at driftwood as it went by. I'd sure hate to be a duck if that old devil had his gun loaded. He told me to come back and tell you this was his busy day."

High kept his word, reporting with his two boys in tow, together with an extremely dirty, shifty-eyed man whom he made no effort to introduce.

"Hanley," he said gruffly, "I want ten dollars, a quart of good likker, and you folks to keep out of the road." He squinted at the site and a few timbers already cut. "Gimme two days. You fellers might get to cutting timber. This mill must be turning out sawdust by then, or we'll pitch her into the river."

On the morning of the third day, feeling pretty doubtful, Luke, accompanied by Tom Short and Clyde Brown, walked down to the mill site. Luke's pocket was heavy with ten silver dollars, and Tom carefully carried the small jug of whiskey. To their delight, smoke was lifting from the stack of the upright boiler. High and Eddie were the only people in sight. There was a small log on the carriage, and when the riverman saw his employer approaching, he signaled to the boy who sent the carriage carrying the log against the rapidly moving upright saw. A second trip and the first pitch pine plank dropped on the rolls. High waved his hand, and Eddie shut off the engine.

Luke gravely counted the ten bright dollars into a dirty palm, and Tom proffered the jug. Both were taken without thanks, and High gestured to the mill. "Used to run that old coffee grinder for Ely when he was cutting wild cherry. It's a pity to waste a good mill like that on pitch pine."

The weeks dragged along, with Luke and Clyde cutting and getting timber down to the mill, using one of the Brookland horses for the skidding.

One evening, Luke talked with Ben Royal. "I'm going to get High to saw for me. I'll work off weeks here for Brookland and use my pay for High."

Royal grinned. "You're getting to be a lumberman, my friend, robbing Peter to pay Paul and trading sawdust for elbow grease."

High proved amazingly cooperative, even about the financial setup. "We won't fall out about money. A dollar an' a half will be the pay, fifty cents for Eddie, the dollar fer me. If you're short of money, I could even lend you some."

He imperiously took a cigar box from the mantel. It was full of banknotes, silver, and some gold. "Always made a little money and always saved some of it. There ain't much chance to spend much around these parts. There's damn near enough there in that box for John Caines to buy Parvin's seat." He replaced the box and became confidential. "Now's your chance to stop foolin' with these black folk that slip up this way nights. Let that job to Fred over at Keating. You run your lumber and get yourself a stake of money. That stuff talks when the time comes."

Luke had been warned so often that it was an old story, and High appeared to read his thoughts. "I know, young feller. Likely you've been warned too much. Jest now, there ain't much movin'. The time you figger there ain't any snakes about is when you git nailed."

* * *

Clyde Brown was a good woodsman but a silent man. He and Luke worked side by side with axes and the big saw, and the cut timber was piling up. The woods, under the hot August sun, was studded with pitch pine tops. Luke never did like this month. It reminded him too often of his experience in Crossville. Clyde, however, seemed to enjoy the heat and grew more cheerful day by day. Luke wondered at that, for the man had seemed dour while in the Brookland camp, walking off in the woods after working hours, a custom he still continued, although mornings found him cheerful.

A mile below Rattlesnake Run was a small abandoned farm. The little house was in good condition but usually vacant. Luke had passed it often as he went down to Baker's Bend. He had seldom looked at it, however, since it was all but hidden by trees that shut it off from the road. On his last visit with High, when he was passing, he thought for a moment that he had seen the flutter of a woman's dress, as if someone had run round the house to be out of sight. However, his mind was on the mill and he did not investigate. Two weeks later, he had cause to remember.

Brown was a free man. He had been born in Point Haven and was proud of his status. In spite of the talk about kidnapping black folks, he had gone in and out of Pine Bend as he wished, which was probably Brookland's reason for being worried about him. On this particular day, which was Saturday, with no work in the afternoon, he had been in town. Luke had gone over to the Brookland camp and returned more or less unexpectedly. Clyde, wearing his best shirt and pants, sat at the rough little table, turning something over in a big hand. As Luke walked in, he stuffed what he had into his pants pocket, but there had been time to see it was a small, cheap breastpin such as Race's Hardware in Pine Bend sold.

Luke said nothing, and the two men prepared their supper together. When it was finished and the dishes washed carefully, Luke filled his pipe. Clyde, who did not smoke, left the shack as he did so often, ostensibly for his walk in the woods. At the edge of the chopping, he turned westward as Luke saw by peering through the little window.

". . . the time you figger there ain't any snakes . . . ," High had said.

Clyde Brown was a steady man and a good one, but he was young. The thought of High made Luke remember the lonely little house and the flutter of a dress.

He waited for full darkness and went down the road, feeling foolish. Clyde had gone out like this night after night since he had known him. The man was a confirmed night prowler. The place was nearer than he thought. When he came in sight, he stopped dead. There was a light in the back of the house.

Luke moved cautiously through the trees and across the rough mat of tall grass until he could look through the window from which the light came. The little room was crudely furnished. There was a small fireplace for cooking, a table, two chairs, and a straw pallet covered with a rumpled quilt. Clyde Brown sat on one of the chairs, and when the half-dressed girl on his lap turned, Luke recognized Claudy. She held the breastpin in her fingers. Her free arm was about the big man's neck, and she was kissing him warmly.

Luke stepped away from the window and heard the light tinkle of the girl's laughter as he moved off. He remembered too well Hester's cold smile that day up at Lymansville and her hatred for black men. Before he could make up his mind about what to do, if anything, he was walking down the road. Downriver on the far side, he saw the twinkle of light in High's house. The old man would have an idea and advice.

He made the two miles at his best pace, turned off the road, and came down to the tiny plank wharf directly across the old riverman's home. Luke was about to whistle and had lifted both hands to cup the sound when he saw the batteau moored just below him, and a warning hiss came from the brush. In a moment, he was joined by Mose and Eddie. Both carried guns.

High spoke softly. "Something hes been up at the old Tuler place lately. Mebbe you found out tonight. Your man, Brown, hes been layin' up there with a woman. Tonight, there's four horses and two men down the road a piece. Hell's to pay. Hev you got any pitch hot?"

With High leading, the three moved up the road. After a mile, Eddie caught Luke's sleeve. They all stopped and heard the sound of horses coming slowly after them.

"When you think there ain't any snakes—"

"Yes," Luke whispered. "You're right, Mose."

When they reached the Tuler place, Luke again looked through the window. Clyde was sprawled on the pallet. A half-empty whiskey bottle stood on the table. Claudy was looking down at the sleeping man. She picked up a dress that hung over a chair and slipped it on. After she had watched Clyde another minute or so, she crossed to the table and took a long drink from the bottle. Then she tiptoed to the back door, opened it carefully, and came out. She paused, probably listening for the sound they all heard—the soft tramp of shod hoofs coming close on the road. Claudy stood for a full moment, a dim shape in the semidarkness, then whistled a soft whip-poor-will's call,

Luke and his companions pressed their backs against the house. There was light enough to see the shapes of two riders and four horses come into what used to be the yard of the place. The men swung down, and one spoke in a loud whisper to the girl.

"Hold the horses, Claudy. We'll go in and get him."

He and his companion moved quickly toward the back door. In the next instant, Mose and his son knocked them senseless with gun barrels. Claudy screamed. There was a surprised yelp from the house, the door jerked open, and the half-dressed Clyde stood there.

"Git!" High yelled and fired his gun.

Clyde took off up the road, his large feet making little splattering noises in the sand as he ran. Claudy dropped the reins she held and started after the runner, but Eddie caught her arm, whirled her about, and slammed her hard against the house.

High came close to Luke. "Keep out of sight," he whispered. "We'll manage."

Father and son worked in the dim light as though they had rehearsed the business. They jerked the gear off the horses one by one and sent them galloping down the road with blows of a whip that one of the men had dropped. Then High jerked Claudy forward. With a savage move, he ripped her dress and swung the whip one stroke across her bare shoulders.

"Now run, you damned trollop! If I ketch you on this river agin, I'll cut yer hide off. Run!"

She let loose the scream she must have fought back at the cut of the whip and obeyed, running like a deer into the darkness.

"Sure can give tongue," High said callously. "Let's git these men going."

With gun muzzles pressed to their victims' stomachs, the two river-men forced the groaning riders to their feet and lined them up against the house. There they compelled them to strip off their coats, pants, and shoes. High shifted his gun, picked up the whip he had dropped, and cracked it.

"Git!" he commanded again and swung his lash at the bare legs of one man, who plunged away in a clumsy run. His companion followed so fast the old riverman missed his stroke at him.

"Work fast, boys," Mose commanded. "We'll burn most of it in the fireplace."

They lugged the clothing and three saddles—one horse had been barebacked—into the candlelit room. Eddie piled the straw of the pallet into the fireplace, pitched the men's clothes on top, and touched the candle to the inflammable bedding. Mose had his knife out, slashing the saddles into useless pieces of mutilated leather. They did not take the time to search the house.

"We better git," Mose declared. "Them slave ketchers might be back fer their stuff. Whut did you do with their pistols?"

"I got 'em, Pop," the boy replied, and the three went outside after pitching the candle into the blazing fireplace.

Luke spent the night with his friends. Before he went to bed, Mose got on his snake theme again.

"Thet over there is what I meant about snakes. Me and my boys keep watchin'. If they didn't, I'd whale hell out of them till they did."

The little shack was empty when Luke got there in the morning. Clyde Brown's few belongings were gone. He had been paid at noon,

Saturday, so there was nothing to bring him back. A month later, Luke learned from Fred that he had come to Keating, remained for a few days, and then went on up to New York State.

Luke had all of a long quiet Sunday to think about the occurrence. It sickened him that Hester might have been involved in the affair. On the other hand, Claudy girl might have been working on her own. She was entirely capable of it. There was no telling how Clyde Brown encountered her; perhaps it was on one of his walks. But Luke was certain that someone had furnished the girl with information and that she had come to the region just to trap Clyde, who, of course, was like putty to her blandishment.

Monday morning, he walked over to the Brookland camp, where he found Ben Royal in his office. "Clyde went through here Sunday morning. Said he'd quit."

"Yes," Luke answered. "He was paid Saturday, then he walked out on me."

Ben Royal was a dependable man with whom he had shared confidences for years. Yet Luke was not going to tell what happened at the Tuler house until he had seen one or both of two men: Rush Geen and Brookland. There was still the possibility that Hester had not really been involved.

Royal looked at him a little doubtfully. "Another thing. Your lawyer, Jonathan Shaw, is in Pine Bend. He wants to see you. For a working man, you were sure hard to find yesterday."

* * *

Luke's first stop in the town was at Race's Hardware, and he had just purchased two files when a voice hailed him eagerly.

"Luke, Luke Hanley!" Shaw shouted. "I've been looking for you."

Fred Race, the proprietor, saw the two men shaking hands and came over. "Luke, Mr. Shaw has been looking for you. Take him into my office where you can talk."

They thanked him and went into the littered cubicle, where they found chairs. Shaw explained that he was handling the right of way along the river for the railroad and had come along splendidly until he had encountered John Caines, who had refused to either cede or sell the right to cross his property.

"Of course. Eminent domain could be invoked. But that means delay and viewers sympathetic to Caines." Shaw stopped, waiting for Luke to comment.

"What's his reason, Shaw? The railroad means something to all of us. There's no real loss to any of us in the narrow strip you'd use."

Shaw nodded and gestured with his hands. "Luke, there are only two types of people who'd block our buying. One of these would be those who won't sell because they hope to gain something by not doing it. The other is made up of folks who can't sell for some reason, and that's usually a bad title."

He slapped the desk lightly with his palm. "I propose to put enough pressure on your friend Caines to make him admit to which class he belongs." Abruptly the attorney seemed to change the subject. "Your father worked on this river for a man named Unger?"

"Yes, that was when I was pretty small. Mother told me he was with him for years as a woods boss."

Shaw's shoulders came forward, and he became very earnest. "Clifton Unger was a big operator in his day. John Caines bought his first tract of timber—fifty acres—from him. The tract we want to cross and where we're blocked originally belonged to Unger. Caines bought the whole business at a tax sale, but the title then no longer belonged to Clifton Unger. Records in the courthouse are in bad shape. We cannot find who the owner was who did not pay his taxes."

Luke was listening politely but with little real interest. Titles to land in the timber country were often bad and lawsuits common.

Then Shaw startled him. "The reason I mentioned your father was because Unger, himself, was an ardent Abolitionist. He was also a very wealthy man."

Luke stirred in his chair. He was sure Shaw wasn't telling the whole story, and it irked him. "There's nothing new about Caines grabbing land at tax sales. The sheriff's with him, so are the other folks in the courthouse. He tried to grab the Haliday place that way. The man's a damned buzzard, hovering over the properties of the unfortunate or unlucky."

Shaw returned to his breast pocket a small piece of paper he had been holding. There were names on it, but Luke did not see them. Now he offered some advice to Shaw.

"If you want to know something—almost anything—about this timber country, see two men. One is Mose High down at Baker's Bend. The other is Squire Jacoby over at Crossville. Jacoby was my father's closest friend."

The lawyer fidgeted but made no comment on the information. "I'll have to be moving now. Got to go on up Weston way. Don't forget we have a date to catch some trout."

Luke was in town until mid-afternoon and was about to start back to camp when a flashy buggy drawn by two dun horses passed. He looked up. Linda Caines and Nedrow were in the rig. Linda waved her hand to him, and Nedrow raised his hat as a matter of duty. Luke stood still, unpleasantly stirred at this reminder of the unsuited pair's relationship.

Tired from his long walk, he stopped at the Brookland camp. Sometime in the night, he was roused by Tom Short.

"Listen," the big man whispered. "Tammie wants you. There's a boy outside with a horse."

Luke rubbed his eyes until he was wider awake, then fumbled for his pants. If Tammie wanted him in the night like this, the matter would be important.

Luke found the boy, Caleb, who worked at Tammie's Place. He was mounted and led another saddled horse. "Tammie wants you, Mister. She said to hurry."

When they rode up, the big building was dark except for a small window in the back kitchen. Luke's light rap was answered at once by Tammie, whose opulent figure was wrapped in a loose robe, and the heavy braids of her yellow hair were wound round her head. "Quick, Luke, I'm scared."

She picked up the small lamp and led the way into a room where all shades were tightly drawn. A man lolled in a deep chair, and when Tammie raised her light, Luke saw it was Rush Geen.

"Bullet in his shoulder," she explained. "It's out, but he's weak from loss of blood."

Geen opened his eyes at the sound of voices, recognized his friend, and managed a smile. "Bad shape, Hanley. Couldn't stop . . . blood."

Tammie gave the wounded man a sip of brandy, and he revived enough to talk. "It was a deputy sheriff and Clate Baumheit. They jumped my camp. Baumheit's got a bullet in the leg somewhere. His shot got my shoulder." His face twisted, and he waited for more strength to continue. "Got two horses, bills of sale for both. The deputy has another man, and they're hot after me. Take me to Joerg's Run, Luke. Get Brendy. I can ride if you'll lead the horse."

He sat forward and showed some of his old fire. "If they catch me before I can get Brendy, it's bad. He'll get the jump on them, file for assault. Then I'm clear."

Luke grinned. "Quit talking, Rush. Pull your clothes together and let's ride."

Geen staggered as he rose and looked at Tammie.

"The horses are fed and ready," she replied to the question in his eyes. She turned to Luke. "Make him take it easy. He's pretty weak."

Luke walked back through the kitchen and outside, where Caleb had two saddled horses. Tammie followed with Geen, and the three helped him into his saddle.

She gave Luke a small bundle. "There's food here and liquor." Her face was close. "Take good care of him."

Luke brushed her forehead with his lips and mounted the second horse. "Don't worry, Tammie. I sure owe him a lot."

It was a nightmare ride back through the timbered hills. Again and again, Luke was completely lost, but Geen, wounded as he was, kept telling him which way to go. Once, when he seemed pretty weak, Luke helped him from the saddle. They ate a little of the food Tammie had sent, and Geen drank some whiskey, gagging.

"Never liked the stuff," he said weakly.

Morning showed gray in the east when they turned westward along a brawling creek and entered a small, natural meadow where a tiny log cabin stood with a pole corral behind it.

"Made it," Geen said grimly as Luke helped him from the saddle.

The cabin was fitted with pole bunks and a stove. It was getting lighter by the minute, and Luke supported the injured man to the bunk, where he wrapped him in a blanket. After a fire was going in the stove to take away the morning chill, it was quite comfortable. Geen ate some of Tammie's food but refused the whiskey. Luke went out and unsaddled and fed the horses from a bag of grain in the cabin Geen managed to point out. The horseman, propped up against a saddle, now talked freely.

"The trail to the left leads to the Pike. Three miles up and again left, you'll find a farmhouse and George Brendy." He managed to pull some papers from his coat pocket and extend them. "Give these to George. They're bills of sale for the horses. I'll be all right here, but bring him back."

When Luke left the cabin a half hour later, Geen was sitting up. He had insisted that his revolver be placed alongside him on the bunk.

"Case a bear comes," he said. "Make George hustle. Sometimes he's slow."

Luke had no trouble finding the Pike. After a half-hour's riding on that, he found the road turning left that led him to a good-sized farm and comfortable-looking buildings. Brendy appeared as he rode up and dismounted. He listened to what had happened to Geen without showing much emotion and put the bills of sale into his pocket.

"We'll go to Rush soon as we and the horses have eaten a bite."

In half an hour, they had finished a substantial lunch washed down with coffee Brendy said had been made from parched wheat.

"I like it," he said over his second cup. "It's nourishing and don't keep you awake."

They rode back at what seemed to Luke a slow pace, and found Geen again flat on his back. Brendy turned smartly efficient, examining the wound and then cleaning it thoroughly before he rebandaged it.

"Tammie ought to be a doctor, Rush. She's got that wound in good shape. Loss of blood makes you weak."

Thinking the pair might want to talk, Luke went out and curried the two horses after he unsaddled them. Both were good animals of the type called "carriage horses." When he reentered the cabin, Geen, with his arm in a sling, sat on the edge of the bunk.

"Guess we'll have to send you back. That deputy down there might check and find you away. All I need now is more time." He cleared his throat and gestured toward Brendy. "George thinks he knows something about our mutual friend, Caines. One of his men tipped off the deputy and Baumheit that I was camped down there. George will talk to Shaw, who's after that right of way."

Luke frowned, understanding the young horseman and his eagerness to settle obligations. "Don't be in such a hurry to settle accounts, Rush. I've had a nice ride and learned some new country and how much guts a man can have."

They gripped hands, and Luke went out with Brendy. As soon as they resaddled, the one-time lawyer led the way along the trail.

This time they rode hard, and Luke was put to it to follow his leader. When he figured they were less than a mile from the Brookland camp, he pulled up and called to Brendy, who turned his mount and rode back.

"Get down, Brendy. I want to talk a little."

Both horses were warm. The men dismounted and tied the animals. Then they seated themselves on rocks so they faced each other.

"I wanted to talk this over with Rush but doubted if he was able. Now I'll do it with you. Perhaps you'll know what should be done."

Speaking rapidly, Luke told of Hester's bitterness against black men without hinting at the experience on the farm that she had partly revealed to him. He told how he had seen Claudy at the Prentis Hotel and then of the Clyde Brown episode.

"It's making her hard, Brendy. She's changed a great deal since I worked on her father's place. Do you see anything that can be done?"

Brendy stroked his sparse beard for a moment. There was frankness in his faded eyes as he looked into Luke's. "Actually, I never liked the girl. She hurt Rush badly a few years back. Yes, I believe the girl had something to do with turning in runaways. I'm sure that Claudy has, but, of course, you know that." He rose. "I'll have to get back to Rush. In a day or so I'll talk to him. If anybody can keep her from mixing in this filthy business, he can."

They shook hands and parted there since it would not be wise to ride into the camp in case there were observing visitors about.

By early October, Luke was well pleased with his pitch pine venture. Logs had been cut, skidded into the mill, and sawed into two-inch-thick planks. Long, low piles stretched out along the little mill tram road over which they had been taken from the saw. Drying was important, reducing the weight of this heavy lumber, and the long dry weeks had been excellent curing weather. It also was fast making the woods a tinder box with each wilted pitch pine top a potential torch.

Since Clyde Brown had taken his unceremonious departure, different men from the Brookland camp had helped Luke; Pritchett, Tom Short, or someone else. Today, Luke was not doing much and was alone. He had just finished checking the amount of board feet in a pile of planks when the sound of an approaching horse and rig made him step out into the open road. It was a smart open buggy drawn by a spirited horse. To his amazement, the driver was Linda Caines.

"What a road," she cried in mock exasperation. "It's nothing but stones, big rocks, corduroys—"

"And dry mudholes," he finished for her. "Let me help you down."

Today she was wearing no hat, and the shawl scarf about her shoulders was pushed well back from the sheen of her heavy hair. Apparently, she had not heard Luke's offer but was looking at the mill and the piled lumber. Then she pointed with her whip. "If that was white pine, Luke, you'd really have wages. There'd be a market for it right up around here. By the way, I saw you in town the other day."

His face began to color with embarrassment, and she leaned forward.

"Luke, I didn't run out here to talk lumbering. There's news, dangerous news. It was telegraphed in to Point Haven and then on up the railroad to where they're working. We got it only hours past."

She stopped and took a long breath. Luke noticed she was wearing the little locket that had been on her slim throat that day in Crossville. Her steady, frank eyes lifted and met his. "Last night, Kansas John Brown captured the United States Arsenal at Harpers Ferry. Men were killed. He's leading a slave insurrection against slaveholders, and his men are heavily armed. No one knows how far the trouble will spread, but the Governor of Virginia has called out the militia, and United States Marines have gone to Harpers Ferry."

Luke's lips shaped a soundless whistle of surprise, and he seized the rim of the buggy wheel near him with his big hands.

Linda was speaking severely. "It's because you are always getting into trouble that I drove out. Everybody in Pine Bend is excited, and I don't want you to do something rash. Already some are talking of going down there to help Brown. Don't get mixed in it, Luke. Just now, you're getting on your feet as a lumberman, and folks talk well of you. Keep it that way. Don't meddle with this slavery thing now. It's too big."

He moved closer until he caught a hint of the perfume she wore. There were so many things he wanted to say to this slim girl who had done so much for him. The news she had brought was shocking, but he was thinking only of her.

"Well," she asked sharply, "don't just stand there. What are you thinking of?"

He smiled and shrugged his lean shoulders under the threadbare shirt he wore. "Just this, Linda. That I really must amount to something, or you just wouldn't go on doing things for me. If only—"

She must have read in his eyes what he wanted to tell her. Expertly, she turned her horse and rig and drove down the rough road at a smart clip. When she had gone, Luke remembered that, once again, he had failed to thank her.

CHAPTER EIGHTEEN

LUKE FOUND it impossible to return to his work. In spite of her engagement to Nedrow and the bitter hostility of her father, Linda had driven out to help him. At every turn of the bitter road through the years, she had been there, giving advice and hoping it would be taken. He had seldom followed it to the letter, but each time she came, he felt stronger, "taller," he had told her once. Now, with the memory of her perfume in his nostrils, he could not believe that someday she would be the wife of the corpulent lawyer to whom she was now promised.

He walked about the place, trying to get settled. An axe stood beside a log near the shack. The handle felt good in his hands, and when he had chopped through the log in two places, he was steadier and able to consider what he had been told.

To have news telegraphed back into the woods like this was an event in itself to cause excitement. This same thing must have been done all over the North and would be hailed everywhere with mixed emotions.

John Brown was a dangerous figure who had become nationally important through his savage fight against slavery on the plains of Kansas, but Harpers Ferry was just a dot on the map of northern Virginia. Luke, and probably a majority of other people, had not known there was a government arsenal there. Brown had probably gone about what he assumed to be his business with the cold efficiency he had used in the west when only the presence of the newly elected Governor Geary, who was a Pennsylvanian, had brought about a troubled truce between the warring factions.

Luke put away his scaling rule and the axe he had used. When he had checked the mill to see that the fire under the boiler was safely extinguished, he went over to the Brookland camp and, to his surprise, found it deserted, even by the cook. Horses munched grain from their feed boxes, wagons were in their places, and tools were neatly stacked, but the men had gone. The dining room tables showed that a hasty lunch had been eaten. Luke helped himself to what cold food he could find and went on up toward Pine Bend.

Tammie's Place was locked, an unusual occurrence. She was usually about somewhere. Still, he was unprepared for the fever of excitement and the commotion he encountered when he reached the little town. Horses were tied at every hitching post and rail, and the streets were thronged with noisy men, anxious women, and whooping children. Little groups gathered about the two hotels. It did not seem possible that this forested country could turn out so many people. Luke had the feeling that every living person west of the county seat was here on the streets of Pine Bend.

He pushed through the crowd in front of the Race store and carefully read the placard pasted on the window:

John Brown of Kansas starts to free slaves. Captures government arsenal at Harpers Ferry, Virginia. Militia and Marines called out to suppress him. Hurrah for John Brown!

Someone had deluged the last few words with tobacco juice to express his lack of sympathy with the tone of the notice. As Luke walked on, he saw further evidence of mixed feelings. Half a dozen fights started and ended with only a few blows struck. Most of the crowd veered toward the Hoffman House, where a big man stood on a barrel, haranguing. It was Tom Short, and he had been drinking.

"Walk up!" he yelled. "Walk up, you mossy-footed knot-bumpers. Walk up and enlist. This here company's going down to help Old John Brown give them slave drivers hell. Come one, come all!"

Someone upset Tom's barrel, and he fell. Immediately, there was a free-for-all. Luke had pushed forward and grabbed Tom by the shoulder to yank him out of the melee he had created when a drum across the street sounded, and everybody stopped milling about to see what was happening.

Out of the town hall, a small frame building, came a squad of men led by John Caines. There was no mistaking the neatly dressed figure nor the calm assurance of his walk. With his companions clearing the way, he reached the place where Tom Short's barrel had collapsed and held up his hand.

"Neighbors, there's no need to start a war up here among ourselves. Quiet down and let the government manage things. Fighting here won't help or hinder John Brown. From the news, the man is in arms against your government and mine."

He stopped to give emphasis to his final words. "Any man from my jobs caught fighting here today will come to my office for his time."

There were several derisive catcalls, then a burst of hand-clapping as Caines walked down the steps and across the street to his office. Luke watched the crowd, grudging the skill with which Caines handled these people. Two-thirds of the men worked on the man's operations or depended on the business he created for a livelihood. With times bad, the man who lost his job was in a sorry way.

On his way out of town, Luke encountered Tammie, who readily agreed to have her boy, Caleb, drive him down to Point Haven.

"Likely you want to meddle," she said sarcastically. "It could be that the United States government might manage it without you, Luke."

He did not care for her sarcasm. Somehow, he had built up within himself a shell of resistance to being warned. The only real opening to this was held by Linda Caines.

Brookland had guests when Luke reached the beautiful home beyond King's Shore. Erritt was there from Lymansville. There were two men from Williamsport: a Mr. Seiger and Jared Jones, both interested in the Underground. One of the Jenkins cousins was down in King's Shore, on the lookout for further news that might come in by telegraph. Brookland and his guests assembled in the living room, and he talked first.

"This is the second day, gentlemen, and the country is terribly wrought up. I never knew news to spread so fast. Last word was that Brown's holed up in the firehouse of the arsenal. That's a brick building. He had nineteen men. The Virginia militia is there and the United States Marines under Robert E. Lee and Colonel 'Jeb' Stuart. The end is only a matter of time. No one could hope to hold out against the government. I think Brown wanted to get the arms from the arsenal but got trapped somehow. Now let's all listen to Mr. Seiger; he's just returned from down there."

Seiger was a thin man with a thoughtful, clean-shaven face who reminded Luke a bit of Jim Haliday. He spoke slowly and carefully.

"As you all know, I guess, I was down in that country. Just got back this afternoon and hurried up here. I went down to see Brown, who I thought had some runaway slaves for me to bring up. When I visited him, it was on a little farm just inside the Pennsylvania line. He gave his name down there as I. Smith."

Luke started, remembering the visitor at the Dyer farm.

"He said he had nineteen men, which included his two sons, that he hadn't any runaways but he was about to make a stroke that would wake up the nation on this slavery business. Six of his men were out scouting the country, but he could accomplish what he wanted with the rest. Now that I was there, he wanted me to go along with him down to Harpers Ferry to look around.

"It wasn't much over a ten-mile drive, and nobody paid much attention to us. Of course, Brown wears a heavy beard, but lots of men do. Once in the town, he excused himself and was gone over an hour before he returned to our rig.

"Remember, men—it's a hilly place. Two rivers meet there, the Potomac and the Shenandoah. The B. & O. railroad goes up through the break in the mountains where an old canal used to be, and another rail line goes on to Winchester. So the place is a crossroads of rivers, roads, and rails.

"On the way back, Brown talked, and I tried to argue him out of his plan, but it was like talking to a wall. Like Mr. Brookland told you, he wanted to raid the arsenal for guns and ammunition to arm a force of white and black folks. Frankly, gentlemen, I was scared and didn't know what to do. Likely my duty was to report to the authorities, but by the time I went through Harrisburg, the blow had been struck, men had been killed, and Brown cornered."

Brookland cleared his throat when Seiger finished. "John Brown's a fanatic, has been for years, and believes that force alone will liberate the slaves. He ran an Underground station on the Delaware River at the village of Richmond before any of us did anything for runaways. Granted that the whole business looks like lunacy, still, Brown, by this move, will bring the whole issue squarely before the American people."

Erritt spoke with the assurance of an old friend. "There's talk buzzing round about organizing companies to go down and rescue Brown, but that's poppycock. Likely by now they've hanged him on the nearest sycamore."

He slapped the table with a broad palm for emphasis. "But that bloody-minded old devil has lighted a fire to bum till this slave issue is settled on a national basis. Remember what that prairie lawyer said not long ago: 'A house divided against itself cannot stand.' That man's a leader capable of making clear the issue Brown may have bungled."

"Lincoln," the silent Mr. Jones said, half musing. "Lincoln is only one man. Can he ride the whirlwind and harness it to his will?" He got up and walked to a window, where he stood listening while Brookland talked again.

"There's one thing, men, that likely brings us together. We know some of Brown's raiders may get away. We know a few of them, including Owen, his son, have been in our area often. He was your visitor on the Dyer farm, Luke. We know some of the hardened fighting men who were with Brown: Hazlitt, Stevens, and Cook. It isn't likely they'll trap them all. So, if any get clear, they'll come north and need help. They'll look to us to get them to Canada."

Three of them nodded, and Luke said nothing for a moment. He was stirred by the odd feeling that Linda Caines had anticipated something just like this and had been trying to warn him against becoming involved. It might be that she had heard her father's opinion. In that case, Caines would be alerted and only too ready to capture such a fugitive. He thought of Smith, his advice, and his prayer at the table. Abruptly Luke spoke, knowing in that instant, with a thin, sick feeling inside him, that he was shutting the doors to the advice given him and burning any bridges over which he might turn back.

"We'll have to get word round fast about what we expect. Let's get some messengers. I wish we could watch—"

"John Caines," Seiger finished for him and then continued. "I have some money, five hundred dollars, from the Philadelphia Abolition people. We'll use that for expenses so our men can afford to stop their regular work to watch. First, we'll advise our station men. Next, in case any of the fugitives are located, messengers will spread the word 'no news.' That will mean the opposite and warn every man to be alert."

There was general agreement, and Brookland broke the tension by asking his guests to walk about the place while they waited for further word. Luke found himself with Erritt, striding toward the big barn.

"Friend," Erritt said, "we could be thinking the same thing. Will Brookland trust the wrong person?"

Luke frowned. He had not thought of it until now. "You mean Hester Haliday?"

The station keeper nodded soberly. "I told you he was in love with the girl and might confide in her. If one of those men gets away, there will be big rewards, thousands, not hundreds of dollars."

For a moment, Luke wanted to tell the story of Clyde Brown and Claudy, but he said nothing, and his friend looked at him queerly.

Ad Jenkins came in later with electrifying news. Brown had surrendered when a field piece was used against the firehouse doors. One of the old zealot's sons and five others of the small band were dead. Reports had it that six men had escaped and that Virginia was officially offering a reward of a thousand dollars each for their capture. Marines under Stuart had reduced Brown's stronghold.

"Six men," Brookland commented grimly. "Let's get back to our places fast. I'll use the Jenkins boys as my messengers. Luke, get back to Hyner Run. Trust Ben Royal all the way."

When the others were gone, Brookland talked privately with Luke. "If one of Brown's men came our way, likely it would be Owen, whom you knew as Smith. That is if he escaped. He knows the Pike country and would work his way up to Lymansville. I don't want him there even a few hours. Our camp on the river is too public. You, with Pritchett or Tom Short, move back into the woods to the shack at Power's Fork. That's spar country, and your action will seem natural to any casual observer. I'll take care of hauling some of your planks to the railroad so you won't lose time or money."

Luke was ready to start when his friend stopped him in the hallway.

"Listen, friend. I have to say this. We've been together a good while and pretty close in many ways. In a day or so, if it is possible, I'm going to do something that may hurt you, something that I have postponed a long while because I did not want to get in the way of a younger man. Now it's the only safe thing to do even if it breaks our friendship."

Luke studied the sharp lines about the mouth of the tall man. Whatever Minor Brookland was or would be, he was sincere, entirely so. Luke went out puzzled, and there was no further word between them.

He returned to Point Haven by train but remained in that town long enough to get more news. When it came, it confirmed Brookland's report. Six men had escaped the trap in Virginia. Two had already been captured, but those at large were John Cook, Albert Hazlitt, Aaron Stevens, and Owen Brown. The reward offered was for the capture of the men, not their death. Virginia wanted to try them publicly.

Luke and his two friends moved back into the little camp, taking with them, at Royal's suggestion, a light team and wagon loaded with supplies for a long stay. Once they had made the cabin habitable, the three friends started to cut spars. Each day, however, one of them rode down to the camp for news.

Ten days passed, and then two weeks. Luke was thinking of his talk with Linda and hoping none of the men came this way.

But there was in him a strong dread he could not explain. It was as though, after years, matters were coming to a real head. Helping any of these fugitives was not like taking some refugee to safety. This would be a serious offense against the United States government, and Luke remembered the uniform he had once worn.

* * *

On the fifteenth day, a boy was waiting at the main camp. Luke had taken his turn as a news carrier this evening. When he had assured the messenger that he was Luke Hanley, the boy spoke frankly.

"Sir, Mr. Erritt said I should say 'no news' about the Dyer farm."

Luke studied the nervous messenger, then took out a silver dollar and gave it to him. The boy grinned, mounted his horse expertly, and left at a fast trot. Likely, he would ride most of the night through dark woodland roads.

Luke did not enter the camp. The fact that the fugitive had reached Erritt indicated that the man must have tried to get to Lymansville, and Brookland had been afraid of that. Returning to the camp at Power's Fork, he told his friends of the message and said that he would go to the Dyer farm in the morning.

The bay gelding made good time. When Luke rode into the neglected field where so many things had happened to him, the house looked deserted, but there were two saddled horses eating in the barn. He tied up his own mount and was walking toward the house when Erritt appeared.

"Our friend is in the brush," he said. "Come on inside. It's Owen Brown, all right. He's mighty nervous, close to a wreck, and that bothers me."

They entered the house with Erritt still talking. "Mr. Brookland brought the man up himself. We understand United States Marshals are patrolling the New York State border. All railroads are being watched. So we'll have to hide him in the hills instead of taking him on his way."

Luke felt a certain dismay. Brookland had taken the fugitive exactly where he dreaded. He looked sharply at the station keeper, who waved a pudgy hand, understanding the unasked question.

"Yes, we figured she would find out, but Brookland took her out of circulation. She's on her way down country with him."

Luke continued to stare, his pulses drumming as he remembered Brookland's apologetic words.

His friend went on. "She's Missus Minor Brookland now. She was married to him two days past, and she'll be too busy settling down in the big house to bother about other things."

"Married?" Luke said.

"Well," the other continued, "she was single, so was he, and our friend's a mighty good catch for a girl that wants to get ahead in the world."

Confused at what he had just heard, Luke scarcely noticed the entrance of the man he had known as Smith. He turned at the sound of his voice. The mustache was gone, the heavy eyebrows were clipped close, and the thin face was even thinner, almost emaciated.

"Hello, Luke," he said, extending his hand.

Luke murmured a few words of sympathy about the father, and the son frowned.

"Yes, they took him as might have been expected. Likely he'll hang. I'm thankful my brother was shot fighting. Six of us were on patrol and escaped."

He seated himself wearily at the table and half apologized for his presence. "It didn't seem wise to cross into New York State just now. I thought of holing up for the winter with our friend, Fred."

Luke tried to reassure the man and to make him welcome, but the news he had received made it hard for him to be natural. "We'd better get to our camp. This place can be pretty public, as I've learned."

Erritt, behind Brown's shoulder, nodded, and Luke caught the gesture.

Out at the barn, Luke untied his horse. "You get aboard, Brown. I'd rather hoof it."

They had barely reached the cover of the woods when three horsemen clattered down the lane from the Pike, and even at this distance, Luke was sure the stout leader was Marshal Bay. He swore irritably, and Brown slipped from the saddle, tossing him the reins. With an incredibly swift movement, he drew a huge revolver from under his coat. Luke could not help but note that all friendliness and weariness were erased from the hunted man's face. It had become cold and patiently watchful. There was no doubt what he would do if he felt cornered. Luke thought of Linda's advice, which he had ignored. If Brown killed or wounded an officer, it meant the men helping him were guilty of the same crime, and these hills would no longer be a refuge for any of them.

Erritt appeared at the cabin door as his visitors rode up and dismounted. It was, of course, too far to distinguish what they were saying.

"Two saddled horses in the barn," Brown said. "The fat's in the fire if them men know their business." He drew a second revolver, and his sternness relaxed a little. "Go on, friend. Hide in the timber. No need for them to see you."

Luke didn't move, and the fugitive actually smiled. "Don't worry. Three men can't take me."

The steady way his strong hands held his weapons supported this wild statement. The brass caps of the revolver nipples shone wickedly.

At the buildings, Erritt was walking toward the barn with the officers, gesticulating toward the stout marshal. The two men entered the barn and came out in a minute or so, leading two horses. Only the one wore a saddle. After a five-minute interval, the officers rode away, Erritt following them at a leisurely pace.

Luke smiled at Brown. "How did he hide that other saddle? It was on the horse when I rode up. Erritt's smart, but how did he do it?"

Brown did not comment. In fact, he talked little on the way to the cabin at Power's Fork. Pritchett and Short greeted him in friendly fashion and grinned when he insisted on being called Smith.

The weather was getting colder, and Pritchett had to get back to his forge to point horseshoes for the teams that would be working on iced roads before long. Brown worked steadily with Luke and Tom. His only unusual act was to keep close to his coat with a revolver in it. In the evenings, he talked freely about almost everything except the raid on Harpers Ferry.

Two weeks passed with either Tom or Luke going down for news every day or so. There was plenty of it. John Brown had been tried for treason against the United States and was sentenced to hang on the second of December, in Charlestown, Virginia. The son took the word stoically, but when the rabid Governor Wise of Virginia wrote President Buchanan that there was a plot in Pennsylvania to rescue the old warrior, Owen laughed derisively.

"Wise is haywire. God knows we had no outside help beyond some money given to my father. They won't rest till they've hanged us all. Less than a score of men, some armed only with pikes, have scared the entire slave-loving South."

Newspapers carried glaring headlines in accounts of the excitement in the North, which did not subside until a committee headed by the man who had framed the Fugitive Slave Law reported there was no conspiracy in the North, nor had there been one. In the Deep South, newspapers and leaders talked of seceding from a Union which could not protect their property.

On the morning of the third week, Tom Short got Luke aside. "Somebody's hanging around this camp. Last night, that Barney horse was restless till I slipped out and quieted her."

"Maybe it was a bear prowling," Luke suggested.

"It could be, though it's late for them to be out. I'd damn well rather it was. This thing's getting on my nerves, them pistols and all. He sleeps with 'em."

"It is on mine, too, Tom. Let's watch, turn and turn about."

They tried being sentries for a few nights, and Luke thought he heard a horse somewhere north of them but was not sure. Losing sleep was hard on men who worked during the day, and finally, Luke proposed a solution.

"We've watched over Brown a good while. Go down and tell Ben Royal to send for Fred. We'll put our man over at Keating for a while."

Fred arrived the evening of December first. It was cold with a light snow blowing. He was genuinely glad to see Owen Brown and carefully addressed him as "Mister Smith."

"You come and visit with us a spell, Mister Smith. Them folks won't come where we is."

Brown thanked the man gravely, but it was plain he was nervous and with reason; his father was to be executed the next day.

"I'll go with you tomorrow evening, Fred. Let's stay here that day and not travel."

They worked during the morning but came in a short time before noon. Luke cooked the meal, and the food was on the table. Short and Brown were walking toward the benches and Fred was following when he stopped and stood as though he were listening. Brown, next to him, held the same attitude. In a minute, he placed a hand on the black man's shoulder and asked a question in a low voice.

"You felt it, too, son? It's all over now."

Fred brushed tears from his eyes with the heel of his hand, and Owen Brown quoted from the Bible that he knew so well. "*The Lord giveth and the Lord taketh away. Blessed be the name of the Lord.*"

His voice nearly broke. After supper, when they were in the shed feeding the horse, Tom asked a question. "Did them fellers really hear something?"

Luke lifted the lantern and adjusted the wick a trifle. "I wouldn't know, Tom, but they say a dog howls when his master dies, and the papers said John Brown was to hang at noon."

Fred and his charge left in the evening to the relief of the two lumbermen who planned to stay in camp a few days longer to finish some spars. The night after the fugitive had departed, Luke and Tom were routed from their first sleep by a heavy rapping at the door. Luke slid off his bunk, turned up the lantern wick, which was kept alight, and glanced at Tom, who had placed two big bare feet on the floor and was reaching for a double-bitted axe. Luke opened the door.

Three men were just outside in the circle of light shed by the lantern. One was Deputy Marshal Bay.

"I've a warrant to search these premises."

Anger came up in Luke's throat like a taste. He turned to his companion. "Never mind the axe, Tom. It's that damned pot-bellied marshal."

Bay pushed into the room, followed by his men, and he was scowling. "Hold your tongue, Hanley, or I'll have your mouth shut for you."

Luke faced him, his big hands knotted. "Bay, this is the third time you've bothered me. If you lay your hand on me, I'll wipe this floor with your fat face. Hell, you've seen the whole place. There's only one room, and the roof leaks. Get out and poke around the barn. The horse won't mind the smell of you. Tom, hand me that axe."

Short passed over the tool, concern on his heavy face.

Luke balanced the axe in one hand. "Now get out. Run back to John Caines, and tell him not to send the pups when the old dog's afraid."

The marshal looked at the axe and into the raging face not six inches from his own. Followed quickly by his men, he went out, with the lantern light glinting on his gold watch chain when he turned at the door.

After everything was quiet again, Tom asked his friend, "Would you have used that axe?"

Luke sat on a bench with his big hands between his bony knees. The axe was over beside the stove. His voice was thick when he answered. "I don't know, Tom. But every time I see him, there is sheer, rank murder in me. Every piece of bad luck that has come to me found him close by."

Short spat carefully into the stove and commented, "To me, he don't look worth hanging for. If I felt like that, I guess I'd go down and raise hell with his boss. Like you said to our fat friend, that would be John Caines."

CHAPTER NINETEEN

BAY'S SURPRISE visit left Luke unnerved and irritable. The marshal had become a symbol to him of all that threatened the humble runaways in their drive for freedom and of the type of persecution that had come so close to breaking up the Haliday home. Even worse was the knowledge of the dangerous extent to which the man could arouse him. The escape of them all had been too narrow. It showed him how dangerous this game was in which he, as a marked man, played. Bay had come to the Dyer farm and now to this cabin deep in the woods.

After the few days it took Luke and Tom to finish spars, they came down to the main camp, and Luke talked with Ben Royal.

"The whole thing was just too close, Ben. Somebody has been watching and talking. It would have been bad enough for Brown and me, but I feel as if I pulled Tom close to penitentiary doors."

Royal smiled. "Tom likes trouble. If he wasn't led into it, he'd create it so he could fall in."

"Ben," Luke resumed. "I'm going down to have a talk with John Caines. Seems to me I have been dodging the man, taking too much advice about what he might do. I'm sure he sicked Bay on us."

The woods boss shrugged his heavy shoulders and spoke philosophically.

"Well, son, some has it, some hain't. Some folks like to tease bulls, others just likes their beef cooked. So far as I'm concerned, I try never to grab anything I can't hold when I get it or let go of when I have to."

The day was a dreary one, with a light dusting of snow on the rutted road and the nearby rocks. Luke did not turn in at Tammie's Place but followed the bluffs on to the little town. As he walked, he thought of the difference between Ben Royal and Tom Short. Both men were, he felt, instinctively cautious. Tom's idea when something threatened was to plunge at it and destroy its power to hurt him. Ben would go in slowly, watchfully, neglecting no advantage. Both men got results.

Caines' office was a two-room affair built against the side of the town hall, and smoke curled from its chimney as Luke mounted the caulk-marred steps and rapped sharply. At a muffled bid to come in, he entered a room where the only furniture was a row of benches about the wall. Through an open door, he saw a man working at a table.

John Caines lifted his attention from his papers to his visitor, and his face did not show emotion of any kind. As usual, he was immaculate, from the string tie of his white shirt to the polished boot tips that showed under the table. Today, he wore a brown suit.

"Ah, it's Luke Hanley, in from the pine woods, I hope."

The final two words could have meant anything, but they irritated Luke almost as much as the way Caines inspected his visitor's worn clothing. Luke refused the offer of a cigar but did take the indicated chair, facing the lumberman.

"Well, Hanley, is this a business call or just a friendly visit? I hear you are using teams to get your pitch pine to the rail head."

Luke knew his irritation placed him at a disadvantage, and he felt Caines knew it as he leaned back in his chair easily and made a tent of his fingertips.

"Hanley, Senator Parvin is resigning his seat in the state senate, and I aspire to that position. It looks as though Governor Packer should appoint me because of the friends I enjoy along this river and what I could do for this country in the way of legislation. In that post, I could even be of service to you, as a rising young lumberman. Also, I could show you, even now, a way out of some of your many predicaments."

Frowning, he picked up a pencil and tested its sharp point on the table. "You have surely had your share of misfortunes, most of which you have foolishly blamed on me. You did save me from embarrassment by entering the navy, where you should have remained. I am pleased that you are now a hard-working lumberman like the rest of us up here. If we can keep back this railroad, there will be a future in our rafting—"

Abruptly, Luke gained his feet and looked down into the suave face of the man he had come to hate. He shook his head like an angry bull. "No, I shouldn't have come here nor listened this long. You're behind every bit of deviltry in this country; log stealing, kidnapping, my own trial. Your last move was to sick that big-bellied marshal on me. There's only one question in my mind, and I propose to find the answer. I'm just an ordinary man, and I want to know what you really have against me to point so much trouble my way?"

"Right," Caines cut in. "You are just an ordinary man touched with delusions."

Luke's long body leaned forward, and he pounded the table. "You started after me in Crossville, where I heard the horses of your men run at night. You stole my pistol, tried to fasten murder on me—"

Caines' control broke, and his face slowly shaped itself into a mask of fury. Keeping his eyes on the young man before him, he reached into a partially open drawer. Luke did not see the pistol until it was lifted and a white thumb was pulling back the hammer. His quick blow caught the wrist, and the weapon dropped. With a forward lunge, Luke grabbed Caines' shoulders. The older man twisted, cursing, but was no match for the fury of his attacker. Flecks of spittle stood in the corners of his mouth as he was shaken savagely. His collar tore open, and his coat ripped. Finally, with a terrific shove, Luke threw Caines over a chair into a corner. Seeing the pistol on the floor, he snatched it up and hurled it through a window, some of the broken glass falling on the prostrate Caines.

"Damn you, John Caines," he gritted, "damn you to hell." Still feeling futile and unsatisfied, he went out of the office.

He had not gone half a block before he met the blacksmith, Axelroth. There was no way of telling whether he had heard the commotion back there in the office.

Luke blocked his way. "I don't like your face; get off the walk when I come along."

The smith's loose mouth ripped out a foul oath, and Luke struck him twice with all the force of his anger behind the blows. Axelroth went down but came up snarling. Heavy and powerful with great sloping shoulders, the smith was a terror in a fight, but he was no match for his opponent today. He went down twice and remained on the ground the second time, his face cut and his nose broken so that he was a gory mess. Bystanders who came up looked on with open mouths, but neither the young man walking away nor the bloody figure who scrambled up and scuttled toward Caines' office paid any attention to them.

Luke walked slowly out of town, occasionally rubbing his knuckles on the sides of his pants. He knew he had behaved as Tom Short might have done, and he had accomplished exactly nothing except venting a little physical punishment on the man he hated and on his chief henchman. He turned into Tammie's Place, where the only customer was just walking out.

Tammie came out from behind the bar and looked smilingly at him. "Come sit down. You've been fighting again. Who was it this time?"

"Your esteemed blacksmith, Tammie. Before that, I messed up John Caines a little."

"My God!" she said explosively. "You sure manage."

She stepped behind the bar, then started to pour a glass of wine but changed her mind and poured whiskey. Luke followed her to chairs that faced each other. He drained the whiskey at two gulps.

Tammie set her glass of wine on her chair arm and talked. "Most men up this way, when they want to blow off, get drunk. Likely likker is bad stuff, but I wish to high heaven you'd get yourself good and drunk instead of bustin' out like this. Axelroth's mean enough to tie a rattlesnake to a crippled dog. John Caines—"

She interrupted herself by pursing her lips into a low whistle, and Luke grinned at her.

"He pulled a gun, Tammie. You ought to see him with his collar open."

"Mebbe I have," she snapped. "Listen, you damned fool. I know you never listen to good advice. But Caines owns the county attorney, the sheriff, and most of the houses and timber in this neck of the woods. He's got men working fer him that'd do anything from rape to murder. Next fall, he'll be state senator; after that, the Lord knows what. And you, Luke Hanley. You're just Minor Brookland's trouble boy. You've got no money, no home, no girl. Nedrow took away Linda Caines, and Brookland got your Hester."

The whiskey fumes were rising into Luke's nose from the glass he still held. He felt a tremendous sensation of release. This woman had ripped the veil from things and had really called the turns.

He jumped up and pulled her to her feet. "But, Tammie, I've got you. To hell with Caines, and the same with Brookland and the women."

He whirled her round and round in a crazy dance until her hair was flying and her face was flushed. Finally released, she leaned against the bar. "It's the whiskey," she muttered. "You can't handle it on an empty stomach."

He grabbed her in his arms again, and Tammie lifted her face. He kissed her again and again. "Tammie, my own, I'm bound downriver. Maybe I'll go to Brookland and break up the honeymoon of the girl that sold runaways for a price."

He released her and stalked out the door. Alone, Tammie pushed back her heavy, loosened hair. Her eyes were swimming with tears as she spoke aloud. "The damn fool," she mumbled. "My God, he don't know what John Caines'll do to him!"

She had picked up Luke's empty glass, and now she stared at it, seeing that in her confusion, she had used a tumbler, not a whiskey glass. With a savage gesture, she flung it against the wall.

"Drunk," she whispered brokenly. "He was drunk, after all."

The woman who cleaned up the place came in just then from behind the bar, and Tammie pointed. "There's broken glass over there. Some fool broke a tumbler."

* * *

Luke did not stop at the Brookland camp. He had walked a long way but did not feel weary. At Baker's Bend, he called across. Eddie ferried him over so he could spend the night with Mose High and his family.

High was glad to see him, but his first greeting was derisive. "Glad to see you, Luke, only this is the first time you come smelling of cheap whiskey."

The talk during the evening was of hunting, fishing, and the weather. Finally, High got round to one of his theories. "Chestnuts was mighty wormy this year. There was places where even the bear didn't eat 'em.

That's a sign of troubles ahead. One such year, an old she-bear kilt three of my pigs; another, the big mill at Point Haven burnt down."

Luke tried to show a polite interest, but the riverman was paying little attention to his visitor's reaction. He just wanted to talk.

"Things is going to break. That lawyer was here twice, and he'd talked with George Brendy. You know him?"

Luke nodded and winced when his host poked him vigorously in the ribs.

"Both of us told him things. There's gonna be a hell of a lawsuit."

Suddenly interested, Luke asked, "About what?"

High put on an act, tiptoeing to the door to see if anyone outside was listening, then returning to speak almost in a whisper.

"About how John Caines got title to that big strip of land along the river. Son, we'll get us to bed now. Tomorrow, when thet likker is off your breath, go down to the county seat and soak up some news."

Ordinarily, Point Haven had merely been a stopping place for Luke on his way down to Spring Haven or back to the lumbering country. Now, he had no desire to visit the lovely old house where he would find Hester the mistress. So today, he walked aimlessly about, finally entering the reading room attached to the office of the Clarion. There he consulted the racks of back numbers of the local triweekly newspaper. He was shocked to see that Virginia had sentenced four more of Brown's men to the scaffold. Reading further, he found the opinion of a Pennsylvania judge who had allowed the extradition of these men captured within the jurisdiction of his state:

> We are satisfied that a monstrous crime has been committed and that these prisoners helped in its commission. We, therefore, yield them to the requisition of the Governor of Virginia to stand trial for the said crimes.

"Damned old goat," Luke muttered aloud, and a severe-looking woman at a nearby desk snapped at him.

"We do not swear here, my man. This is a reading room."

Luke, embarrassed, picked up his battered hat and rose. He had about reached the door when the matron spoke again.

"Please replace the paper you were reading in the proper rack."

He turned obediently, put the paper where it belonged, and looked at the woman a moment. "Yes, ma'am," he said humbly. "Hope I did that right, ma'am."

When he was outside, he saw she was watching him through the big window. He winked at her boldly. She stared back for a moment as if aghast, then her lips twitched, and she winked back.

The courthouse was three blocks away on a street lined with brick office buildings, most of which showed signs of lawyers or notaries. Luke was walking along slowly when he saw the small card set in a curtained window: JONATHAN SHAW, ATTORNEY AT LAW.

He did not stand on ceremony but pushed open the outer door and entered a waiting room. Shaw, papers in his hand, was just emerging from the inner office and yelled with pleasure at the sight of Luke. "Well, I'll be damned. Here he is, the very hatchet-faced son of a gun I wanted to see!"

Tossing his papers on a table, he led his visitor to the inner office and pushed the door shut. "Get a cigar, find a chair. I've a lot to spill if you can get runaway slaves and John Brown out of your head for a while."

The folder he pulled from the desk drawer was crammed with papers, and the lawyer opened it as he started talking. "Up in Pine Bend, I found that your father had once worked for Clifton Unger. What do you know about that, Luke?"

"Mighty little. He did work upriver for years and for Unger most of the time. But I was small then. After Father took up Abolition work, he grew pretty close-mouthed. Mother worried about the risks he took, she told me later. Her fears made him tell less and less of what he was doing."

"He left no property when he died?"

"Only the little house and a big garden. Mother and I had tough sledding until I was old enough to pull a saw and swing an axe in the woods."

Shaw studied his papers a few minutes, then leaned back and stared at his visitor through half-closed lids. "I told you once that there were two classes of people who wouldn't sell right of way. One was made up of those who looked for a bigger profit or some advantage for themselves.

The other—those who couldn't sell. I'm going to make John Caines classify himself. Then I can go after him."

He tapped his papers with a not-too-clean forefinger. "Sixteen, seventeen years past, John Caines owned two little hotels, one in Driftwood and one in Crossville, which he considered his home. He bought a small tract of timber from Clifton Unger, which adjoined the thousands of acres on which the big lumberman was then operating. To pass that tract of land, the railroad would have to detour forty miles through the mountains.

"Now, my friend. Some of your chums along the river have been feeding me tips. Unger died less than two years after he sold land to Carnes. Four years elapsed, and during that time, Caines bought the remainder of the Unger lands at a sheriff's sale for unpaid taxes. I went up to Worcester, Massachusetts, and talked with the Unger heirs. He had been a wealthy man, and none of them knew much about the Susquehanna River lands except that they thought these tracts had been in his wife's name. The will had not mentioned them. They were sure of that."

Shaw snorted loudly, making Luke think of a startled deer. "Conveniently, a lot of county records were lost in a flood, but Caines had the perfectly good title issued by the sheriff after the sale. Now, my shotgun-shooting friend, I'm about to ask the court to appoint a special grand jury to smell out the rats in the entire business.

"Clifton Unger was a rabid Abolitionist and contributed heavily to that cause. Your father was also of that persuasion and worked for the man over a period of years. A year after your parent died, Caines made his big play."

"You mean—" Luke excitedly tried to interrupt but was waved down.

"Don't get excited. I don't think Caines is crude enough to take part in a mob killing. I'm after a timber steal, not a murder, and I have enough depositions to compel a court to appoint a jury whether Caines interferes or not."

He laid papers one on top of the other. "Deposition from Moses High, one from Squire Jacoby, another from George Brendy, Esquire. Here's still another from the postmaster in the town where your father was shot."

There was a long silence in the office between the two young men. Luke was adjusting his thinking to what he had just heard.

Shaw began to speak again, slowly, even guardedly. "Your father and Unger were more than employer and employee. They were friends and had a tremendous common interest. This is sheer speculation. Unger, who had many other financial interests, could have turned over those lands for the Abolition cause in your father's name. His death was convenient, and the transaction probably secret, perhaps only by word of mouth. Your father died, and the taxes were not paid, so Caines bought his way into Easy Street for a few hundred dollars. The timber made him rich. It is no wonder he wants to round out his career in the state senate. Perhaps he may have higher ambitions. I, my friend, am trying to find that our mutual friend belongs to the class of those who cannot sell because of a fishy title. Why would an astute man fight the coming of a railroad that could mean so much to the people he wants to represent in legislative halls?"

Shaw's conjectures were disturbing. Luke's father's death had come at too opportune a time not to have been planned. It would explain Caines' attitude toward the son of the elder Hanley, if the lumberman were concerned in his death. Luke jumped up and paced the room until the lawyer went after him sternly.

"The main reason I wanted to talk to you was to be sure you'd keep out of trouble. I want to be sure you are not sheltering one of John Brown's men in your hills. Remember, my friend, they'll send you to the penitentiary for twenty years for helping one of those fugitives. With the present sentiment in the South, if you were tried for such a thing, say in Virginia, it could mean the gallows. Damn it, I wish I could lock you up and keep you out of trouble. Or are you in it already?"

Luke laughed, but there was no mirth in the sound. "Not much. I manhandled that blacksmith, Axelroth, and took Caines' gun away when he tried to shoot me."

Shaw swore bitterly. "Of course you don't and can't see. Deep in you is that queer sense of loyalty to people or a cause that has made martyrs through the ages. I may admire it, but it's a damn poor risk for a man. You will keep trundling fieldhands north in defiance of the law. Likely you'll chambermaid for Owen Brown if he comes your way. Now listen. I'm a lawyer and know. If that fanatic is cornered, he'll shoot. If you're with him when that happens, you'll hang, like I said before. Can't you see that you might be the key to this Caines stuff, and if you stop him, your blessed Underground could be turned into a regular boulevard? The fact that he's been fighting you for years could be our trump card."

Both men were talked out, Shaw particularly. They lit cigars and swung their feet up on the desk. From his position, Luke could see through the open door and the window directly beyond it. His cigar was half consumed when he swung his legs down. "Jim Haliday passed. Are we through?"

Shaw answered sardonically, "Yes, I'm done wasting breath for one day."

Haliday was about to enter a store but turned when his name was called. This time he was unaffectedly glad to see Luke.

"You ought to come out to the house. Things is like old times with Hugh back and married. Hester lives close. We don't bother with strangers at night anymore, though mighty few seem to be coming through these days. Mother says she can sleep nights again."

Luke did not question his friend and found it hard to talk to him since it brought up unpleasant memories. Even Corbet, who had been more of a friend than a mere animal, was dead. "I will be out someday, Jim. Now I'm bound upriver to cut spars."

There was a catch in his throat when he finally shook hands and left Haliday. Perhaps his feeling was deepened because Shaw had shown him the really precarious position in which he was. He could close his eyes now and see the walnut-butted revolvers come out from under the skirts of Brown's coat. The man was dangerous to those who would take him, to himself and to his friends.

Thinking of Erritt and Lymansville, he took a train to King's Shore. The mirror at the end of the car was directly before him as he slouched in his seat. He did not like his face, leaner now than ever, and he remembered that he had failed to get his hair cut. Now close to thirty years of age, he knew he looked ten years older, and he felt a little dismayed.

From King's Shore, he took the stage to Lymansville and enjoyed the long cold ride over frosty hills and through the dark timber. It was nice to go into Hillside and be welcomed, then to sit with Samuel Erritt before his fireplace while they talked. There was news; Rush Geen had brought a suit against the men who had attacked and shot him. Brendy managed his case so cleverly that it was settled out of court and twenty-five dollars paid for damages. No runaways had been coming through since the John Brown raid. Southern people were watching their slaves more closely. Erritt agreed about the danger of having Owen Brown on the chance that he might shoot someone and involve all his friends.

"Yet," he questioned, "what can the poor devil do? He's seen his father captured, knows his brother was killed, and that hangman's rope is waiting for him as it did for the others."

Luke agreed with the statement. "We're probably stuck with him, like it or not. Every friend I have seems to be warning me to get out of the runaway business. What do you think?"

The station master tossed a chip on the flames. "Luke, you can't help yourself no more than your father could. You'll stick as he did no matter what price is asked of you."

Later, when he had heard of Shaw's plans, he seemed to have just one comment. "I'm not too interested in the land aspect of Shaw's planning. Somebody from your father's home territory sent word down country that he was coming to that meeting. Whoever he was, he killed Abner Hanley as surely as if he had fired the shot."

When Luke had finished his visit, Erritt took him back, once more, to the Dyer farm, from which he walked the few miles down to the cabin on Power's Branch. Smoke curling from the chimney startled him. When he pushed open the door, Owen Brown sat on the bunk, his right hand under his coat.

News had been so hard to get at the Keating settlement that Brown had returned to be kept posted by Pritchett and Short. He was depressed at the accounts of the hangings resulting from the Harpers Ferry raid and talked a long time.

"My father offered himself not once but through most of his life. He dared everything in Kansas, and it was hair-raising to ride with him by night and sleep with guns always ready. There would be clashes, the stab of gunfire, cold, hunger, pain. He swore his sons to keep fighting so long as a slave was held anywhere." He paused before reminiscing further. "Generally, he read the evening family lesson from the Old Testament, and he liked the prophets. Often, when we were children, we asked him to read from the Gospels. He would do it, but the next night we'd get two chapters from Jeremiah."

Luke listened and mused. The Harpers Ferry raid looked like the work of a crazy man. But in apparent failure, John Brown was a success. He had set the slavery issue squarely before the people of the United States through his grim sacrifice of himself and his little band.

* * *

A week after Luke's return, he received a letter from Jonathan Shaw. The special grand jury he wanted had been appointed, and its foreman was Squire Jacoby of Crossville. The lawyer's letter told further that State Senator Daniel Parvin had tendered his resignation, and Governor Packer would appoint his successor. In July, Parvin would step out of the office he had held so long. During the lapse of tune, the executive would have an opportunity to consider his successor carefully. John Caines was being mentioned on all sides. The letter concluded with a final reference to the work the grand jury would do.

"Now we'll find what is buried in the backyard. I'm convinced that it will smell to heaven when we dig it up. Keep your hands clean. Remember, you may be a key person in the investigation, and I don't want you in the penitentiary or hanged before we have made use of you."

As Luke read his letter over carefully in the little cabin, Owen Brown sat close to the lantern, busily oiling one of his revolvers.

CHAPTER TWENTY

HEAVY SNOWS shortly after the first of the year practically isolated the upriver lumbering country, and there was, therefore, little likelihood of officers coming up to continue the search for Owen Brown. The fugitive became more relaxed and talked more. He was concerned greatly about Hazlitt and Stevens, two of his father's men who were to be hanged during the first week of March.

"Just young fellows," he commented. "Hazlitt is the typical cowboy and a fine rider. Stevens looks older because he wears a beard. These boys were always the life of the camp, skylarking or singing. They came all the way from Kansas with my father."

Further talk brought out the fact that Brown had finally decided to try to get to Canada when weather permitted. "I don't think the Canadians would extradite me. My father has a good name up there, and they've always sheltered runaway slaves."

Tom Short was a confirmed checkers player and was delighted to find their guest was one also. The two men would play through the evenings while Luke either read or did surveying problems from the book Brookland had given him long ago.

During the January thaw, Luke went up to Pine Bend for some files used in touching up their axes. Returning, he stopped in to see Tammie. He felt full of spirits this day, probably because the Brown problem was closer to a solution. Tammie was alone and friendly. He ate supper with her.

"You know," he joked with her, "we ought to get married. If I lived on your cooking, I could cut twice as many spars as anyone else on this river."

"Yes," she retorted. "About the time we got things working, you'd land in jail. You're a mighty bad risk, my long-legged friend, and it's mostly your fault."

He kissed her noisily when leaving and, on the walk back to the camps, found that she had put a small bottle of her homemade wine in his pocket. It was an article she never sold, and he had the fancy she shared it only with him.

Ben Royal had pushed through a good winter's work and had the entire cut of timber rolled out on the ice directly inside their little boom, waiting for the thaw. He was uneasy, but Luke assured Royal that trouble in the former season was due to Luke's having charge.

One letter came through during the winter. It was from Jonathan Shaw and consisted of exactly one line: *The jury is making real progress. Keep out of trouble.*

Luke was annoyed at being warned again, and he tore up the letter. Actually, he had little choice of action. Brown was here whether it meant arrest and the penitentiary or not.

As the weather softened and the ice began to move in the river, the much-hunted fugitive became restless. "I'll go up to Keating again for a few days. Look for me in four days. Maybe I could help a little with the rafts."

All hands worked feverishly, preparing for the great spring float of timber. No one paid any attention to hours. Work proceeded while there was light, and often men would be out on the raft, boring holes used for the pinning on of the lash poles, by lantern light. No one wanted to have a poor raft, particularly since one had been all but lost the previous season.

Brown's four days slipped by without notice. It was on the fifth morning that Pritchett mentioned it to Luke.

"He said he'd be back in four days. Where is he, I wonder?"

Luke had been sharpening an auger bit and now tested it on his thumb. The quiet months had made them careless—now things were moving on the river. Roads were open if muddy, and people were passing up and down. There was a thousand-dollar reward for Brown, enough to tempt any of these woodsmen who would not earn that much in three years of hard labor.

"We'll wait for afternoon," he promised the anxious smith. "Then we'll see."

But at noon, he was uneasy and talked to Ben Royal. Since the horses were not working, Luke took the fastest one and started for Keating, careful to detour Pine Bend and Weston. In late afternoon, he reached the junction of the Sinnemahoning Creek and the West Branch of the Susquehanna. After tying his horse securely, he went up the creek and crossed the rickety bridge to a scattered collection of buildings. One of the first men he encountered was Fred, who insisted on taking him to his cabin.

"My wife's away, but you stay for supper and the night."

Luke explained his errand, and Fred was aghast with alarm. "Mister Luke, Smith ain't been here since last fall."

Brown had left the Brookland camps five days before. He was a good woodsman and knew the way. There was only one answer—he had been captured. Fred offered to turn out his people to make a search for traces of the fugitive and pick up any news available.

Luke returned to his horse and rode fast to Weston. It was dark when he arrived, and to him, the place looked normal, with no indication that anything out of the ordinary might have taken place. Certainly the open capture of the wanted fugitive would have stirred up the town if it had happened here. Stores and hotels were open, with people moving about. Once Luke thought he sighted the squat figure of Axelroth, but that was all.

Pine Bend was closed up for the night. When he and his tired horse reached the camp, Ben Royal, despite his long day's labor, was waiting in the office, thoroughly shocked by the news.

"We should have sent a man with him. Now, if they've got him, we're all in trouble up to our necks. They'll hang him. After they check back and prove where he stayed all winter, every man of us is in the soup."

In the morning, the worried woods boss talked to his men, placing the story before them and strongly hinting at the trouble that would come to them all if Brown was tried.

"You've all been mighty decent about Owen Brown—Smith to you. Now we got to do something for him and ourselves. The raft work'll have to go on, but I want some of you to drift into Pine Bend come evening. Drink a little, but keep your eyes and ears open and your mouths shut."

All of them promptly agreed to help. Royal selected six of them and gave each a dollar of the Abolition Society's money.

"That's expenses. Me and Luke will go down and see Mose High. A sparrow can't scratch its left ear on this river without that old cuss knowing it."

Two days brought nothing about the fugitive. Even High knew little except that his boy, Benny, had seen Brown walking openly on the road above Pine Bend the day he left camp. The news brought back was that both Caines and Axelroth were in Weston and that everybody was talking about Senator Parvin's resignation and the strong possibility that Caines would get the post.

In five more days, the river had become a vast moving sea. White water no longer showed over the rocks, and water birches along the shorelines bent against the tug of the current. The first Brookland raft slipped away downstream on the morning of April fifth. Caines' first floater went by near noon of the same day. Tom Short and Pritchett remained behind after the second Brookland raft pulled out.

Luke was desperately uneasy. From his talks with Shaw, he knew how serious the situation was and how fraught with danger for his friends at the camp and those more active in the Underground, like Erritt, Brookland, and the Williamsport men who had been in the conference at Spring Haven. The raft would carry the news to Brookland. At its tie-up, a messenger would go to him.

"Caines has two more floats," Short reported. "One's a whopper— four sections and two deckhouses."

Luke knew his presence in town would occasion talk if Brown had been captured. But he could no longer stand it, so he went to Pine Bend and visited for an hour with Race, the hardware man, and several old rivermen. Nothing unusual was mentioned; talk was all about rafting. Then he went back to Tammie's.

Here a number of men were drinking at the bar where Tammie was serving. Luke, as he finished a glass of beer, felt sure the blonde woman was uneasy. When he set down his glass, his shoulders shut out the rest of the room, and as she faced him, he caught her slight gesture. A few minutes later, he said good night, nodded to the men in the room, and went out. Immediately, he slipped back to the kitchen door, which opened before he could turn the knob, and Tammie pulled him inside.

She was distraught. "I warned you again and again, but you did not listen, kept on playing with fire. Now, I never did this before. I just let things come and go without telling nobody. This time, though, I got to talk, partly for you and partly for the men you've got tangled. Caines' men hang around here, and I hear some of their talk. They've got Owen Brown in a deckhouse on Caines' big raft. The plan is to take him clear downriver, then over into Virginia. Then the marshals will arrest you and everybody mixed up in hiding the man—Brookland with the rest of you. Remember, if they know you got the news from me, they'd kill me."

"Good God!" Luke exclaimed, then he saw the tears in her eyes, slipped his arm about her shoulders, and wiped them away with his handkerchief. She reached up and held his hand for a moment.

"This is shooting stuff, Luke Hanley. Caines will have Axelroth and his toughs on the raft as guards. Here's the thing I've dreaded. You'll—"

She was crying in earnest now, and he held her tightly for what comfort that might bring her.

"Tammie," he whispered. "I'm stumped. I don't know what to do. They'll hang Brown; that's bad enough. But think what they'll do to us and men like Tom Short."

At that moment, all his appetite for risks had left him. He was afraid, desperately afraid. After all, he had gone through one trial himself.

Tammie lifted her head, anger in her eyes. "That Brookland sits down there at ease, holding his little doxie, while you pull his chestnuts out of the fire. You've done that for years."

He shook her gently. Pulling her close, he spoke half musingly. "Guess we ought to get married, Tammie. Like I said before, I'd lumber and you'd cook. We wouldn't bother about the strangers at night or who killed my father or men with a thousand-dollars reward on their heads."

Her eyes were shining as she studied his face. Abruptly, she pushed back her heavy hair and spoke bitterly. "No, Luke, it's too late for that. There's things you'd never forget or forgive, and you're not in real earnest anyway. I'm Tammie, you see. Go ahead, Luke Hanley, risk your neck. But don't do a single damn thing till you talk with Mose High. That old buzzard is crooked enough to get you out of this mess if anybody can. Thank God, Rush'll be here late tonight."

This time, Luke followed Tammie's advice. He did not stop at the camp but went straight down to Baker's Bend and crossed the river in a leaking flatboat. He went directly to the point with High, telling him the whole story of Brown and the present situation.

The riverman listened closely, then filled his black pipe and leaned back, his eyes shining. "Son, I been pickin' up timber along this big crick close to forty years, and both my boys has me beat. What you want's no job. Caines starts his rafts close to noon. His first tie-up is on your side of the river, about a half-mile above here. He's a good raftsman, runs slow and keeps his men rested for bad water." He spat so strongly into the fireplace that the feeble blaze was all but extinguished. Then using a slab to indicate a raft, he explained. "They tie up to a big slipp'ry elm, one rope at the back so's the front end with the guide sweep will point out toward the main current. In the mornings, they untie one fastenin' and slide right out into the current. Thet's Caines' way, and his bosses foiler it. You got to have a hundred feet of half-inch rope, mebbe a little more."

He frowned and looked at his visitor. "Kin you swim in ice water—say, a couple hundred feet?"

"Yes."

The riverman continued. "The Caines raft ties up. After dark, you or some other damn fool swims out and hitches his rope to the front sweep blade while a couple or three men hold the other end of the line on shore. One man cuts the inch hawser that holds the raft to the slipp'ry elm. It starts out from shore, edgin' toward the current. Wisht I could show you in daytime how it'd act. The men holdin' the rope trot along a little then they pull. The guide sweep will turn the raft in, and there's rocks where that crick comes in from the north. She'll pile up, the whole damn business. Make that rope two hundred feet, pay it out till you're sure the raft's moving well. Then's the time to wreck her."

This time he finished drowning the fire with spittle and he chuckled. "Mind you, the trick'll work. It has before. When she hits, it's up to you fellers with axe handles."

He raised a dirty forefinger. "Mind, no shootin'. If John Caines is aboard, I don't want him kilt. He buys logs from me, and don't ask too many questions. And don't shoot Axelroth. There ain't another smith on the river that can make grabs like he kin."

Eddie had come in to listen while his father talked and asked promptly if he could help. His father nodded, and Luke was delighted to have someone along who understood the job. The three went down to the boat landing.

"I just want Eddie for the know-how, Mose. We'll do the rough stuff."

High paid no attention to the promise. He had a last word. "Pay out lots of that thin line. The faster the raft moves, the harder she'll hit. There's a good current now, even inshore."

* * *

Rush Geen arrived at camp in the morning. Tammie had probably sent him over. There was no use hiding anything. Luke explained his plan to the men left after the first raft had gone.

"Ben, you and the crew take the second raft out early tomorrow morning. Tom, Pritchett, Rush, Eddie, and I will take on the job. Five men'll be enough. I'll do the swimming; Dan and Eddie will handle the ropes. Rush and Tom will be the boarding crew."

The Brookland raft left as scheduled. In the lobby, Luke counted out ten dollars to each man. "You men are losing some time. There's raftsmen's wages. I figure on about two days' time."

Geen picked up his money from the table and was about to replace it when he caught Luke's wink and pocketed it. Eddie High was delighted. The other men worked hard for a living and did not demur.

After all plans were completed and the materials needed were assembled, the time dragged. Luke went over everything again: the half-inch rope in two coils for ease in handling, an old axe handle for each man, a sharp axe to cut the raft cable. Luke knew Geen carried a revolver under his coat, but none of the rest of them would be armed.

Shortly after the noon meal, the vigilant Eddie shouted. "She's comin'! Comin' fast!"

The big raft out in the middle of the river was as Tom Short described. She was a full four-section affair with two deckhouses set well apart.

Geen was counting. "I see six men. Wish I had a field glass."

The great brown mass of timber moved majestically along at the speed of the current. From the shore, her deck, the round side of the logs, looked all but awash. The sweeps were tremendous things, and the watchers could see she carried four fending oars on their side.

Luke grinned, trying to conceal his excitement. "All right, boys, let's travel with her."

Short and Pritchett carried the rope, Geen the axe handles, and Eddie proudly bore the axe, which would be used to cut the raft's hawser. Pritchett had sharpened its two bits to razor edges. It was easy to walk along and keep the raft in sight, and it was not likely they would be seen since the road was generally fringed with brush or trees. Toward evening, they noticed that the side oars had been lowered, slowing down the heavy craft. Then, to their dismay, it passed the place where High said Caines' rafts usually tied up, but Eddie assured them.

"They'll swing in just below, and it's just like this, rocks and all. The crick current will keep her headed out better."

He was right. As the short spring day ended, which had been a trifle overcast, promising a pitch-dark night, the raft came to shore and was snubbed by one of its crew who had jumped on land. It stopped. Then slowly, the front end swung until it angled away from the shore as Mose High said it would do.

"She's right—just like Pop said," Eddie cried exultantly, chewing tobacco and spitting at every third word or so.

"Eddie," Luke gibed the boy, "I thought you'd quit chewing."

The young would-be riverman jerked his shoulders and grinned in the fading light. "Jiggers, Mister Luke. I'm too damned worked up to hold fast to a pipe with my teeth."

Fire showed in the raft's sand boxes, and the odor of cooking drifted to the watchers. It was quite dark now in the brush, but the big floater's outline showed against the dull, lingering gleam of the river.

Two hours dragged by, and Luke changed his plan a little.

"Tom, you cut the snubbing rope and come in over that end when she swings. Give a peeper's call when you're ready. No, we'll give the call when we have the rope fast."

He frowned at himself in the darkness for having confused his directions, then Tom Short touched him on the shoulder and surrendered the coils of rope.

"Careful now; it all ain't worth drowning for. I'll wait for the peepers."

While the big woodsman slipped away into the darkness to locate the snubbing rope, the others studied the outlines of the raft. It hung as Mose and Eddie said it would, jutting out from the bank like a thumb does from the palm of the hand. The cooking fires had about burned out, and a light showed in one shack. Likely the forward sixty or seventy feet of the big floater would be deserted. Sticking out a full fifteen feet would be the blade of the front sweep, which was Luke's target.

The four men moved onward silently, waded a small brook, and stopped. Nobody spoke. To cover the fact that he was scared, Luke sat down on the ground and took off his shoes. These, with his coat, hat, and woolen pants, he piled on a big rock beside the brook where he could find them again. Shivering, he waited for Eddie to slip a loop of the rope over his shoulder and knot the two coils together.

"You ready?" the boy asked, and Luke tapped his shoulder with his hand.

"If you get stuck," Eddie whispered, "yank the rope. We'll pull you back."

Slowly, Luke waded into the river, and the icy grip of it had him, sending panic through him so he partially turned to come back. But he could dimly see Eddie tossing the rope on the water in coils so it would not drag on the swimmer. Taking a long breath, he ducked his body into the water and began swimming.

The water fought him like the hands of a strong man pushing against his body. He had only a hundred and fifty feet to go, but it was taking all the strength of his wiry body to make any progress. Eddie was paying out the line expertly, only its weight was impeding the swimmer. After what seemed like hours, he suddenly went under, and for a second, he thought he had an attack of cramps. When he came up, his head struck something, and his thrown-up hand touched what he realized must be the plank blade of the sweep. He held on thankfully for a full minute while his breath and strength returned. Then he slipped the loop of line from his shoulder and fastened it securely to the sweep.

He had just finished when the sound of running steps came forward and stopped about where the sweep post must be. Luke flattened his head against the sweep. He could see, against the sky, the form of a man who held something in his hands that might be a gun. He went back, and Luke heard him call, "Twasn't anything. There's nothing out there."

Holding on to the rope, Luke worked his way back to the shore. His companions slapped his chilled body with their palms while he pulled on his clothes. On the raft, a man came out of a deckhouse and hung a lantern on its side, then hurried indoors.

Eddie, because Luke's lips were too cold for it, gave the signal. Geen and Dan took their end of the rope and ran downriver from the big floater. To Luke, hours seemed to pass while the raft lay motionless. Then, by the light of the lantern on the deckhouse, he saw he was mistaken. It was moving and gaining speed. Minutes later, the raft crew realized something had happened and came rushing out.

A stentorian voice yelled, "Man the sweeps! We're loose!"

Eddie had darted forward. As he disappeared, Luke saw the front end of the big raft veer. Geen and Pritchett pulled on the line, which turned the blade of the front steering oar. The floater was coming faster. It gained momentum, approaching shore. Tom Short came running up. Then the raft struck head-on.

At Eddie's suggestion, all five of the attackers had, earlier in the evening, darkened their faces with ashes. Like black pirates, they now swung aboard the disintegrating raft. The weight of its own timbers snapped off the lash poles, and one of the deckhouses was flat on the deck. Dan Pritchett felled the man at the front sweep with a blow. In spite of his crippled arm, Eddie, with Geen, had waded into a dark knot of men, swinging axe handles viciously. Tom Short was using his axe on the remaining lash poles.

Satisfied with the way the melee was going, Luke rushed to the remaining deckhouse, kicked open the door, and heard a man groan. The riding light outside came through the cracks enough to show him that the figure tied on the bunk was Owen Brown, who had also been partially gagged. It took just a moment to cut him loose.

Brown spluttered, spat out bits of cloth, and stamped his legs. "My guns—they're in the other cabin."

Luke yanked the rescued man through the doorway. A dark figure was dashing toward him, and Luke swung his axe handle viciously and with effect.

Geen ran up. "Get ashore," he hissed. "She's breaking up."

There was no pursuit. Caines' raftsmen had been mercilessly mauled in the surprise attack. Luke and his friends went slowly back toward camp. When they found they were not followed, they curled up bone-tired in a hemlock thicket on great piles of boughs, huddled together to keep warm, and slept through the remainder of the night.

When they reached camp in the morning, Rush Geen spoke to the man they had rescued. "Now, Brown, it's too risky for you and us to have you in these parts. Luke and his friends have taken all the risks anybody could expect from them. I'll take you up the old Boone road to Erie. From there, it'll be no trick to get into Canada. My lawyer friend, George Brendy, says there will be no extradition."

All of them felt a little sorry for Brown as he shook hands with each at parting. He thanked everyone individually, then rode away with Rush Geen. Luke, watching them go, felt tremendous relief. It had been a tight corner for them all, tighter than they realized. He was thankful, too, that the walnut-stocked revolvers, which Brown had asked for when released, were now probably under six feet of mighty cold river water.

Pritchett summed up. "Well, that's that. You know, lately, every time he'd come in, I could hear jail doors clang."

CHAPTER TWENTY-ONE

GEEN RETURNED after four days and talked with Luke, who had gone back to his pitch pine operation. It was quite plain that the horseman, usually undisturbed, felt relief and expressed it frankly.

"We met one of my boys up the old Boone road, and he took Brown on up to the lake. Luke, I'm sure glad he didn't get them damn pistols off the raft. The man is deadly, and a killing up here would have put ropes round all our necks."

They both agreed that the fugitive would find sanctuary in Canada.

"You know, Rush, maybe that Brown raid struck a blow against slavery, but it surely dried up the Underground. Nobody's coming through anymore unless they take a different way."

Geen frowned and kicked a stick with his boot. "That don't make me too sorry for you. Maybe now you can lumber for a while in peace and get a stake. Tammie's the one that worries me now. I know nobody of your outfit will talk—"

Luke interrupted him. "Rush, I didn't tell a soul who tipped me off. None of the men even asked me."

Geen nodded. "Yes, that's all right. But some of the Caines crowd may put two and two together."

He picked up an axe, spun the handle in his brown hand, and then sank the blade into a log almost up to the eye as if he needed an outlet for the tension within him. "You watch out for her, Luke. Don't get careless about either Caines or his man Axelroth. Neither ever forgets an injury, and they'll wait years for revenge. Axelroth does most of the dirty work; he's been riding over the country for Caines close to twenty years."

"How did Tammie know?" The question was out before Luke thought, and Geen frowned. His answer was evasive and much the same given him by the woman herself.

"She has lots of friends, and news just sifts into her. Many of Caines' men come into her place, and she's always been so close-mouthed that they get careless. Don't ever forget the risk she took. I wonder sometimes that she ever told you of Brown's kidnapping."

Luke thought about the whole thing after Geen was gone but could not bring himself to feel Caines was so dangerous. He had seen the man's mask drop in anger and had seen him cringe under pain. Besides, with his ambition to be appointed senator, he would not likely resort to any open violence, and he would probably curb his henchmen.

So the time passed in a monotony of steady days of labor. Luke worked alone. Most of his money was gone, so he could not afford to hire labor. Sometimes he dropped down to Tammie's Place and, when they were alone, talked with her. Brookland had not been upriver for months. As the talk about Caines being appointed to Senator Parvin's place grew stronger, Ben Royal and Pritchett speculated with Luke as to why Brookland, with his influential friends, did not try for the post.

"I guess he just don't want it," Ben said. "When I was down the other week, I spoke about it, and he just smiled. Said he was happy and had no other plans."

Luke was tempted to ask about Hester but did not. He often thought about her and found contentment in her present status. She had been a wonderful comrade, and he knew their approach to a romance had been a passing thing that died during their long separation. At Spring Haven, she would be happy with her husband. He could open new fields to the girl and satisfy the ambition in her that made her so different from many other young people.

During the May term of court, Judge Adam Faris received the secret report of the special grand jury he had set up at Shaw's instigation. He announced that the material would be studied carefully by him in conference with Judge Harkness from the next judicial district. The two judges would then report to a special court session on July ninth. Luke, who had gone down to the county seat at Shaw's request, discussed the progress of the case with the lawyer.

"You can bet, my friend, that Jacoby and his men have done a thorough job. They have been all over the lumbering country, taking testimony. Two of them went up to New England to see the Unger heirs and their counsel, and two went down to Exeter where your father was shot."

Luke looked at the eager lawyer and asked a foolish question. "Who pays the bill for all this?"

Shaw fidgeted and then shrugged his shoulders. "The county is supposed to, but my company has entered into an agreement to cover all costs if Caines' titles are confirmed."

Apparently, John Caines had paid no more attention to the investigation than he had to the wreckage of his raft. He was traveling over the four counties that comprised the senatorial district, building up the idea that he was the logical person to succeed the venerable Parvin. Of course, he controlled the local leaders in his own county; he was fast extending that influence to men in other areas. Wages had been raised on his operations, and the men were insured against injury, a policy originated by Brookland and some of his friends. Luke saw Caines twice in Pine Bend and noticed the assurance of the man.

No rain had fallen for over a month, and it was becoming extremely dry, especially in the choppings, where masses of treetops lay in long windrows. Brookland's premises were bad, but Luke's were more dangerous since the pitch pine tops were more flammable than white pine. Besides, he had long rows of carefully piled and now well-seasoned planks along the tram road from his mill. He gave up smoking while at work; the danger of fire was too great.

One hot afternoon, he had a visit from Fred, and the two had a long talk about the Underground Railroad.

"Them folks down south is watchin' my people too close fer them to git away now that Brown had skeered them, and there's so much war talk. I'm bound down yonder to pick me up some that wants to git off like Harriet Tubman does."

Luke looked at the big man. The short years had made a change in him. "Look out down there," he cautioned, and Fred smiled.

"This here time I ain't gonna listen. I heered them white folks telling you not to go on helping folks git clear, and you paid them no mind."

Luke laughed and gave him what was left of the committee's money. He watched Fred leave, filled with regret. It had always been a comfort that he was in Keating, keeping the place safe from slave snatchers, and he had risked his liberty, perhaps his life, at the trial.

Tammie's spirits had lifted, and she was herself once more. She no longer thought something would happen because of the information she had passed on. She would often visit with Luke, even when customers were in the big room.

Again, she was full of advice. "When spring comes, load that pitch on a raft and float it to market. Brookland's teams surely didn't haul much. You ought to be getting some money out of your work."

Luke smiled ruefully. He couldn't even tell her how hard up he was just then. She lost her temper at his smile and launched a tirade against Brookland. Luckily, no one else was in the big room at the time. "Go down and read the riot act to the stuck-up cuss. Tell him he promised to haul planks for you. Get him off his high horse and away from his new woman long enough to be fair to you. The government'll be needin' them planks."

Tammie's vehemence amused Luke, and he did not stop smiling. If his planks remained on the piles, it was as much his fault as Brookland's. The presence of Brown in the area had complicated things to the point where ordinary work was just neglected. But walking back to camp later, he thought a lot about Spring Haven. He had come to love the place, with its arches of trees, the rooms with their dark walnut furnishings, and the sunlight filtering in through tiny windowpanes. The Jenkins cousins would be working in the fields. Brookland's spare figure in worn corduroys would loom in the doorway as he answered the summons of the brass knocker.

"Damn homesick fool," he grunted aloud as he walked on.

July brought no relief from the drought, but it did bring tremendous excitement from the county seat. County Attorney Nedrow resigned suddenly, ostensibly to take up private practice. Two days later, Elias Page, sheriff for a generation, resigned. This local news came upriver along with much war talk, but the Pine Bend people were more interested in the county excitement than in the national emergency. Also to intrigue them was the fact that the filling of Senator Parvin's place was imminent.

To Luke, some news that came down the river from the Sinnema-honing country was significant. A free black man working on one of the lumbering operations had been kidnapped by three men of the Baumheit stripe. The woodsmen with whom the man had worked set up a pursuit and overtook the kidnappers. First handling them roughly and releasing their prisoner, they resorted to the old cure for those who incited public displeasure—tar and feathers. The rumor had it that one of the kidnappers was still close to death from the manhandling he had endured. To Luke, it indicated a marked change in public opinion.

In Washington, Southern leaders were demanding a revision of the constitution, which prohibited the importation of slaves. President Buchanan, an old man and a Pennsylvanian, was bewildered and swayed by representations from both North and South. He sought peace in his day. But arguments in congressional halls and the debates of Judge Douglas and the prairie lawyer, Abraham Lincoln, did not interest these men of the great pine country. To them, there was only the one issue—peace or war.

On July ninth, the date set for consideration of the special grand jury's report to be made public, Luke was in the courthouse with Attorney Shaw. The place quieted when Judge Faris, looking older and feebler, took his seat. Inside the railing was Nedrow and another lawyer representing John Caines, who was not present. Shaw and Luke were just outside. The grand jury occupied their regular place. There, his noble head and thatch of white hair made Squire Jacoby stand out. At the judge's direction, the old man rose, faring both the court and the audience. His face was sober as he spoke.

"Your Honor, two months past this special grand jury, of which I have the honor to be foreman, presented our findings concerning the matter of the Clifton Unger lands along the Susquehanna. You and a companion judge have studied our claim and asked that we make the contents of the papers submitted public this day."

Judge Paris, his thin fingers toying with the gavel before him, cleared his throat. "That is correct. You may proceed, Mr. Jacoby."

The squire spoke slowly and distinctly enough so he could be heard all over the big room. He told of the jury's travels and the taking of depositions. The attorney for the Unger heirs had searched through the papers of the deceased lumberman and discovered a note of the same date as the man's will. It was probably written as an explanation as to why the property was not included in it. Jacoby held up a yellowed sheet of paper. "This is the note, ladies and gentlemen."

He read: "*Your father's lands along the upper Susquehanna were given by me several years back to a trusted employee, Abner Hanley, to be used for the Abolition cause, which he and I support with all our hearts. Signed, Father.*"

The old squire waited for the murmur in the room to subside, then told of a visit to the town of Exeter in southeastern Pennsylvania. "Your Honor and ladies and gentlemen, we found that this same Abner Hanley registered in the Speedwell Hotel of that place. He had a packet of papers. At first, he told the clerk he would leave these with him, then changed his mind. That night, a meeting of an Abolition Society, which he attended, was broken up by a gang of roughs. One shot was fired through a window, and it killed Abner Hanley."

Luke found himself leaning forward, gripping the railing with his big hands. Then he forced himself to sit back while Jacoby went on.

"The county records for the years in question were found to have been lost or destroyed, perhaps in one of our floods. Therefore, we went to the land office in Harrisburg and learned that, two days before his untimely death, Abner Hanley had recorded a deed to the Unger tracts west of Pine Bend. Due to the death of the new owner and no one having been advised of his ownership, no taxes were paid. In a tax sale, which we did not find advertised, these timber lands were sold by the sheriff to John Caines, who now holds a county title to the property on which he had lumbered for years."

Judge Faris had to use his gavel vigorously to quiet the clamor in the room, and Nedrow, speaking for his client, John Caines, asked and obtained a fifteen-minute recess. Luke remained in his seat, and Shaw returned just as the foreman resumed.

"There are many items in our report which suggest gross misconduct by officials and perhaps criminal acts by others. The judge has suggested that, in the interest of saving time, I present only the gist of our findings and recommendations. It is our opinion that the lands now being used by John Caines are the rightful property of the Abner Hanley estate, now vested in his son, Luke Hanley. We suggest, pending trial, that there may have been some collusion between the rioters at Exeter and John Caines."

The audience went clear out of hand, and only a threat to clear the room restored order so that the now-weary Jacoby could continue.

"Your Honor, we recommend that you set aside the injunction against the railroad company, allowing it to cross the lands in question. This is in the public interest; damages to be fixed by viewers appointed by the court. Further, we propose that John Caines and ex-Sheriff Page be brought before this court to be tried for false conversion of property. If found guilty, then triple damages covering all gains from lumbering on the said property should be assessed and collected and paid to the rightful and legal owner, Luke Hanley. Your Honor, the special grand jury rests and has already placed the evidence it collected in the hands of the court."

This time, Judge Faris rose to his slim height and grimly forced order after ten minutes of uproar. Then he sat down and spoke rapidly. "This Court directs the arrest of John Caines and Elias Page. Pending trial, they will be released on bail of five thousand dollars each for appearance at the November court. This hearing is adjourned."

Nedrow and his companion remained in their seats as if stunned while members of the audience pushed forward toward Luke and Shaw. The lawyer pulled his friend out into the hallway, where two reporters from the Clarion cornered them.

"Hanley," one demanded, "what will you do with all that money? You'll be a rich man."

Luke grinned at him. "You are ahead of your horses, my friend. It's not my money, and anyway, no one has it yet."

Shaw pulled his friend away, and when they reached the office, Luke spoke excitedly. "What did Jacoby mean? Did Caines send word to have my father shot? Is that true?"

Shaw nodded. "Probably, but we have no real proof. However, now we know why Caines has hounded you, trying to get rid of you. Also, I know he fought the right of way because he could not sell."

Luke paid no attention to Shaw's second statement. "You know, two or three years back, I'd have started to hunt Caines and demand a settlement—"

The smiling lawyer interrupted his friend. "Luke, there's no telling you how much you have grown since first I met you. You're a bigger man than the hellion that opened fire on a deputy sheriff. You probably don't know it, but you've made a lot of friends who trust you. Now, like the newsmen, what will you do with that money if you get it?"

Luke studied a long moment, then shook his head. "I don't know, Jonathan. It wouldn't be my money anyway, and the Abolition cause really doesn't need it now. No, I couldn't use it." He had turned away in some embarrassment at the praise given him and did not see the expression on Shaw's face when he made his comment about the money.

Luke had to remain in town for a few days while he went over old surveys with the lawyer. During this time, he was bothered by the curious and those who wished to congratulate him and advise him on what to do with the Caines money when it came to him. So he had a chance to see *The Clarion* when it came out with its headline account of the special grand jury's report to Judge Faris. Practically every paragraph began with a lead line.

"Grand Judy indicts lumberman John Caines and ex-Sheriff Elias Page for criminal fraud . . . held for high bail . . . November court. Jury recommends triple damages . . . fortune at stake. Unger lands belonged to Abner Hanley, a well-known county Abolitionist shot at Exeter. His son says the money is not his . . . what will become of the money?"

Shaw laughed when he had read the account and then tossed down the paper. "They'll surely hang that money on you, my strong-minded friend."

Luke smiled at him and then surveyed his worn clothes. "Well, I could use some of it for a new suit. Dammit, there's a hole in these pants."

On the morning of the fourth day, when Luke was about to start back upriver, he had walked into Shaw's office to say goodbye. A woman was seated in the outer office, and the lawyer introduced him. "Mrs. Street, this is Mr. Hanley; Luke, this is Mrs. John Street—she is Miss Caines' aunt."

There was a strong family resemblance to Linda in the woman's face. She rose and gave her hand briefly to Luke. "I am a sister of Linda's mother. She lives with me now. Remember, please, she did not send me to you. That is my idea. If you are the man people seem to think you are, come to her. I think she needs you."

* * *

Luke was taken to a large house on a quiet street. Outside the door, Mrs. Street turned and looked at her companion for a moment without speaking, then they went in.

Linda was seated near a window of the large living room. As her aunt and Luke entered, she turned, and her lips parted a little in surprise. He crossed the room with long strides, took her hands, held them a moment, and then sat down facing her.

"I didn't know you lived here, Linda. You're thin; have you been sick?"

"No," she answered. "I'm all right, and I've lived here since I broke with Father months past."

Mrs. Street had disappeared. Linda rose, crossed the room, and closed the door while Luke stood waiting for her return. She hesitated a moment as a swimmer does before plunging into icy water, then, without preamble, she was talking as if she had expected him to come and hear her story.

"When I was sure at last, I broke with my father. Two days past, I saw him again when he wanted me to come back. He was in a fury. When I accused him, he finally admitted everything. Years ago, he had become a member of a southern anti-Abolition society. Now I'm sure he is the head of it in this state, but he would not admit that. Luke, as far back as Crossville, he wanted you out of the country. Now you know it was because of that timberland business. The society, Knights of some kind, planned to kill your father and other Abolitionists. My father knew what was going to happen at Exeter and could have saved him. Perhaps he planned it; he wouldn't tell me much about the society."

She drew a long breath and looked into his eyes for a moment. Perhaps she read encouragement there, for she hurried on.

"He was desperately jealous of my mother without cause and hated Fred Horton; had him run out of town once when I was a little girl.

There were always messengers coming and going at our place, usually after night. Likely this was society business. Well, one messenger was Axelroth. Father told him about Horton's return and that he wanted him driven away. Horton must have been stubborn. Axelroth beat him first, then shot him and carried the body to where it was found.

"No, Luke, I didn't know these things then. I only suspected that terrible things were going on. So I told that story in the hearing at Crossville, and I've tried my best to stand between you and Father since.

"Listen, there is a fury in him. First, he wanted money. When that came, he wanted political posts. He felt that with the secret society working for him, he might get national importance. Sometimes I think, under that smooth exterior, he is mad, and I hope so. Now, he'll—"

"Nedrow?" Luke questioned.

She stopped, and her eyes widened. "Oh, that; it was over months past. He was the prosecutor, I—" She came to her feet and half turned away from him. "I can't talk anymore, Luke. You can go to the authorities. He didn't fire the shots, but he is guilty of two murders. Only God knows what more. You are a violent man, you can—"

Luke had her hands, and they were cold in his work-roughened palms. He raised them and placed them with his across her lips. He could not bear to look at her emotion-tortured face. He wasn't thinking of John Caines nor the evil he had done. His mind was on this girl, what she was and what she had done.

Just for a moment, the awful shadow of what stood between them crossed his mind. He was holding her hands tighter. "Don't say anything more. It's over now." He took one hand free and stroked the smoothness of her hair. "I couldn't hurt you, Linda. I couldn't."

She was crying softly as he led her to the door. Outside Mrs. Street was in the hallway and slipped her arm about the girl's shoulders. They stood there as he walked out, but Linda did not raise her head to look at him.

CHAPTER TWENTY-TWO

IT WAS a real tribute to the organizing powers of John Caines that his upriver interests did not collapse under the impact of the news that came from the county seat. Lumbering went on as usual; men reported for work, and payday occurred the day after the grand jury report was made public. They were talking about these things in the Brookland camp when Luke returned. He came in at once for strong ribbing about the fortune coming to him, and he took it in good grace.

"Right now, boys," he assured them, "I have two pairs of pants—one with a hole—three shirts, and four dollars and eighty-five cents. How many of you knot-hounds can match me?"

Tom Short shook his head dubiously. "It ain't a hole, Luke. Them pants is just ripped. I got six dollars."

They soon tired of their ribbing, and the talk then was of the dry weather and fire danger. Woods bosses along the river prohibited smoking at work. Two men in Pine Bend had been dismissed for not obeying the order. The creeks and the river were low. Luke thought of his own place, the pitch tops and the piles of dry planks.

The night of his return was spent in the little shack on his mill site. He wanted to be alone and think things through. John Caines was probably head of the Knights of the Golden Circle in the state. Owen Brown and others had mentioned that order. This would account for the organization, which had both fought and fattened on the runaway slave situation. Probably that interference would stop when Caines was brought to trial. Anyway, as Fred and others had said, no one seemed to be coming north anymore. The John Brown raid had its effect, and so did the talk of the imminent war.

He thought of his father. Five years ago, he would have felt it his duty to track down and punish Caines himself. Now, he knew the man was broken. His own father was dead—nothing now would bring him back or erase the times through which he, as a boy, and his mother had passed.

He went out on his little porch and was about to light his pipe but stopped. His mind was on Linda Caines now, her courage, what she had done for him, the strain tightening her lovely face. That he was here now was probably due to her and her quiet defense through the years. Suddenly, he was obsessed with a feeling of acute humility. There was so little of him that warranted what she had done, and the barrier was still between them as it could always be.

In the brush, the crickets were sounding their dry litany. The warm air was charged with the odor of dead treetops and the pitchy aroma of the piled planks. A year and more of hard work was stacked along that narrow spidery tram road. Every cent, with the exception of what was in his pocket, was tied up in the lumber Mose High had sawed on the rickety mill.

There was little use in working; he saw that in the morning. He did not want to go up to the Brookland camp, so he struck back over the mountain with the vague idea of cruising the country for more stands of pitch pine. It was pleasant to swing along. Except for thoughts of Linda, he had in him a strong feeling of release. The problems were solved. He knew now why things had moved against him. After a long walk in the darkness, the sun was just showing for the morning.

He spent most of the day behind the mountain, returning by way of an old path that led through a gap close to the eastern end of his chopping. He had been thinking hard. Now, he stopped as he caught the sound he had been afraid to hear for months.

It was the lifting roar of fire.

To the west, a broad, low arc of yellow flame rose from the stacks of pine tops. The whole end of the chopping was ablaze. The light wind played tricks as he ran forward. Now it was from the east, then from the west. The fire was drawing its own draft from the heat it released. Beyond his own operation was more conflagration; the Brookland chopping was also burning.

Luke had seen many forest fires, but none like this. It moved with the speed of a trotting horse, carrying a banner of black smoke above the flames. He had run too far and had come into a trap, passing through a break in the circling fire wall just where his mill and the little shack stood.

Momentarily, panic held him. The temptation was to run blindly, but he knew he could not get out the way he had come. There were blankets in the shack. If he could get them, throw one over his head, he might break through along the now almost dry creek bed.

The fire had reached the end of the tram road, hungrily eating a pile of resinous planks, when he reached his door and kicked it open. Inside, his eyes smarting from smoke, he stumbled over a small crouched figure on the floor. It was a tiny, huddled old woman who was mumbling over and over, "I'm ketched, I'm ketched."

Luke recognized old Grandma Crull, who lived in a filthy shack not far from Tammie's Place. She was reputed to have set fires on the ridges to promote huckleberry growth. Lumbermen had put the fear of the law in her, and she had stopped the practice, but now, beside her on the floor, was a small tin can, smelling strongly of kerosene.

"Granny," Luke said, shaking her lightly, "did you set this fire?"

"Yes," she answered, suddenly quite calm. "I set it, and it'll burn us. I came to burn the mill. The wind twisted."

Grimly, the young man looked down on the bedraggled figure standing before him with wisps of dirty gray hair protruding from under a sunbonnet devoid of starch. Her closed, blackened hands twisted nervously. Over her cracked shoes were tied leggings made of lumberman's socks. Oddly, even in this strained moment, Luke remembered how mountain berry pickers wore such socks as protection against snakes.

"You got any ideas about getting out, Granny?"

Confusion possessed her again. She shook her head and picked up her can, which he snatched from her and flung out the door. Minutes were precious. He grabbed a blanket and soaked it in the bucket of water he had brought into the shack the night before. There wasn't enough of the precious liquid for a second blanket. The old woman squalled when this wet one was flung about her and she was snatched up in his arms.

The flames reached the shack as Luke and his burden partly fell, partly scrambled, into the creek bed. Fire was on both sides, with high flames arching the road and creek. It was hot, like plunging into the door of a furnace, as Luke bowed his head, held his breath, and drove forward. One of the woman's skinny arms was across his shoulders, and he felt her claw-like fingers digging at his neck.

He fell for the third time in his plunging run and rolled over, trying to protect his burden with his body. Half-stunned, he got up after a moment and realized that he was through the fire. The blanket-swathed figure on the ground lay still.

He pulled away the cloth anxiously, and Granny sat up, tugging at the sunbonnet that was still on her head.

He spoke grimly to her, jerking a shoulder in the direction of the fire. "They paid you to do it, didn't they, Granny?"

Her reddened eyes searched his face. "You're Hanley, ain't ye?"

Luke waited till she pushed back her bonnet and cackled. Then he took a step toward her, and the wizened face drew tight in perplexity. She lifted a dirty finger to her mouth as a child might do. "Tammie gives me whiskey. No 'twasn't her. He was a short man, black-like, bald-headed. Him, it was giv' me the two dollars and the coal oil."

Luke pointed. "Granny, you get the hell down that road before somebody sees you. I ought to break your neck."

Her dirty paw came up, and she touched a burned patch on his sleeve. She was cackling again in what she meant for laughter. "Been a long time since Granny wuz carried by a young feller. You got any money for an old woman as needs most everything?"

Luke fumbled in his pocket with a blistered hand and pulled out his money. He had been wrong in camp. It was a dollar less. Gravely he put a dollar bill and eighty-five cents in silver into the clutching fingers. "Now git!"

She trotted away, making little chirping noises and jingling the coins in her hand.

Cutting back through the unburned woods, Luke encountered Ben Royal, who looked at his burned shirt and singed hat.

"Tried to get through and got caught," Luke explained, and Royal frowned uneasily.

"The fire'll take the east corner of the pine job. The men are working a fire line up to the ridge top. Maybe we can stop it at the crest. They'll start the backfire just after it's dark. Your stuff's gone, though."

Pitch was the kindling wood used in the stoves of these mountain people to start fires. It is simply resin-soaked yellow pine, and Luke's small lumber yard had been crammed with the flammable stuff, stored and dried in the sun. Everything over there would be burning now, and Granny Crull would be with it but for his rescue. He thought bitterly of the crone, but likely she didn't have enough mind left to realize what she had done nor the enormity of evil in the man who had hired her. From her description, it must have been the blacksmith, Axelroth, John Caines' right-hand dispenser of evil.

Luke moved up the road and came to a place where he could look over his chopping. There was nothing alive over there now. The shack had crumpled to a mass of coals. Debris from it was tossed into a pile of plank edgings. The flame from the pile lifted, waving back and forth in the capricious air currents. Then the fan of it touched the side of the mill, and burning dust and gas flowed through its timbers like molten water. The heat touched the boiler. Suddenly it exploded, scattering flame like great bright feathers upward toward the brassy sky.

Luke turned away, unable to watch the place longer. Perhaps he had built his hopes too high in this, his first chance to get ahead. Mill, shack, tools, even one of his old coats, were gone. His fingers in his pocket fumbled a dollar bill and one coin left there.

Royal's men worked diagonally up the ridge side, and others were arriving from up and down the river to check this conflagration that threatened everything for miles. They used forked sticks, clearing leaves and debris down to the soil. Axes cleared away the brush for this work, and three or four workers used shovels. Behind the pathmakers came trusted men who would set the backfire when Ben Royal gave the word.

The long flank of backfire began to flame up just at dusk, making a bright line up the ridge. Men watched it carefully, seeing that it burned toward the main fire and did not jump back across the line which had been made. Men moved along under the pall of smoke. Occasionally, they called signals to each other.

The main fight was just over the ridge, where there was a tangle of laurel and scrub oak with an occasional dead pine top. Heated rocks in the path of the main fire exploded with the sound of gunfire, and flames began to show above the ridge line. Night came. Twice, the backfire jumped the path, and men fell upon that danger with tools, coats, and tramping shoes. Warning calls went up and down along the line. Then, as if on signal, the men stopped and stood watching.

The main fire approached the crest while the backfire was still two hundred yards away. Heat lay in the brush like a blanket. Yard by yard, the backfire crept toward its antagonist. Then with a tremendous roar and one long upsurge of flame, the two met. Minutes later, the fury was spent and wasted. The danger was over. Far out toward the end of the fire, a man yelled a cry of triumph; a second took it up, then others, until the yelling reached back down the ridge to where the wagons and buggies, which had brought the fighters, waited.

Doctor Nice had come out from Pine Bend to treat those who might be hurt. One worker had a broken leg, and there were several bad sprains from working among the rocks. He treated several burns in the Brookland camp kitchen and was finally alone with Luke after attending to his injuries.

"We won't bandage those places, Luke. They are superficial. Too bad about your lumber."

He washed his hands carefully in a basin. While he dried them, he asked a question without looking at his patient. "Any idea how it started?"

"Yes," Luke answered without explanation. "Yes, I have." It was easy to catch a ride into Pine Bend, for half the town had come out to the fire. He had a notion of dropping off to see Tammie, but remembering Geen's anxiety about her, he decided he should not be seen in her place tonight. To him, his trail was clear, and it led to the fountain of all deviltry in this area.

There was no one in Caines' office, but a dim light shone from a small kerosene lamp. A cold, half-smoked cigar lay in an ashtray. Luke worked methodically, yanking things down onto the floor. When he was about to pitch the lamp into the pile, he stopped, remembering the town hall to which this office building was attached. He walked out and tossed the still-burning lamp into the street.

At Axelroth's smithy, he smashed the lock with a stone and used one of the smith's hammers to wreck the shop and the living quarters at its back. This time, he did set a fire in the debris he had created, and yellow flames showed through the windows as he tramped on.

That night, he stopped twice to rest but slept only for a short time. It was daylight when he stalked into the office on the Caines job and thoroughly frightened the young clerk who had just come in. He stared at the wild-eyed man with the burned hands and assured him neither Caines nor Axelroth was about.

Something of his rage had burned out when he was back at the Brookland camp the following day, having caught a ride downriver. The place was deserted. The men who were not cutting timber were probably patrolling the fire lines. Luke found something to eat in the kitchen cupboards and made a package of food to take back to the little camp on Power's Fork.

Depression was riding him like a physical burden. He walked as though he were half asleep. It would be days before he could shake off the feeling of hopelessness. The fire and his loss had hit him hard.

The little clearing was before him in the oncoming dusk. Behind the cabin, he caught sight of the rear quarters of a horse. The door was ajar a few inches. Still holding the package of food in his right hand, he kicked open the door. In the shadows at the rear of the room, a squat figure moved.

"This is on me, Hanley," a voice gritted. There was a stab of fire, a ripping report.

The blow on Luke's shoulder was like that of a heavy sledge. He sank to his knees. He tried to lift his head and identify his attacker. A savage kick in his side brought from him a retching grunt of pain, then something crashed down on his head, and the darkness became complete.

Axelroth, breathing heavily, stirred the still form on the rough floor, thrust the revolver back into his trouser band, and went out to the horse.

CHAPTER TWENTY-THREE

THE CONCERN of Tom Short and Ben Royal following Luke's disappearance after the fire led them on an intense search for him. In Pine Bend, Royal learned of the destruction in Caines' office. Then Tom went up to the little cabin on Power's Fork, which he had shared with Luke and Owen Brown. The terribly injured man was alive but delirious in the afternoon of the day he was attacked.

Luke knew little of being found and taken down to the Brookland camp, but he did have a moment or so of lucidity shortly after Doctor Nice examined him.

The physician was speaking to Ben Royal. "The bullet may have touched the lung, and he has been horribly beaten. There may be some concussion from the head blows. Get him to the Point Haven hospital . . . pneumonia."

He tried to move as he heard the crisp statement, but then a wave of nausea blotted out his reason again. Mercifully, he knew only moments of the long ride downriver, his body swathed in blankets and resting on straw in a wagon bed.

In a week, he became fully conscious once more, but he was so weak he could not recognize just where he was or exactly what had happened. His nurse was a stout, comfortable woman who reminded him a little of Tammie, and he tried to call her that.

"Tammie."

Mrs. Hill, the nurse, bent low. She had scarcely caught the syllables, but she warned him not to talk.

"You've been a sick man; bullets, a bad beating, and other things. Wait a while, then you can talk."

He was stronger the next day, and she told him he would recover completely, but it would probably take several weeks. "You've got to get well for your friends. There's a lot of them. When they brought you in from that wagon, you sure didn't look worth saving."

He grinned at her and tried ineffectually to raise his head, but she pressed him back with a soft hand against his forehead and continued her remarks.

"They sure come right and left. That dirty old Mose High's been here twice. Then there was a tall man and his yellow-haired wife who sat up with you two nights and you raving like nobody's business."

She stopped talking about his visitors then, but she began again in the evening. Luke had identified the tall man and his wife as Brookland and Hester, and he was warmed at their concern, especially since Hester had come here to help him.

"Mister, a lot of wood hicks came. We only let them have a minute at a time. Then there was a woman, a girl she was, I guess."

Her eyebrow's puckered, and she lifted a plump forefinger to emphasize what she was about to say. "If I had knowed she'd kiss you, I'd have had the hospital barber shave you whether you was sick or not. I never saw her before, but she had the blackest hair and deep brown eyes. No, she didn't talk, but she was with me and you most of a long bad night."

"Linda," Luke whispered to himself. In spite of everything that lay between them, she had been close to him through a whole night.

After a pause, Mrs. Hill concluded. "You must be a heller with the women when you're shaved."

Luke laughed. The exertion hurt him, but he felt better.

Brookland came the first day the patient was allowed to sit up. The big man looked at Luke doubtfully, but when he took the shaky, welcoming hand, his face lit with relief.

"Thanks, Minor," Luke said. "They told me that you and Hester sat up with me. I wish I could have visited with you both. They told me, too, that my bill here is covered by the insurance you have on us men."

Brookland's hand made a deprecating gesture. "That's only good business. I get you fellows back quicker and in better shape to go to work this way."

The two men talked for a full half-hour. Brookland confirmed that Luke's operation on Rattlesnake was a total loss. Besides, more than a hundred acres of good white pine had been destroyed. Oddly, neither referred to the Owen Brown interlude. Finally, when he saw how weak Luke still was, Brookland left with the promise to return in a few days.

There was much to think about as the sick man's strength slowly came back. He would sit for hours on a side porch, looking at the wooded hills across the river. He was sure the man who had attacked him was Axelroth, though he had not seen him clearly in the shadow.

"*This is on me.*" Those had been the man's words. If it had been the smith, he was getting his revenge for the beating he had received and for the loss of his shop. Luke thought bitterly of the fact that no one from the sheriff's office had come to ask questions about his assailant. Most of his thinking, though, centered on Linda Caines and her visit to the hospital.

On the day Mrs. Hill told him marked the end of his third week in the hospital, she announced another visitor who proved to be Squire Jacoby. He was puffing a bit from climbing the stairs and took the chair beside Luke's with evident relief.

He came to the point of his visit almost at once. "You look strong enough, my boy, to hear all the news. Your friends have delegated me to bring you up to date. I suppose you have been wondering?"

Luke nodded. Something about the old man's look made him brace himself for a shock.

"To begin, the bail on John Caines was raised in light of new evidence that has come in. He refused to surrender himself and evaded the sheriff. Nedrow threw a fit, but Caines was declared a fugitive from justice. Your fire was set, and Granny Crull finally owned up. She showed the money you gave her, too."

He wiped a finger along his nose to hide a smile.

"It beats me what some men do. If you had insurance on that property of yours, there might be a warrant out now for collusion in attempted arson. Axelroth hired her. He's the one who shot you. Now, the hardest part." His grave eyes searched Luke's thin features, and he cleared his throat. "Tammie's dead; buried the first week you were in here."

Luke came half out of his chair, his eyes wide in amazement.

Jacoby hurried on. "Axelroth was on a round of murders. He had a double grudge against you and thought he'd killed you. From there, he came down and killed Tammie with an iron bar. That was because he felt she had informed you about Owen Brown's being on that raft. Rush Geen found her a few minutes before she died. None of us will ever know now exactly what there was between Rush and Tammie, but they were very close to each other."

Luke's sound arm was braced against the chair, and his face was drawn as the squire continued. "Rush did exactly what you would have expected. He found Axelroth, sent a charge of buckshot through his belly, then beat the man to a pulp with a poleaxe while he died. After that, he must have started right after Caines. It could be Axelroth talked a little before he was shot, trying to get some mercy."

Jacoby rose and walked stiffly to a window, which he looked out a moment before returning to his shocked listener. "Lots of people knew where Caines had been. It was in the house he owned in Pine Bend. But both he and Rush disappeared. It was George Brendy who found them in a little cabin on Windfall Run. Both men were dead, and only God knows just what happened. Rush Geen could be a mighty savage antagonist. Tammie, for whatever there was between them, had been brutally murdered, likely at Caines' orders. We know that our big would-be senator had a broken arm, and there were burns on his chest. Geen had been shot twice in the back with a derringer found in Caines' hand. Likely it had been hidden up his sleeve. But before Rush died, he managed to shoot out Caines' eyes."

Luke shook himself, trying to fight back the nausea he felt. He knew Rush Geen, had seen how the savage in the man could rise. Now he drew a long shaky breath while Jacoby started to speak more thoughtfully.

"I suppose, Luke, we'll never know everything about your father's death or that of Fred Horton. Caines was in them both. The man was a devil, driven by unholy ambition to have money and high place. Murder, fire, and political corruption were merely tools to him. It could be Rush Geen saved the county from hanging the man. Perhaps this was the best way."

Both men were silent. Luke thought of Tammie, her loyalty which had cost her life, her warm-heartedness, and her bluntness. His eyes were wet with tears.

Jacoby's voice seemed a long way off. "Now, the last of it. I've known Linda since she was a child. The only good thing about Caines was that he worshipped that girl. I have talked to her again and again; she has confided much in me. Quite early, she had suspected her father, had learned that he was the agent of a militant anti-Abolitionist society. To make it short, through the years she stood between John Caines and you. She told me she had a legacy from her mother's estate and had not used any of her father's money, even as support, for years. Finally, she broke with him entirely."

Jacoby touched the sick man's knee with his fingertips. "Luke, few men in the world ever had a friend like she has been to you."

The younger man bowed his head to hide the emotions he could not control.

The squire rose and looked down at him for a moment. "Underground days are all over now. Armies will be taking over from you men who cared for strangers in the nighttime. War's close. Erritt is over around Driftwood, organizing a company, so it will be ready when the guns open."

The old man was not sure Luke was listening. He waited a moment more, then tiptoed from the room.

All the threads were untangled at last. It did not seem possible for one man to have caused so much misery to satisfy his vaulting ambition. And John Caines had come close, very close, to attaining his goal. Things had broken just in time to keep him from becoming state senator. In that position, his influence would shortly have made him secure. Two of Luke's friends had died. As he sat here by his bed, it seemed to him that they had died for the same cause that had left him without a father.

Brookland and Hester came that evening. There was a new expression on the girl's lovely face. She walked to Luke's chair, bent, and kissed his forehead while her husband smiled down at them.

"I haven't too much time to talk, Luke," the big man said. "Hester and I have come with a proposition. Senator Thaddeus Stevens has called me to Washington. There is to be a new administration, and I am to be used in a position I may not name just yet. Our Hester here will live in a city and have her chance to study music under real teachers."

Luke looked at her, his eyes shining. He could never forget the appeal of her voice. She smiled. Then a cricket called from the window sill, and one of her eyes drew down in a wink as her husband continued.

"There are some other things, but this is first. You are to take charge of all my affairs up here: the farm, the lumbering, everything. Hester and I want you to live at Spring Haven. That is to be your home. You love it, and we could not leave it in hands that did not cherish every inch of it. When we come back for a visit, have the little cottage ready for us. The house is yours." He got up and smiled down at the nonplussed man in the chair. "Dammit, Luke, get well. We need you outside. We'll pick you up the day after tomorrow when you are discharged from the hospital."

* * *

When the hour came for him to leave the hospital, Luke walked downstairs with Mrs. Hill. At the door, he kissed her. "Remember," he whispered to her, "you said I must be a heller when I shaved."

Brookland was waiting outside with a smart team of bays and drove fast through the streets of the county seat. Of course, Luke thought they were going to Spring Haven. Instead, they drew up before Point Haven's best hotel, the Faron. Hostlers took the team, and Brookland, grinning at his companion, led him across the lobby to where a clerk beckoned them, then opened a wide door.

Luke was all but pushed into a big, plush parlor that boasted deep carpets and heavy drapes at the windows. There seemed to be a throng of people. Jim and Emma Haliday were there. Attorney Jonathan Shaw, Tom Short, Ben Royal, Dan Pritchett, and Moses High, who was neatly shaven for the occasion. As the clerk pulled the door shut behind Brookland and Luke, another door at the far end of the big room opened, admitting Judge Faris, who was accompanied by two others who looked like reporters or lawyers. Luke's friends were smiling as he was pushed into a chair facing the judge, who remained standing, a paper held in his right hand.

"Friends," he said in his judicial voice, "there has been so much excitement in our county lately that we may have forgotten that Governor William Packer is to announce a successor to State Senator Parvin whose post is now vacant. The governor is a citizen of our neighboring county; he knows us well and realizes that a man of parts had to be selected to succeed our illustrious Senator Parvin. Today, through his letter, I have the privilege of naming the governor's appointee, who will later be confirmed by the state senate itself."

Luke looked at Brookland with satisfaction. Undoubtedly, he was the man for the post. Luke was pleased at being here to hear him named. Brookland had poise, integrity, and was a leader of men. Faris was reading from the letter, and Luke missed the opening lines.

". . . we have checked carefully to find the proper man. It is our feeling that he should be comparatively young due to the onerous work incident to the office of a state senator. We have considered the advice of outstanding Pennsylvania citizens, among whom are: United States Senator Thaddeus Stevens, Judge Faris, and Squire Jacoby, all of whom are personally known to me. Therefore, in light of personal service rendered by him to his fellow men at great cost to himself, and because of his devotion to the region's best interests, we do appoint and invest with all emoluments and privileges as state senator of the twenty-sixth district, a lifetime native of our county—Luke Hanley."

A burst of applause swept the room, then those assembled were all on their feet, moving toward the stunned young man to congratulate him.

Judge Faris was the first; he spoke with a smile. "Son, once I thought I had to send you to the county jail—now I send you into state politics. I am afraid you may have to regret I did not follow the former alternative."

So far as Luke was concerned, the next half-hour was complete confusion. Brookland advised him there would be a testimonial dinner that evening in the hotel.

Luke looked ruefully at his friend. "Minor, I wanted to run up to Pine Bend with the news. She—"

Hester had moved up beside her husband. Her smile was warm, understanding. "That won't be necessary, Luke."

She called a hotel clerk over, and he, too, was smiling as he approached. "Take the senator up to room one-eighty-two, please."

Luke followed the man and noticed his steps fell soundlessly on the deeply carpeted stairs. The clerk knocked discreetly at the door, opened it a crack, and announced, "Senator Luke Hanley to see you, miss."

Linda Caines turned from the window out of which she had been looking and met Luke in the middle of the room. He held her trembling hands. There was none of the old teasing light in her eyes. Today it was just pride. Her lips were parted a little, but he gave her no time to speak.

"Linda, this is the first time I have ever had anything worthwhile. Will you marry me?"

Tears came to her brown eyes, but she wiped them away quickly on a wisp of cambric. "There have been such awful things, Luke—"

"But they're all over now," he promised and drew her close.

She gave him her lips. Moments later, he spoke in mock sternness.

"You have not answered the senator's question, young woman."

She drew back her head, something of the old impishness in her smile. "Perhaps I'd better. Sometime past, I announced that we had spent a night together. It is high time you made an honest woman of me."

* * *

The doors of the big dining room opened, and the guests stood beside the long table, gleaming with silver and crystal. At the end, directly before the plate of the guest of honor, stood a well-polished castor filled with its cruets of condiments. It had come from the Haliday home.

Luke, with Linda holding his arm, walked slowly to the table. He saw the castor and, reaching out, touched it almost involuntarily.

Brookland brought him back to face the situation. "Ladies and gentlemen. Judge Faris married this couple an hour ago. I present Senator and Mrs. Luke Hanley."

The applause was quick and long. Luke bowed slightly in acknowledgment. Brookland's best black coat fitted him rather tightly across the shoulders.